TRIGGER HAPPY

TRIGGER HAPPY

A NATHAN STARK, ARMY SCOUT WESTERN

WILLIAM W. JOHNSTONE

AND J. A. JOHNSTONE

PINNACLE BOOKS
Kensington Publishing Corp.
www.kensingtonbooks.com

PINNACLE BOOKS are published by

Kensington Publishing Corp.
119 West 40th Street
New York, NY 10018

PUBLISHER'S NOTE

Following the death of William W. Johnstone, the Johnstone family is working with a carefully selected writer to organize and complete Mr. Johnstone's outlines and many unfinished manuscripts to create additional novels in all of his series like The Last Gunfighter, Mountain Man, and Eagles, among others. This novel was inspired by Mr. Johnstone's superb storytelling.

PINNACLE BOOKS, the Pinnacle logo, and the WWJ steer head logo are Reg. U.S. Pat. & TM Off.

ISBN-13: 978-0-7860-4028-5
ISBN-10: 0-7860-4028-9

First Pinnacle paperback printing: June 2021

10 9 8 7 6 5 4 3 2 1

Printed in the United States of America

Chapter 1

Emerging from breakfast in the Fort Randall mess hall, Nathan Stark and his fellow scout Moses Red Buffalo paused to gaze off in the direction of a low hill about half a mile southwest of the fort's wall.

They watched four buzzards circling in the sky above the crest of that hill, taking turns swooping down to a particular spot, landing for a minute or so, then rising again. Something up there—something dead—was providing the scavengers with their own breakfast.

"Noticed a couple of them up there yesterday," said Red Buffalo. "Didn't think too much of it. Figured they were probably picking clean the remains of a jackrabbit or maybe a coyote." Red Buffalo frowned. "Now there's four and they're still mighty busy with it. Got to be some bigger critter, wouldn't you say?"

"Reckon so," Nathan allowed.

"Make you curious?"

"Curious enough to walk up there and take a look, you mean?"

"That's what I was thinking."

Nathan gave him a dubious look. "Ordinarily, I'd tell

you to go ahead and have at it. My curiosity ain't that strong and whatever it is those buzzards are picking at is long past any help. But, seeing how today is shaping up to be about as boring as yesterday and the day before that, the notion of a hike in the cool morning air to do some exploring, pitiful as that amounts to, is at least *something* to do. So yeah, let's go have a look."

The pair headed for the front gate, reporting tersely to the sentry on duty that they were going to check something out and then angling in the direction of the distant hill and the circling buzzards. As civilian scouts under no current direct orders, they had far greater freedom to come and go than the uniformed soldiers of the garrison.

In his middle thirties, Nathan Stark was lean, though solidly muscled, with wolfish facial features and a mane of thick dark hair. He wore a flat-crowned Stetson, faded red bib-front shirt, buckskin trousers, well broken-in boots. A Colt Peacemaker rode in a holster on his right hip. On his left was sheathed a ten-inch bowie that he had pried from the dead fingers of his slaughtered father.

For his part, Moses Red Buffalo, a full-blooded Crow Indian, was of indeterminate age, somewhat stockier in build, perhaps an inch shorter. He wore his glossy black hair in two long braids trailing down from a brown slouch hat with an eagle feather stuck in its snakeskin band. A buckskin vest over a thin cotton shirt and fringed buckskin trousers tucked into high black leather boots completed his outfit. He, too, had a holstered Colt strapped around his middle and a bone-handled knife thrust in his belt. He also carried a Henry repeating rifle.

The pair gave off an unmistakable air of competence, alertness, and dangerous readiness as they glided lightly, silently, across the expanse of Dakota prairie grasses and began their ascent up the slope of the hill. The approach of the intruders caused the buzzards to squawk and flap their wings in protest.

Red Buffalo swung the muzzle of his Henry out ahead, slashing the air and snarling, "Scat, you ugly black varmints! Clear out before I blast you into more piles of putrid meat for other scavengers to feast on!"

"Here now. I thought Injuns, especially you bein' a Christian one and all, walked in harmony with God's creatures, great and small."

Red Buffalo scowled. "Filthy birds! They are not God's creatures. They are the spawn of the devil!"

Educated in his younger years at a Catholic mission school, Red Buffalo had become a devout Christian—one of many beliefs the two scouts did not share.

Nathan was considering some further remark to needle the Crow, but before he could decide what it should be, he was struck by a viciously foul odor that caused him to stop in his tracks and turn his face away.

"Egad!" he exclaimed. "Whatever's giving off that terrible stench is something a hell of a lot bigger than the carcass of a jackrabbit or even a coyote."

Red Buffalo faltered a bit from the same terrible stink but continued on a few more steps—close enough to come within sight of the bloated, shredded form at which the birds had been pecking. He halted, winced distastefully, and said, "You're right, it is neither of those things. It is the body of a man!"

That was enough to bring Nathan the rest of the way forward. Gazing down, he grunted, "I'll be damned. I wonder who . . ."

"Whoever it is—or was—his clothing and boots mark him as a white man," Red Buffalo stated.

"Yeah, you're right. Say, wait a minute . . ." Then Nathan exclaimed once again, "Well, I *will* be damned! You'd never know it by the ruination that's left inside them, but I recognize those duds. That shirt, the fancy leather belt . . . we're looking at what's left of none other than Dietrich Bucher."

"Yes, I see it now, too," agreed Red Buffalo.

"So the low-down, stinking snake didn't get away after all!" declared Nathan.

A week earlier, Dietrich Bucher, a third scout assigned to Fort Randall, had come up missing in the wake of an attack on the fort by a war party of renegade Sioux under the leadership of a chief called Hanging Dog. Bucher had been part of a gunrunning scheme that could have resulted in a bloody massacre of the troops if not for Nathan's efforts.

Bucher had been unaccounted for following the battle, neither among the surviving or the dead, and most believed he had cut his losses and escaped.

Here was the proof that hadn't happened.

As the two men continued to gaze down at the ravaged remains of the German, Red Buffalo said, "No, he didn't get away. It's kind of puzzling, though, that he ended up here."

Nathan frowned. "What do you mean? The Indian attack backfired on him just like it did on his partners. What's so puzzling about that? I say it's well-deserved payback suffered by the whole lot of treacherous varmints."

"I got no trouble with that part of it," Red Buffalo said.

"What I'm saying is I find it curious how Bucher came to fall in this particular spot."

"You and your curiosity."

"Don't you see? How did he manage to get struck down clear up here? Could have been a wildly stray bullet, I suppose. But otherwise, the fighting was all down on the flat, closer around and in the fort. Look at the ground hereabouts"—Red Buffalo swept his free hand—"there's no sign of Indian ponies or any other activity having taken place anywhere near here. And if a Sioux made a kill this far apart from the rest of the fighting, wouldn't he have taken Bucher's cartridge belt and boots? Not to mention his scalp."

Nathan's frown deepened. "No, he's still got that. Leastways what the blasted birds didn't tear away."

"Don't you see at all what I'm getting at?" Both Red Buffalo's expression and his tone conveyed frustration. "Another thing. If this body has been up here a whole week, don't it seem like—"

The rest of what he was going to say was cut short by a sudden wind-rip of sound—a peculiar *thurrrp!* of disturbed air that would have been indecipherable to most people but was all too familiar to the experienced ears of Nathan and Red Buffalo.

It was the sound of a bullet sizzling through the sixteen inches of space that separated them as they stood discussing their grisly discovery. And unless there was the slightest doubt, the confirming boom of the heavy rifle that had hurled the menacing slug reached them a ragged second later.

By then the two men were peeling away from each other and pitching themselves to the ground.

Chapter 2

Nathan hit the dirt and rolled to the side until he came to a halt in a slight depression filled with higher, thicker prairie grass. He sensed, without seeing, that Red Buffalo was executing a similar maneuver. The high grass wasn't going to protect Nathan from another bullet, of course, but with luck it would make him a harder target for any further attempt by the bushwhacker.

But an anticipated second shot didn't ring out.

Nathan bellied tight to the ground. He swept off his hat with his left hand and with his right drew his Colt. Then, edging forward a few inches, he cautiously parted the high grass and peered out.

"What the blazes was that?" Red Buffalo called from a few yards away.

"Somebody was trying to part the hair on one of our heads with a bullet," Nathan answered.

Red Buffalo grunted. "A bullet makes an awful dull razor, though a right smart skull splitter. Who's gotten proddy with you lately?"

"Ain't got the time nor inclination to rattle off that whole list. You spot where the shot came from?"

"No, not yet."

"There!" Nathan said abruptly. "That brushy ridge due north. See the powder-smoke haze in those bushes?"

"Got it," Red Buffalo replied. A moment later his Henry roared once, then a second time as he sent some return fire back in the direction of whoever had opened up on them.

Extending his right arm, Nathan triggered the Colt in his fist three times, rapid-fire, and blistered the air with some lead of his own.

"You realize, don't you," said Red Buffalo, "that a hand-gun doesn't have the range to make it as far as that ridge?"

"Maybe, maybe not," Nathan replied. "But the same ain't true for that Henry of yours. Did you do any good?"

"No, not as far as I can tell," Red Buffalo admitted grudgingly. "But I darn sure gave the bushwhacker some-thing to think about."

"Hell, I did that much," Nathan scoffed. "Burned some powder, let off some steam. Made sure the dirty so-and-so knows he missed me and that I am annoyed by the attempt."

"Annoyed enough to go after him?"

"You really have to ask?"

"No, I guess not."

"Whoever it is don't seem to be in a hurry to plunk away no more. Probably still best to wait a bit, though. Not be in too big a hurry to poke our heads up. In case he's laying back waiting for another crack at what he missed the first time."

"Uh-huh."

As it turned out, neither Nathan nor Red Buffalo had to worry about being the ones to poke their heads up. The shooting had not gone unnoticed by men down in the fort.

In a matter of minutes, four riders came boiling out the front gate and then made the sharp turn to proceed up the hill toward where the scouts were hunkered down.

Nathan recognized Corporal Cahill at the head of this detail. He had come to consider Cahill one of the more tolerable troopers at Fort Randall. He was young and inexperienced, but eager to listen and learn and work his way up through the ranks by effort, not favoritism.

When the riders were three quarters of the way up the slope, Nathan shoved himself up on one elbow and shouted, "Corporal! Dismount your men and walk them on the south side of their horses! There's a bushwhacker up on that high ridge to the north and ain't no telling when he might decide to open up again!"

Cahill promptly responded to the suggestion, ordering his men to quit their saddles and walk behind the chests and forefeet of their horses.

No more shots came from the ridge to the north.

When Cahill and his men reached the crest of the hill, Nathan and Red Buffalo pushed guardedly to their feet, all the while keeping a sharp eye on the distant ridge.

"Are you two all right?" Cahill asked. "We heard the shooting. You say you were fired upon from ambush?"

"One shot," Nathan told him. "The rest of it was our return fire."

"Do you think you scored a hit on the scoundrel? Is that why only the one shot?"

Nathan shook his head. "More likely we just drove him off. But keep your men spread out and a close watch, just in case he's waiting for us to let our guard down and give him a bunched-together target."

The men accompanying the corporal quickly fanned out, not waiting for an order.

"Any idea who it was? Or why he shot at you?"

"No, but we damn sure aim to find out," Nathan assured the corporal.

Cahill snapped a nod. "We'll report back to the fort and then form a more fully provisioned detail to ride in pursuit."

Red Buffalo, who had remained keenly focused on the ridge, now turned his head, saying, "That would waste valuable time. If we've put that ambusher on the run, as it appears, he'll be able to gain several miles on us before we set after him in the way you suggest."

"Moses is right," Nathan was quick to add. "If that varmint has lit a shuck, we need to start after him pronto!"

"But—"

"I'll take full responsibility," Nathan said, cutting off Cahill's objection. "Let me and Moses take two of your horses and head out right away. You'll have plenty to take care of here, mounting a burial detail."

The young corporal looked bewildered. "Burial detail? I don't understand."

Nathan jabbed a finger in the direction of Bucher's carcass. "Was up to me, I'd leave the scurvy snake to the buzzards and worms. But since he was attached in a scout capacity to Ledbetter's command, I imagine there's all sorts of proper protocol the good colonel will want followed."

His attention drawn to Bucher's remains, Cahill recoiled in horror when he got a closer look. All natural color drained from his face, replaced by a somewhat greenish tint, and for a moment Nathan thought the lad was going to throw up. By force of will, Cahill managed to keep his breakfast down.

The same wasn't true for one of the other soldiers, however. Happening to be standing closest to the carcass and getting a better view when he turned to look down, this trooper immediately doubled over and spewed more foulness onto the hilltop.

"In case you missed it, that's Dietrich Bucher," Red Buffalo said to Cahill. "What's left of him."

"What happened to him?" the corporal asked in a ragged voice.

"We don't know," replied Nathan. "We were drawn up here by the buzzards. This is how we found him. Before we could determine anything more, somebody started shooting at us."

"Do you think the shooter is responsible for Bucher's death?" Cahill wanted to know.

"No way of telling," said Nathan. "Since he took what you'd have to call an interest in me and Moses showing up here, you got to figure he at least knows something about it."

"All the more reason to take after him with the least delay," Red Buffalo added.

"Yes, I can hardly dispute that," said Cahill.

Nathan said, "So let us see to that and you go do what you need to do about reporting to the colonel and the rest. Probably be a good idea to get Captain Northby, the fort doctor, up here, too. Maybe he can figure out what killed Bucher and led to him being left here like this."

"Yes. Of course," Cahill responded dully. His gaze had once more returned, as if unbidden, to the ravaged carcass. "I . . . I must do those things."

Chapter 3

While Cahill was still in a somewhat stunned state, before it occurred to him to try and raise any further objection, Nathan and Red Buffalo commandeered a pair of horses—along with a Winchester for Nathan—and rode north away from the cluster of soldiers.

Since a slight chance still remained that the ambusher might be hanging back and biding his time for another try, they took the precaution of splitting apart and swinging wide to either side of the ridge where they'd seen the haze of powder smoke. Then, from opposing directions, they slowly, cautiously converged on the spot.

Red Buffalo got there a few minutes ahead of Nathan. When Nathan arrived, the Crow was kneeling behind a line of low, spiny rocks and studying the ground before him.

Without looking up, Red Buffalo said, "This is where the ambusher shot from. The way the grass is flattened, it looks like he bellied down, probably rested his rifle barrel on these rocks so he could steady his sights on us."

"Let's be glad he didn't steady them any more accurately than he did."

Red Buffalo stood up. "No sign of a spent cartridge,

the shooter must have picked it up and taken it with him. Reckon he had a horse tied somewhere down below."

"He did," Nathan confirmed. "I spotted sign of it when I was on my way up. Matter of fact, there were two horses tied down there."

"Two? You mean the shooter has a partner?"

Nathan shook his head. "No. When the horses took off—about a half hour ago, I judge—only one of them was carrying a rider. One of the animals was shod. The other one, the one carrying the rider, wasn't."

Red Buffalo's brow puckered. "You saying our shooter was an Indian?"

"I'm saying it was somebody who favored climbing on an unshod mount. Draw your own conclusion. We won't know for sure until we catch up with him."

"But why two horses? Where did the second one come from?"

Nathan turned his head and looked back toward the grassy hill where earlier they'd made their grisly discovery and then been shot at.

"If I had to guess," he replied, "I'd say it might have belonged to Dietrich Bucher."

"Does that mean you think our shooter killed Bucher, too?"

"Like I told Cahill, it seems likely he's connected in some way. How, I don't know. Bucher sure as blazes wasn't no fresh kill, not even close." Nathan scowled. "So if the hombre who took a potshot at us *was* his killer, going back at least a couple days or more, then why was he still hanging around to make the try on us?"

"Like I said at the outset," Red Buffalo reminded him, "there are some very puzzling things about all of this."

"Yeah, you called it right enough," Nathan allowed.

"Something else just occurred to me," said Red Buffalo. "The sound of the shot that came rolling down from this ridge after the bullet passed between us . . . that seemed like the boom of a mighty powerful gun, not just another Henry or Winchester. Wouldn't you say?"

"Yeah, now that you mention it. But what difference—"

Red Buffalo interrupted with, "Didn't Bucher carry a Sharps Big Fifty buffalo rifle? He still had his boots and belt, but there was no rifle left laying back there."

Nathan's scowl returned, darker than ever. "I'll be damned. Maybe Bucher's horse and now maybe his rifle, too, both in the hands of an ambusher hanging around for some mysterious reason. *Puzzling* don't begin to cover it."

"There's one thing neither puzzling *nor* mysterious," Red Buffalo declared. "The reasons behind it may not be clear, but it's a certainty that whoever fired that shot meant to kill one of us."

Nathan clenched his teeth. "Then here's another certainty. We're going to catch up with that bushwhacking skunk and throttle some answers out of him! We take him alive, we'll find out what we want to know."

Red Buffalo cocked one eyebrow. Then, referring to Nathan's well-known hatred for all red men, resulting in him becoming widely dubbed *the Indian Killer* due to the many campaigns he'd joined relentlessly fighting them, the Crow said, "Won't that go against your grain? If the ambusher favoring an unshod pony turns out to be an Indian, I mean. You saying you'd refrain from killing him if you had the chance, in order to get some answers?"

Nathan glared at him. "You're an Indian and I've put

up with you without killing you, haven't I? Maybe I'm losing my edge."

"Or maybe," Red Buffalo replied, a hint of a grin tugging at one corner of his mouth, "I'm just more charming than most Indians."

"Thing to remember is that I said we'd take this skunk alive for the sake of getting some answers. Red man or white, once we get those I never mentioned anything about *leaving* him alive."

A dozen miles due north of the ridge from which he had taken his errant shot at the hated Indian Killer, a young Creek brave called Black Sun urged his pony up the ascending floor of a narrow arroyo that climbed into an expanse of broken, rocky terrain. At the top of the incline, the arroyo flared out into a flat oval surrounded by higher rock walls. Along the base of these tall cliffs grew a line of stubborn grass and a few patches of tangled brush. From a notch at one point in the cliffs, a spattering of freshwater poured down from some elevated spring.

After crossing the flat area, Black Sun slipped from the back of his pony and released the animal to go drink and find graze in the line of grass. He did the same for the saddled horse he had been leading on a tether. As the horse moved away from him, the brave's eyes came to rest on the stock of the buffalo rifle thrusting up from the scabbard hanging on one side of the saddle.

Black Sun scowled fiercely at the weapon and cursed it under his breath. Then he cursed himself for giving in to the temptation of attempting to use it before he was fully prepared.

The lure, the legend of the Big Fifty—cursed far ahead of Black Sun by the men of many tribes for its effectiveness at helping to wipe out the vast herds of buffalo which were the very lifeblood of their people—had been too much for the young man to resist. What a satisfying thing it would be, he'd thought in a moment of hate-fueled foolishness, to not only kill the despised Indian Killer but to do so with the equally despised weapon that had also caused so much harm to his race.

Unfortunately, Black Sun hadn't had sufficient time to familiarize himself with the gun. Although he had become an adequate marksman with other rifles he'd acquired in the past, the distance involved for the shot he attempted that morning, coupled with the fierce kick of the Big Fifty, had resulted in missing his target—the target he'd wanted to hit far worse than any previous one he'd ever taken aim at.

Black Sun once more uttered a curse. But along with it, he also made a silent vow to himself. A vow to never again be so impatient and foolhardy. He had not tracked Nathan Stark, the Indian Killer, all this way—all the way from Indian Territory—to fail at meting out the vengeance he was obsessed with delivering as payback for the slaying of his father and brother at Stark's hands.

For weeks the Creek brave had trailed Stark, only to arrive at Fort Randall here in the Dakotas just ahead of the clash with Hanging Dog's renegade Sioux. Black Sun had barely escaped a Sioux war party himself and it was on that occasion that he'd fled to the safety of this place where no one else seemed to venture.

Following the battle at the fort, he cautiously emerged to assess the aftermath. During that time he had been filled with dread that Stark might have fallen during the battle, a victim of the Sioux, robbing him of his chance for revenge. Monitoring the activity at the fort from surrounding concealed vantage points, Black Sun had been relieved to spot Stark still alive and engaged in the cleanup and repair.

It was one day as he continued this reconnoitering, watching and waiting and planning for his chance to strike at Stark, that Black Sun had spotted the man with the Big Fifty Sharps also monitoring the fort from the grassy hill.

When it became alarmingly evident that the man was preparing to line up a shot at the very same target Black Sun was interested in—again a threat to rob him of his revenge—the Creek brave had ghosted up behind the man and prevented him from succeeding. That much had gone well. He not only managed to yank the man's head back by his hair and slit his throat before he knew what was happening, but he'd also had time to roll the would-be thief over onto his back so that, before he died, he saw Black Sun's face and heard his explanation of *"Mine!"* ahead of the eyes going dull and the last bit of life draining away.

After making the kill, Black Sun had taken the man's rifle and horse and returned to his rocky hideout, wondering why the man—a white eyes—had reason for also wanting to kill Stark and what, if anything, it might mean for Black Sun's effort to do the same.

In the end, the young Creek decided, it changed nothing. With the rifleman eliminated and neither the presence nor death of this would-be killer even known to Stark, Black Sun still had the chance to finish what he'd come so far to do.

So he'd returned to conducting his vigil of the fort, watching for the opportunity he so desperately wanted. He'd spotted Stark moving within the walls a handful of times, but he never ventured anywhere Black Sun could close in on him. Not for the first time, the vengeance seeker weighed the risks of sneaking *into* the fort under the cover of dark and attempting his strike that way. If he was forced to wait much longer, he told himself, he would have to work up the nerve for such a measure . . .

And that was when the idea first struck him about using the Big Fifty.

The range and power of the rifle were renowned for that very reason—the impressive distance at which it could deliver deadly impact. If the Indian Killer was providing Black Sun no opportunity to get close enough to use his knife or tomahawk, then maybe here was another means to deliver his revenge. It wouldn't be the same as sinking a knife blade or tomahawk edge into Stark at close range, so they were eye-to-eye and he knew who was killing him—the way the rifleman had—but the deed of ending his life would nevertheless be accomplished.

With this possibility in mind, Black Sun had ridden even deeper into the remote, broken land and spent the afternoon practicing with the Big Fifty. He had only a limited number of cartridges, but he fired off enough rounds to convince himself he could hit what he aimed at. And any hit from one of the Sharps's heavy slugs was certain to be fatal.

Early this morning, then, Black Sun had returned to take up his vigil over the fort. As he'd been doing ever since acquiring the rifleman's horse, he led the animal along on a tether. In case he had to flee suddenly, having a backup mount could be very useful in escaping pursuit. This morning, the big-bore rifle riding in the horse's saddle scabbard now meant an added reason for having the additional horse along.

As he neared the fort, sticking to the various points of higher ground that surrounded it to the north and west, Black Sun had abruptly spotted something that changed the course of the whole day and sent his heart thudding with wild excitement.

Not far ahead, ascending the low, grassy hill where he had slain the rifleman days earlier, he was able to make out two men. A moment of closer scrutiny provided a revelation almost too marvelous to believe. One of the men was none other than Nathan Stark, the hated Indian Killer!

Black Sun quickly swerved his horses to cover behind the back slope of the north ridge. Tying them there, he pulled the Big Fifty from its sleeve and proceeded frantically up to the peak of the ridge. His course was clear now. Everything was falling into place, like an omen he could not deny. The rifle had fallen into his hands, the possibility of using it to achieve his revenge had entered his thoughts, and now—for the first time—the Indian Killer had exposed himself in a manner perfectly suited for that.

Too much open ground led up to the grassy hill for Black Sun to ever reach Stark unseen for an up-close strike, and the second man being present added yet another obstacle to any such attempt.

That left using the rifle for a long-range kill shot. As the omen meant for it to be.

But then it had all gone wrong. The shot missed. Panicking, knowing he had only two more cartridges for the

Sharps, Black Sun had fled the scene and immediately headed back to his hideout.

At first he told himself he must have misread the omen. But then he decided that no, the omen was too clear. In his eagerness to gain his long-awaited revenge he simply hadn't steadied his aim properly and the fault— the failure—was all his.

But as he paced agitatedly back and forth across the clearing, he refused to accept what had happened as ultimate failure. The only way it would ever be a complete failure was if the life was gone from him and breath still remained in Stark. Then he would have failed to avenge his father and brother and to right the humiliation of being the one left alive. If it came to that, he would not deserve—or want—to go on living.

Having seen that Stark and the other man back at the grassy hill were on foot, Black Sun believed that his hasty departure put enough time and distance between him and any pursuit. In case anyone *did* come after him at some point, the young Creek had followed precautions to mask his sign—until he reached the broken land where he took his refuge. The rocky, rugged surfaces here, he told himself, would serve their own purpose for hiding the marks of anyone's passage.

Feeling confident of this, he nursed plans to remain here, just lying low for a couple of days, allowing Stark to wonder and worry about the shot that had barely missed him. When some time had passed without further incident, the Indian Killer would start to relax and become less guarded . . .

And that was when it would be time to start stalking him once more.

Chapter 4

Black Sun woke to the sound of a pistol hammer ratcheting back to full cock. Opening his eyes, he was surprised and shocked to find himself gazing into the muzzle of a Colt .44 held only inches from his face. When his eyes widened with even greater alarm, he saw the grimacing face of Nathan Stark on the other end of the Colt.

"You little red heathen," Nathan snarled. "I should have left you dead back in Indian Territory."

A sudden surge of anger erased the fear that had momentarily numbed Black Sun. Eyes burning with hate, he bared his teeth and responded, "Why didn't you? I begged you to at the time. After you slaughtered my father and brother, I pleaded with you not to spare me and leave me with only the shame and humiliation of failing to avenge them. But you, who called yourself the great Indian Killer, would not grant me so little."

Nathan's own eyes narrowed into fierce slits. "That's right. Like I told you at the time, I ain't in the business of granting favors to mewling savages."

Standing two feet past Nathan's right shoulder, his Henry rifle leveled in the general direction of the Creek they had caught napping in the presumed safety of his remote hideout, Red Buffalo frowned and said, "Wait a minute. Are you saying you know this bushwhacking scoundrel?"

Without turning his head, Nathan answered, "Ain't like I *know* him, exactly. But me and Cullen, my old partner, had a run-in with him and some of his pack back when we were leaving the Nations to report up here to Fort Randall. The others who were with him didn't fare out too well."

"But you let this one live?"

"That's what you just heard, ain't it?" Nathan said irritably.

Red Buffalo's brows lifted. "If this is an example of what happens when you leave a live redskin in your wake, maybe I got a better understanding of how you came by your reputation for not making a habit of it. With the exception of yours truly, that is."

"That's only because we've been stuck with each other ever since you got assigned here, too," Nathan told him. "Keep in mind, we ain't reached the point where I'm able to put you in my wake yet."

"I will indeed keep that in mind," Red Buffalo remarked. "But in the meantime, what about our friend here? Have you learned your lesson yet where he is concerned? If you don't want to do him the favor of killing him, I'll be happy to take care of it for you."

"Don't worry, I learned my lesson. But first," Nathan said, "there's the matter of getting some answers, remember?"

Black Sun's eyes flashed. "You will get no answers out of me, you gutless cur. Nor will you"—his glare shifted to Red Buffalo—"you betrayer of your own people! You lick the boots of this white devil who has slain members of every nation and tribe on the frontier. How can you even call yourself a man?"

Red Buffalo replied softly but sternly. "I call myself a child of the Christian God. The only feet I bow before are His. And through Him, I recognize evil and the hand of the only true devil, Satan. Sometimes evil dwells in white men, sometimes in men of other colors. Wherever I find it, that is what or who I fight against."

For a moment, Black Sun appeared baffled, left at a loss for words by this statement. But then he quickly found the words to respond.

"I recognize the devil, too! Evil is in your tongue, twisted by cowing to the white eyes and learning to spout the lies and wicked views they are born to."

Nathan abruptly swung the barrel of his Colt in a chopping sideways motion, rapping it across Black Sun's jaw. The young brave's head rocked back. After a moment, his eyes blinked back into focus.

"All right, let's try this," Nathan said, shoving his face closer to Black Sun's. "I'm going to tell you what we're going to do to you if you *don't* answer what we want to know. Since I'm a white eyes and you think all I speak are lies, you probably won't believe me. So I suppose I'll have to prove it to you. I'll give you a minute to think about it. Think real hard. Make sure to keep in mind that if you force me to commence proving, it's gonna turn mighty unpleasant for you."

"And if you think you are experiencing shame for failing to avenge your father and brother," Red Buffalo added, "that is nothing compared to the shame you will place on yourself when you start screaming like a squaw bringing forth a child or wailing like the old women who mourn the passing of their sons in battle."

Black Sun's eyes shone bright as they darted back and forth between the two men.

Sighing wearily, Nathan said to Red Buffalo, "Might as well go get a fire going. Stoke up some nice red-hot coals. I don't think the young fool is going to cooperate. Reckon we'll have to do it the hard way."

"You are the fool!" Black Sun suddenly blurted. "You are hated by many men, far more than just me. So many I doubt you even know."

Nathan twisted his mouth wryly. "Son, if you think it comes as a surprise to me that I got enemies strung from the Rio Grande to the Yellowstone hot springs, I got a big disappointment to spring on you."

"The disappointments of my life only grow," Black Sun muttered sullenly. "I wish now I would have let the man with the big gun go ahead and kill you when he meant to. He had the skill to not miss, as I did. Then I could have settled for the satisfaction of desecrating your grave, making a necklace from your bones, and taking your skull back to the medicine man of our tribe to use as a bowl for mixing his potions."

Nathan's eyes bored into those of the young Creek. "The man with the big gun," he echoed. "You mean the man whose body we found on the grassy hill where you shot at us earlier?"

Black Sun averted his eyes and hung his head, saying, "Yes."

"And he was aiming to shoot *me* from that hill?"

Black Sun's head did not raise. "Yes. You were in an open area down in the fort, walking with a woman. I stopped him. Before he died, I let him know that I wanted you for myself."

Red Buffalo, who'd turned away to go build a fire, had abandoned that task to stop and listen to the conversation taking place. He returned to stand beside Nathan.

"When did this happen?" he asked Black Sun.

The young Creek frowned in thought. "Five sunrises ago."

Nathan and Red Buffalo exchanged looks. Red Buffalo said, "I'm not sure what Bucher was up to, but I'd say we got the rest of our answers."

Nathan nodded. "Close enough, I reckon."

Black Sun's face lifted. "So will you kill me now? Quickly?"

Nathan gave him a hard look. "Are you still so damned determined to die?"

"I must. One of us—you or me—has to die. It is the only way."

"Either way, what will it change? Will it bring your father or brother back?"

"It's the way it has to be," Black Sun insisted stubbornly.

"You sacrificed a great deal to track the Indian Killer this far," Red Buffalo pointed out. "That took great courage and it took even more to be prepared to confront him in the very shadow of a fully garrisoned army fort. Further, in the process you took the life of a truly evil person, one who betrayed his own kind and was responsible for the killing of many men, both red and white. Do these things not amount to sufficient atonement on your part for the past deeds that haunt you?"

Black Sun seemed to waver for a moment, but then

shook it off and snarled, "No! You are trying to twist my thoughts, the way the white eyes have twisted yours. But it is no good! I am clear on how it must be."

"So what you want," said Nathan, "is to die in this lonely, remote place where no one will ever even know."

"My spirit—and those of my father and brother—will know!"

"Your spirit!" Nathan spat caustically. "When I kill you, I will scalp you. If you are not whole, you will not be worthy to enter the spirit world. Your soul will drift forever between the winds. What's more, after I take your scalp I will tie it to the tail of my horse so that every time the animal does its business it will repeatedly foul the only thing left of you."

"You have a filthy mind!" Black Sun said. "None other could think of such a thing!"

"Maybe so. But if you give me no other choice, that's how it's gonna be." Nathan leaned back away from his captive and straightened up. Then, frowning down at the Creek, he added, "But I'm going to give you one last chance. Get on your pony and ride far away from here. Only make sure you understand this: if you return, if I lay eyes on you or so much as catch your scent ever again, I will kill you without hesitation."

Black Sun pushed to a sitting position on the blanket where he'd been further humiliated by being caught off guard and napping, believing no one could track him to this spot. His gaze shifted warily back and forth between Nathan and Red Buffalo.

"Go! Show some sense," Red Buffalo urged him. "Take your pony and a waterskin—no weapons, nothing more— and ride as fast and far as you can. Maybe, just maybe, you will survive long enough to become an old man one day and gain the wisdom to look back on this as a blessing you probably never deserved."

Something in his tone seemed enough to convince the young brave. Black Sun rose to his feet and glided hurriedly to his pony, scooping up a bulging waterskin on the way. Once mounted, he paused to take a long look at the two men who were releasing him. His expression was unreadable. Then, abruptly, he heeled his pony into motion and galloped away.

Chapter 5

Nathan and Red Buffalo stood in silence until Black Sun was gone from sight and the sound of his hoofbeats had faded.

Turning his gaze to Nathan, Red Buffalo said, "Do you believe we have seen the last of him?"

"How the hell should I know?" Nathan grumbled in response. "In case you didn't notice, I've gone soft in the head. This ain't the time to trust my judgment on much of anything."

"Yes, I was wondering about that."

"You didn't stop him, either," Nathan pointed out.

Red Buffalo shrugged. "I'm not the one he's bent on killing. And unless your memory is softening, too, you should recall I *did* make an offer."

Nathan made a sour face. "Well, what's done is done. At least for now. The thing we need to worry about is getting back to the fort and facing Colonel Ledbetter. He already hates my guts, though maybe not quite as bad as that Creek does. I'm sure we can expect some bellyaching from the colonel about us commandeering these horses and riding out without reporting to him first."

"I expect you're right." Red Buffalo sighed. "Nothing like looking forward to a good chewing-out to round off an already eventful day."

A handful of minutes later, the scouts were mounted and on their way down through the arroyo, Red Buffalo leading Bucher's horse. The sun in the cloudless sky overhead had arced past its noon peak and was turning the afternoon oven-hot. The sunlight bouncing off the bleached, baked rocks of the broken land seemed to increase the heat even more and the higher upthrusts of rock effectively blocked the mild breeze that would be found out on the grassy plain. Until then, Nathan and Red Buffalo sweated in silence.

They were nearing the outer edges of the badlands when the attack came.

As they entered another narrow passage between nearly the last of any tall, ragged cliffs, Nathan took the lead and Red Buffalo shifted back behind him with Bucher's horse bringing up the rear. Suddenly, from a recessed ledge about eight feet up on the rock wall to the right, Black Sun leaped directly down onto Nathan. In his right hand Black Sun clutched a melon-sized chunk of rock with several jagged, sharp angles. He raised it above his head as he dropped and then swung it down and forward, aiming to drive it against the back of Nathan's head as he alighted heavily onto the rump of the scout's horse.

"Vengeance *will* be mine!" Black Sun cried.

Only a desperate move by Nathan saved him from getting his skull caved in. Sensing Black Sun's movement as he made his leap and hearing his enraged vow, Nathan twisted frantically in the saddle and whipped his right arm up and back, ramming blindly with the point of his elbow.

Fortunately for him, the elbow came around just as Black Sun landed behind him. It collided hard with the side of the Creek's face, knocking him sharply to one side. At the same time, Nathan's arm blocked the brave's own descending arm. The rock he was attempting to brain the Indian Killer with swung short and only grazed its target.

The sudden arrival of Black Sun's added weight and the struggle on its back caused Nathan's horse to bolt. This was enough to spill both men and send them toppling to the hard, unforgiving ground.

Nathan landed mostly on his right hip, with Black Sun pressed underneath his upper body. Despite that to cushion the impact, the landing was jarring and drove much of the wind out of him. He could only imagine that the punishment to his adversary must have been worse.

Yet it didn't seem to matter. The obsessed young brave instantly began kicking and shoving wildly to try to get untangled from Nathan. Before Nathan could gain a tight enough hold on him, he succeeded.

Black Sun rolled clear and scrambled nimbly to his feet. In his hand he still clutched the chunk of rock, his only weapon. But in his driven, wild-eyed state, he seemed determined it would be sufficient. Baring his teeth to issue another menacing cry—"Die, you white-eyed devil!"—he rushed forward, swinging the rock as he came.

Nathan, who hadn't yet fully gained his feet, could only throw himself back and to one side, dodging the bone-crushing threat of the rock as it whistled through the air mere inches from his face. Black Sun's momentum carried him three or four steps past before he could halt.

Immediately, he wheeled back around to face the hated Indian Killer.

But by now Nathan was upright and braced on one knee, facing Black Sun in return. The scout's face wore no expression, but a flinty hardness shone from within the narrowed slits of his eyes. He watched Black Sun's knees bend into a slight crouch, getting ready to hurl him forward once again. The hand holding the rock started to rise.

When the rush came this time, Nathan palmed the Colt on his hip, drew it in a smooth motion, pushed it forward, and triggered a single shot. The bullet that exploded from the muzzle hit Black Sun just above the bridge of his nose. In the same instant, another shot rang out and a second slug slammed into the young brave's chest an inch to the left of his sternum.

The double impact hit Black Sun like he'd been swatted by a giant, invisible hand. He was knocked into a floppy, loose-limbed backward somersault that deposited him on the ground in a lifeless heap.

Nathan slowly rose the rest of the way to his feet. Pouching his iron, he cut his gaze to Red Buffalo. The Crow remained poised in his saddle, Henry rifle still extended from the hip, a waft of bluish smoke curling from its muzzle.

"I didn't ask for your help, you know," said Nathan.

"Uh-huh." Red Buffalo casually returned the Henry to its saddle scabbard. "It's just that the way you kept putting it off, I wasn't sure you'd ever get around to killing that fool."

"I told him what would happen if I ever laid eyes on him again."

"Yes. You did."

Nathan set his jaw and then added with obvious reluctance, "All the same, I'm obliged you saw fit to pitch in."

"It's what partners do."

"End result was him getting what he wanted." Nathan turned and walked a few paces to where his spooked horse had stopped. He took up the reins, planted a foot in the stirrup, climbed into the saddle.

"We going to just leave him like that?" Red Buffalo asked.

Nathan frowned. "Well, I sure as hell ain't gonna break a sweat burying him, if that's what you mean. I gave him every break. I repeat, he got what he wanted."

Red Buffalo gazed down at the crumpled form he had helped kill and a look of vague sadness came and went from his face. He said, "When we get back to the fort, I expect arrangements will have begun for some sort of proper funeral for Bucher. I guess that's the Christian way, even though he was a coward and a traitor and a reprobate of the lowest order. Somehow, especially by contrast, it doesn't seem fitting for this man—who had courage, even if that of wrongheaded conviction—to be left for coyote bait."

Nathan shrugged. "If you think he rates a burial, have at it. I'll see you when you get back to the fort."

Red Buffalo didn't respond, just continued to look down at the body.

Nathan wheeled his horse and rode away. He didn't go very far, though, before he hauled back on the reins. For a long moment he remained very still in the saddle, just staring straight ahead, as if concentrating hard on something. Then, heaving a sigh, he turned back.

"Ah, hell," he said. "There's a gully off to one side over here. I suppose it wouldn't hurt to wrap the young idiot in his pony blanket, put him in there, and cover him over with rocks and such so the critters can't get at him."

Red Buffalo nodded, a satisfied smile briefly touching his lips. "Yes. That would be good."

Chapter 6

"It should come as no surprise, Stark, to hear me state that I have found your low regard for proper protocol largely a thorn in my side ever since your arrival here."

The look Colonel Wesley Ledbetter fixed Nathan with was as stern as his tone. He held it for an extra second, then shifted his eyes to Moses Red Buffalo before addressing him.

"As for you, mister, I was reserving any hasty judgment. Inasmuch as you arrived later and it was clear from the start that you and Stark were hardly on friendly terms, I had hoped that your conduct would be more suitable. Unfortunately, only by the slimmest margin has that been the case."

The two scouts stood at a rough approximation of attention before the colonel's tidily arranged desk in his well-appointed office. Ledbetter sat ramrod straight behind it. Only the three of them were present in the room. A coal oil lamp burned at a low setting on one corner of the desk, and through the drawn-back curtains of the office's single widow, the long shadows of dusk could be seen settling over the fort.

"Your unsanctioned foray earlier today in pursuit of this, this *bushwhacker* as you describe him, is yet another example of behavior I find unacceptable," Ledbetter went on. "At the same time, I cannot ignore the fact that some of your unruly behavior has proven to be of great benefit, such as giving us warning of that recent surprise attack by the Sioux."

The colonel paused, looking at neither Nathan nor Red Buffalo directly, but scowling instead at the empty space between the two. During the awkward moment this went on, the scouts exchanged quick, puzzled sidelong glances. The expected reprimand seemed to be taking a curious turn.

His focus abruptly returning, Ledbetter leaned back in his chair and laced his fingers over his stomach.

"You may or may not appreciate the quandary such a situation would present even the most seasoned commanding officer," he said. "Observing it being faced by another, I might even find it rather amusing. Do you understand the dilemma?"

Nathan cleared his throat. "Uh. No, sir, not sure I do. Speaking for myself, that is."

"Same here," Red Buffalo didn't hesitate to add.

The colonel leaned forward and rested his forearms on the desk. "The thing is, under ordinary circumstances I would not hesitate to quickly and thoroughly dispense disciplinary action for such behavior. The fact that both of you are civilian scouts presents the first complication. The fact that such behavior—or misbehavior, to be more precise—has, at least in the past, been of value greatly offsetting a few fractured rules . . . well, as they say, there's the rub. If any commander lets one or two individuals—no matter how talented they may be—get away with bending the rules, how does he then hold the line on the next subordinate who steps over? And the one after that?"

Neither Nathan nor Red Buffalo attempted a response to the clearly rhetorical question.

"Even before today's incident, I was wrestling with how, going forward, I would handle the situation you two presented. And then, out of the blue, a dispatch rider arrived early this afternoon with the answer." So saying, the colonel reached into a side drawer and produced a sheet of paper that he pushed across the desk toward the scouts. "There it is. Read it for yourselves. Both of you have been reassigned from Fort Randall and ordered to report with all haste to a Captain Joshua Earl in the Montana Territory."

After a quick scan of the paper, Nathan said, "Montana is a mighty big chunk of real estate. Whereabouts we supposed to hook up with this Captain Earl?"

"If you look closer, it says there," Ledbetter told him. "North of Judith Basin, up toward the Milk River, just below a small mountain range called the Wolfheads."

"Blackfoot country," Red Buffalo said with an edge to his voice.

"That's right," the colonel confirmed. "Actually, most of the Blackfeet have moved on out of the area and gone up into Canada. But a stubborn handful under a subchief called Thunder Elk—much like the trouble we just experienced here with Hanging Dog and his renegade Sioux—are terrorizing ranchers and settlers around the town of Telford. Since there's no fort in the area, Captain Earl and a company of soldiers are being sent from Fort Billings in the south to chase the troublemakers up into Canada also, or deal with them as otherwise necessary. You two have been selected to aid them in that task."

"For as long as anyone can remember, the Blackfeet have been bitter enemies of my people, the Crow." The edge in Red Buffalo's voice grew even sharper as he stated this. Looking over at Nathan, he said, "As much as you are renowned for hating *all* Indians? That is how much it has been ingrained in me to hate Blackfeet."

Nathan cocked an eyebrow. "Even the Christian part of you?"

"In the Bible, one can find passages to serve many purposes," Red Buffalo replied. "When it comes to the Blackfeet and the long suffering they have inflicted on my people, I believe the Old Testament teaching of 'an eye for an eye' would suit me for this undertaking."

Now both of Nathan's brows lifted. "Well, then. This sounds like it has the makings to be right interesting."

"In any event," said Ledbetter, "the terms of the dispatch instruct you to proceed with all haste. Taken literally, I'd say you should make plans for riding out tomorrow. I'll see to it you have access to whatever provisions you deem necessary."

"What are you going to do for a scout after we leave?" Nathan asked.

"I've been assured that a replacement will be soon provided," responded Ledbetter. "With the recent defeat of Hanging Dog and his followers, the immediate need is minimal. In truth, except for this morning's events, I expect the past few days have been even a bit boring for you two."

"Whether it has or hasn't," said Nathan, "it seems like

the higher-ups have arranged to make sure we ain't gonna be bored when we get to Montana."

"Indeed," said the colonel. "And as for this morning's incident, I trust you agree that the death of the Creek brave who shot at you and his story of how Bucher met his end concludes that whole matter sufficiently? Dr. Northby confirms that Bucher died several days ago, which matches the Creek's claim. What Bucher was doing hanging around *after* the Sioux raid and allegedly planning to kill you, Stark, we can only conclude must have been an attempt by him to get even with you for your part in spoiling the gunrunning operation he and the other traitors had going. Do you have any objection to calling it closed and reporting it in that manner?"

"Suits me." Nathan spread his hands. "It fits that way, and we ain't likely to ever learn any different."

"Very well. You are dismissed." Ledbetter stood up behind his desk. He pressed his knuckles down on its surface, appearing awkwardly indecisive about something. Then: "I expect I'll see you tomorrow before you leave. But . . . well, let me add at this time that, despite the differences we may have had, you men have provided considerable benefit to this post in your time here. On behalf of all, I wish you well in Montana. Captain Earl could do worse than to have the pair of you assigned to him." Ledbetter gave them a curt nod. "That is all."

Chapter 7

At shortly past nine o'clock the following morning, Nathan and Red Buffalo rode out through the front gate of Fort Randall and swung their horses west toward Montana. Nathan was astride Buck, the prized buckskin stallion that had served him faithfully since before his time in Indian Territory. Red Buffalo rode a sleek black that Nathan had never heard him call by name. A third animal, a heavy-chested packhorse loaded with provisions for the two-week trip that lay ahead, followed along on a tether.

The sun was a brilliantly shimmering ball climbing in a cloudless, cobalt blue sky. With even less breeze stirring than the day before, all signs were indicating another scorcher.

As they plodded along, the fort falling gradually behind, Red Buffalo said, "Ain't surprised the colonel ended up not finding time to see us off this morning. He let a little too much humanity slip out last night. Reckon he must've figured he couldn't afford to risk overdoing it."

Nathan grunted. "Could be. But that ramrod shoved up

his backside is pretty securely in place. I don't picture him making a habit of letting it slip very often."

"Yeah. I'd have to go along with that."

They rode another minute or so before Red Buffalo spoke again. "I was kinda surprised, though, by a certain other person not being on hand to see us off. That is to say, seeing off you in particular."

Keeping his eyes straight ahead, Nathan said, "You worried about my love life? Or are you just trying to stick your nose in where it don't belong? And to be clear, where it ain't got no business and ain't welcome."

"I don't consider it *sticking my nose in*," Red Buffalo replied indignantly, "to inquire after two people who are . . . well, close acquaintances. I came to consider Miss Cordelia a friend. Not as good a one as she clearly was to you, but—"

"That's enough," Nathan said, cutting him short.

The subject under discussion was one Cordelia Blaine, an attractive red-haired widow who played a prominent role at Fort Randall when it came to the education, both scholarly and religious, of the garrison's children. Her late husband, Stephen, had been an army officer stationed at Fort Sill at a time when Nathan was also assigned there.

The two had become friends and Nathan had been invited to take supper with the Blaines on several occasions. Not a social creature by nature, especially not at that point when his vengeful rage against Indians following the slaughter of his parents and pregnant wife was burning at its hottest, Nathan had nevertheless greatly enjoyed those visits.

As it was in the habit of doing, however, the army saw fit to send Nathan and Stephen on different paths and over time they lost track of each other. It wasn't until his arrival at Fort Randall, with Delia already there, that Nathan learned Stephen had been killed in an Indian skirmish a couple of years earlier in Colorado.

Once past that initial piece of sorrowful news, it seemed only natural for the two old friends to gravitate toward each other once again. It became common for Nathan to take supper at Delia's place.

On a few occasions, after Red Buffalo was brought in as an added scout for the fort, Delia invited him, too. The tensions that flared the first time, given Nathan's deep hatred for all Indians, had made for quite a memorable evening.

Gradually, Delia's patient, gentle urging for Nathan to try and control some of his blind rage had helped him form a tenuous acceptance—and even a grudging respect—for the Crow's undeniable skills as a fellow scout and not just another hated Indian.

In the course of all that, the feelings between Nathan and Delia had deepened as well. They learned they'd always shared an attraction for each other. Properly restrained, of course, when Stephen was part of the picture.

But now, under current circumstances, those restraints were no longer in place. Something else that still had to be considered, however—a restraint in its own way—was Nathan's ongoing urge to mete out revenge against what he saw as the entire red race, those responsible for slaughtering his parents and pregnant wife. Despite what he did not try to deny were increasingly romantic feelings between Delia and him, both knew he wasn't ready to make a complete commitment to anyone or anything else until he somehow came to grips with his bloody obsession.

In their time together, especially since the Sioux attack on the fort when the fighting had drawn Nathan away from Delia and his fears for her safety had nearly driven him mad, they had talked of little else but how to resolve these conflicting emotions.

And then the dispatch had arrived, ordering Nathan to join another campaign hundreds of miles away.

Nathan had gone to Delia's directly from the meeting with Ledbetter. She'd already heard the news. They talked into the wee hours about what this meant to whatever relationship they were building and what to do about it.

Being a civilian scout, Nathan could have refused the Montana assignment and broken further ties to the army. But they both knew he wasn't ready for that. In the end, they'd decided to treat this like a test to see how strong their feelings truly were. If they both felt the same when the Montana business was finished, then either Nathan would return to Cordelia at Fort Randall or send for her to join him wherever he was. It was the best that could be made of a bad situation.

After Nathan shut down Red Buffalo's remarks, the pair rode in silence for a spell. Finally, Nathan said, "If you must know, Delia and I said our good-byes last night. It was a little rough, as you might guess. She didn't want to go through it again this morning, in front of everybody."

Red Buffalo nodded. "I guess I can understand that."

"She said I should tell you good-bye for her and let you know she considers you a friend and hopes the two of you meet up again somewhere along the way. I guess I should have told you that right away and not bit your head off when you tried to ask."

"You can't help being you," Red Buffalo said fatalistically. "Reckon it's enough that you did get around to letting me know."

"She said more, too," Nathan added. "Said for you to stay safe . . . and mentioned something about being obliged if you'd help get me back to her in one piece."

Red Buffalo rolled his eyes. "Oh, come on now. That's a mighty tall order. I'm all for keeping my own self safe. But looking after your sorry hide as well? I heard what you told that Creek about having enemies scattered from the Rio Grande to Yellowstone. I plan on being busy killing Blackfeet. I don't know how much spare time I'll have to look around and see who's coming after you next."

"Guess you'll have to settle for doing the best you can, then," Nathan said. "Besides, remember the request came from Delia, not me."

"Come to think of it," said Red Buffalo, "considering how far we got to go before reporting to Captain Earl, we're apt to run into a half-dozen or so hombres out to get you before we ever make it that far."

"Look on the bright side. Comes to that, it'll keep the trip from being boring," Nathan told him.

Chapter 8

The ride from Fort Randall to Telford wasn't boring or fraught with danger. The natural beauty surrounding them much of the way was anything but boring and some of the more rugged stretches offered plenty in the way of adversity. The weather stayed reasonable, a few particularly hot days and a couple of stormy nights, but quite tolerable for the most part. Game and fish were plentiful to supplement the provisions on the back of their packhorse.

On the thirteenth day, a Thursday by their reckoning, they were into the Milk River region. The Judith and Moccasin mountains lay behind, and the low, shadowy line of the Wolfheads could be seen along the distant horizon to the north. The only thing left now was to locate the town of Telford.

With the sun nearing its noon peak, they came upon some fresh wagon tracks angling toward the northwest. A short time later, topping the crest of a rolling hill, they spotted a cluster of three covered wagons halted on a low flat just ahead. The smoke of a cooking fire rose from their midst and the aroma of biscuits baking drifted faintly to the riders.

"We've steered clear of folks most all this time," said Red Buffalo. "But it occurs to me that this bunch is likely headed for Telford, same as us, and maybe could give us an idea how much farther. Plus, it'd be worth riding up to ask, just for the chance to get a closer smell of those biscuits."

"If they're stopped for their nooning like it appears and they got an ounce of hospitality in 'em, they ought to invite a couple of lonely fellow travelers for a sit-down and offer us a *taste* of those biscuits. Come on, let's go find out."

As they neared the wagons, a heavyset man stepped out from between two of the rigs. His expression was amiable enough, but a double-barreled shotgun was clenched in the crook of his right arm, its muzzles pointed downward at a forty-five-degree angle. Behind the driver's box of the far-right wagon, a younger, leaner man edged into sight. The snout of a Winchester rifle poked into view, held at the ready across his chest.

Nathan mentally commended the men of this group for showing some readiness. It paid to stay on the cautious side out here on the frontier.

After he and Red Buffalo were close enough to rein in their horses, Nathan said to the man with the shotgun, "Howdy to you. We spotted your wagons and smoke from back up a ways."

The shotgunner nodded. "Uh-huh. We saw you riding down." He looked to be a year or two short of fifty, with ruddy cheeks where they peeked out from a full beard and shrewd eyes. He wore a collarless white shirt, red suspenders, and pin-striped trousers tucked into high black boots. His expression remained amiable as he appraised

Nathan, but when those shrewd eyes came to rest on Red Buffalo, the man's mouth pulled notably tighter.

"Don't worry," Nathan said around an easy grin. "He's a tame Injun. Mostly. I've managed to keep him from scalping anybody since way last winter."

The man continued to regard Red Buffalo and his mouth stayed tight.

Red Buffalo spoke for himself, saying, "Pay no attention to my companion. He is as inaccurate as he is unamusing. It's been nearly a full year since my scalping knife has seen any activity."

It took a second or two before the bearded man suddenly broke into a grin of his own. "If you two are a couple of owlhoots trying to get me to lower my guard with lame humor, then you're almost there."

"Actually," said Nathan, "we're a couple of civilian army scouts on our way from Fort Randall in the Dakotas to join a company of soldiers who've been stationed up this way near the town of Telford. We came across your tracks earlier and had a hunch you might be headed there, too."

"Indeed we are. By our reckoning, we'll be there well before sundown. That's what made us decide we could afford to stop for a rest and to take a noon meal. My name is Amos Handley, late of Billings."

"My name's Nathan Stark. This"—Nathan gestured—"is Moses Red Buffalo. We've been sent to scout for and assist the soldiers in their mission to deal with some Blackfoot Indians who've been causing trouble hereabouts."

"Yes, we heard there were some Indian concerns up this way."

"And you came on anyway? Without escort?" Red Buffalo asked.

"Mr. Handley and I consider ourselves reasonably competent," said the young man with the Winchester, emerging from behind his wagon and stepping forward. "Furthermore, our understanding is that the Indian trouble has been confined to the north of Telford."

"Could be," allowed Nathan. "Been my experience, though, that Injuns who are willing to be 'confined' will stick to a reservation somewhere and not go raising hell to begin with."

The young man frowned and appeared to give this observation some serious thought. He was tall, trim though solidly put together, not too far into his twenties. He was clad in homespun clothes, scuffed boots, wore a short-billed cap one size too small with strands of straw-colored hair poking out all around. Nathan thought he might as well have had a sign hanging around his neck that read SODBUSTER . . . but he'd stood ready behind that wagon and he held his rifle like he knew how to use it.

"This is Joe Raymer," Handley introduced. "He and his wife, Margie, are newlyweds, just starting out. They're bound and determined that up here in the Telford area is where they can make a go of it."

"We got us a cow and a bull and a homestead grant for a section of land," said Raymer, a mix of pride and eagerness in his voice. "You bet we're gonna make a go of it."

"Amos!" a rather strident female voice called from the other side of the wagons. "If you're not going to shoot those strangers or chase them off, then bring them on in to break bread with us so we can all finish eating and proceed on our way!"

Handley smiled sheepishly and his ruddy cheeks reddened a bit more. "My wife, Esther," he said. "Come on, if you're hungry. Your Indian-fighting background ought to have you toughened up sufficiently to face the sharp tongue of my better half."

The meal with the wagon travelers went well. Esther Handley, stout and round-faced with iron gray hair pulled into a severe bun, indeed turned out to be loud and a bit brassy, but it was quickly evident that her bark was worse than her bite.

Joe Raymer's wife, Margie, was the complete opposite: a petite, doe-eyed, strawberry blonde, she spoke seldom and softly, almost to the point of near silence. The single occupant of the third wagon was an attractive, dark-haired woman of thirty or so who'd been introduced as Andrea Fontinelle.

The Handleys were relocating after their Billings restaurant had burned down. Esther's brother, an elderly widower in failing health, ran a dry goods store in Telford and had extended a welcome invitation for them to move in with him and help run the business. The Fontinelle woman spoke somewhat vaguely of being on a quest to try and locate a wandering uncle, her only remaining kin.

The conversation was pleasant, the stew served in generous portions was delicious, and the biscuits met and exceeded their enticing aroma. Nathan and Red Buffalo were both adequate trail cooks, but it had been quite a spell since they'd eaten such good food.

During the course of the meal, it was decided that the scouts would ride the rest of the way to Telford with the wagons.

"As Joe said earlier, he and I considered ourselves up to the challenge of any trouble," Handley remarked. "But I'll admit that, as we get nearer to where the Indian trouble has been reported, it's comforting to have a couple extra guns on hand. Comforting, too, to hear that the army has been assigned to the area in order to clear up the problem for good."

Everything had been cleared away and the wagons were nearly ready to roll again when more riders were spotted heading toward them, this time from the west.

"Looks like this is our day for visitors," said Handley.

"Well, it's poor timing on their part," Esther declared. "The pots and vittles are put away, and that's that."

The approaching horsemen, four in number, advanced at a hard gallop and didn't slow down until they pulled reins only a few yards from the wagons. This brought a churning cloud of dust rolling over and past them and then spreading to the wagons and beyond.

As before, Handley stepped out to greet the new arrivals. He held his shotgun again, but this time wore a less amiable expression as he squinted against the swirling dust.

"You fellas seem to be in a mighty big hurry over something," he said.

One of the riders, a lantern-jawed specimen with a wide, thick-lipped mouth that looked like it was made for curling into a sneer, responded, "We're busy men, mister.

We go everywhere in a hurry because we got lots to take care of."

Handley nodded. "Good to have a purpose in life. You gents from around here?"

Nathan moved up to lean casually between two of the wagons, a few feet in back of Handley. Young Joe Raymer and his Winchester had once again taken up a partially exposed position behind the driver's box of his wagon. For the time being, Nathan motioned Red Buffalo to stay out of sight. He was making a quick appraisal of the four riders and didn't particularly like what he saw.

Two of them appeared to be standard-issue ranch hands. Unshaven, faces weathered by long hours in the sun and wind, six-guns riding on their hips in faded, cracked, and stiff-looking holsters.

The other two men, however—including the one doing the talking—were cut from a different bolt of cloth. Their clothing was of a better grade and their faces had seen some time in the out of doors, but not nearly as much. They sat their saddles a little less comfortably and their eyes and body language conveyed an air of insolent arrogance.

But mostly it was the way they wore their guns riding low on their hips in tied-down holsters that were well oiled and supple. And the smoke wagons nestled in them—top-quality shooting irons—rode high for easier grasping.

Unless Nathan missed his guess, he was looking at a pair of hombres who made their living doing gun work.

In response to Handley's question, the lantern-jawed spokesman said, "Yeah, you called it right. We're from around here. Got our roots sunk here, you might say.

Which leads me to observe that you folks appear to be rolling in after pulling up roots from somewhere else."

"True enough," Handley admitted. "My wife and I are relocating to Telford to aid her brother in the running of his dry goods store there. Miles Rafferty is his name, you may be familiar with him."

"No, can't say as I am. But then, I don't spend a lot of time dealing in dry goods," replied Lantern Jaw.

"Neither do I," spoke up the rider to his right, the other hombre Nathan had marked as a gunman. He appeared somewhat taller and leaner than Lantern Jaw, with beady, suspicious eyes and a mouthful of horsey teeth that were revealed when he spoke. "But I been around enough to know that a cow and a bull ain't generally no part of running a dry goods operation. How do you explain hauling such critters all this way for the purpose of doing town work, mister?"

Before Handley could reply, Joe Raymer stood a little taller behind his driver's box and said, "The answer's simple. Those animals don't belong to Mr. Handley and therefore got nothing to do with the business he'll be involved with."

"You see," Handley offered by way of further explanation, "the three wagons in this group are traveling together, but those inside of each have different purposes upon reaching Telford. As I said, my wife and I—"

"Yeah, yeah, we got all that and we don't really give a damn," Lantern Jaw said, cutting him off. "But what we do care about is fat, plodding cows moving in. Because that signals hayseeds and sodbusters and next will come chickens and pigs and hell, who knows, probably low-down sheep if the tide ain't stopped quick and permanent."

"This is a free country," Joe said stubbornly. "Folks have a right to try and make a way for themselves—"

Lantern Jaw cut him off, snarling, "It's a free country because that's how cattlemen *made* it! Paving the way, bringing in beef, driving off the Indians—hell, *still* fighting the stinking redskins! That wasn't done so a bunch of pig farmers and corn growers could move in and start plowing up the good grazing ground that was tamed by the sweat and blood of others."

Nathan stepped forward from out between the wagons. "Tell me," he said in an easy drawl while his eyes conveyed a flinty hardness as they locked gazes with Lantern Jaw, "how much sweat and blood did *you* shed when it came to taming any piece of this land?"

Chapter 9

Leaning forward in his saddle and resting his left forearm down on the pommel, leaving his gun hand free, Lantern Jaw shifted his gaze past Handley and brought it to rest on Nathan.

"Well, now," he said. "I see for a fact it's how the man said. These three little wagons surely are carrying quite a variety of folks, ain't they? You don't strike me as no sod-buster and you sure as hell ain't no store clerk. So what is it that brings you to our part of the country, stranger?"

Nathan replied, "For starters, let me tell you what I *didn't* come for—and that's to get lectured on who does or don't rightly belong here and then to get grilled about my personal business, which I figure I'll share when and with who I take a notion."

Lantern Jaw remained leaning on his pommel but he went tight across the shoulders and the fingers of his right hand opened and closed slowly.

The beady-eyed number to his right showed his horsey teeth in a wide, crooked grin.

"Say now, Lester," he said. "If I heard right, that fella kind of warned you off sticking your nose in his business.

Which, seein's how you was just making some friendly inquiries, seems downright rude."

"Does for a fact, Curly," agreed Lantern Jaw, now identified as Lester. "And something we definitely don't need no more of around these parts—besides sodbusters, that is—are rude hombres who think they're gonna sashay in and start throwing their weight around."

"And who are you," huffed Handley, "to think you have any right to say what new arrivals are wanted or needed hereabouts? I see no badges to give you that kind of authority!"

"Badges?" Lester barked a nasty laugh. "We don't need no badges, you old fool. We got something way better than that." He reached back with his free hand and slapped the rump of his horse. "You see the M-Slash-G brand on this nag? That stands for Bennett McGreevey, the he-wolf of this whole territory. The ranch is just part of what he owns and runs around here. And when I said a little while ago that we keep busy taking care of things? Well, the things we take care of are for Mr. McGreevey . . . and he don't like rude strangers and he most of all don't like stinking sodbusters!"

"How about the Blackfeet?" Nathan asked. "Reckon they don't qualify as sodbusters, but from what I've heard they sure have been showing some rude behavior lately. Is that a problem you fellas are gonna take care of for this McGreevey, too?"

Lester scowled. "Injun fighting ain't our line. A company of soldier boys have been brought in to handle that problem."

"Lucky for you, eh?"

"What's that supposed to mean?"

Nathan shrugged. "Take it how you want. To my way of thinking, giving a hard time to a few farmers and home-steaders out breaking their backs trying to work a piece of land, or pushing around some other poor slob you decide to take a dislike to for whatever reason . . . that's a lot easier than butting heads with a pack of howling red-skins out for hair. Wouldn't you say?"

The one called Curly went rigid in his saddle. "You calling us yellow?"

Red Buffalo glided into sight behind Nathan and then stepped wide off to his left. Holding his Henry rifle up and ready across his chest, he said, "If he ain't, I am."

Lester pushed up off his saddle horn and bared his teeth in an angry grimace. "Say, what the hell is this?"

"It's called bumping up against somebody who ain't intimidated by your threatening spiels and your pushy ways," Nathan told him.

"If it's trouble you and your ragged-ass bunch are look-ing for, then—"

Nathan cut him off. "You're the ones who came barging into this camp and started running your mouth. Nobody was acting quarrelsome before then."

Nathan reached down and unexpectedly, smoothly drew his Colt. Leveling it in the general direction of Lester and Curly, he grated, "But now that we've reached that stage, there's no sense pussyfooting around it any longer. You and your pal Curly look like you're handy and probably pretty fast with those shooting irons strapped on your hips. But I don't think you're fast enough or stupid enough to try anything funny with two guns already drawn against you."

"Make it three," said Handley, lifting the barrel of his shotgun.

"Four," spoke up Joe, stepping around the end of his wagon.

The two cowhands behind Lester and Curly went a little pale and their eyes shifted around nervously. The two gunman stayed outwardly calm, their expressions cold and hard. But they made sure their hands remained still and in plain sight.

Lester's thick lips finally got around to forming that sneer that Nathan had been expecting. "Mister, you are making a bad mistake."

"I've made 'em before."

"You follow through with this one, it might be the biggest—and last—you ever do."

"How much longer are we gonna stand here and listen to this gasbag blow gut wind?" Red Buffalo wanted to know. "I've heard about all the threats I care to. I say it's time for them to either put up, or shut up and make dust out of here."

"Oh, we'll clear out, all right," said Lester, his sneer widening. "The stink of would-be pig farmers is starting to sour my stomach anyway. You're a brave bunch now, all clustered together with your guns bristling out like a pack of porcupines. But it won't always be that way. And as soon as it ain't, you'll be seeing us again."

Nathan sighed. "I figured you'd say something like that."

"Meaning what?"

"Meaning, for starters, is there a sheriff or marshal in that town of Telford?"

Curly snorted. "Oh yeah. We got us a real rip-snortin' town tamer."

Nathan nodded. "Good. Then, come tomorrow, that's where you can reclaim your guns."

Curly's jaw dropped. "What?"

"You heard me." Nathan thumbed back the hammer of his Colt. "I ain't hardly stupid enough to listen to a man threaten me repeatedly and then let him wander off fully armed and still hot under the collar so's he can decide to try and bushwhack me around the next bend."

"We ain't bushwhackers!" Lester protested.

"No, not today you ain't going to be. I'm going to make sure of that. Because you're going to shuck your guns and leave 'em here with us before you ride off. Then, after you've had a chance to cool off, you can pick them up tomorrow from your local town tamer."

Lester's face turned bright red, almost purple. "To hell with you! I don't hand my shooting irons over to nobody."

"Fine by me," responded Red Buffalo. "If that's how you feel, you can always go the put-up-or-shut-up route, like I suggested before. Me, I'd just as soon you tried it."

The two wranglers farther back began immediately, though with careful slowness, unbuckling their gun belts.

Curly looked increasingly uncertain, borderline panicky. He said, "That damn Injun is crazy, Lester. Look in his eyes. The other one ain't much better. I think they mean it. They got the drop on us and they'd be all too happy for an excuse to cut us down!"

"I wouldn't rate your partner particularly high on brains," Nathan drawled. "But he's showing some now, Lester, and you'd be smart to listen to him. You tried to play a bad hand here today and couldn't bluff your way through it. Now's the time to fold your cards and walk away from the table."

Nobody said anything more for several seconds. Lester aimed a glare first at Nathan and then at Red Buffalo.

Finally, slowly, he reached down to loosen the tie-down thong on his holster and then began unbuckling his gun belt. Curly followed suit.

In a hoarse voice barely above a whisper, Lester said, "All right, you win this hand. But there'll be another, I guarantee it . . . And you won't have to wait very long."

Chapter 10

Miles Rafferty shook his head and uttered a dry chuckle. "Whooee. I sure would've liked to see that. I'm not saying it was wise on your part to brace Lester Fallow and Curly Messingill that way, mind you—or, worse, Bennett McGreevey by extension—but I would've bought a ticket to see those two bullies eat crow!"

"Well, keep your spare change," Nathan advised him. "Because unless I miss my guess, they'll be coming around sooner or later to try and get even with Moses and me."

"How about that, brother?" Esther Handley asked. "You called those two scoundrels 'bullies' a minute ago. Bullies are often cowards who slink off once confronted and go in search of easier targets to push around. Might that be true of this pair? Or is Mr. Stark right in his assessment that we haven't seen the last of them?"

The expression that had accompanied the chuckle from Rafferty now faded and turned sober. He was a very thin, frail-looking man, several years older than his sister and quite a physical contrast to her stoutness. He shuffled slowly amidst the shelves and countertops of his cramped dry goods store with the aid of a polished hickory cane that looked considerably sturdier and nearly bigger around than he was.

Nathan, Red Buffalo, Joe and Margie Raymer, and the Handleys were all gathered in Rafferty's modest living quarters at the rear of his store. Upon their arrival in town, Andrea Fontinelle, claiming a severe headache, had separated from the others and gone to secure a hotel room while the rest came here. Outside, dusk was settling over Telford, sending alternating bands of shadow and orange-gold light stabbing in through the windows.

"Alas, dear sister," Rafferty replied in response to Esther's question, "I fear Mr. Stark is right. Fallow and Messingill aren't the types to slink away in the manner you describe. They're bullies, to be sure, but they back it up with genuine toughness and they're both mighty handy with those temporarily confiscated six-guns."

"Be that as it may," interjected Amos Handley, "let's not forget that both Stark and Red Buffalo have proven highly competent in their own right. They sent those two skunks packing with their tails between their legs once. I wouldn't hesitate to put my money on them doing so again if that's what it comes to."

"Thanks for the vote of confidence, Handley," Nathan said. "But keep in mind we sort of caught those varmints by surprise earlier today. They came looking to hoorah some wagons full of settlers and homesteaders, not expecting to run into a couple of rougher cobs like me and Moses. By the time Moses stepped out with his Henry and they realized they weren't facing such an easy job, they were already under our guns."

"And our guns, too," spoke up Joe Raymer.

Red Buffalo nodded. "That's true. But Nathan's point

is that, even though he and I are no strangers to violence, we are not what anybody would consider 'fast guns.' If Lester and Curly had recognized sooner what they were faced with and gone for their guns first, things likely would not have gone so well for us."

"But Mr. Handley and I had our guns out right from the get-go," Joe insisted.

Nathan looked at him. "You ever shot anybody, boy?"

Joe blinked. "Well . . . no. I never even aimed a gun at anybody before."

"It ain't something that comes easy for the average person. There's a hesitancy, a natural reluctance to it for men who haven't been hardened by gun work," Nathan told him. "Yeah, you and Handley were observant and took a protective stance when you saw riders approaching. First me and Moses, then those other four. That spoke well for you. But if gunplay had broken out with men like Lester and Curly, I'm afraid that even with rifles already in your hands, likely you wouldn't have acted fast enough to do you much good."

"I've been thinking about that, too," said Esther. "You're both better suited if it comes to more trouble. Amos and Joe are not. They haven't been 'hardened,' as you put it, by situations involving gun work."

"Oh, I don't know about that," protested Handley. "As a younger man I wore a uniform in the Mexican War, you'll recall."

"Yes, as a *much* younger man, dear husband," Esther reminded him. "Since then, the only uniform you've worn is the apron of a cook in our restaurant, and until you picked up that old shotgun the other day, your hands have held little besides the handles of pots and pans."

"Mrs. Handley is right," said Red Buffalo. "If Lester and Curly come looking to deliver payback to Nathan and me, that's one thing. We have the experience and capabilities to deal with something like that. But if they also mean to make trouble for Mr. Handley and Joe for the parts they played . . . that is more concerning."

"How about it, Rafferty?" Nathan asked. "How strong a reaction would you expect out of these varmints? And what about the law in this town? Once we turn Lester's and Curly's guns over to him and explain the situation, won't he have some control over keeping them tamed down?"

Rafferty made a sour face. "I'll answer the last part of your question first. Our town marshal is a lazy tub of lard named Fergus Feeney. He has a shrew of a wife and seven or eight kids at home and the only reason he wants a job at all is to have an excuse to get away from them. As far as looking to him to tame down Fallow and Messingill? He couldn't tame a sparrow with a broken wing."

Nathan grimaced at this response.

Rafferty went on, "The only 'taming' that gets done around town is by Feeney's deputy, Rafe Ridgway. He's great at busting the heads of drunks who get out of line in the saloons and whorehouses, and running snake oil salesmen and other riffraff out of town. And he's pretty handy with a six-gun, too. Cut from cloth not too dissimilar to the like of Fallow or Messingill. In fact, it's a common rumor around town—and one I happen to subscribe to myself—that Ridgway takes his orders more from Bennett McGreevey than from the marshal. Sort of McGreevey's more *respectable* hired gun."

"You don't paint a particularly favorable picture of your town," Red Buffalo said.

Rafferty shrugged. "It has its flaws, like most any place. Also has a lot of promise. I may not live to see it, but I believe Telford will one day be a fine and prosperous community. McGreevey's heavy-handed ambition will see to that until, ironically, I expect it will grow beyond the dominance he currently enjoys. That's when it will reach its full potential."

"McGreevey again," echoed Nathan. "That name keeps coming around. Started with Lester being in a big hurry to bring it up back on the trail. Called him the he-wolf of the whole territory, him and his M-Slash-G brand. What's his story? He that much of a high muckety-muck?"

"McGreevey's story?" Rafferty pursed his lips. "Guess it's not too different from some of those cattle barons you hear about down in Texas. McGreevey's was one of the first big herds in this area. He was largely responsible for the town starting up. Owns several prominent businesses in addition to his ranch. He's been named a delegate to Congress as part of the push for statehood. He has ambition and ego and he sees Telford and all things branded M-Slash-G as just the beginning. He means to ride that delegate post to much bigger things. And if he needs to grind a few people under his boot heel along the way, so be it."

Red Buffalo cocked an eyebrow. "Heavy-handed and heavy-booted, too, eh?"

"That's the way it is."

"Lester and Curly had a lot to say about how unwelcome farmers and the like were to the area," said Nathan.

"Were they speaking strictly for themselves or did that come from McGreevey, too?"

"What do you think?" Rafferty responded wryly. "In the first place, Fallow and Messingill don't spend time thinking up opinions of their own. And McGreevey is first and foremost a cattleman. The thought of farmers and other settlers moving in and slicing up the land that, in his opinion, was God-provided for raising beef gouges hard against his grain.

"So far, all the homesteaders and smaller operations have taken root across the fringe land up nearer the Wolf-head Mountains, not down in the basin where the big cattle outfits are. But the way McGreevey sees it, there's plenty of other places in Montana and elsewhere for that kind of thing . . . but not in his backyard."

Nathan frowned in thought. "Seems to me that having a range war boil up in his backyard, as you call it, wouldn't present a very favorable picture to the paper-pushers back East. Not as a place settled enough to be considered for statehood. And what about the Blackfoot flare-up? Strikes me as yet another concern for McGreevey's domain."

"I'm sure it is," Rafferty allowed. "But McGreevey's hardly one to just sit back and fret. That's why he's got Fallow and Messingill and a handful of other gun toughs signed on to his crew for the sake of applying added pressure to the farmers. Some he's managed to buy out, a few others he's discouraged with thinly veiled threats. Now it appears he's building up to do more than just threaten the stubborn ones still hanging on.

"It's ironic to think that, since they're picking off the smaller spreads that make the easiest targets and are mostly the kind McGreevey wants to get rid of, if the

Blackfeet were left alone they'd be doing McGreevey a kind of service. The only trouble with that is the words *Indian uprising* are even more off-putting to Washington than talk of a range war.

"So who do you think it was who pulled the strings to get a whole company of soldiers sent up here? McGreevey's delegate status definitely carries some weight. If the army can promptly push the Blackfeet up into Canada, as I understand is the plan, and McGreevey's tactics with the settlers work . . . Well, then there won't be much to stand in his way."

"Sounds like we got the easy part, just helping to chase off the Blackfeet," said Red Buffalo. Then, eyeing Nathan, he added, "Was we to stick around too long—long enough to see and hear more about McGreevey's heavy-handed ways—I got a hunch that one or both of us might take a notion to stick our noses where it wouldn't be healthy."

Nathan returned his look. "And chasing Blackfeet *is* healthy? Besides, if Lester and Curly come around looking to settle a score with us, we might not have any choice but to stick our noses where McGreevey's business overlaps."

There followed a long, somewhat tense silence.

Until Rafferty said, "You've all had a long trip and must be weary. With the passing of my wife nearly two years back and my bum knees growing steadily worse, I set up this apartment here as my living accommodations. Saves me walking back and forth each day from our house. Which means the house has gone virtually unoccupied of late, making it the residence I wrote that would be available to you and Amos when you arrived, sister. It may be a bit musty from lack of use, but except for any personal touches you'll want to make, I think you will find it quite acceptable. There's plenty of space, including a spare bedroom where, if the four of you wish to work it out, the young couple might also want to spend the night. In the morning, then, they can proceed with their own plans."

"That sounds wonderful. Certainly Joe and Margie are welcome to spend the night there with us," said Esther.

"If it's not too much of an imposition, yes, that does sound wonderful," Margie responded in her typical shy manner.

"There's room out back to park your wagons and even a small barn to stable your animals," Rafferty told them.

"It's settled, then," Handley proclaimed. "Just give us directions, Miles, and we'll take you up on your kind offer."

Rafferty turned to Nathan and Red Buffalo. "I'm sorry I don't have anything to offer you gents. I certainly would if—"

"Don't worry about it," Nathan told him. "Moses and I are plenty capable of fending for ourselves."

"Come to think of it, I suppose you'll want to be reporting to the army encampment, anyway. It's north of town only a couple of miles. You can't miss it."

Nathan grinned. "I'm sure we'll be able to find it . . . but in the morning. I think Moses will agree with me that the army can wait long enough for us to squeeze in a night's sleep in a soft hotel room bed and maybe a hot bath if we can scare one up somewhere."

"The Telford House just a couple of blocks up the street can meet those needs—and at a fair price," Rafferty suggested.

"Another need we'll want to take care of before leaving town," Red Buffalo reminded everyone, "is paying a visit to the marshal's office and dropping off Lester's and Curly's property, as promised."

Rafferty beamed a wide smile. "Doggone it. Something else I won't get the chance to see, but would pay admission if I could. Guess I'll just have to settle for listening to Marshal Feeney whine and whimper over being put in the middle of such a situation." He coughed up another chuckle. "Doubt I'll have any trouble hearing him, either, not even from all this way down the street."

Chapter 11

"So you just shucked your hardware and rode off without it, is that what you're telling me? Didn't even put up any kind of fight? Jesus!"

Bennett McGreevey had demanded an account of the incident be repeated to him for a second time, but still he seemed scarcely able to believe his ears.

Lester Fallow and Curly Messingill stood before him in the expansive den of his sprawling, well-appointed home at the M-Slash-G ranch headquarters. They shifted their feet uneasily on the thick carpeting and tried to find somewhere—anywhere—to look other than meeting McGreevey's glare.

Finally, Fallow responded somewhat defensively, "Wasn't really no chance to put up a fight, Mr. McGreevey. They got the drop on us before we had any clue they were gonna get their hackles up. All of a sudden there was four guns on us."

"*You* had four guns, too! And you and Messingill are supposed to be a couple of the best at using them. That's what I'm paying you for!"

Messingill made a sour face. "Meaning no disrespect

to Smitty and Nolan, boss, but they were two of our four guns. They're okay fellas, but they're just a couple of ranch hands—not gunmen. They started unbuckling at the first growl of a cross word."

"That still left the both of you!" McGreevey insisted.

Fallow started to let some irritation show. "Yeah, and it still left four gun muzzles trained on us. We might be fast with our shooting irons, but anybody'd have to be plumb loco to slap leather in the face of that. And two of the hombres aiming those muzzles—the Indian and that wolf-faced ranny—looked mighty comfortable behind 'em. I don't rightly know how they fit in with that wagon bunch, but it was plain they meant business. And no matter how much you're paying us, we'd have a hard time spending it plugged full of holes. We wouldn't be of much use to you in that condition, neither."

McGreevey stood up and came around the end of his desk. He kept moving, pacing across the width of the massive stone fireplace built against one wall, streaming a plume of smoke from the fat cigar clenched between his teeth.

He was a tall, solidly built man in his middle forties, with classically handsome facial features and thick dark hair combed straight back from a sharp widow's peak, streaks of white at the temples. His attire was simple though of the finest quality: rich brown trousers tucked into high, gleamingly polished black boots, lemon-colored shirt, maroon string tie knotted at the throat through a silver stud as big as a boiled egg.

He paused for a moment at the end of the fireplace. Then, turning back, he removed the cigar from his mouth and said, "Damn it all, I realize you must have done all you could. For your own pride, if nothing else. But surely you can see the bigger problem this could cause for us, right? We're trying to discourage more blasted nesters and farmers from coming in and at the same time crowd out the stubborn jackasses already here. Accomplishing that rests largely on you two. But now, if word spreads how you got your guns taken away by the members of some piddling little wagon train, what kind of message do you think that's going to send? That people can stand up to you and live to tell about it!"

The lower half of Fallow's lantern jaw jutted forward and his brows pinched tight to form a scowl. "In the first place, another run-in with that pair—the Indian and the wolf-faced hombre—will make sure *they* ain't spreading any talk about what took place between us. We'll be ready for them next time."

"Not just ready. Damn well looking forward to it," Messingill amended.

"That's right. And after we're done with them," declared Fallow, "if there's anybody else around who thinks they're ready to try their luck, we'll show them that what happened out on the trail was nothing but a fluke and we ain't to be trifled with."

Through clenched teeth, Messingill said, "All we need is time to get our guns back from Feeney in the morning and then hunt down that pair. Unless they lit a shuck out of town or are lying low somewhere, we can have the whole business squared away by noon."

Encouraged by McGreevey's apparent tolerance for this release of anger and humiliation that had been building up in the two gunmen ever since the incident with the wagons, Fallow kept going.

"Why wait until tomorrow for our own guns? What makes you think we can trust those skunks to do what they said they would? We could head out to the bunkhouse right now and borrow some guns from the fellows there. The lead from one six-gun does just as good a job as from another, long as the trigger puller knows what he's doing. I say we go on into town tonight and look those varmints up. Settle things with them all the faster and make sure they don't run their mouths."

Messingill's head bobbed eagerly. "By grab, I'm up for that. Let's do it!"

"Now hold on," said McGreevey, the cigar back in his mouth and the words rolling out in a cloud of blue smoke. "I understand and applaud your enthusiasm to get the problem taken care of. However, acting too hastily could also have its drawbacks."

"How so?"

"I'm not sure, exactly. But it occurs to me that learning a little bit about that pair—and the others they were traveling with—might be worthwhile before goading them into gunplay." McGreevey paused, puffing some more smoke thoughtfully. Then: "You say there was a cow and a bull tied to one of the wagons, obviously the start-up for another small operation destined to fail. But is the whole group connected to that undertaking, or did they just happen to be traveling together? If so, what is the intent of the rest in the other two wagons? And where do the two troublemakers fit in?"

"We don't know none of those things. We never got the chance to find out," Messingill said sullenly.

"Uh-huh. That's my point," McGreevey told him. "I was planning on going into town anyway, once we were finished here. I think it may be even more beneficial for me to follow through with that, and for the two of you to hold off. Stay here, cool down, get a good night's sleep. Tomorrow will be soon enough for you to settle your scores, and in the meantime, there's a good chance I can learn some answers—possibly some important ones— about who it is you're aiming to settle with."

"Don't really matter, not in the long run," Fallow grumbled stubbornly. "Whoever they are won't change what they got coming to 'em."

"No. Perhaps not, as you say, in the long run," McGreevey allowed. "But what I'm able to learn may have a bearing on how and when we proceed where they and perhaps some of the others are concerned. So. We'll do it my way. Understood?"

After getting themselves all worked up for another confrontation with the men who'd humiliated them earlier in the day, it wasn't easy for Fallow or Messingill to hold back now. But McGreevey had the bankroll and that meant that—as long as they wanted to keep drawing from it—he called the shots.

"If that's the way you want it, boss," Fallow said reluctantly. "But I wish you'd at least let us ride into town with you. You know, just to keep an eye on things."

"Things will go fine," McGreevey assured him. "You boys stay here. Get some rest, like I said. Who knows? Maybe I'll have some luck and be able to get my hands on your guns while I'm in town. If I do, I'll bring them back and have them waiting for you when you crawl out of bed tomorrow." He chuckled. "Be like kids waking up on Christmas morning with presents under the tree."

Messingill snorted. "When I was a kid I was raised

with nine brothers and sisters. The only thing I ever got for Christmas was a pair of hand-me-down shoes to wear for going out to help chop and haul firewood so we didn't all freeze to death."

"I'll settle for a present tomorrow of you just turning us loose to go after those two, boss," said Fallow.

McGreevey canted his head to one side and exhaled a perfect smoke ring. "There's an old saying about being careful what you wish for . . . You might want to keep that in mind while you're busy getting rested up tonight, Lester."

Chapter 12

The clerk at the Telford House Hotel was a gangly, bespectacled young man with prematurely thinning hair. He also appeared to have a nervous tic, but Nathan wasn't sure if that was always present or was perhaps brought on by the sight of him and Red Buffalo striding into the lobby with their saddlebags and bedrolls slung over their shoulders.

"Like two rooms for the night," Nathan announced as he reached the desk.

The tic under the young man's left eye gave a little jump before he stammered, "I, uh . . . That is, the hotel policy don't . . . I can't . . . I'm not allowed . . . to rent a room to an Indian."

Nathan regarded him for a long moment. The clerk struggled to meet his gaze. And what he definitely avoided was making any eye contact with Moses Red Buffalo.

Nathan glanced over at the Crow. His expression was blank. Nathan had a pretty good hunch this wasn't the first time he'd run into such a thing.

Turning his eyes back to the clerk, Nathan said, "Well, then, there really ain't no problem. You see, *I'm* the one renting the rooms—both of 'em. This fella here is just my manservant."

"Manservant?"

"Yeah. You know what that is, don't you?"

The young clerk look bewildered and the tic under his eye became busy again. "No . . . No, I don't reckon I do."

"A manservant," Nathan explained, "is a fella whose job is to look after the needs of another fella. That's what Red Buffalo—that's his name—is to me. He lays out my clothes, polishes my boots, runs errands, and fetches things for me. Like that. Sort of a traveling butler. Only he ain't in my house doing those things, he goes around with me and takes care of 'em, understand?"

The clerk didn't look any less bewildered.

Nathan kept pushing. "You can see, can't you, how me being here at the hotel and him having to stay somewhere else would mess up the whole arrangement? I need him close by, in an adjoining room, to be available for any chores I want done. It ain't like he'll be running loose, wandering the halls on his own and scaring your other guests into thinking he might be some wild-eyed redskin on the warpath."

By now the young man looked terribly ill at ease and his tic was busier than ever.

"All right, then," Nathan declared as if everything was decided. He took a wad of bills from his wallet and laid them on the counter. "So how much for the two rooms?"

Haltingly, the clerk named a price.

"Fair enough," Nathan said, separating some of the bills and pushing them closer. Then he spun the guest register around so it was facing his way, lifted the nearby ink pen from its well, and scrawled his name on the next empty line. As he was doing this, the clerk reached hesitantly and took the money that had been shoved his way.

Dropping the pen back into its well, Nathan said, "Done and done. All I need are a couple of keys. Oh, and I'm gonna want a bath, too. Reckon that can be arranged, can't it?"

The clerk's eyes widened anew. "For both of you?"

Nathan's mouth pulled into an exaggerated frown. "You loco? He's an Injun. He don't bathe but a couple times a year. And when he does, it's in a creek or horse trough or some such."

Looking relieved, the clerk jerked a thumb and said, "Door at the end of that short hall. Room on the other side has a big ol' tub and a pile of clean towels. Somebody else is in there just now, but should be finishing up any minute. By the time you stow your gear in your room and come back down, it should be clear . . . and I already got a couple pans of freshwater heating on a stove in the back."

"One more thing . . . something to eat. Any chance of getting some grub after I'm done with my soak?" Nathan asked.

"Restaurant just across the street delivers to our guests. Getting kinda late, might have to settle for only sandwiches. But I can holler over and tell 'em to fix up what they got. And I can brew up a pot of fresh coffee to go with it."

Nathan nodded. "Now, that's what I call service." He shoved another bill to the young man, adding, "That should cover the meal and leave you some extra for your trouble."

"Thank you. I appreciate that." For the first time since

the two scouts had marched in, the clerk appeared to relax at least a small amount as held out a pair of keys to Nathan. "Here you go. Rooms eight and ten. And there's a connecting door like you wanted."

Nathan took the keys. For a moment he felt almost sorry for the kid on account of how he'd pressured and manipulated him. But then, before starting up the stairs to the designated rooms, he decided he couldn't resist giving one more poke of the needle.

"Oh, by the way," he said. "Don't be concerned if you see my manservant coming back down and accompanying me to the bath. Like I said, he won't be hopping in and contaminating the water or anything. But I like for him to carry my clean duds and haul away the dirty ones after I strip down. He's mighty handy, too, for scrubbing my back and those hard-to-reach places, if you know what I mean."

The last thing Nathan saw before turning back to the steps was the clerk's nervous tic jumping into motion again.

Nathan was barely a half-dozen steps into the room before Red Buffalo, entering behind him, heeled the door shut with a bang and let loose a highly agitated outburst.

"What was the big idea of handing out that whole line of horse droppings?" he demanded. "You want everybody to think I'm your damn slave or something?"

"Hey, calm down, you short-fused redskin," Nathan protested. "I did some fast thinking to come up with an idea meant to keep your ungrateful rear end from having to sleep in a stable or some such. I thought it was pretty clever."

"Well, I didn't! And it ain't like I haven't slept in a stable before."

"So are you telling me you liked it?" Nathan frowned. "We just spent two weeks on the trail to make it here. And if we go chasing Blackfeet with the army, it'll be more of the same . . . or, at best, we'll get one of those torture-rack army cots." The scout tossed his saddlebags down on the bed, then leaned over and pressed the flat of his hand deep into the cushiony mattress. "But lookee here. A night's sleep on this—like floating on a cloud—ain't that worth putting up with a few stretchers?"

Now it was Red Cloud's turn to frown. He aimed it at the mattress, as if it were somehow betraying him.

"Does look almighty soft," he grudgingly allowed.

"Lookin' don't do it justice," Nathan told him.

Red Buffalo's frown lifted and turned into a glare directed at Nathan.

"I still don't like all that 'manservant' junk! Polishing your boots, fetching every little this and that . . . The only thing you left out was cutting up the meat on your dinner plate and maybe dabbing your chin after you take a bite." The glare suddenly flared hotter. "But you did include how I'm supposed scrub your back and your 'hard-to-reach places'! Why the sam hill did you have to throw that in?"

"Okay, that was maybe laying it on a bit thick," Nathan admitted. "I did it mainly to get the clerk's goat a little more. But come to think of it, look at the opportunity it gives us. You go with me down to the tub, once we close the door there ain't gonna be nobody else around . . . so you'll have the chance for a turn at the tub, too. Right?"

"Wrong! I ain't going down there with you and having anybody, even if it's only that twitchy-eyed kid, thinking I might be in there scrubbing your back or whatever . . . and that's all there is to it," Red Buffalo said firmly and stubbornly. "Besides, you know how us Indians are when it comes to bathing. Once or twice a year is plenty for us and all we really need, even then, is just a creek or watering trough."

Nathan rolled his eyes. "For crying out loud. Are you going to keep groaning and bellyaching until hell freezes over about every little thing I said? I didn't mean for none of it to be took serious, not by you. Like I explained, it was all aimed at trying to wangle you a room and a soft bed. And since it worked, you ought to be thanking me."

"Don't hold your breath waiting for that," Red Buffalo huffed. He kept glaring for several more seconds until some of the heat cooled out of it. Then: "But you're right about putting this to rest now that we've each had our say and cleared the air some. Only don't trot out no more of that 'manservant' business, understood?"

Nathan shrugged. "It's done serving its purpose anyway."

"You'd better go have your bath, then. I'll get settled in the other room and make do with the pitcher and washbasin in there." Red Buffalo started for the connecting door, then paused to look over his shoulder. "I'd advise against soaking too long, though. I got me a powerful hunger, so if those sandwiches and hot coffee show up before you get back, I can't promise to save you any."

Chapter 13

"I'm warnin' you! This door is gettin' busted down and I'll be haulin' your butt outa there in another blasted minute if you don't finish up before then on your own!"

The man standing at the end of the short hall and bellowing these demands as he pounded his melon-sized fist on the door was clad in a buffalo-skin vest. The rest of him added up to about as big, shaggy, and smelly a specimen as the critter who'd originally worn that hide.

Also occupying the hallway—very reluctantly, it was clear—was the Telford House's gangly young desk clerk. He stood several feet behind the impatient door pounder, hunch-shouldered and wringing his hands fretfully. Despite obviously wanting to be just about anywhere else instead of here, faced with this situation, he was manfully attempting to do his job.

"You simply must understand, Mr. Haliway, that you'll have to wait your turn." The clerk's voice, rather high-pitched and timid under the best of circumstances, now sounded even weaker and a bit quavering as it came on the heels of Haliway's booming words.

Haliway spun to face the young man. The bulky buffalo-hide vest made him appear even more massive than his natural height and girth supplied on their own. Additionally, the scowl that blazed from wild eyes set in a weather-seamed face framed by a thick, tangled beard was fierce enough to blister paint.

"Now, doggone it, Waldo, you know my routine and the arrangement I've had with you and your pa for over a year now. I come into town on the first Saturday of every month and I stop here for a bath on my way to Miss Marvelle's place. You know dang well she won't let me frolic with her or any of her gals if I show up unwashed and smellin' of campfire smoke and the blood and guts of the critters I trap and kill. So, since I'm feelin' a particularly strong urge for a frolic this evenin', that means I'm wantin' this here bath real bad and ain't in no mood to wait around for it!"

"But, Mr. Haliway, there's a big problem."

"Don't start in on that takin'-my-turn malarkey. I'm warnin' you, Waldo. We got an arrangement, remember?"

"That's just the thing. It's *not* Saturday, Mr. Haliway," wailed Waldo.

Nathan had been able to hear most of this exchange as he'd come down the stairs and crossed the hotel lobby toward the hall where it was taking place. He paused at the mouth of the hallway now to observe the big man's reaction to what the clerk had just told him.

In a way, the scene appealed to Nathan's rough sense of humor. The hulking giant towering over the trembling smaller, young man who was trying bravely to stand his ground. And the look on Haliway's face—surprise followed by befuddlement quickly mixed with suspicion—only added to it.

"What the hell you mean it ain't Saturday?" roared the big man. "I carve a notch in my trap-springin' stick every mornin' when I wake up, just to make certain I keep track. And in case I get woke sudden-like by some howlin' critter caught in a nearby trap, then I make sure to make the notch later on. That's how I know when the first Saturday rolls around!"

"I . . . I don't know what might have gone wrong, Mr. Haliway," replied Waldo. "But what I do know is that today is only Thursday. I can show you on the calendar out at the desk if you like."

Haliway's face darkened with anger. "You know I can't read, Waldo. Are you tryin' to trick me into thinkin' I'm loco or something, you little runt?"

"Oh no! No, sir, I would never do anything like that."

Haliway suddenly swung his right arm, whipping its fist in a whooshing backhand blow to one wall of the hallway, punching a pumpkin-sized hole that sent dust rolling and chunks of plaster rattling to the floor. Then he swung the hand forward, grabbing Waldo by his shirtfront and lifting him up on his tiptoes.

"You know what, runt? I don't give a damn what day of the week it is. I'm here in town with a powerful mood to frolic and that means I need a bath. So are you gonna tell whoever's in there to clear the hell out, or am I gonna use you like a battering ram to knock down that door and clear 'em out myself?"

Nathan had seen and heard enough. Ordinarily, he made it a point to step wide of other folks' trouble. But all at once he felt a protective urge toward Waldo. After he himself had hoorawed the kid some, he guessed he wasn't ready to see him endure still more, especially not physical harm.

Besides, by Nathan's reckoning, the next turn at a bath was *his*, not Haliway's.

Edging deeper into the hallway, Nathan spoke in an easy drawl that was nevertheless plenty loud enough to be heard. "Begging your pardon, gents. But in addition to making a lot of unpleasant racket, y'all are blocking my way to the bath I already paid for."

Haliway continued to hold Waldo up on his toes. Slowly, he swiveled his head and glared at Nathan. Waldo also turned his head, as best he could, and gazed at Nathan with wide, pleading eyes.

"What did you say?" growled Haliway.

"I think you heard me," Nathan replied calmly. "I said I find your racket disturbing and you're also blocking my way to the bath I'm on my way to take."

The big man let go of Waldo. The sudden release caught the clerk by surprise, causing him to almost collapse before he used the wall to keep himself upright.

"Get out of here, Waldo. Go on and wait out in the lobby," Nathan advised him.

The kid complied as fast as he could slip past Nathan and scurry away.

When he was gone, Haliway turned to face Nathan full on. The span of his shoulders nearly filled the hallway. He said, "You were right about me blockin' your way. What do you figure to do about it?"

Nathan regarded him for a long moment. Then, sighing, he transferred the clean clothes he was carrying draped over his right forearm across to his left. This resulted in fully revealing the Colt holstered on his right hip.

"That buffalo hide you're wearing looks like a real sturdy garment," he noted. "Expect its original owner thought so, too . . . until a bullet or arrow or whatever taught him otherwise. You see the lesson there? Or is it going to take a couple pills from this equalizer I'm packing to convince you the same?"

Haliway bared his teeth in a sneer. "I shoulda known. A bold talker, yeah . . . but only when you got a shootin' iron to back up your words."

"And a tub of guts like you, rag-dolling a young fella one-third your size," Nathan responded. "You call that a more acceptable kind of boldness?"

"I call it what it is. Anybody, big or small or young or old, gets in my way, I move 'em *out* of the way! They get what they see. I don't have to resort to no stinkin' guns or other weapons. I get the job done with *these*!" He held up his two fists, and from closer up, each one looked about equal to the size of Nathan's head.

Nathan told himself that if he had a lick of sense, he ought to be clearing leather right about then. But something about Haliway's taunting, boastful claim—*"Anybody, big or small or young or old"*—rankled him deep.

That, combined with the way he'd seen Haliway treat Waldo, brought on a red haze that shouldered good sense off to one side. It was time, came a voice out of the haze, that somebody put this big slob in his place . . . and did it without resorting to using a gun.

Baring his own teeth in the wolf's smile that any who'd previously seen it—the ones who lived—tended to never forget, Nathan said, "I got in mind to show you where you can shove those"—a tip of his head indicated the fists Haliway continued to hold up—"and this time it won't be down somebody else's throat. Since it'll be just a little while before I take that bath I'm planning, I reckon I can stand the stink and grime of tussling with you long enough to teach you some manners."

Haliway's mouth twisted menacingly. "More bold talk. If you're willing to back it up by shucking that hardware, we'll quick enough see who gets taught what!"

With his free hand, Nathan yanked open the buckle of his gun belt and peeled it off. He hung it over the clean clothes still on his left arm and glanced around for someplace to set the bundle aside.

Bad mistake.

Chapter 14

The second Nathan's attention was diverted, Haliway hurled himself forward. An enraged roar rumbled from his chest and he covered the distance separating them with stunning speed. Nathan wheeled back to face him but got only partway turned before Haliway slammed into him with all the force of the bull buffalo that had once owned the hide wrapped around him. Nathan's clothes and gun belt went flying.

The impact drove the scout back and surely would have knocked him off his feet if his attacker hadn't thrown two thick arms around him and clamped them tight as they both went staggering wildly out into the lobby. They still might have collapsed to the floor in a tangle if their momentum hadn't run them up against a wide, thickly cushioned couch positioned for guests to lounge outside their rooms. Nathan toppled backward onto the couch with Haliway continuing to ram into him as the couch skidded for a couple of feet on the carpet until upending and tipping jarringly onto its back.

If not for the couch's thick padding, the big man's crushing weight landing on top of him probably would have driven all the breath out of Nathan. It pounded out plenty as it was, but he retained enough to twist and flail desperately in order to prevent being pinned in place. He got some assistance with this by means of Haliway partly overshooting him and then being unable to check himself on the couch back's slick leather surface.

Nathan rolled away and clambered to his hands and knees, spinning to face Haliway. The big man had rolled in the opposite direction, pivoting on one hip and then also pushing to his hands and knees. Momentarily disoriented, his head swung one way and then the other as he looked for Nathan.

Now it was Nathan's turn to take advantage of a slight distraction and strike where he saw an opening. Remaining on his hands and knees, his head at roughly the same level as Haliway's, Nathan scuttled forward as fast as he could across the short distance separating them. As Haliway's head swung the rest of the way around, Nathan tilted his face downward and rammed the crown of his head as hard as he could straight into the big man's mouth and nose.

The jolt of the solid impact accompanied the crunch of mashed cartilage and broken teeth. Haliway howled in pain and rage and Nathan felt hot blood soaking through the hair on top of his head.

The blow had been telling, but Nathan knew better than to count on it for more than it was. His opponent's eyes would water involuntarily for a minute or so, impairing his vision some, and the mashed nose would take a toll on his breathing the longer this wore on—but right at the moment, there was still plenty of fight left in the big man.

Well aware of this, Nathan scuttled backward on his hands and knees just as fast as he'd gone forward, shoving to his feet only when he was a safe distance away. This maneuver paid dividends when Haliway wasted no time raring back onto just his knees and then, swinging blindly due to his watering eyes, uncorked first a vicious round-house right and then a left. If Nathan hadn't been so quick to get out of the way, either of those connecting would have taken his head off.

Wanting to take as much advantage as he could of Haliway's blurred vision, Nathan quickly skirted the upended couch and closed on his opponent from the right side just as he was gaining his feet. Before the giant got fully upright and balanced, Nathan leaned in and pounded a right hook to his ribs. Shifting his weight and straightening up a bit, he then followed with a straight left to the side of Haliway's neck, just below the ear.

Somewhat alarmingly, the blow to the ribs seemed to have little effect. The neck punch, though, at least caused its target to stagger half a step in reaction.

But immediately, while Nathan was still formulating his next move, Haliway leaned back from the way he'd staggered and threw a slashing elbow that surely would have been a bone breaker had it landed. Luckily for Nathan, the big man's vision was still impaired enough to send his aim high, thus allowing Nathan to duck and escape the attempt by a whisker's width.

Twisted around and again pulled slightly off-balance by the missed elbow thrust, Haliway's full girth now loomed momentarily unprotected directly in front of Nathan. Nathan planted his heels and drilled a pair of hard punches—right, then left—into the other man's heavy gut.

As with the blow to the ribs, though, this failed to get anywhere near the hoped-for result. Haliway emitted a short grunting sound as each fist landed and little clouds of dust and grit puffed from the buffalo-hide vest—but that was pretty much the extent of it.

Nathan was so stunned by the failure of two solid gut punches to double Haliway over, like they would any normal man, that he lapsed for a second into a perplexed, unguarded state.

That unguarded second gave Haliway, now with his vision clearing even as thick blood continued to pump from his nostrils down over his tangled beard, all the time he needed to retaliate in a heightened rage. He twisted his powerful shoulders and swung a thick, bearlike arm, slamming the boulder-hard fist at its end straight to the point of Nathan's chin.

The scout was knocked backward, heels digging frantically to keep his feet from flying out from under him, arms windmilling crazily as fireworks exploded inside his head. The only thing that kept him from ending up on his back was the fact that his wild staggering took him across the lobby until he bumped hard against the wall beside the mouth to the short hallway where all this had started. Nathan pressed tight to the vertical surface, clinging to it as a means to keep upright while he tried to will the fragmented pieces of his brain back into focus.

Haliway, in the meantime, had become very focused. "Now I got you!" he bellowed as he hurled himself once again into a bull-like rush toward Nathan. The only thing that slowed him was nearly tripping over a corner of the upended couch. He solved that annoyance quickly enough by kicking the couch aside like it was a stick of kindling wood, then continuing with his charge.

But the couch's brief intervention provided Nathan an

extra moment to clear his senses. That enabled him to make a single desperation move as Haliway's furious mass came barreling to crush him against the wall.

Nathan twisted away at the last possible instant and flung himself into a diving roll across the hall mouth. This left Haliway to slam full force into the now-empty wall, without Nathan there to absorb the impact of the collision and to cushion the big man from the unyielding surface. Haliway hit so hard that two or three pictures hanging off toward the front desk fell clattering to the floor and an entire stretch of wall shuddered as if caught by the shock of an earthquake.

Bounding to his feet, rejuvenated by his successful escape, Nathan watched as Haliway took an unsteady step back away from the wall. His eyes were glassy and his knees appeared spongy. A fresh gash on his forehead was pouring down a trickle of blood to add to that continuing to leak from his flattened nose.

But the big brute still didn't go down. He stood there, teetering like an oak in a strong wind.

Nathan knew he had to find a way to finish chopping that oak down before it quit teetering and stabilized itself again. Wasting no time, he lunged back across the hallway mouth and grabbed Haliway by one sagging arm and a wad of shirtfront. Tightly maintaining these holds, he pivoted fast and hard back toward the opposite side of the hall, pulling Haliway with him like one child whirling another in a game of swing-the-statue. When he had Haliway staggeringly in motion and at a pretty good clip, he aimed him at the corner on the other side of the hall mouth, where the hallway wall veered at a right angle from the lobby wall, and let go.

In something of a repeat performance of what the giant had endured only a minute or so earlier, Haliway again went crashing against an unyielding surface, this time suffering the added bite of the sharp corner.

That *had* to be the end of it, Nathan told himself, his breath coming in rapid gusts and rivulets of sweat running down over a face that was still partially numb from Haliway's blow.

As the scout watched, Haliway's knees buckled partway and he slid a half foot down the wall and then stopped. His breathing, too, was labored and a low, rumbling sound that might have been a groan escaped him. But, with the help of the wall, he was still mostly upright.

With a weary sigh, Nathan stepped over to him. He shifted a bit into the hallway so Haliway could lift his bloody face and look up at him when he spoke.

"You agree it's finished, then?" he said. "You agree I get the next bath and you wait your turn?"

Haliway's eyes were bleary and one of them was puffed nearly shut. When they tried to focus on Nathan, the scout wasn't sure they comprehended who or what they were even looking at.

Another rumble came from deep in the battered man's chest. It took a moment for Nathan to realize he was trying to say something. But then, all of sudden, the words became very clear.

"I ain't finished yet, damn you!"

And with that—unexpectedly, amazingly—Haliway shoved away from the wall, surged full to his feet, and plowed into Nathan with renewed fury!

Their two bodies thudded heavily together. Caught by surprise and without any time to get set, Nathan was driven back by Haliway's greater weight. He had all he could do to maintain his balance and keep the big man from wrapping him in another bear hug that would pin his arms to his body and make him all but helpless.

Fighting to prevent this, he jerked one arm free and used it to slam a forearm blow to the side of Haliway's jaw. The strike rocked the giant's head back on his shoulders but it didn't keep him from plowing forward—which meant Nathan kept staggering backward.

They tipped to one side and bounced off the wall there, then lurched a ways farther and bounced off the wall on the other side. Nathan landed another punch to Haliway's head, but it was short and choppy, barely making him flinch. Feeling increasingly desperate, Nathan began attempting to gouge at Haliway's eyes, but his fingers kept slipping in the sweat and blood, failing to find their target . . .

And that's when the combined weight and momentum of the two combatants rammed into the door at the end of the hallway. The flimsy barrier held for just a second and then gave way with the shriek of twisting hinges and splintering wood.

Somewhat puzzling was the sound of another shriek— that of a woman—joining in. But Nathan had precious little time to wonder about the meaning of that.

The second or two of resistance provided by the door, only to have it suddenly yield, was too much for Nathan to continue maintaining his balance. He fell back and toppled to the floor with Haliway once again landing on top of him. Only this time there was no lobby couch to provide any cushioning, making the landing hard and painful and all the more punishing by being ground under the bulk of his adversary.

But a stroke of luck—for want of a better word—actually came from this. While Nathan was slammed to the floor and pinned there, Haliway's momentum, as before, carried him some distance farther. In this case, it carried him to the point of his head slamming forcefully against the base of a large copper bathtub that occupied the middle of the small room.

The loud *bong!* produced by this impact was not only music to Nathan's ears but, more important, it succeeded in accomplishing what he'd been laboring to do for the past several minutes.

It knocked Haliway cold.

Dragging himself out from under the limp, unconscious form, Nathan scarcely had time to breathe a sigh of relief before he caught a flash of movement out of the corner of his eye. He had time to further note that this movement was coming from the shapely form of a woman barely covered by a towel knotted over her bosom.

Any lingering appreciation of this, however, was prevented by yet another flash of movement—that of a galvanized washbasin streaking downward toward his head.

Vaguely, before he, too, was rendered unconscious, Nathan heard that bonging sound again . . . Only this time it wasn't nearly as pleasant.

Chapter 15

The first time Nathan tried to open his eyes, a stab of bright light caused him to promptly squeeze them shut again.

"Looks like he's starting to come around," said a voice he recognized as belonging to Red Buffalo.

To which a woman's voice responded, "Thank God."

Mentally, Nathan clawed a little further out of the fog of unconsciousness. A woman . . . The one from the bath? He recalled the faceless, shapely female form he'd gotten an all-too-brief glimpse of after he and Haliway crashed through the door. And then . . . Was it she who had bent the washbasin over his head? And could the woman he'd just heard speak be one and the same?

Nathan eased his eyes open, more slowly this time, and was able to keep them that way. The bright light that had assailed him before came from coal oil lanterns pouring out illumination. He saw that he was in his hotel room, lying on the bed. Red Buffalo stood looking down at him.

As they locked gazes, the Crow lifted his eyebrows and quipped, "How was your bath?"

Nathan made a face. "Very funny."

"I just can't leave you alone for a minute, can I?"

"That was the trouble. I *wasn't* alone." Nathan raised one hand and brought it to rest gently on his bruised ribs. "There were at least three other hombres who showed up to spend some time with me. And they were all wrapped in the same buffalo-hide vest."

Waldo, the desk clerk, stepped up beside Red Buffalo. His pale forehead was puckered with anguish.

"Mr. Stark, I can't tell you how grateful I am for the way you came to my aid. I went to try and find some help for you in return, but I'm afraid it wasn't in time. Not before your fight with Mr. Haliway was already over with."

Nathan frowned. "Haliway," he said, echoing the name bitterly. "Where is that big brute? Bolted down somewhere with logging chains, I hope."

Red Buffalo and Waldo exchanged glances.

"Actually," Red Buffalo said, somewhat hesitantly, "he's in the other room."

"What other room?"

"Mine. The one adjoining this one."

Nathan pushed up on one elbow, the sore ribs causing him to grimace. "Are you loco?"

"The doctor is in there with him," Waldo said.

"Well, I hope the marshal and a posse of deputies are in there, too, protecting the doc." Nathan scowled. "Better yet, I hope the army supplied a cannon to train on that varmint in order to keep him in line."

"Aw, Beauregard ain't so bad," claimed Red Buffalo. "Yeah, when he ain't been to town for a spell he can be a mite bristly, but otherwise . . ."

"Wait a minute! You saying you know that character?" Nathan demanded.

"Matter of fact, yeah, I do." Red Buffalo sighed. "Been a few years since I've crossed paths with the old cuss, but was a time me and him used to scout for General Harker down in Kansas. That's where he shot the bull buff he made his vest out of. Said it was the first critter he ever bagged that'd yield a hide big enough to cover him."

Nathan grunted. "Too bad it didn't go the other way around and leave a buff somewhere out on the Kansas plains wearing Haliway's hide."

"The main thing," Red Buffalo said, "is that *your* hide is still intact. Not many men are lucky enough to go fist and boot against Beauregard Haliway and come out of it in as good a shape as you."

"I guess *good shape* depends on which side you're looking at it from. And as far as luck, if it wasn't for that bathtub lending a hand—"

Nathan stopped short, recalling again the rest of what happened after Haliway brained himself on the tub. Pushing himself up a little straighter, he tried to see past Red Buffalo and Waldo for a wider scan of his surroundings.

As if sensing why his words had halted and what it was he was looking for, a woman came forward and stepped up between Red Buffalo and Waldo. She was dark-haired and attractive and, though now fully clad in a flowing skirt and high-collared blouse, the ripe curves still in evidence under the snug blouse appeared a reasonable match for what Nathan had glimpsed down in the bathroom.

But what was more of a certainty was the identity of the woman. She was Andrea Fontinelle, the rather mysterious member of the three-wagon train Nathan and Red Buffalo had accompanied into town after the trouble with the M-Slash-G men back on the trail.

Gazing coolly down at Nathan, she said, "You seem to make a habit of coming to the rescue in situations where I am at some peril, Mr. Stark. I fear my hasty departure when we arrived in town earlier today left unspoken my gratitude for what you and Mr. Red Buffalo did to help our wagon train. And now I've made that display of rudeness pale in comparison by bashing you over the head for your latest efforts on my behalf."

Nathan was speechless for a moment. Then: "So you *were* the lady down in the, uh . . . And it was you who hit me with the washbasin?"

"Yes and yes," replied Andrea. "After all the hollering and commotion from out in the hall, when you and that bear of a man came crashing through the door I had no way of knowing which of you might mean me harm. I didn't recognize you in the chaos of the moment, so when you lifted your head and looked like you were going to stand up, I . . . well, I guess we've established what I did."

She paused, her coolness slipping for a moment, spots of blush appearing on her cheeks before she added, "And if *that* action seems unladylike, you need to remember there were certain other considerations, personal ones, already placing me in an unladylike position."

Nathan swung his legs over the edge of the bed. He wanted to stand up but sensed he wasn't quite ready. He settled for holding up one hand, palm out.

"No hard feelings, ma'am. Not on my part . . . and I hope not on yours. Neither one of us ended up in a position we exactly wanted to be in."

Andrea started to say something in response but was interrupted by voices coming from the adjoining room.

They drew nearer, increasing in volume and the level of excitement discernible in their tone.

"You really ought not be up moving around so quickly," said a voice unfamiliar to Nathan. "You've received some serious head trauma and should minimize activity for at least—"

"People die layin' in bed, Doc," a gruff voice that Nathan recognized all too well as that of the big brawler now identified as Beauregard Haliway cut him off. "If the grim reaper is comin' for me, he's gonna have to do some chasin'. I ain't gonna make it easy for him."

Nathan didn't miss the tension suddenly showing on the faces of Andrea and Waldo, and felt the same reaction in himself. Additionally, Red Buffalo took a step away from the side of the bed and brought his right hand to rest on the handle of the Colt holstered on his hip.

Swiveling his head, Nathan saw two men coming through the connecting door of the adjoining room. One of them was an average-sized gent with tousled brown hair, wearing a rumpled white shirt with the sleeves rolled up and gripping a bloodstained towel in one hand.

Crowding him along was the towering form of Haliway. His vest had been removed and the homespun shirt now straining to cover his torso was also streaked with blood. The gash on his forehead was freshly stitched, purplish discoloration was starting to form around both eyes, and his mangled nose was stuffed with thick wads of cotton, wispy tufts of it poking from each nostril.

Red Buffalo took another step, planting his feet wide and saying in a warning tone, "Now, Beauregard . . . you promised to behave."

Haliway looked at him and blinked. "I know what I

said, Moses. I ain't fixin' to do no different. But I heard this feller talkin'"—here he turned his gaze to Nathan—"and I wanted to see how he was doin'."

His tone, to Nathan's surprise, seemed earnest, genuinely caring. The scout held the big man's eyes for a moment, then said evenly, "To tell the truth, there've been times I felt a lot sprier."

Haliway blinked again, didn't say anything right away. Then, all at once, he threw back his head and emitted a throaty laugh.

"Times you felt a lot sprier . . . Man, do I ever know what you mean. I feel exactly the same. Ha! And the reason I do is on account of you bein' plenty doggone spry when we was in the thick of it a little while ago, eh? I tell you, that was the best tussle I been in in a long time—and even longer since anybody left me layin' cold the way you did."

"Well, I did have a little help from that bathtub," Nathan allowed, repeating his line from earlier.

Haliway released another bellowing laugh. "'A bathtub lending a hand' . . . I like a feller with a sense of humor, I swear. If I gotta get thumped by somebody, that makes it a little easier to swallow."

"There's nothing humorous about the condition either of you men are in," the doctor said officiously. "You both suffered serious damage and need to be taking it easy in order for your bodies to start the healing process."

"I'd start healin' a lot quicker if I had the proper kind of medicine to help things along," said Haliway. He eyed Nathan. "How about you, feller? You join me in a jolt or two of tonic if we was able to get our hands on some?"

Feeling strangely relaxed now in the presence of this affable-seeming giant who only a short time ago had been trying to tear him apart, Nathan admitted, "I've been known to soothe a few past pains that way."

"If it will help get the two of you to settle yourselves down, I have no objection," the doctor said, even though no one had really asked his opinion.

Haliway cast his eyes appealingly on the desk clerk.

"Little Waldo," he said with a sudden syrupiness in his voice, "I didn't hurt you none when I crowded you down in that hallway, did I, lad?"

"You didn't do me any good!"

"I know, I know. I'm sorry as can be for what tiny little bit of a shakin' I may have gave you. And I already told you I'll pay for the broken door and any other damage," Haliway promised. "All the time I been comin' here, I never did nothing like that before, did I? What's more, over that time I've come to think of you as practically a . . . well, a nephew. You could tell that, couldn't you?"

Waldo looked highly skeptical. "You want me to go fetch a bottle, don't you? That's what you're driving at, right?"

Haliway frowned. "Well, if you know, you little smarty, then why are you makin' me drag it out so? You've got a couple of guests—and any others present who'd care to join 'em—in need of refreshment that borders on medical salvation. Are you willing to tend to the business of serving us or not?"

Red Buffalo spoke up at that point, saying, "Before you get to that, Beauregard, I think there's another piece of business—an apology—that needs to be taken care of."

"An apology? By who—me?"

"None other."

Haliway frowned. "But I already apologized to everybody—"

"No, not everybody," Red Buffalo cut him off. "Not the one you interrupted most of all with your shenanigans. That would be"—he gestured with a sweep of his hand—"Miss Andrea Fontinelle, whose privacy you invaded in a most shameful way."

Now it was Haliway who blushed. Furiously.

"Oh Lord," he murmured, his usually booming voice suddenly quite small as he had difficulty bringing his eyes to meet the gaze of Andrea. "Moses is most surely right, ma'am, and I don't know how to tell you how much . . . well, how truly sorry I am for my miserable behavior. I'm no stranger to letting the wildcat inside of me howl too often, I can't deny that. But never . . . well, almost never . . . in the presence or earshot of a fine lady like yourself. So for slippin' the way I did this evenin' and as a result causin' you discomfort or embarrassment . . . I . . . I am an ashamed and regretful wretch."

By the time he was finished, the flinty look Andrea had started out giving him had softened notably.

But before she could respond in any way, the sound of excited voices and a bit of commotion came from out in the hall. Suddenly, the door to Nathan's room burst open. As all heads turned to look, three people came pouring in—two with an unmistakable show of eagerness, a third with shuffling reluctance.

Chapter 16

The first of the trio to enter was a tall, thin man in a swallowtail suit jacket. His physical features too closely resembled an older version of Waldo to be anything other than the lad's father.

Right on his heels came a short, attractive middle-aged woman with piled-high blond hair, gaudy icicle earrings, and heavily applied makeup. Her dress of shiny red silk had a plunging neckline that barely contained her generous bosom and left displayed a slash of deep cleavage that the shawl she wore draped over her shoulders and tried to hold closed in front seldom succeeded in covering.

Behind her, dragging his feet and edging forward reservedly, came a badly overweight man of average height. He had anxious eyes, a bulbous nose, and roll after roll of chins where his throat should be. A marshal's badge was pinned on the lapel of a threadbare corduroy jacket that was years past being able to button over his swollen stomach.

"Father!" Waldo greeted the man in the swallowtail suit jacket. His tone was a curious mix, sounding partly annoyed yet partly relieved.

"When I heard there'd been a disturbance here requiring the doctor be urgently sent for," explained the older hotel man, "I thought it best I also put in an appearance. I know everything is in your capable hands, son, but it only seemed prudent. Same for bringing along the marshal."

Oblivious to this exchange, the blond woman zeroed in on Haliway with a cry of "Beauregard!" and launched herself in his direction with such intensity it caused Red Buffalo to sidestep for fear of being trampled. The doctor standing beside Haliway did likewise.

"When I heard a mountain of a wild man had been beaten bloody, I knew with a sinking feeling in my heart it had to be you," the woman wailed, giving Haliway scarcely time to get braced before she slammed against him and wrapped him in an embrace—at least as much as her arms could reach.

After she'd given him a good squeeze, something that had to have been a bit painful for him in his condition, though he neither resisted nor gave any outward display of discomfort, she took a step back and examined him more closely.

"You poor dear! Look at you! How many low-down bullies did it take to gang up on you in order to do that much damage? Where are the dirty rats? I'll not only give them a piece of my mind, I'll—"

"Take it easy, Marvelle darlin'," Haliway stopped her. "You've got it all wrong. It was a fair fight, strictly one-on-one. And, though it pains me to admit it more than the soreness of all these bruises you can see, I got the thrashin' I deserved."

Marvelle's jaw dropped and her eyes flashed. "Say it

ain't so! There's not a man in Telford who can beat you in a fair fight."

"There is now, my dear. My hope is that he's only passin' through, mind you," said Haliway, one corner of his mouth lifting in a wry grin. "But for however long he's here, he's got the right to that claim and I'll have no hard feelin's about it. In fact, me and him were just tryin' to arrange—"

The hurried clump of heavy boots came from the hallway. All faces once again turned to look and this time they saw a blade-faced man in a dark Stetson step into the open doorway directly behind the marshal. In stark contrast, this new arrival was lean and hard-looking, all sharp angles, with suspicious slits for eyes and a mean twist to his mouth. Pinned to his black leather vest was a deputy marshal's star.

"We got trouble here, Marshal?" His tone was almost hopeful, and though the words were directed to the marshal, those suspicious eyes were raking everybody else in the room.

"I don't know yet," replied the marshal, all of a sudden appearing emboldened, no longer hanging back and giving the impression he didn't want to be there. He even took a step forward, hauling his bulk deeper into the room as he added, "But I aim to find out."

"Judging by the damage I spotted down in the lobby when I came in just now," said the deputy, "there don't appear much doubt some kind of situation got out of hand."

"The responsibility for that damage has already been acknowledged and will be paid in full once the cost for repairs is known," Waldo was quick to say. Unfortunately he couldn't keep his eyes from darting tellingly in Haliway's direction as he said it.

The marshal, Fergus Feeney, didn't miss this. His own eyes went to Haliway. "You. I might have known. Seems like there's some kind of 'damage' whenever you show up in our town."

"That's not true . . . well, not *every* time," argued Marvelle. "And when Beauregard *is* at fault, he admits it and makes right for his part."

"Yeah, and the troublemaker only keeps getting away with it because he scares the hell out of everybody who might not otherwise agree to his idea of making it 'right,'" declared the deputy, Rafe Ridgway.

Observing this, Nathan recalled Miles Rafferty's assessment of the law in Telford and it seemed clear that his opinion hadn't been far off. It wasn't hard to see that Marshal Feeney was a lazy slob who didn't show much spine unless Deputy Ridgway was around to back him up—and that Ridgway was the type who loved his role because it meant being able to talk tough and strong-arm folks from behind a badge.

Looking to push tonight's situation as far as he could, Ridgway turned to Waldo's father and said, "How about it, Eakes? This is your hotel, your lobby. Are you another one who's gonna settle for some pay-for-the-damages promise that probably never will be kept? The big bum makes a living trapping varmints and getting paid a handful of coins each for their hides. How much of that do you think you'll ever see? He comes into town once every few weeks for some drinking and whoring and then he's immediately broke and all he's good for is heading back out into the wilderness again."

"You find anybody who says I promised payment for damages and then didn't make good, I'll show you a liar," Haliway growled ominously. "And if it's you makin' that claim, callin' *me* a liar, Ridgway, then we're gonna be on our way to some more damage right here and now."

Marvelle put a restraining hand on Haliway's massive chest. "Pay no attention to that bag of wind. He's just trying to get your goat. Don't give him the satisfaction. You're already injured enough, you don't need a bullet from him too . . . which is the only way he could ever take you."

Ridgway chuckled dryly. "You sunk down to letting a whore do your fighting for you now, big man?"

Red Buffalo made a long, quick stride and this time it took him, Marvelle, and the doctor to hold Haliway back. But it didn't stop him from bellowing, "Hidin' behind that badge don't impress me none, Ridgway! You keep eggin' me on, you'll get what you're askin' for!"

The deputy spun to Feeney. "You hear that? That's threatening an officer of the law! You don't expect me to put up with that, do you?"

"Take it easy, Rafe," the marshal told him. "If we threw everybody behind bars you put a bur under the saddle of, it'd be a full-time job building expansions onto the jail."

"You, too, Fergus? Come on," Ridgway protested, "he's already got the doc and Madam Marvelle and the Injun taking up for him. Hey, wait a minute!" The deputy's glare shifted to Waldo's father again. "What the hell is an Indian doing here anyway? What kind of place are you running, Eakes?"

Waldo didn't give his father a chance to try and answer.

"The Indian is here on my say-so," he explained. "He's with Mr. Stark and he had absolutely nothing to do with what happened. He wasn't even—"

"Any time there's an Injun around there's bound to be trouble," Ridgway snapped. "Any chowderhead knows that!"

"I'll thank you not to refer to my son as a chowderhead," Eakes responded defensively. "I left him in charge because he is perfectly capable of running things when I am not around. If he made such a decision, I trust he had a good reason."

Ridgway sneered. "You so-called citizens make me sick. You expect badge-wearers like me and the marshal to stick our necks out and keep the peace, protect you from bad hombres and the like . . . But then, if we come down a little too hard and step on some of your toes in the process, that's a different story. Then you think you have the right to tell us when to back off and *not* do our jobs!"

Once again, Nathan had heard enough. He pushed up from his sitting position and fought hard to hold steady in his stance.

"If you want to talk about sticking out necks and protecting folks," he said, gaze leveled straight at Ridgway, "let me tell you about the *Injun* that has you so riled up, among other things."

He gave it a second, waiting for the deputy's glare to settle on him, as well as the looks of the others to also swing his way. Then he continued, "His name is Moses Red Buffalo. He's a civilian scout for the army. Has been for a number of years, meaning he's fought in campaigns all over the frontier and now has arrived here—along with me—to report for duty with the company of soldiers that's been sent to deal with the Blackfeet problem you're having hereabouts. So, like I said at the outset, Deputy, taking risks and protecting folks don't *just* come with wearing a badge. And if trouble breaks out when this particular Indian is around, it's usually for a good cause."

Ridgway's mouth twisted into something that wasn't quite a sneer but nevertheless showed he wasn't impressed, either. "If you and your pal are scouts for the army, why are you here and not out at the encampment?"

"Because we got in late today, and after two weeks on the trail from Fort Randall in the Dakotas, we reckoned we'd earned ourselves a night's sleep in a soft bed before reporting for duty in the morning. We got Waldo's okay for letting Moses stay by virtue of me running a bit of a shuck on the lad. I apologize for that now . . . but he shouldn't blame himself, nor should anybody else."

"If you two are here to serve the army on our behalf," said the elder Eakes, "then apology or blame, either one, is hardly necessary."

"That sounds to me like a pretty good sentiment all the way around," declared Marshal Feeney. He motioned to his sour-faced deputy. "Come on, Rafe, there's no need for us to hang around any longer. It's getting late and I think these folks have got enough of a handle on things here to sort out the rest of what they need to. We've still got to make our patrol through the remainder of town, though. Maybe we'll run across a couple of rowdy drunks who'll give you reason to chunk them over their heads with your gun barrel, and that will help cheer you up."

Chapter 17

Next morning, Nathan and Red Buffalo ate an early breakfast at the Hot Griddle Restaurant, just across the street from the hotel. This was the same establishment that had sent some food over the previous night—food whose delivery got interrupted by the fight between Nathan and Haliway. It arrived mere minutes before the trouble broke out and Waldo had placed it on a shelf behind the front desk, where he subsequently forgot about it until things were tamed down and everyone else had left.

Sheepishly and full of apologies, he had brought the tray up to the two scouts, who were hungry enough to be grateful anyway. They became even more forgiving once they sampled the fare, which consisted of wrist-thick roast beef sandwiches and a pitcher of buttermilk rather than coffee due to the lateness of the hour, and found it to be delicious.

That experience made the choice of where they would take breakfast this morning a mighty easy one.

Arriving shortly after the Hot Griddle's doors opened for the day's business, they had the place almost to themselves at first. It didn't take long, however, before a steady stream of other customers started showing up.

Nor did it take long for many of these newer arrivals to cast furtive glances in the direction of Nathan and Red Buffalo, often accompanied by some quiet exchange of words. For the most part, none of this appeared unfriendly or unwelcoming, but it was notable and a bit unnerving all the same.

"I'm just guessing, mind you," said Red Buffalo around a mouthful of scrambled eggs and ham, "but it looks to me like word has spread pretty quickly about the two of us. Either that, or they can't help staring due to the dashingly handsome figure I cut."

"If they're staring at you," muttered Nathan, "they're probably wondering which one of their neighbors is yet to be discovered scalped in his bed."

"They ought to know better than that," Red Buffalo scoffed. "It's a well-known fact that Indians don't do no fighting or scalping at night. Or so I've heard."

Nathan grunted. "Yeah, I've known more than a few men, some who even claimed to be experienced Indian fighters, who believed that foolish yarn. A good number of 'em ended up dead . . . killed in middle-of-the-night attacks."

"Well, then, let's hope nobody in Telford wakes up dead this morning. Because, if they do, it'll probably get blamed on me. But remember, that means you'll also get roped into it, too."

"Me? How?"

"Are you joking? After that spiel you gave up in your hotel room last night about me—about the two of us—don't you see how that's going to leave us tied together in everybody's minds?"

Nathan made a sour face and paused with a piece of buttered biscuit halfway to his mouth.

"Man, you sure know how to ruin a good breakfast, don't you? All my spiel last night was meant to do was put that pompous, badge-wearing jackass in his place. I hate men like that—men who take a little bit of authority and use it like a club over others—almost as bad as . . ."

When his words trailed off, Red Buffalo finished the statement for him, saying, "Almost as bad as you hate Indians?"

Nathan glared down at the black pool inside his coffee cup for a long moment before replying, "Everybody has some kind of hate in 'em."

"Too true," Red Buffalo allowed. "But as far as what anybody in this town thinks, it'll soon be behind us. We'll be gone from here in short order and commenced on our scouting chores for the army. Once we're up to our necks in heathen Blackfeet, what anybody in Telford thinks about either of us won't matter much."

Nathan eyed him. "You sound almost eager to wade into those 'heathen Blackfeet.'"

Red Buffalo's tone turned somber. "You just said everybody's got some kind of hate in 'em, right? Like I told you before, it is ingrained in every Crow, including me, to hate all Blackfeet clear down to our core. As far back as I can remember, I started hearing stories of the many atrocities committed by them on my people. My hate was seared in early and deep, deeper than even my conversion to Christianity could erase. When my journeys took me through territories to the south, away from Blackfeet land, it seemed I would never have an outlet for that hate . . . Now, through this turn of events, it looks like I will."

"You may find," Nathan said, his gaze returning to the

black pool inside his cup and his own tone sounding nearly as dark, "that no matter how much hate you let out, there's still more piled up wanting to be released."

Red Buffalo gave a faint nod. "If that's how it is, then I guess I'll discover for myself. But no matter, I'm ready to go in search of the answer."

Nathan raised his cup, drained it, set it back down heavily. "In that case, we'd best head out and get ourselves introduced to Captain Earl. Not just for the sake of starting after your answers, but also for the sake of covering our butts against stepping off on the wrong foot by failing to report to him in a timely manner."

Red Buffalo regarded him. "Now, don't take this wrong and fly off the handle, but Beauregard wailed on you pretty good last night. Not to mention the lick that Fontinelle lady got in. We go sashaying out to the army encampment, are you feeling up to reporting for duty?"

Nathan grimaced. "I'll manage. The doc has got my sore ribs and whole middle wrapped up tighter than a hatband around a cow's belly. And I've had worse headaches after a night of too much who-hit-John. Thing is, since word about us appears to be spreading pretty quick through town, if it reaches the captain before we do, he might look on our foot-dragging with disfavor. And hearing I got some ailments due to brawling while lingering in said town ain't likely to gain me much sympathy."

"Okay, if you say so. I'm all for avoiding getting off on the wrong foot with the captain if we can," said Red Buffalo. "But ahead of reporting in to the captain, there still remains one other piece of town business we're supposed take care of."

Nathan's brow puckered in puzzlement for a second, and then he realized what Red Buffalo was referring to.

"The hardware. The guns we took from Lester and Curly and said we'd leave off at the marshal's office."

"Uh-huh."

"Damn. I wish we would have thought of that when we had Feeney right there in our hotel room last night."

"That might have been a good idea . . . then again maybe not," said Red Buffalo. "With Deputy Ridgway there, too, it could have just started another flare-up. The way he was primed to make trouble for somebody—especially us, after you got done putting him in his place—there's a good chance he would have tried accusing us of theft or some such."

"*Tried* is the main word there," grated Nathan. "And if he's around again this morning, no reason to think it'll be any different."

"We could leave the guns with Waldo, tell him the story behind them, ask him to see they get delivered to the marshal," suggested Red Buffalo.

Nathan shook his head. "No, we already put that kid through enough. Besides, if we did it that way it would really make us look guilty in the eyes of Ridgway, maybe Feeney, too. I don't know how often we might be coming back to town, but we don't need them breathing down our necks every time we do."

"Not hardly."

Both men stood up. Nathan said, "Let's go gather up our gear, get checked out of the hotel, and find the marshal's office so we can get that business over with. Then we'll ride out to the army encampment and ask those soldier boys to kindly point us in the direction of some Blackfeet."

Chapter 18

Bennett McGreevey stood at the window of a spacious, elegantly decorated apartment that occupied the second floor above a ladies' apparel shop prominently located on the main street of Telford. With his left hand, McGreevey held back the edge of a lacy curtain to give him a less obstructed view of the street below. At his right shoulder, Deputy Rafe Ridgway stood gazing down at the street with him.

"There they go now, leaving the hotel and headed in the direction of the marshal's office, presumably to drop off the guns they confiscated," said McGreevey. His eyes tracked Nathan and Red Buffalo as they moved along the boardwalk below.

"I'd like to be there when they show up," growled Ridgway.

"No, it's just as well you're not," McGreevey countered. "Given your temper, especially after your run-in with them last night, there'd be too much risk of the meeting getting out of hand."

The deputy frowned. "Depends on your notion of what 'getting out of hand' amounts to, I guess. Seems to me those two have already got more out of hand than they should be allowed. First, trashing the hotel lobby and disturbing the peace—with the help of that big oaf Haliway—and then the one called Stark getting mouthy with me like he done. And now you're telling me they're parading around with property that rightfully belongs to Fallow and Messingill. How is that not stealing?"

"How about because of the circumstances under which the property was acquired and the fact they're now turning it over to the proper authority?"

"Turning it over because they know there'd be hell to pay if they didn't. And as for how they got those guns," Ridgway said stubbornly, "it'd be just their word against Lester and Curly."

"The word of the two scouts backed up by those other witnesses—a total of five in all, as I understand it—from the three wagons Fallow and Messingill decided to go harass in the first place." McGreevey let the curtain drop and turned away from the window. "You see, Rafe, your temper and your intensity sometimes cause you to over-look little details like that."

McGreevey moved away from the window. He was clad in a dressing gown of high-quality material, maroon in color, belted over matching pajama pants and a pair of soft leather slippers. He passed into the apartment's dining area, where a glass-topped table with ornate wrought iron legs painted ivory was set with a tray of china cups, a silver carafe of coffee, and another tray holding an array of pastries and fruit.

Ridgway followed along, looking almost pouty. "Kinda figured I've always earned my keep," he said sullenly.

McGreevey took a seat at the table, poured himself

some coffee. Didn't offer the deputy any. After he'd taken a sip, he said, "Your work is quite satisfactory. I never said otherwise. If it wasn't, I wouldn't keep you around. My point was simply that sometimes you need to be reminded of your boundaries. In turn, I look to you to pass that reminder on to others, meaning, in this instance, Fallow and Messingill."

Ridgway's expression displayed nothing. He wasn't quite sure what McGreevey was driving at, but wanted neither to show it nor to ask.

McGreevey took an apple from the fruit tray and began polishing it carefully on the sleeve of his robe. As he polished, he said, "When I left the ranch and came to town last evening, I told Lester and Curly I would get together with them this morning and we would discuss how best to deal with the strangers who got the drop on them and took their guns. As you might imagine, they were mortified by the experience and raring for the chance to face those strangers in order to set things straight."

Ridgway's mouth spread in a wide smirk. "Oh, hell yeah. They've got to have burs under their saddles something fierce. I know I would . . . *if* I was ever sloppy enough to allow my six-guns to be took in the first place, that is."

"The thing is," McGreevey said, "I ended up remaining unexpectedly here in town last night. So I haven't seen Lester or Curly since I left them believing they would soon get another chance at the men who'd humiliated them."

The deputy frowned. "You make it sound like you're fixing to hold them back from getting that chance."

"I'm afraid I am, yes." McGreevey looked genuinely regretful for that statement. "Given what has now been learned about the identity of the two strangers—that they are scouts soon to be joining the company of soldiers I arranged to be sent here to drive off the Blackfeet—I don't want them interfered with. They may prove crucial to the success of the soldiers' mission. Lester and Curly are just going to have to live with a little personal disappointment, at least for now."

"That's bound to be a tough lump for 'em to swallow. I know it sure would be for me, like I said before. *If*, that is, I was ever to—"

"Yes, yes, I heard you the first time," McGreevey said, cutting him off. He finally got around to taking a bite of the apple and then chewed what he'd bitten off almost angrily. "You've seen that young captain they sent us. Him and a company of only a hundred and twenty men. They've been here more than a week and as far as I know haven't come within spitting distance of any savages. And being led by that boy officer, I'm not sure they'd know how to act if they *did* flush out a war party."

Ridgway's brows pinched together. "Their captain is mighty young, that's for sure. But some of those in his command look to have a fair bit of bark and experience on 'em."

"I hope so!" McGreevey took another bite of his apple. "But none of that will matter if they can't find the damn Blackfeet! That's where these newly arrived scouts could make a difference."

A swish of movement from across the room caused both men to look around. Their gazes were treated to the sight of a lovely woman emerging from a narrow hallway off to one side.

She was of average height, a few years past thirty, with

precisely arranged silver blond hair and a finely chiseled face dominated by almond-shaped blue eyes. Her supple form was wrapped in a robe of powder blue with a scooped front that highlighted the thrust of a high, firm bosom and revealed a shadowy hint of cleavage. The flowing bottom half of the robe reached to the carpeted floor and made it appear almost like she was gliding on air as she proceeded forward.

"My goodness," she said upon reaching McGreevey and leaning to give him a quick, light kiss on the cheek. "You're being awfully loud and vulgar so early in the morning, aren't you?"

McGreevey harrumphed. "These are very busy and very trying times. Any man caught deep in the whirlwind of them, as I am, has the right to release a little steam now and then."

"Of course you do," the woman agreed. She sank lightly onto a chair beside McGreevey and poured herself some coffee. Her gaze shifting to Ridgway, she said, "Good morning, Deputy. Let me guess, the rude old bear hasn't even offered you a cup of coffee, has he?" She spoke with a faint German accent.

Ridgway, feeling boyishly shy and awkward the way he always did in the presence of Elke Klein, wrinkled his brow and replied, "That's all right, ma'am. I've got to be going anyway, and there'll be plenty of coffee waiting at the marshal's office."

"Yes, you do need to be on your way," McGreevey concurred. "But I want you to stop by the office only briefly, Rafe. Just long enough to pick up the, er, items we were talking about and take them out to Lester and Curly at the ranch. Will you do that for me? Explain the situation to

Marshal Feeney. Then, once you're at the M-Slash-G, tell Lester and Curly about the things we've recently discovered and make sure they understand not to proceed with any of their earlier plans. Tell them to just sit tight until I make it back out there myself and can explain things in more detail."

"They ain't gonna like hearing to hold off, especially not coming from me," Ridgway told him.

McGreevey regarded him flatly. "I don't give a damn what they *like*. They work for me, I call the shots. I'm counting on you to make sure they're clear on that. Are you and I clear?"

"Yes, sir. I'll see to it they get the message . . . and follow it."

After Ridgway had departed, Elke took a very dainty bite from one of the pastries and then said, "You know, don't you, that he hates your guts?"

McGreevey smiled tolerantly. "More accurately, he hates not having my power."

"Because you having it makes him subservient to you?"

"Something like that. Never mind that his association to me, along with his badge and gun, already make him a powerful man around town and through much of the territory. He wants more." McGreevey's smile turned cold. "The fool doesn't realize that no amount of power in the hands of someone like him could ever achieve what someone like me can. He has neither the vision nor the imagination to go beyond that."

Smiling coyly, Elke said, "Yes. I can certainly testify to your imagination, based on just last night."

"But with you around to distract me, my own potential might be seriously jeopardized," McGreevey responded.

"Uh-oh. Does that mean my chance at being the wife of Montana's first governor might also be in jeopardy?"

"You wouldn't be satisfied with being the mistress to Montana's first governor?" McGreevey's tone had adopted some of Elke's teasing lightness, yet at the same time there was an edge to it.

"Shouldn't the question be broader than that?" Elke countered. "If you want to talk about truly jeopardizing something, wouldn't the baggage of continuing to have a mistress rather than having a wife who *used to be* your mistress fall into that category?"

"What we have going now hasn't harmed me any," McGreevey pointed out. "Our relationship is the worst-kept secret in Telford. Yet as long as we go through the minimal pretenses of discretion, no voices of any consequence have been raised against my push for statehood or my delegate status or the greater aspirations I've made no secret of."

Elke arched a perfectly penciled eyebrow. "Could it be that no voices are raised against you because you own about seventy-five percent of everything as far as the eye can see for miles around? You have this territory in the palm of your hand."

"You're damn right I do." McGreevey's lips spread into a wide, smug smile. "And before long, after a few more things fall into place, I'll be able to start closing that hand and then matters won't be just in my palm . . . They'll be in my grip."

Chapter 19

"Greetings and welcome, gentlemen. You may stand at ease. You will soon find that, in this outfit, particularly under our current circumstances, I am not a stickler for by-the-book behavior at every moment of every day. What I do expect, however, is strict obedience and performance of duty when it counts toward the completion and success of our mission."

Captain Joshua Earl, not yet thirty, tall and trim and square-jawed handsome, made this declaration while standing erect behind a sturdy folding table positioned in the center of his command tent. His voice was well modulated, practiced, without any discernible accent.

Standing before the captain, relaxing now from an approximation of being at attention that each had been attempting, Nathan and Red Buffalo tossed each other a quick sidelong glance. The message contained in this unspoken exchange was: *Say now, this sounds like a good start.*

The young captain continued, "Since civilian scouts are rather notorious when it comes to not being sticklers for protocol themselves, I suppose that statement may have been unnecessary in present company. I always think it best, however, to lay things out plain."

"Not a bad policy, Captain," Nathan replied.

"Not a bad one at all," Red Buffalo agreed.

Earl smiled. "I especially wanted things plain between us for some very particular reasons. You see, I have thoroughly read the reports on each of you and it's quickly evident that . . . well, what I said a minute ago about scouts not being sticklers for protocol seems well suited to each of you. With perhaps a bit of an edge, reputation-wise, going to you, Mr. Stark."

Nathan shrugged noncommittally. "I've been around longer and worked under more commands. Reckon it's put me in a better position to gain that, er, reputation."

"But if I keep getting partnered with him," said Red Buffalo, "maybe my reputation will grow."

Earl shook his head, still smiling. "All that's of little or no consequence, really. Because what else is in the reports I read is how skillful each of you are as scouts and how worthwhile you've been to the various commands you've served, regardless of incidentals that seem generally petty to me. Those scouting skills are what *this* command needs and needs badly. Do you understand?"

"Sort of what we figured when we got sent here," Nathan told him.

"We've been encamped here for ten days. I've sent out patrols daily," the captain reported, his smile now gone, "without yet encountering any hostiles, not even a sign of one. I have men in the company who are experienced at fighting Indians—though not necessarily Blackfeet—

but none who are very competent at tracking. The terrain to the north, where the raiding parties keep fleeing, is mountainous, either rocky or heavily wooded or both. It provides good concealment for the raiders while at the same time making it very difficult to follow their trail."

Red Buffalo nodded. "Like Nathan said, that's why we got sent here."

"I like the confidence I'm sensing in both of you. How soon will you be ready to get started?"

The scouts once again exchanged glances. Then Nathan said, "'Bout any time you want, Captain. If you show us a place to stow our gear and maybe share a map of the area, particularly where the hostiles have hit most recently and the mountainous spots where they've been fleeing into . . . that should be plenty to get us going."

"Excellent!" Earl exclaimed. "I'll have Private Hanks show you to your quarters and naturally give you time to get settled and prepared. In the meantime I will call an officers' meeting for, say, two hours from now at which time I will introduce you to the rest of my staff and have the maps you requested ready."

Neither scout gave any response.

"One thing more," said Earl. "The mission I was given when sent here was simple and direct: these renegades under Thunder Elk are to be removed from the northern Montana territory—either by wiping them out or driving them up into Canada where most of the rest of their tribe is already on a reservation. I, personally, have no prefer-ence one way or the other. I harbor no deep animosity toward the Blackfeet, nor any member of the red race, for what it's worth, Mr. Red Buffalo. Nor do I feel any special empathy for their plight.

"I simply accept the conflict between white men and red men as being far greater than me. Nevertheless, at present I have a small slice of it to resolve and I mean to do so as expeditiously as possible.

"Which brings me to your renown as Indian Killer, Mr. Stark. First off, let me offer my profound condolence for the tragic loss that led to you becoming so known. Further, let me be clear that whatever course of action you pursue as part of this Blackfeet problem has my complete sanction . . . as long as said actions are meant to expedite the completion of the mission and not merely serve your thirst for personal vengeance.

"That is all for now. I will see you again in two hours."

"If I didn't know better," Red Buffalo said, "I might think I was still back in that soft hotel room bed, dreaming."

Nathan scowled. "I'm almost afraid to ask, but what are you talking about?"

Red Buffalo turned from where he'd been looking out the front opening of the tent they'd been assigned.

"The way this morning has gone," he said, making a catch-all gesture with one hand. "Starts out with a fine, reasonably priced breakfast. Then turning Lester's and Curly's shooting irons over to the marshal goes nothing like we expected. No fretting or accusing, practically no questions, just a lame warning about keeping any future trouble between us and them outside of town. And now we get here to the army post and we find ourselves dealing with a commander who seems fair and reasonable and actually *compliments* us on our past service and our reputations for being top scouts." Red Buffalo shook his head. "Come on now. You telling me you're used to things going that smooth in the normal course of events?"

From where he sat on the edge of one of the tent's two cots, repairing some leather stitching on his knife sheath, Nathan replied, "No, I can't argue that it's normal for things to go along that smooth. But by the same token, I don't see where a body ought to rail against a good stretch when one *does* come along. And remember, the day is young. We ride out on a scout this afternoon through territory neither of us has ever been in before, so there'll be plenty of time and opportunity for things to turn *un*smooth in a hurry."

Red Buffalo grunted. "You're just saying that to cheer me up."

"The hell I am. I got no problem at all with suffering through a stretch of easy going for a while."

Red Buffalo sat down on the other couch. "But a stretch of easy going may include having no Indians to kill. That's of no concern to you?"

"A little bit of ease-up don't mean there won't still be plenty of Indians out there to kill when the time comes." Nathan continued to focus on his stitching, then added offhandedly, "Besides, if I get too hard up, there's always you."

"You have the advantage of being satisfied with killing any and all Indians that come along," said Red Buffalo, getting used to the kind of needling comments Nathan came up with. Red Buffalo went quiet for a long count, his expression hardening as his gaze seemed to penetrate the wall of the tent, seeing something far beyond. When he spoke again, his voice, too, seemed harder and somewhat distant. "Me, I'm out for Blackfeet. And unlike our boy captain, who's about to find he has more than one Indian Killer in his ranks, I'm not willing to be satisfied with just chasing them over the damn Canadian border."

Chapter 20

"No, sir! It ain't gonna go that way. I won't have it!"

Curly Messingill tromped back and forth on a patch of dusty grass out back of the M-Slash-G bunkhouse as he spouted these words. His face was flushed bright red with anger.

Standing with one shoulder leaning against the outside of the building, Rafe Ridgway patiently watched Messingill pace and let him rant until he had to pause to catch his breath. Then, sighing, the deputy said, "I'm afraid that *is* the way it's going to go, Curly. The boss has got his mind made up. I understand it's a galling thing to choke down, I surely do. But you're going to have to cool off and find a way to live with it."

Messingill abruptly stopped pacing and turned to stand facing Ridgway. His gun belt was once again around his waist, holster tied down snug.

"What if I don't?" he challenged.

Ridgway remained leaning, his relaxed pose in sharp contrast to the other man's rigid tenseness.

"Do you really have to ask that question, Curly? Are you that stupid? Under different circumstances, I suppose maybe you could refuse an order from McGreevey and simply get fired. Go ahead and ride away. But there's too much riding on things this time around, and you damn well know it because you're up to your eyeballs in it."

"Yeah, *I* know that," countered Messingill. "Seems to me McGreevey is the one who might be forgettin' it. I know too much for him to jerk me around and expect me to put up with it no matter what. I got my pride, you know."

Ridgway's narrow eyes grew even narrower. "There's an old saying about pride . . . how it goes before a fall. Ever hear that one?"

"Maybe. Even if I did, I never understood what the hell it meant."

"Try this for size, then. A minute ago I told you you'd have to find a way to live with doing what McGreevey wants, holding off on going after those strangers we now know are scouts for the army."

"I don't give a damn who or what they are," Messingill insisted. "Nobody gets the drop on me and strips me of my guns and then can expect me *not* to come looking for payback. Not the low-down curs who done it, and not even Bennett McGreevey! Now that you've brung my shootin' irons back to me, Rafe, I'm bound to use 'em for deliverin' that payback."

Deep inside the slits that were Ridgway's eyes, the flames of a cold fire flickered.

"You didn't let me finish making my point before you so rudely interrupted me," he said, his voice suddenly colder, too. "When I said you'd have to live with doing what McGreevey wants . . . the unspoken part was that you could choose to die over *not* doing it."

Suddenly, as silently and effortlessly as a curl of smoke,

Ridgway was no longer leaning against the building but was standing upright, feet planted wide, facing Messingill full on.

Messingill remained rigid, motionless. His eyes widened, though, and his chin sagged as if in disbelief.

"You'd do that, Rafe? You'd pull iron on me over something like this?"

"I will if you give me no choice, Curly."

"But you're a lawman. Quittin' McGreevey ain't breakin' no laws, and neither is lookin' to settle the score with those two who done me wrong."

Ridgway spat out a short, caustic laugh. "I'm a lawman like you're a cowpuncher, Curly. We're neither of us no more than hired guns for McGreevey, and no matter how much of a pain in the rump he is, I like being on the right side of the money he dishes out. If he succeeds in pushing through statehood and ends up the damn governor— which he very well may—then I want to be on the right side of that, too."

"So what does me or Lester settlin' up with a pair of mangy army scouts have to do with any of that?" Messingill wailed.

"For cryin' out loud, Curly, for once try thinkin' with your brain and not just your gun hand, will you?" This came from Lester Fallow, who until then had been standing quietly off to one side in front of a dilapidated old buckboard. "You think I don't want to go after those scouts as bad as you do? I tossed and turned all night, itchin' to get my hands back on my guns, thinkin' of nothing else but how I'd use 'em on those two."

With a renewed show of eagerness, Messingill said, "Then you're singin' the same tune as me, right?"

"Same tune for sure . . . but all in good time," Fallow countered. "Didn't you hear what Rafe told us about McGreevey sayin' we needed to hold off? Not forever, just for the time being. You can see how an Indian uprising could ruin the whole statehood thing and all the rest of McGreevey's plans, can't you? And you've seen how poorly the ranchers and homesteaders—and even the army, so far—have fared against Thunder Elk's raids. So if that pair of scouts can provide an edge, well, it makes sense for McGreevey not wantin' 'em interfered with. *For now*. But after they've served their purpose, then there wouldn't be no more reason for us to hold off gettin' our turn at 'em."

Messingill looked torn with indecision. Turning back to the deputy, he said, "Is that right, Rafe? Is that what you think about McGreevey's feelings? That he wouldn't have no problem with me and Lester settlin' up with those scouts *after* the Injun trouble is over and done with?"

"Seemed plain enough to me," confirmed Ridgway. "And in the meantime, he's still needing you and Lester to keep the nesters and farmers from clogging up the range. You stick to that, keep doing the good job you been doing, and you'll have your own shot at being on the right side of what lies ahead for this whole blasted territory."

"That don't sound too bad to me, Curly," encouraged Fallow. "Sure seems worth havin' a little patience when it comes to those scouts . . . knowin' we'll get our chance at 'em in the end."

Messingill looked almost won over but he still had a question. "What if the Blackfeet get 'em first?"

Fallow considered for a beat, then one side of his mouth pulled back, baring his teeth in a humorless grin.

"Would that be such a bad trade? Losin' our turn to an Injun torture knife?"

At last the tenseness lifted from Messingill and he said, almost relieved, "No, I reckon not. If things were to work out that way, it wouldn't be a bad trade at all."

Chapter 21

"Not too far past that rise straight ahead," said Sergeant Thomas O'Driscoll, pointing, "is the latest homestead we know of those red devils strikin'. That was day before yesterday. They did their bloody work and their robbin' and then, as usual, shot back north toward their mountain hideout."

He swung his thick arm in that direction to add clarity to his statement.

O'Driscoll was a big, beefy trooper, ruddy-faced as much from the copious amounts of liquor he'd consumed in his fifty-odd years as from exposure to the elements, with decades of army service under his belt and citations for bravery in battle equaled only by the number of times he'd been busted back in rank due to his fondness for the bottle.

"This homestead marks about the farthest south and the closest to town they've struck so far," the sergeant went on. "Their pattern seems pretty clear, though. They're workin' their way down more and more out of the mountains. Just a matter of time, once they get all the scattered little places picked off, before they start hittin' the herds of the bigger ranchers down in the basin. Barrin' us stoppin' 'em, that is."

"So when the smaller spreads were getting pecked away at, they were pretty much on their own," said Red Buffalo. "But now that the big, moneyed outfits are on the brink of getting hit, it's serious enough for the army to be called in. That the way it went?"

O'Driscoll's face scrunched up with an expression that seemed to convey annoyance, but whether it stemmed from agreeing or disagreeing with the Crow's assessment wasn't clear. All the sergeant said was, "The army goes where it's sent, when it's sent. I been around a long while, mister, and that's how it's always been."

Nathan joined in, saying, "The bigger ranches down in the basin, one among those belongs to a Bennett McGreevey, ain't that right?"

The three men were striding abreast at an easy pace, on foot to give their horses a walking break. The soldiers of the twenty-man patrol sent out under O'Driscoll's command, also on foot and walking their horses, stretched out behind them. The sun hung just past its noon peak in a cloudless sky and a light, gusting breeze came and went in the pleasantly warm air, stirring faint swirls of dust from the bare patches in the grassy, rolling terrain that spread out all around them.

"McGreevey," O'Driscoll said, echoing Nathan's mention of the name. "Way I hear, he ain't just *among* the big ranchers in the basin, he's the biggest . . . by half again of all the others combined, if the stories are true. What's more, he owns a good share of the businesses in the town of Telford."

"He-wolf of the whole area, we've heard him described," summed up Red Buffalo.

O'Driscoll cocked a shaggy brow. "That's an accurate way of puttin' it, I reckon. You fellas got some particular interest in McGreevey?"

"Just some things we heard," Nathan replied. "We got in late and stayed over in Telford last night. Like you said, he casts a pretty big shadow over the town so his name popped up more than once."

O'Driscoll reached up with a big paw and scratched the side of his neck. "What else I hear is that he's a, whatya-call, *delicate* for makin' our Montana Territory a state."

Nathan grinned. "You mean he's a *delegate*. I never met the hombre, but I've got a pretty good hunch there ain't much delicate about him."

"Well, whatever you call it," grumbled O'Driscoll, "I don't see why fellas like him—or anybody, for that matter—push so hard for statehood. Why not leave at least a few places wild and free? I've been in other territories that got turned into states and right away there was lawyers and politicians and town councils and what have you, all layin' down *statutes* and boundaries and so forth until in no time at all it got so's every way you tried to turn there was some blamed rule against it . . ." He shook his head. "Naw, I know enough to know that ain't no way for the likes of me."

"But you're in the army. Have been for more than three decades, the captain told us," said Red Buffalo. "Ain't the army full of rules and regulations you have to follow?"

"There's rumors to that effect," the old sergeant allowed. Then, after a moment, the lower half of his whiskey-ravaged face split into a sly grin. "But for some, the army's book of rules is sorta like the devil ye know. For an old horse soldier who's been around as long as me, you learn to slip and slide in and out of the more meddlesome ones and even get a chance to tweak the devil's nose now and then."

Nathan and Red Buffalo glanced involuntarily at the stripes on his sleeve.

O'Driscoll added, "Of course, as these wee little three stripes indicate after all my time in this man's army, the devil *does* tweak back once in a while. Still, I'd rather give and take my tweaks soldierin' in a territory over a state any old day. That was my point."

Nathan sighed. "Comes down to it, reckon me and Moses have chalked up our share of dodging meddlesome rules ourselves."

To which Red Buffalo remarked, "Speak for yourself, white eyes. I am a good Christian who always walks the straight and narrow."

O'Driscoll cast a somewhat uneasy sidelong glance and said, "He's kidding, right?"

"Hard to tell about this particular one," Nathan replied. "Other Injuns I've known lie half the time then don't tell the truth the other half. Can't say much 'kidding' ever enters into it."

O'Driscoll decided to let it go at that. "Well, we need to get that burnt-out homestead looked at and then make our swing north if we're gonna give you two enough daylight to have a chance at picking up any sign." He stopped walking and called back over his shoulder, "Halt and prepare to mount!" The men in the column did as ordered. When, a moment later, the sergeant called, "Mount!" they swung smoothly up into their saddles, as did O'Driscoll, Nathan, and Red Buffalo.

As promised, a handful of minutes later the blackened shell of the most recently attacked homestead came into sight as they topped the rise O'Driscoll had indicated. The place didn't look like it ever amounted to a whole lot to begin with, but whatever sweat and hope and dreams had taken it as far as it did were certainly ended now, crushed and turned to ashes.

"Ebner, we were told, was the name of the family who lived here," O'Driscoll related as they rode down to the place. "A ma and pa and a couple of boys who were just comin' of age. Had some hogs and chickens, a milk cow or two. A decent-sized stand of corn over yonder by the creek. Seems like they were makin' out okay, maybe on their way to gettin' by still better . . . but Thunder Elk and his braves took it away. Their lives and all the rest. But you can bet the livestock meat and the corn and whatever else they hauled off made the lives of their own a lot better off."

"Their own? Women and children part of this renegade band?" Nathan asked.

"Took squaws and brats with 'em when they left that Canadian reservation," O'Driscoll answered. "Nobody can say for sure how many, though, because nobody has got close to wherever they're holed up to see. Same for the size of the raiding parties they send out. Never been any survivors to say how many hit 'em. Somewhere north of thirty seems to be the generally accepted number, based on what sign they've left behind. But that ain't sayin' all the fightin' braves go out at once."

"They'd leave a few behind to watch over their camp,

but most of the able-bodied men would join the raids," said Red Buffalo confidently. "Especially now that you've shown up."

"The army, you mean?" O'Driscoll frowned. "We ain't never had no kind of run-in with 'em yet. They might not even realize we're here."

"They do." If anything, Red Buffalo's tone was even more confident.

Nathan had dismounted and was slowly circling the charred remains of the cabin on foot, leading Buck along behind him. His eyes were cast downward, sweeping from side to side as he walked, scanning the blackened rubble as well as the trampled ground around it. As he got to what had been the back corner of the cabin, his eyes lifted and he stopped. His gaze settled on a grassy hillock about twenty yards out where lay a row of four fresh graves marked by simple wooden crosses.

His eyes remaining trained on the piles of heaped earth, Nathan said over his shoulder, "So they killed the mother, too, rather than taking her captive."

It wasn't really a question but O'Driscoll, who remained mounted, as had the rest of the soldiers as well as Red Buffalo, saw fit to answer anyway.

"The Blackfeet ain't been takin' captives in any of these raids. Which ain't to say the red devils haven't been usin' some of the women mighty hard before they kill 'em and ride on."

Nathan's face was turned in such a way that none of the others could see the look that had come over it: features turned to stone, mouth pulled into a grimace as tight and thin as a knife slash, an icy glint in his eyes that, no matter where they were aimed, were seeing something visible only in a tortured internal place.

Watching, Red Buffalo could not see these things either; but he didn't have to. He knew what was happening by the sudden rigidity that ran through Nathan's whole body, the way his shoulders raised ever so slightly and then locked as motionless and hard as if they'd turned into a steel rod spreading his shirt.

Red Buffalo had seen this come over the man he was partnered with only once or twice before. But there was no mistaking or forgetting it. There were times, when talk of females who'd been captured or abused by Indians came up, that Nathan's thoughts were jerked uncontrollably hard to the painful memory of his three-year-old sister being abducted by the same savages who'd slaughtered his parents and pregnant wife. The events of that day were what resulted in Nathan's overriding hatred for all red men and what had spawned, ultimately, the Indian Killer who continued to roam the frontier seeking blood for blood.

These episodes of revenge sustained Nathan Stark, gave him a wretched sense of getting even one dead Indian at a time for the deaths of his loved ones, but they did little to address the hauntingly unanswered question of what had happened to his sister . . .

Was she still alive? If so, where? In what condition? Given the years that had passed, would he even recognize her now? . . . Everywhere Nathan went, as he scouted and killed and increased his reputation for relentless vengeance, he kept his eyes and ears open for something, anything, that might give him a clue as to the fate of red-haired little Rena. And despite his physical strength and toughness, the agonizing emptiness of learning nothing was sometimes nearly more than he could bear.

Watching Nathan now, recognizing what he was going through, Red Buffalo felt helpless to be able to say or do anything that might ease his torment. And then, ironically as he found himself hoping the somewhat awkward moment would pass, not only for Nathan's sake but for the sake of keeping O'Driscoll and the other men from growing curious about what was going on, Red Buffalo's gaze drifted beyond Nathan and he spotted, way out on the horizon, something he felt also rated the attention of the others.

"Nathan," he said. He didn't raise his voice or put any particular inflection in the word, yet there was an intangible something in his tone that told Nathan—as well as O'Driscoll and the rest within earshot—he had something important to say.

Pulled from his dark reverie, Nathan turned to see what Red Buffalo wanted. As soon as he did, the Crow extended his arm, pointing at what had caught his eye. He said, "There . . . See it? That dark smudge way off, that thin curl of black against the sky?"

Nathan's head swiveled back, his gaze following the line of Red Buffalo's pointing finger. O'Driscoll and several soldiers in the column did the same.

"Smoke. Something burning," Nathan said decisively. Then: "What's out that way, Sergeant? Another homestead, a remote ranch?"

"Nothing," O'Driscoll said. "We swung a patrol out wide after discoverin' what happened here. Their report was nothing but emptiness in that direction."

"A grass fire maybe?" suggested a soldier mounted behind O'Driscoll.

"No. A grass fire would be throwing a line of smoke much wider than that," responded Red Buffalo.

"Whatever it is, it was damn sharp of Moses to spot it," Nathan said. "We need to take a closer look-see, without wasting any time." He stepped around to Buck's side, planted a foot in the stirrup, swung smoothly up into his saddle. Eyeing O'Driscoll, he asked, "You and your boys ready to try and keep up, Sergeant?"

The big sergeant threw back his head and snorted. "You just give that buckskin of yours a good swat to set him in motion, lad, and we'll see who keeps up with who."

Chapter 22

The curl of smoke remained in a fixed position, although growing darker and reaching higher as the patrol column galloped hard to reach it.

When they came in sight of the source, they saw it was the remains of a single burning wagon. The collapsed frame and wheels were barely recognizable in their charred, twisted state. A haze of smoke lifted from the smoldering mass and here and there a few small flames continued to lick and crackle stubbornly.

Personal items ransacked from the wagon lay strewn about, and off a few yards from the wagon's rear end lay two gutted and partially butchered bovine carcasses. Near the front end, the body of what had once been a yellow-haired man—the top of his head now a crown of raw, bloody skin and the fringe of hair around his ears soaked crimson—lay facedown. His back was pockmarked by a pattern of ragged bullet holes, along with a single arrow thrusting up from between his shoulder blades.

"Of all the sorrowful luck," groaned O'Driscoll. "We missed having a chance to stop this by only a short time."

"But who are they, Sarge? And what were they doing

way out here?" asked a soldier who'd reined in just behind O'Driscoll.

Before the sergeant could respond, Red Buffalo said, "They were on their way to homestead a section of land that had been granted to them somewhere around here. Those carcasses over yonder are what's left of a cow and a bull they were planning to get started with."

O'Driscoll gave him a look. "You know the people who belonged to this wagon?"

"Met 'em on the trail into Telford just yesterday," answered Nathan, who, like Red Buffalo, recognized Joe Raymer even in arrow-and-bullet-riddled death. "If what you told us a little while ago about Thunder Elk's raiders not taking captives is true, then I expect if some of your boys make a sweep of the area, they'll find the body of the wife not too far off. For what it's worth, their names were Raymer. Joe and Margie."

The sergeant signaled six men to peel off from the column and make the recommended search. It wasn't long before one of the soldiers called out from a shallow gully west of the wagon.

"Over here, Sarge! It looks like they . . . Oh hell . . . Somebody bring something to wrap her in."

"I got it," said Red Buffalo. He heeled his horse into motion, leaning from the saddle to grab a long dress from a pile of clothing that had been flung from the wagon and left in a tangle on the ground. He rode the short distance to the gully and dismounted to help the soldier who'd found her gently wrap the ravaged remains of Margie Raymer.

While they were doing that, Nathan, keeping his gaze averted from the dead woman, rode off at a measured gait to the north, carefully scanning the ground as he passed over it. After he'd covered a hundred or so yards, he wheeled his buckskin and rode back to where O'Driscoll waited at the head of the patrol column. By then, Red Buffalo and a couple of the soldiers were carefully placing Margie Raymer's limp, shrouded form on the ground beside her husband.

"I make it three dozen riders on unshod ponies, plus the shod prints of the team they took from the wagon," Nathan reported. "They lit out due north at a pretty good clip."

"You think they saw us comin'?"

"Not much doubt." Nathan pointed, saying, "You can see we interrupted 'em from butchering the cow and bull all the way. They got most of the meat but didn't have time to scrape the hides all the way clean and make off with them."

"And they took the team for eating later because they didn't have time to start cutting them up here," added Red Buffalo, once more mounted and guiding his pony over to stand alongside Nathan's Buck.

O'Driscoll looked in the direction Nathan had indicated the raiders fled. "Due north from here is a ways off course— more westerly—from where they usually head, straight into the heart of the Wolfhead Mountains."

"You can see a spiny offshoot of the Wolfheads angling west from here," Nathan pointed out. "Means rugged, broken ground they can reach quicker, either to fog their trail to make it harder to follow . . . or to lay an ambush if we crowd up too close."

The sergeant scowled. "You're not suggestin' we hold off goin' after 'em, are you?"

"Not everybody, no," Nathan told him. "For sure, me

and Moses ought to give pursuit. With a trail this fresh, we'll not only be able to stick with it, but we may have a good chance to track 'em all the way to that elusive hideout nobody's been able to get a bead on before this."

"But it sounds like you're sayin' the whole patrol ought not try to engage."

Nathan grimaced. "That's your call to make, Sarge. But remember, you're looking at nearly two-to-one odds. And if they gain high ground ahead of us—which they almost certainly will—and if they know we're coming—which everything indicates they do . . . Look, I can surely understand the urge in a soldier like you, believe me. But charging into circumstances like that is practically a guarantee for heavy losses and in the end may waste the opportunity for locating their main camp."

"How would it be any different for you and Red Buffalo to give chase than for all of us?"

"We could close in on them without being seen. They'd figure if anybody was going to come after 'em, it'd be the whole patrol. They wouldn't be on the lookout for only two men. We could swing wide, move in from an angle they wouldn't expect, and pick up their trail after they were already in the rocks."

O'Driscoll cocked a shaggy brow. "You're awful cocky, awful damn sure of yourself, ain't you?"

"I didn't earn the name *Indian Killer* by making a habit of letting the red devils outfox me," Nathan said flatly.

The two men locked eyes for a long count. Until Red Buffalo finally said, "Somebody make up your mind who's going to do what. Wasting time arguing over it is only letting the trail grow colder."

"Ah, blast your hides, the both of ya! You're right and

I know it, no matter how much it galls me to have to hold back." The expression on the big Irishman's face told how painful the admission was for him to make. "The way it stands now, our full patrol is too many yet too few. You pair of rascals, on the other hand, have a chance at pulling off what you claim."

"There's no shame in not acting foolhardy and avoiding a waste of lives," Nathan said somberly. "Fella by the name of Custer, who I had the honor of riding with for a time before his craving for glory got the better of him, made a strong case for that not too long ago."

"Best get goin', then," O'Driscoll said brusquely. "We'll finish up here and then report back to Captain Earl. From there, we'll all be anxious to hear how you make out."

"Be most fitting for these folks"—Red Buffalo tipped his head toward the bodies of Joe and Margie Raymer— "if they could be buried on the homestead property they were headed for. But since we don't know where that is, if you'd take their bodies to town and notify an Amos and Esther Handley at Rafferty's dry goods store, they'll know what to do."

O'Driscoll nodded. "I'll see to it. Now be off with ye rascals . . . and Godspeed."

Chapter 23

As Nathan had indicated they would do, he and Red Buffalo rode away from the rest of the patrol in a westerly sweep that gradually curved north. With the use of field glasses before starting out, they'd pinpointed a distinctive rocky peak in the mountainous spur of the Wolfheads that was in direct line with the way the Blackfeet raiders were headed. Their sweep was aimed at bringing them around to this peak as a spot where they calculated being able to pick up the raiders' trail again.

Sticking to shallow gullies and draws as much as possible, choosing the grassiest ground covering to minimize the dust kicked up by their horses' hooves, the scouts ate up distance steadily. As they rode deeper into the afternoon, a dull gray cloud cover moved in overhead accompanied by gusts of a cooler wind.

Once they reached the beginning of the Wolfheads' spur and the grassy ground gave way to hardpan and flat slabs of rock, they paused to shroud their horses' hooves with coarse leather stockings designed to muffle the sound of their passage over this rugged surface. The peak that was the scouts' focal point loomed less than a mile ahead.

"If we were about an hour behind the attack on the Raymer wagon," Red Buffalo whispered as they took the opportunity for a short rest in a clump of high, smooth boulders, "then we must be close to three hours behind the raiders now."

"Sounds about right," Nathan agreed.

"If the Blackfeet set an ambush for the patrol, like we figured they'd do once they reached these foothills," Red Buffalo continued, "how long do you figure they'd wait without any soldiers showing up?"

Nathan glanced skyward. "With weather moving in and wanting to get the meat and other plunder from their raid back to their main camp, not overly long, I wouldn't expect. Leastways not the whole bunch."

"Uh-huh. That's what I was thinking. More likely they'd leave behind only a half dozen or so to lay down some covering fire and provide warning in case any bluecoats *did* show up."

"Which is probably what's up ahead waiting for us now. Be harder for us to spot and, even if we do, we'll have to hold off engaging them so as not to warn the rest that we're out here."

"Been thinking the same," said Red Buffalo through clenched teeth. "Been thinking, too, how hard it's going to be for me to keep from opening up on some Blackfeet if any come in my sights."

"If that crusty old sergeant had the will to hold off on a foolhardy chase, then you're going to have to display some will of your own," Nathan told him. "If we're able to spot some lookouts left behind and can be patient enough, then when they finally pull out and head to join the others, we'll be able to follow 'em. That'll be easier and surer than trying to track them through these rocks."

Red Buffalo sighed. "Yeah, I know. Like O'Driscoll said, I know it but it still galls me."

"Well, first things first. That means, to begin with, we've got to spot the lookouts we expect to be out there without giving ourselves away. Let's start with that and then worry about what comes next."

Slowly, cautiously, the scouts progressed deeper and higher into the foothills. At the same time, the overcast sky was growing darker and the cold gusts were becoming stronger and more frequent, eventually turning into a sustained wind that moaned and whistled eerily through the rock formations around them. It might muffle their approach, but the bits of dust and sand it whipped up also stung the eyes and made the horses fidgety.

When they got to the base of the distinctive peak they had aimed for, they found a narrow, twisting canyon passing between sheer, jagged cliff walls and reaching deeper back into the spiny mountainous spur that reached out from the more majestic sprawl of the Wolfheads. Off that way, the lower heights were mottled by the greenery of trees and undergrowth; here, the terrain was almost exclusively bare, weather-scoured rock.

Dismounting and ducking once more into a seam between some clustered boulders, Nathan and Red Buffalo did some further palavering.

"If Mother Nature ever created a more perfect spot for an ambush, I've never seen it," stated Nathan, keeping his voice low so there was no chance of the wind scooping up his words and carrying them to unwanted ears.

"No argument here," responded Red Buffalo. "The only thing missing is any sign of the ambushers."

"Only a handful of things that could mean. Either the Blackfeet never set an ambush to begin with, or they set it at a spot deeper in, or they waited for a while but then gave up and moved on."

"Or we're just not seeing them."

Nathan gave him a look. "*Neither* of us? You got to be kidding."

"No, I wasn't," Red Buffalo said, his expression sour. "But you're right. If any were near, one of us would have seen something."

"Since I can't believe they'd pass up a chance at ambushing the patrol in case it came in pursuit, that leaves only two choices. Either some braves are positioned a ways farther in, or enough time has passed that they went ahead and withdrew with the rest."

"And we can't proceed with trying to pick up their trail until we know for sure."

"Wouldn't hardly seem healthy."

Red Buffalo pushed back one of his long braids that the wind had whipped across his mouth. "We'll have to leave the horses here for now, do our checking on foot— mountain-goat style."

"I've been called a variety of critters in my time, never a goat before," Nathan said. "But you're right about it being time to quit the horses for a while. How about this? You cover me while I hotfoot it across the width of that canyon. Then we'll each work our way back on opposite sides, along the rim of those cliffs, and see what we find deeper in."

Red Buffalo reached up and pulled his Henry repeater from its saddle scabbard. "Ain't gonna argue for hot-footin' rights. So take off whenever you're ready. I'll cover you from here and then we'll have ourselves that look-see deeper in."

After seizing his Winchester '73 to take along with him, Nathan made the scramble across the canyon floor without incident. The wind was growing more stinging, more vicious by the minute, and something about the placement of how the high rocks bracketed the canyon created a funneling effect that sucked the wind into its mouth with even greater force. Nathan cursed this as he made his way up and then started along the jagged rim on his side.

What was worse, he thought, was the way the cloud cover above was looking ever more threatening. No matter what else he and Red Buffalo might find deeper in this canyon, if a hard rain cut loose and lasted for any duration, their chances of picking up the trail of the main body of raiders in hopes of following it to their hideout camp would be seriously diminished.

Nathan willed himself to dismiss that gloomy prospect from his thoughts and stay focused on the task at hand. If there *were* any braves awaiting in ambush somewhere up ahead, they obviously presented a greater and more immediate danger than an ill-timed downpour.

When he heard the first dull boom, whipsawed crazily by the rush of the wind, Nathan's first thought was that it was a clap of thunder. Then another followed quickly and the scout was considering how it didn't really *sound* like thunder, not even knocked around by the wind, when a new sound cut through the rushing air and reached his ears—the unmistakable whine of a bullet ricocheting off rock. When bits of shattered lead and stone scraped his cheek, he knew it had struck only inches from his head.

Nathan immediately pitched to the ground and pressed as flat as he could to the hard surface. The passage along the canyon rim at this point was quite narrow, no more than four feet, with the drop-off on one side and a smooth, slightly sloping wall of higher rocks on the other. It left him little room to maneuver and, except for some small boulders scattered around, no real cover.

The splatter of the ricochet shrapnel across his cheek told Nathan that the shot had come from somewhere behind and below him. Acting on this realization, he squirmed around to face back the way he'd just come, all the while continuing to press as flat as he could. More shots boomed through the howling wind, followed closely by the sound of more lead clattering against rock.

When a fresh pair of rifle cracks spoke from closer by, Nathan realized that Red Buffalo was returning fire from the opposite rim of the canyon. A second after this recognition, he heard the Crow shouting over to him, "They're swarming up behind you, Nathan! Stay low!"

Nathan smiled grimly at the words, glad for the assist but at the same time thinking he'd be damned if he would remain hunkered down and leave all the fighting to his partner. Jacking a round into his Winchester and crowding into a shallow vertical depression in the rock wall at his back, he waited for a break in the latest volley from below.

When it came, he twisted around in the depression and raised up to swing his rifle muzzle in search of a target.

When a wide-brimmed tan hat poked into sight, Nathan stroked the Winchester's trigger, vaguely aware that Red Buffalo was also shooting again from his side of the canyon.

The man under the tan hat went flying backward and it was only then, as he toppled over a slanted rock outcrop, legs kicking high, that Nathan spotted the flash of his cavalry blue shirt and the yellow stripes running down the sides of his pantlegs.

Holy hell! The man was no Indian, but rather a soldier!

Nathan dropped back into his depression as a fresh volley hammered up from below. His heart was hammering, too. What in blazes was going on?

From across the way, Red Buffalo called, "Did you see that?"

"Afraid so," Nathan responded. "You got a better angle than me, did you catch sight of any more? Is it really soldiers down there shooting at us . . . or is it some kind of Blackfoot trick?"

More shots from below.

"There!" Red Buffalo exclaimed. "Yeah, more blue. Five or six of 'em down there. All soldiers. Nathan, I don't think it's a trick. I think they must think *we're* Blackfeet!"

As if to remove any shred of doubt, the thin, wind-whipped strains of a trumpet blowing "Charge!" could be heard coming from a ways off to the east.

Nathan leaned back against the cold, smooth rock wall and groaned aloud. "Aw, hell."

Chapter 24

Captain Joshua Earl paced back and forth within the limitations of his command tent. His mouth was pulled into a straight, tight line, the muscles at the hinges of his jaw bulged visibly, and his forehead was laddered with deep seams above pinched brows.

"This is unfortunate. Terribly unfortunate," he muttered, repeating the words for a third time.

Standing inside the tent with him were Nathan, Red Buffalo, Sergeant O'Driscoll, and the company's two other officers, Lieutenant Benton and Sergeant Purdy. Kirby Benton was a stocky fifty-year-old, average height, with carrot-colored hair, piercing blue eyes, and at the moment, a sullen, antagonistic attitude showing plainly on his weathered face. A dozen years younger, Ben Purdy was compact and well-muscled, very disciplined in his military bearing, with pale, thinning hair and an air of earnest dedication to the uniform he proudly wore.

"The overall responsibility naturally rests on me, and I must, of course, accept some of the direct blame," Captain Earl said, stopping his pacing and raising his voice to be heard over the wind that continued to howl outside, causing the walls of the tent to flap and shiver almost non-stop. The flame in the lantern placed on the folding table in the center of the enclosed space, providing illumination against the dusk that had begun to settle outside, also danced and flickered with little letup. The throbbing shadows it cast, combined with Earl's current somber expression, appeared to age the young officer dramatically.

"It was my decision," he went on, "to send out a second patrol under Lieutenant Benton after O'Driscoll's had already left. Meaning that O'Driscoll had no idea there would be another force anywhere out in the field. Which shouldn't have presented a problem if Benton's patrol had continued due north as intended, well away from O'Driscoll's westerly course." His gaze came to rest on the lieutenant. "Which brings me once again to the question, Lieutenant, of how and why you ended up so far to the west."

"I've already answered that to the best of my ability, sir," Benton answered rather sharply. "As my patrol neared the foothills of the Wolfhead Mountains, we cut what appeared to be fairly fresh sign of a sizable hostile force headed off to the west. It was my decision to follow this sign with two possible outcomes in mind—either to catch up and engage the hostiles or to possibly assist O'Driscoll's patrol in the event they unexpectedly ran afoul of them."

"This sign you cut . . . how many hostiles did you judge it represented?"

"More than thirty."

"Yet you thought it prudent to pursue them with only a twenty-man patrol and not dispatch a rider back here with an advisement of the situation and possibly gain some reinforcement?"

Benton's chin jutted out defiantly. "I thought pursuit my best course of action, sir, with every man I had available. Also, as stated, I had strong reason to expect that, since we were proceeding west, we would be encountering O'Driscoll's patrol and thereby, combined, achieve numerical superiority over the hostiles."

Earl's frown deepened. "But then you found evidence of the sign you'd been following suddenly veering north. So you veered also, sticking with the trail of the hostiles and giving no further thought to O'Driscoll's patrol. Is that what I'm to understand?"

"My thought at the time," Benton replied grimly, "was that if O'Driscoll's patrol had encountered the Blackfeet and were not coming in pursuit . . . well, the outcome for them must have been dire. Otherwise, I couldn't think of any reason why a fully manned patrol *wouldn't* be giving pursuit."

"Now, just a minute, mister," O'Driscoll huffed. "If you're implyin'—"

"Not now, Sergeant!" the captain barked, cutting him short. "You'll get your chance to speak in a minute."

O'Driscoll clamped his mouth tight and stared straight ahead, silent but still clearly fuming on the inside.

Earl's gaze went back to Benton. "So, thinking that the sergeant's patrol had met with serious harm in an encounter with the Blackfeet—or perhaps had not encountered them at all—you nevertheless proceeded to follow this new direction of the hostile's trail. Tell me, what was your estimate of their strength at this point?"

Benton looked to be caught off guard. "I, er . . . I didn't

take time to do any reassessment of how many we were following at that point, sir. There was no evidence that the number had changed to any degree. Frankly, believing the red devils we were pursuing were now in flight after a bloody attack on O'Driscoll's patrol . . . well, me and my men were pretty riled up, no matter what the odds."

"Uhmm." Earl regarded the lieutenant for a long count. "So believing that . . . thinking the savages you were now chasing had just struck a devastating blow to a well-armed, well-trained force of soldiers numbering exactly the same as you and your men . . . it sounds almost as if you continued after them driven as much by vengeance as a reasonable measure of caution."

"With all due respect, sir, I don't feel that is accurate." Benton's eyes had taken on a deep cobalt brilliance. "Yes, our blood was up. I admitted that. But I believe my record shows that I am not an officer given to leading his men recklessly or without due caution. That was why, when the trail led due north into a spur of barren rocks rather than angling back over to the central Wolfheads where it had originated, I reined up on our pursuit and indeed implemented some cautionary steps."

"And these were?"

"Let's just say I can spot the setup for a possible ambush as good as anybody." Benton paused, his tone and a slight curl to his upper lip abruptly conveying a hint of smugness before he continued, "And that's exactly what I spotted in that pile of barren rocks, especially the ragged mouth of that canyon the trail led directly into. It was like the deceptive smile of an evil vixen ready to wrap you in an embrace and then push the point of a knife between your shoulder blades."

"Spare us the colorful imagery," the captain grated. "Just get on with the rest of it."

Tipping his head in the direction of Nathan and Red Buffalo, Benton said, "These fellows can attest to how it went from there about as good as me. Once I smelled a possible trap, I directed the majority of my force down into a nearby shallow draw and sent a four-man reconnoitering team ahead to check the situation more closely. Unfortunately, I allowed one of the four—and I mean no disrespect to the dead—to be Private Selkirk, a young and fairly green recruit.

"As Selkirk and the other three advanced cautiously on the canyon, they had no way of knowing that scouts Stark and Red Buffalo were already there, on foot, making their way along the rim on either side. As best we can reconstruct, Selkirk must have looked up once he got in close and seen a man with a rifle in those higher rocks and panicked into taking what he thought was a defensive shot. From there . . . well, several more shots followed. From all directions. Until Stark finally recognized it was soldiers down below and began calling out, identifying himself and Red Buffalo, when he was able to bring the firing to a halt. By then, unfortunately, Private Selkirk had been struck and killed."

Earl closed his eyes for a moment, breathing deeply and mentally reviewing all he had just heard. When he again opened his eyes, his gaze went to Nathan. "Do you have anything to add to that, Mr. Stark, as far as the encounter at the canyon?"

"No, sir, I don't. It matches what I saw and heard," Nathan answered.

"Red Buffalo?"

"Same," said the Crow.

Now the captain's focus went to O'Driscoll. "Sergeant," he said, "I find no fault in any of your actions regarding this event. Holding your patrol in reserve against a larger force, especially given the potential for what might have been gained by allowing the two scouts to follow and possibly be led to the Blackfeet's main camp, was a difficult yet solid decision."

"Begging your pardon, sir," Benton said in a strained voice, "but is that an implication that my decisions this day were somehow *not* sound?"

"If I have any judgment to pass on your actions this day or any other, Lieutenant," responded a flinty-eyed Captain Earl, "I will convey it quite distinctly and not leave it open to interpretation. So understand this: I feel some of your actions today were *less* than sound, though not worthy of further reprimand. Going forward, I suggest you keep foremost in your mind that our mission here is to get rid of the Blackfeet problem—not to seek personal glory at the expense of lives lost unnecessarily on either side. Is that clear?"

"Yes, sir," Benton ground out through clenched teeth, averting his eyes and aiming a glare down at the ground, not daring to lift his eyes to meet the captain's.

When Earl spoke again, his voice was calmer, softer, barely audible above the shudder of the tent and the howl of the wind outside. "Sergeant O'Driscoll, you sent a detail to deliver the bodies of those slain homesteaders—the Raymers—back to town, is that correct?"

"Yes, sir."

"Prepare another detail to take Private Selkirk's body in first thing in the morning. I will accompany it. I'll arrange for local interment, pending the notification of his family after I've sent a wire to Fort Billings. In the event they want his body transported elsewhere, I'll leave that to be worked out by the brass at Billings."

O'Driscoll nodded. "Very good, sir."

Turning to Nathan and Red Buffalo, Earl said, "There were two bullet holes in Private Selkirk, either of which could have been fatal. So, for what it's worth, you appear to share equal responsibility for his death. Which is not to say, all things considered, any degree of blame or guilt is warranted."

Neither Nathan nor Red Buffalo gave any response.

"With that addressed," the captain continued, "what are the chances, if you two returned to that canyon the hostiles disappeared into after slaughtering the Raymers, that you could pick up their trail again and possibly still be able to follow it to the main camp in the Wolfheads?"

Nathan and Red Buffalo exchanged glances before Nathan replied, "If that wind don't tear loose any rain before the night's over, we might could have some luck. Would have been a lot surer if we'd've been able to stick with it when the sign was fresh. But barring rain, it's worth a shot."

"And if it *does* rain?"

Nathan shrugged. "Nothing to lose by still trying, I reckon."

Red Buffalo added, "Might as well. The fresh meat and supplies those Blackfeet got from the Raymers will help sustain them for a while. That, and the fact they've got to know they came mighty close to a brush with some of the soldiers out looking for 'em, will likely keep Thunder Elk from being in too big a hurry to send out the next raiding party."

"All right, that settles it, then. The two of you get a good night's sleep and figure on heading out for that canyon first thing in the morning." Earl swept his gaze slowly over all who stood before him. "Hardly the kind of day any of us would have hoped for, gentlemen. But one we must now put behind us and forge ahead with resolve for better fortune from here on. That is all. You are dismissed."

Chapter 25

"Was I our young captain and happened to ever find myself in a shooting skirmish with Lieutenant Benton in my ranks," Red Buffalo said as he and Nathan walked back toward their tent, "I would be extra careful to keep him always at my side or in front of me . . . never at my back."

Nathan emitted a dry chuckle. "Wise sentiment. Thing is, I believe the captain is sharp enough to have figured that out for himself. Matter of fact, I think he's sharp enough to have a pretty good handle on most everything. What's more, he ain't too vain—like a lot of officers, especially the younger ones—to admit what he *don't* know and to seek out wiser counsel when necessary."

"Like us, you mean?"

"Could be."

They ducked into their tent and got out of the wind. Nathan groped until he had his hands on a lantern sitting atop a folding table situated between two cots crowded against either side of the cramped quarters. He snapped a match and adjusted the wick until yellowish illumination poured out over them. The walls of the tent fluttered like they were wings trying to lift the structure into flight.

Each man took a seat on the edge of his respective cot.

"So," said Red Buffalo, "you really think we have much chance of picking up that Blackfoot trail again in the morning?"

Nathan shrugged. "Don't look like it's gonna rain, not if it hasn't cut loose by now."

"That's not an answer."

Nathan regarded the Crow through the smoky, throbbing lantern light. "What do you want me to say? Something bold and confident, like if anybody can, we can? Okay, consider it said. But you know as well as I do that a blasted wind blowing as hard and long as this one is lasting can raise hell with ground sign almost as bad as a downpour. But, like I told the captain, we might as well try. We've got to start somewhere, and who knows, we might get lucky."

"Another way of saying, we got nothing better to do. Right?"

"Guess that's what it amounts to . . . leastways not until Thunder Elk sashays out on his next raid."

"But tonight, seems to me there *is* something better we could do. Not in regard to Thunder Elk, but worthwhile in another way."

"What are you driving at?" Nathan asked, frowning.

"I'm talking about going into town. It was me who told O'Driscoll to have his soldiers notify Amos and Esther Handley when they took the Raymers' bodies in. That's bound to have hit the old couple pretty hard. I feel like I ought to be there to commiserate a bit with them, and . . . though I know it ain't something you're big on . . . maybe pray some."

"Yet you want me to come along?"

"No doubt the Handleys would like seeing you, too."

Nathan shook his head. "Man, you sure take some getting used to. I've known a lot of Indians in my time, but—"

Red Buffalo cut him short. "No, you've *killed* a lot of Indians in your time. Hardly the same thing."

"Let's just say I treated 'em how I figured they deserved," Nathan grated.

Red Buffalo let that ride. "Here's something else. You coming into town with me would give you another chance to see that dark-haired woman, Miss Fontinelle," he said. Then, after a pause, he added, "Though, in your case, I can't exactly say you'd be seeing *more* of her."

"Don't start with that," Nathan warned.

"I can't help the facts," Red Buffalo responded, spreading his hands. "You *did* practically take a bath with the lady."

Nathan scowled. "One minute the Christian side of you is talking about going into town to pray, the next you're letting your dirty heathen mind show through."

Red Buffalo stood up. "I'm going into town. You do what you like."

Heaving a sigh, Nathan rose also. "You don't give me much choice. I'd better go along to make sure the wind don't blow you away. Otherwise I'll have to face a chewing-out from the captain in the morning if you're not around to head out with me on our scouting assignment."

Chapter 26

"They were so young and so full of hopes and dreams. To meet such a sudden and horrible end is almost too tragic to bear."

As she spoke these words, seated at the kitchen table in the tidy home provided by her brother, Esther Handley wrung her hands vigorously together where they rested on the tabletop in front of her. Her stout frame seemed sunken with sadness on this occasion and her usual brassy loudness was very subdued.

Seated at her side, also showing the weight of grief, Amos Handley said, "I keep thinking how our greatest concern for them was the harassment they might be in for from McGreevey's thugs. But then to be set upon by the Blackfeet like they were, before ever even reaching the property they were so anxious to see and feel under their feet . . . it's just a dreadful thing."

Nathan and Red Buffalo sat across the table from the couple, cups of coffee and slices of thickly buttered bread placed before them, served at Esther's insistence upon their arrival.

"I don't know what more to say, other than the prayers

I've offered," Red Buffalo said. "It's a sad irony, I guess, how close the cavalry patrol Nathan and I were riding with came to showing up in time to save them. It always tests one's faith, things like this . . . But you have to believe, in the end, that the Lord has His reasons. And tonight, Joe and Margie are safely at His side."

Amos Handley favored Red Buffalo with a wan smile. "Those are kind and well-spoken words, Moses. Esther and I are of solid faith, but you're right in saying that times like this surely do strain it."

Esther said, "We heard how the patrol came along shortly after the attack. And then we heard that you two took out after the raiders on your own. Thank goodness you're both all right, even though we found out only a short time ago that there'd been a skirmish of some kind in which one of the soldiers was killed."

"Unfortunately, that's true, ma'am," Nathan said, not choosing to go into any more details at the moment.

"It's almost as if our arrival here," Esther said gloomily, "has brought nothing but fresh trouble to an already troubled region."

"Surely you can't hold yourself or Amos responsible for any of what's happened," Red Buffalo admonished her.

"Not directly, maybe. But there's no denying," Esther pointed out, "that a wave of misfortune has certainly swept in with us and affected many we've come in contact with. It started with the trouble out on the trail that drew the two of you in and ended up pitting you against a couple of hard-case gunmen. Then, according to what my brother related to us this morning, you didn't even make it out of town before you ran into more trouble in your hotel last night."

"Your brother doesn't miss much that goes on around town, does he?" remarked Nathan.

"Should he?" snapped Esther with a trace of her old sharpness. "Shouldn't a person stay keenly aware of their surroundings? I'd think that a couple of wilderness scouts would see the advisability in that as much or more than most."

"Meant no offense, ma'am. Point taken."

"To continue making my point, then," Esther said, "I guess the tragedy met by Joe and Margie speaks for itself. And now, only a bit earlier this evening, not long before you rode in, Andrea Fontinelle has become embroiled in her own mess of trouble."

Amos said, "You remember Andrea, right? The pretty brunette who occupied the third wagon of our little train?"

"Of course we remember Miss Fontinelle. What trouble is she in?" Red Buffalo asked.

"I'm afraid we're a little vague on the whole thing right at the moment," Amos admitted. "We had just closed up the shop and were on our way home for the evening when the street started buzzing about it. You recall how Andrea was traveling here in search of some long-lost kin, an uncle, I believe she said? Well, it seems that uncle, once she began asking about him and brought up his name, is a notorious and widely hated individual around these parts. A *squaw man*, was the term we heard cast about on the street."

"He's mated up with an Indian?" Nathan said.

Amos nodded. "Married to a Blackfoot woman, from what I gathered. Lives with her somewhere up in the hills. With the recent trouble, I guess it's not hard to imagine how some folks would harbor hard feelings toward him for such a union. And when Andrea started asking around, she quick got a taste of the same. But then, when those soldiers brought in the bodies of Joe and Margie, things really flared up. A bunch of whiskey-fueled belligerents cornered Andrea in a restaurant and it was ready to turn real ugly . . . until a savior stepped in and made the trouble-makers back off."

"A savior? Who?" demanded Nathan.

A corner of Amos's mouth lifted in a rueful smile. "Somebody whose identity I think you'll find quite inter-esting. It was a big brute named Beauregard Haliway, the same gent I understand you butted heads with last night at the hotel." Here he turned his gaze to Red Buffalo. "And somebody, if I heard right, who happens to be an old friend of yours."

"So what happened after the dustup at the restaurant?" Nathan wanted to know. "Where are Andrea and Haliway now?"

"Down at the jail. Deputy Ridgway took them into what he called 'protective custody' until things settle down."

"He'd be better off putting the ones Beauregard went after in protective custody," Red Buffalo muttered. "And if the big man decides he's tired of being *protected* and wants to leave, that deputy best stand out of his way if he knows what's good for him."

"I had to get Esther off the street when the furor was running high," Amos explained. "Now that it seems to have subsided, I was fixing to head down to the jail and check on Andrea."

"How about we save you the trouble?" Nathan sug-gested. "If feelings toward Andrea are still running hot and some of those whiskey-fueled idiots are still hanging around, they could decide to give you a hard time, too, just for being a friend of hers."

"But what about you two?" Amos protested. "If those troublemakers spot you as friends of Andrea, might they not still . . . ?" The words tapered off, replaced by a somewhat sheepish look. "Oh, I see. That would be a rather different matter, wouldn't it?"

"Yeah, I think it probably would," Nathan agreed.

"With a little luck," added a grim-faced Red Buffalo, "maybe we'll get a chance to find out for sure."

Except for the howling, rattling wind that swirled between buildings and sent clouds of dust leaping and tumbling down the main street like a never-ending stampede, there wasn't much activity in Telford as Nathan and Red Buffalo rode from the Handleys' house to the jail, a sturdy log structure located near the western end of the town.

The scouts hitched their horses and stepped up onto the narrow section of boardwalk that ran across the building's front. Just then, the door swung open and three men, faces tipped down to avoid the bite of the wind, came crowding out. Only Nathan's quick reflexes managed to prevent a full-on collision with the foremost of the emerging men. Their shoulders still connected, though—and with enough force to jar the exiting man to a halt that brought his two companions bumping against him from the rear.

"What in blazes!" exclaimed the jostled individual. When his face now lifted, his mouth was stretched in a snarl. "Don't you have enough brains not to stand in the middle of a doorway?"

"You might try looking where you're going before you barge out through one," Nathan was quick to respond.

The snarling man was about Nathan's height and had some beef to him. Too much of it, however, was carried in a heavy gut that swelled above his belt buckle like he was trying to hide a sack of flour inside his shirt.

Still, his attitude was that of somebody who was used to getting away with throwing his weight around. Which was clearly what he intended to try and do now, as he proclaimed, "When I got someplace to go and business to tend to, most folks around these parts have the sense to get out of my way. But since you're a stranger in town, I'll allow you this one . . . Say, what the hell!?"

Big Gut's words faltered and his jaw dropped as his gaze shifted past Nathan and locked on Red Buffalo standing a half step behind him. When he found his voice again, it was choked with heightened anger.

"Oh no! I ain't making no allowance for no Indian lover who goes around with a stinkin' redskin! If you know what's good for you, both of you had better clear away from this doorway pronto . . . and then keep on going until you're clean out of my sight!"

An instant after his final word was hurled in an agitated spray of saliva, Big Gut's mouth was suddenly forced tightly shut by having the muzzle of Nathan's Colt jammed hard up against the underside of his chin.

"And what if we don't?" Nathan growled, stepping closer and shoving his face to within an inch of Big Gut's. "You want us gone from your sight? If I blow the top of your head off, you bigmouthed slob, that will solve the problem because you'll be done seeing anything ever again, won't you?"

The two men behind Big Gut pulled suddenly, staggeringly away, retreating back inside the jail.

A voice from deeper in the room called, "What the hell is going on out there, Ramsey? Who is that you're talking to?"

Jamming his gun muzzle all the harder, Nathan took a step forward, crowding his way through the door and pushing a backward-shuffling Big Gut—now having been referred to as Ramsey—ahead of him. Nathan sensed, without actually being in a position to see, that Red Buffalo was moving along close behind him and he was equally sure that the Crow would have his Henry rifle raised and ready as he did so.

As the two others who'd been starting to emerge with Ramsey peeled off to one side, Nathan was provided with an unobstructed view into the office area of the jail and could see Deputy Ridgway seated leisurely behind a wide, cluttered desk.

The lawman quickly snapped out of his relaxed posture, however, when he got his own clearer view of what was going on. He went rigidly upright in his chair and his right arm stabbed down behind the edge of the desk.

Red Buffalo stepped wide around Nathan in a long, smooth stride with the Henry held level at waist height.

"Don't be in too big a hurry to react, Deputy," he said calmly. "Trust me, things ain't as bad as they look."

"Oh yes, they are, redskin," Ridgway replied through clenched teeth. "For you two, barging into a town marshal's office with drawn guns, things just turned plenty damned bad!"

"Guess we should explain that these are our varmint guns," Nathan told him. "We use 'em for snakes and rabid coyotes and such when we're out on the trail. When we rode up and found these three critters clogging your doorway, reckon we mistook 'em for outhouse rats and thought you might appreciate having 'em exterminated."

"That's real cute," sneered Ridgway. "You might have some around town hoodwinked because you're scouts for the army. But that don't impress me none. Especially not after the way that young homesteader couple got butchered today, practically under your noses. If you or that pack of bluebellies were worth anything, you should have been tracking down and putting an end to those bloodthirsty savages!"

"You hear that, Moses?" Nathan said with a cold smile. "The deputy here sounds like he's an expert on solving the Blackfoot problem. We ought to notify the captain. Maybe he can get the marshal to loan us his man for a day or two so's we can get the whole business cleared up a lot quicker."

"You go to hell!" Ridgway spat, his face flushing almost purple with anger. "Why are you here? What do you want?"

"We didn't come looking for trouble," Nathan told him. "But neither did we come looking to get pushed around and threatened by a handful of your town's trash." He abruptly withdrew the Colt from under Ramsey's chin, and using his free hand, he gave the fat man a hard shove that sent him staggering over to join his pals. "So keep them out of our way and there won't be a problem."

The deputy's eyes narrowed shrewdly for a moment, his gaze moving back and forth between Nathan and the three townsmen. Then he said, "All right. Just to show I'm willing to try and be reasonable, we can start with that. Ramsey, Pete, Wheeler, go ahead on about your business. You know what we just got done discussing. See to that, and everything will work out okay."

"Not so fast," objected Nathan, holding the trio in place with a wave of his gun. "If it's all the same to you, Deputy, I think it'd be a good idea for these fine citizens to stay right where they are a tad longer. No reason they can't hear what me and Moses came to ask about. Besides, unless all that wind outside is playing tricks on me, I think there might be the stink of bushwhackers in the air tonight, if you know what I mean. Hate to see harm come to anybody, especially now that we've agreed to be reasonable and all."

Ramsey's nose wrinkled. "Now, wait just a damn minute. If you're accusin' me and my pards of—"

"Shut up, Ramsey!" Ridgway cut him off. Then, scowling impatiently at Nathan, he said, "Get to it, then. What brings you here, what is it you want to ask about?"

"It's real simple. We understand a couple friends of ours—Andrea Fontinelle and Beauregard Haliway—are being held in so-called protective custody. We want to have a few words with them."

"Friends?" Ridgway echoed in a mocking tone. "Last night you and Haliway were trying to beat each other's brains in."

"Indian lovers stickin' together . . . that ought to come as no surprise," spouted Ramsey.

Ridgway shot him a warning look. Then, turning his attention back to Nathan, he said, "Well, I'm sorry to inform you that you're a little too late. The people you're asking about were released more than half an hour ago.

Seems your timing when it comes to rescuing 'friends' is about as poor as when it comes to protecting folks from the Blackfeet."

Nathan felt angry heat warming his cheeks, but he held it in check as his eyes went questioningly to the heavy door leading back to the cell block.

"You're welcome to go have a look if you want," Ridgway offered. "But you'll just be wasting more of your time."

"Any idea where they were headed when they left here?" asked Red Buffalo.

"Can't say for certain. But since it was Miss Marvelle—our local madam you likely remember from last night—who once again came strutting to big Haliway's defense, I reckon you can get that answer out of her. After she got done blistering the marshal's ear, he made the choice to let her take 'em away."

"Both of them? Haliway *and* the Fontinelle woman?" Nathan said.

"You heard right." Ridgway's tone and an accompanying crooked smile once more took on mocking qualities. "Maybe Miss Marvelle's angling for a new recruit."

The urge to make a lunge over the desk and drive a fist into Ridgway's smug face was harder than ever for Nathan to hold back. Red Buffalo helped by putting a hand on his shoulder and saying, quietly, "We got what we came for. Let's settle for that."

Nathan released a long, ragged breath and got himself under control.

"If you want directions to Miss Marvelle's place, it's real easy," said Ridgway. "Only a ways farther, just past the edge of town. Big house up on the hill, with a red light burning in the window."

"Maybe you'll get a discount . . . you being friends and all," said Ramsey, guffawing.

This time Ridgway didn't say anything to him.

As Nathan and Red Buffalo started backing out the door, Nathan said, "We'll take our leave now. You gents have a real pleasant evening. And if you venture out, be careful you don't come to no harm in this nasty wind."

When they were nearly through the doorway and he was feeling more emboldened, Ridgway called after them, "You didn't take me up on my offer for a look at the cell block. But if you keep crowding things, you might be in for a real close look before we're through."

Chapter 27

The perfumed, plushly furnished private quarters of Miss Marvelle at the rear of her "house" seemed a world apart from the windy, dusty street outside. Nearly swallowed by high-backed, thickly cushioned armchairs that were as close to floating on air as Nathan could imagine, he and Red Buffalo sat facing Andrea Fontinelle and Beauregard Haliway over a low, glass-topped table upon which their hostess had just placed a tray of china cups and a pot of particularly aromatic coffee.

"There now," announced Marvelle, straightening up from positioning the tray. "Help yourselves. That's a special blend of coffee that I think you will find enjoyable, and there's cream and sugar to add in accordance with your individual tastes. My girl Sing-Su will shortly be bringing in some sweet cakes to go with it."

"You really didn't need to go to so much trouble, Marvelle," Andrea said as she took the pot and began filling cups. "Speaking for myself, providing me haven under the circumstances I've suddenly found myself in is more than I can ever repay you for."

Marvelle waved her off with a flourish of one hand

loaded with sparkling rings on every finger. "Nonsense, honey. If anybody knows how the prigs in a town can look down their noses at someone who isn't doing them a single lick of harm, it's yours truly. It took me a long time to learn how to stand up for myself against their kind, and now that I have, it plumb riles me to see somebody else get pushed around that way. Plus, when I heard that my big wild man here was in the thick of it, too, from trying to come to your aid . . . well, that riled me all the more."

Haliway, upon being referred to as her "big wild man" actually blushed a bit as he was raising a cup of coffee to his lips. In his big paw, the delicate cup looked like little more than a shot glass. "Aw, Marvelle, the way you fuss over a body . . . You know, I'm pretty handy at standin' up for myself, too, even when you ain't around."

Marvelle sniffed. "Well, that's still not going to stop me when I *am* around. I was already pining at the thought of you being off on another trapping spree for the next five or six weeks, knowing you were out loading up on provisions for the trail. And then word came about the dustup at the Hot Griddle Restaurant over Miss Fontinelle and how you got involved standing up for her. I've got to admit I was a mite jealous at first. But when I heard what it was about, I was just plumb proud and I had to come and make sure you were all right. That's what brought me to that dreadful jail."

Nathan cleared his throat. "Begging your pardon, ma'am . . . First, speaking for myself and Moses here, I want to echo what Miss Fontinelle said about appreciating this fine hospitality. And then, if you don't mind, since Moses and me got here sorta on the tail end of everything that happened earlier, I wonder if somebody could fill us in a little more on the details behind it."

Upon arriving at Miss Marvelle's establishment, the scouts had been challenged at the front door by a powerfully built black man wearing a tailored suit with a velvet collar. In a booming voice exhibiting a Jamaican accent, he introduced himself as Montclief, Miss Marvelle's "house man."

At first he insisted the establishment was closed for the night. When Nathan pressed the matter by giving his and Red Buffalo's names and stating they were there to see Andrea Fontinelle and Beauregard Haliway, whom they believed to be personal guests of Miss Marvelle, the reaction changed drastically.

The big Jamaican threw back his head and emitted a thunderous laugh before proclaiming, "Stark and Red Buffalo, of course! Big Beauregard's friends who helped him tear up the Telford House last night. That was a show I am sorry I was not able to witness!"

With that, he'd ushered them on back to Marvelle's private quarters, presented them in a very formal manner, and then withdrew.

In response now to Nathan's request for some further details, Andrea Fontinelle replied, "I'm afraid it was I, Mr. Stark, once again finding myself in some potential peril, who brought it all on. Unfortunately, neither you nor Mr. Red Buffalo were present on this occasion to save me . . . though, thankfully, Mr. Haliway was. And this time I managed to show my gratitude by *not* bashing him over the head with anything."

Haliway grunted. "That made me grateful, too, considering how many scoundrels in that restaurant were doing their best to land a punch on my noggin."

"And this was all brought on simply by you mentioning the name of the uncle you came in search of?" Red Buffalo asked Andrea.

For a moment, before answering, the pretty brunette pressed her lips together tightly and faint spots of color appeared on her cheeks. Then: "That is accurate. Mostly. It doesn't really matter as far as the reaction I got from the people in this town, but for those of you gathered here now, I want to be completely honest. You see, the man I'm looking for, Ned Bannister, isn't really my uncle—he's my father. I'm not sure why I used that falsehood when I started out, but I did, and then I just stuck with it."

"How long since you've seen your father?" asked Marvelle.

"Nearly fifteen years. I wasn't quite eight when he abandoned my mother and me. That was back in Chicago," Andrea explained, "where I was raised and have lived until just a few weeks ago. At some point during that time, fairly early on, I think, my mother was granted a divorce and we went back to using her maiden name, Fontinelle. As far as I knew, she never had any further contact with my father beyond that."

There was a brief interruption at that point when a very slim, very pretty Oriental girl entered bearing a tray of sweet cakes. Marvelle thanked her, calling her Sing-Su, and instructed her to place the tray on the glass-topped table. After doing this, Sing-Su beamed a smile at all present and then departed.

As the three men reached to help themselves to one or more of the cakes, Andrea resumed telling her story. "It was only after my mother passed away three months ago that I discovered, in a trunk in her room, the many letters my father had written over the years. They had all been opened and obviously read through many times. At first, they were all addressed to her and whatever messages they contained were directed to her. In more recent years, however, as I was growing older, much of what he wrote was directed to me. Keep in mind, I never saw any of it until after my mother was gone and I discovered the trunk.

"I don't know why she kept all of this from me. She must have had her reasons. Without understanding why, I . . . I can't really be angry with her. We were too close, went through too much together. Yet it's curious. Even though she hid his letters, she never really spoke ill of my father or tried to turn me against him. She merely said he was a dreamer full of wanderlust who wasn't meant to be a family man."

Listening to this, a part of Nathan felt somewhat impatient, like he was eavesdropping on events from people's lives he didn't necessarily have any business hearing. Yet at the same time, he sensed it was important for Andrea to have the chance to relate these things, to air them out to someone else, apparently for the first time. For this reason, Nathan told himself to be patient until she got to a point where he or one of the others present might be able to offer some further assistance.

"I won't bore you with a lot of things from the letters," she went on, almost as if she'd somehow read Nathan's thoughts, "other than to say that in the portions he wrote especially to me—mentioning some of the places he'd been, describing the beauty of the West—it was clear that he *was* a wanderer and a dreamer. And reading his words, getting a deeper sense of who he was, I discovered that I had some of those same traits. With Mother gone and nothing left to hold me in Chicago—we were living in the same rented apartment we'd been in for years, my job as a bank cashier was nothing but monotony I'd long grown tired of, and my most recent beau had turned out to be a two-timing rat—I gave in to the impulse and decided I would come west and try to get to know the father I'd been so long separated from."

"How did you know where to come looking?" Red Buffalo asked.

"I didn't. Not exactly. But his most recent letter, from nearly ten months ago," Andrea said, "was postmarked Billings. So that's where I decided to start. Luckily, a man at the post office remembered my father and informed me he had moved on up here to the Telford area to do some prospecting in the nearby Wolfhead Mountains. Shortly after that I heard about the Handleys, who were preparing to relocate here following their unfortunate fire, and asked if I could travel with them. Once they agreed, I spent most of the money I had left to purchase a wagon, team, some provisions, and . . . well, I guess you're familiar with the rest. Things actually seemed to be looking promising until I started asking around about Ned Bannister, the man I was claiming to be my uncle."

"Wasn't the uncle part that got you in trouble," declared Haliway. "It was just sayin' his name. That's what triggered the rest of it, the other name too many sorry cusses around here have been attachin' to him . . . *Squaw Man*. With the recent Blackfoot trouble in general, and then especially with that young couple gettin' found butchered earlier today . . . it was like throwin' a lit match into a powder keg. That bunch what had you cornered in the restaurant, the look on some of their faces . . . it was like *they* had turned into savages."

Andrea closed her eyes for a moment, shuddering. "Don't remind me. And when I tried to tell them that the Raymers were friends of mine, that I'd just spent several days on the trail with them, it somehow seemed to make the mob even angrier!"

"Thank heavens my big wild man was there to step in," said Marvelle. "No telling what would have happened otherwise."

Andrea shuddered again. "I want to think about that even less."

"But if the bad feelings around here toward Bannister, your father, are strong enough to make a mob form against you," said Nathan, "how has he been treated? Is he somewhere safe? Amos Handley said something about him living somewhere up in the hills."

Andrea nodded. "That's what I heard, too. I learned that much before the tide turned so viciously against me. But I can't confirm it for a fact. And I have no idea where—or how safe—he is."

"I do," Haliway said bluntly.

All eyes swung to him.

"You know my father?" Andrea asked.

"Do for a fact," the mountain of a man allowed. "Things been poppin' so hectic-like, startin' with that restaurant dustup, I ain't had the chance to tell you before now. But yeah, I know your pa. I've run into him regular over the past few months durin' my huntin' and trappin' rounds up in the Wolfheads. I've even et supper a few times with him and Shining Water. That's the woman he's, uh, took up with."

Chapter 28

Nobody said anything for several beats.

"What's everybody gawpin' at me for?" Haliway grumbled. "I didn't hear nothing about Miss Andrea lookin' for a Ned Bannister until just a few minutes before the rowdiness broke out at the eatin' joint. Then, like I just said, I never had the chance until now to say anything."

Andrea blinked several times, obviously taken aback by what she'd just heard. Her voice faltering slightly, she said, "What is he like? I mean, is he all right? Does he know how people in this town feel about him? How does he get along up there alone? That is, him and his . . . woman."

"He gets along just fine," Haliway told her. "Him and Shining Water built themselves a snug log front over a shallow cavern in the side of a cliff. Got a good store of greens and flour, plenty of smoked meat, even got a water drip back in there so's they can hole up comfortable even in a big snowstorm. Your pa pans for gold in the good weather and scoops up enough color to take over the border to a settlement in Canada where he buys any extra provisions they might need. So yeah, he knows how they feel about him down here in Telford and so long as they leave him alone, he don't give a hoot."

"How about the Blackfeet? How does he keep clear of them?" Red Buffalo wanted to know. "And for that matter, how do you, what with your traipsing up and down out of those high reaches?"

"That's what I keep asking, and trying to convince the stubborn old goat to quit doing," chimed in Marvelle.

Haliway scowled at Red Buffalo, as if he'd betrayed him with his question.

"As for me," he said, "I been dancin' in and out of Injun skirmishes most of my whole adult life and still got all my hair. Not too different from you and Stark there, so don't poke at me with fool questions like that.

"As for Ned Bannister, more by accident than design, it turns out his Shining Water is the daughter of one of the old chiefs up on the Canadian reservation. Her father sets a mighty high store by her. She's a widow, and the story goes that her late husband, before he fell accidental-like off a high ledge and killed hisself, was powerful mean and abusive to her. So now that she's took up with Bannister, who treats her like the princess she rightfully is, the old chief looks with favor on the union.

"Which, in a roundabout way, means that Thunder Elk, even though he's a renegade currently runnin' loose from the reservation, knows better than to mess with the chief's daughter's happiness. Ain't none of 'em exactly friends, mind you. They just make it a point to steer clear of one another."

"What a fascinating story," Andrea murmured, her eyes shining. "It's practically like . . . like something out of Shakespeare."

Haliway frowned. "Don't know about no spear shakin'. Ask me, it's just another case of human critters gettin' tangled up one way, then gettin' untangled, then tangled up in a different way all over again. Seems us humans, as a whole, never get any smarter about certain things."

"Will you take me to him?" Andrea said eagerly.

"What?"

"My father. You know him, you know where to find him. Will you take me so I can meet him?"

Haliway looked like he couldn't have been more caught off guard if she'd suddenly asked him to balance his coffee cup on the end of his nose.

"My goodness, honey. You're asking to venture into some mighty dangerous territory," said Marvelle.

"More dangerous than what I'm facing if I remain here in town?" Andrea countered. "You just heard Mr. Haliway describe the looks on the faces of those people who were crowding in on me at the restaurant. 'Savages,' he called them. So what if I'm at risk from one set of savages or another? Is there any reason to believe the townsfolk will all of a sudden feel or act any different tomorrow?"

Haliway dragged a paw down over his thick beard. "Wailin' wildcats, gal. You're askin' a heap from me. I mean, I want to help you out but . . ."

"I can pay you, if that makes a difference," Andrea urged. "I don't have a lot of traveling expenses left, but I could sell my wagon and team. They're good stock, they should bring a decent amount. And I'll furnish my own provisions for the trip."

"Not to be, er, overly blunt," said Nathan, "but what about your father's feelings regarding such a notion? I expect he'd have some concerns about your safety, too.

Don't you think he deserves some . . . well . . . warning before you suddenly show up?"

"*Deserves*, Mr. Stark?" Andrea snapped back. "Who in this life gets everything they deserve? Did I deserve to be a child abandoned by one of my parents? Did my mother and I deserve to be left to fend for ourselves in a society where female earnings are low and desperately hard to come by? Besides, the tone of those later letters where my father directed portions directly to me, was that of a man who *longed* to reconnect with the daughter he'd left behind. Maybe that's a wish-fulfilling fantasy on my part, but I believe it with all my heart and I mean to pursue it with fierce determination."

Nathan felt an admiring smile tug at his mouth. "Yeah. I reckon that shows pretty plain," he muttered.

At that moment, a light knock on the outer door to Marvelle's quarters was followed by the muscular Montclief stepping on through. Gripped leisurely in one hand was a Greener shotgun. "Begging your pardon, madame," he said in his deep, syrupy voice. "But there's a situation building out front that I think you need to be aware of."

Marvelle's carefully penciled brows lifted. "A situation you can't handle on your own?"

"I can if you want me to," Montclief told her. Hefting the shotgun, he added, "I got rock salt loaded in one barrel to send a message and, if that's not enough, double-ought buck in the other and more shells of the same in my pocket. Just say the word on using my own judgment and I'll take it from there."

"Gracious!" Marvelle exclaimed. "It's that serious?"

Montclief nodded toward a bank of frilly-curtained

windows over on one wall. "See for yourself. Appears to me to have the makings for turning mighty ugly."

Marvelle moved to the windows, Montclief striding over to stand there with her. After a slight pause, Nathan, Red Buffalo, Haliway, and Andrea left their seats and went to the windows also.

Marvelle's quarters were included in a single-story wing that jutted out away from a two-story portion that made up the main part of the structure. Thus, the wall containing the windows they now all flocked to look through provided a view of the main building's front entrance. As Marvelle parted the curtain, the sight that greeted them was a roiling knot of men, close to twenty in number, crowded in a semicircle around the front entrance. They were stomping their feet and shouting unintelligible words. Several were brandishing torches whose flames snapped and whipped wildly in the wind.

"What in the world do they want?" gasped Marvelle.

"Me," Andrea said with chilling certainty.

"I'm afraid the young lady is correct," Montclief confirmed. "They're insisting she be turned over to them so they can run her out of town and, in their words, 'make sure the Indian-loving hussy gets the message she is never welcome back!'"

"Be a cold day in hell before that ever happens," rumbled Haliway. "The likes of them gettin' their hands on this child!"

"What about the marshal or Deputy Ridgway?" asked Marvelle. "How can they be unaware this is happening?"

Nathan's glare raked over the men up front in the rowdy pack and he had no trouble making out the big-bellied features of Ramsey, recently seen at the marshal's office and jail. Bracketing him, their mouths gaping wide with shouts and their faces distorted by expressions of blind hate, were the ones called Pete and Wheeler.

Through Nathan's mind raced the words he'd heard Deputy Ridgway say to these three when he was attempting to dismiss them from his office: *". . . go ahead on about your business. You know what we just got done discussing—see to that, and everything will work out okay."*

It seemed pretty clear now what *"we just got done discussing"* had been referring to.

"I don't think you have to worry about the town law being unaware of this," Nathan said in response to Marvelle's question. "But at the same time I'd bet against expecting 'em to do a damn thing about it."

"Uh-huh. The safe bet," added Red Buffalo, indicating he was thinking along the same lines as Nathan, "is that they've already played whatever role they're going to."

"Then that leaves no choice but to take matters in our own hands," declared Haliway. "And that means goin' out front to side Montclief in puttin' the run on those sorry curs who came to run off somebody else. You with us, Red Buffalo? Stark?"

"I'm up for me and Nathan siding Montclief," said Red Buffalo. "But it seems to me, big friend, there's a better purpose for you."

"Whatya mean?" Haliway demanded.

Red Buffalo pointed. "Miss Andrea. Take her to her father, like she asked. As she said a minute ago, even if we beat back that mob tonight, things around this town aren't going to get any better for her. Not tomorrow, not the day after. Maybe worse . . . for her and for anyone befriending her. Maybe even Miss Marvelle."

"You don't need to worry about me," Marvelle huffed. "I got the goods on too many men in this town for any of those high-minded polecats to bother me much." But then, focusing on Haliway, she added, "But that don't change the fact Red Buffalo is right about Andrea. She's been through enough. You saved her once, you big lug, now you need to again."

Haliway frowned. "You mean right now? Tonight?"

"What better time?" said Nathan. "While we've got the bunch out front distracted, you can leave the back way and have her out of town before anybody's the wiser. You said you had your provisions ready, didn't you?"

"Yeah, I took care of that this afternoon," Haliway allowed. "I've got 'em stored at the livery stable, with my two horses. I was figurin' to head out first thing in the morning, as soon as this crazy wind dies down."

"You're big enough so a little bit of wind ain't gonna blow you away," Red Buffalo told him.

"I'm not arguing the idea, but what about my things, my own provisions?" an anxious-looking Andrea asked. "I have nothing ready."

"I'm sure Haliway has enough provisions to get you as far as your father's place," Nathan said. "In the meantime, me and Moses will see to it your team and wagon get moved to that little barn behind the Handleys' house. I'm confident they won't mind. And I expect that, between the two of them, Miss Marvelle or Mrs. Handley will be willing to gather your personal items from your hotel room and hang on to them until such time as we can figure out a way to get them to you."

"This is all happening so fast!" Andrea said a bit breathlessly.

"It had better happen—one way or another—even faster," proclaimed Montclief, still watching out the window. "That mob out there is not easing up. It appears as if they soon may get worked up enough to try breaking down the front door."

"All right, then, you three get out there and stop 'em!" snarled Haliway. "I'll take the girl to her pa, like y'all want." To Nathan and Red Buffalo, he added, "I'll get in touch with you fellers in a few days. We'll work out whatever else we need to from there. Now go on out front and bust a couple skulls for me!"

Chapter 29

The mood out front of Miss Marvelle's was indeed ugly. Like the wind that whipped the flames of the torches they brandished, the whiskey-brave pack of men—the stink on their collective breath too strong to be completely carried away even by the howling gusts—were being whipped into an increasing frenzy by the goading of Ramsey and his two cohorts.

"It's like dry rot in the corner of a barn floor or the first bad apple in a barrel," Ramsey was ranting. "If you don't carve it out and get rid of it right away, it'll spread faster than the poison of a rattler bite! We didn't waste no time running Squaw Man Bannister out of town, did we? Now here comes his supposed kin, spawned by what kind of unholy coupling, you gotta wonder, looking to follow in his footsteps. It don't matter that she's pleasing to look at. A witch with pleasing curves on the outside can still be an evil crone down deep. And how much more evil can you get, I ask you, than to appease the bloody red devils your kin is in thick with by serving up to them some fresh victims in the forms of that innocent young couple this Bannister brat claims were her friends?"

This was the kind of vile hate being spewed when Nathan, Red Buffalo, and Montclief stepped out through the front door to confront the waiting mob.

Ramsey, who had been facing toward his audience, now turned to the emerging trio, his mouth automatically spreading into a sneer. "Well, well, well. Lookee here. The brave protectors of the damsel in distress."

"Those are the first true words I've heard you speak," said Montclief, the flickering glow of the torch flames dancing in sharp orange-gold contrast across the features of his ebony face. "Now hear my words and be wise enough to believe them. You are trespassing on private property and are ordered to depart at once. Should you fail to do so, the consequences may be most severe."

"Whooee! You hear that, boys?" Ramsey crowed over his shoulder. "This uppity varmint is threatening us with severe consequences. We better run away scared and find a safe place to hide."

A ripple of mocking laughter passed through the mob.

It was cut short a moment later, however, when Montclief aimed his Greener a couple of feet over their heads and discharged one of its barrels. A powdery white eruption resulted, much of it immediately whirled away by the wind yet leaving a mist of pulverized, lightly stinging salt granules to rain down on the unruly pack. It was startling enough to make several of the men duck or jerk away, causing almost more damage from bumping into one another than from any result of the blast.

"That," Montclief declared, "was the last warning you will get! If I trigger the second barrel, many of you will leave here in pieces!"

Nathan and Red Buffalo fanned out wide on either side

of the big Jamaican, Nathan resting his hand on the butt of his holstered Colt, Red Buffalo with his Henry held at the ready.

"And if that ain't convincing enough," grated Nathan, "we got plenty of plain old lead to add to the mix."

The crowd, though momentarily rattled, managed to hold together and not scatter. But many of their expressions appeared less certain.

Ramsey remained bold.

"What kind of man are you?" he challenged Nathan. "Big brave army scout! *Indian Killer*, I hear some call you. What a joke! Judging by that Crow you hang around with, looks to me like you're just another Injun lover. And all of you nothing more than pimps for the town whore and her newest attraction."

In the course of saying these things, the big-bellied fool made two serious mistakes. First, he got too personal with his insults. Second, trying to impress his followers, he allowed himself to edge forward and get too close to the target of those insults . . . and this time Nathan wasn't able to hold himself in check.

Snarling "You foulmouthed pig!" the scout lashed out with full fury. He didn't think about his Colt or the lead he'd threatened to throw from it a moment earlier; his response was purely visceral, coming from a primitive core that, instinctively, sought to pound and rip with bare hands.

His fist drilled square into the center of Ramsey's face, flattening his nose and caving in his front teeth. Following that initial punch, Nathan lunged forward with his whole body, slamming a shoulder into the fat man's chest even as he was backpedaling wildly and only kept upright by the others he was driven back against.

As a result of Nathan plowing deeper into the mass and several of the men swarming in tightly around him, any chance for Red Buffalo or Montclief to use their firearms against the greater odds was suddenly limited. At least, they couldn't *shoot* with them, for fear of hitting Nathan.

But that didn't mean Red Buffalo's rifle and Montclief's heavy Greener couldn't still make effective clubs capable of providing a different sort of advantage in close quarters. So, wading in behind Nathan, that's exactly how they began using them.

Muzzles were rammed into stomachs, wooden stocks and butts were slashed across the sides of heads. A few of the torchbearers tried to retaliate. Kicking feet came into play. And through it all, Nathan kept landing hammerlike punches, first pounding Ramsey into a bloody heap and then going after anybody else within reach.

Hastened by darkness enveloping the scene as many of the torches became extinguished—either dropped and trampled underfoot or smothered beneath fallen bodies in a few cases—the melee began to break up. With a barely conscious Ramsey being dragged away by Pete and Wheeler, each of whom had also gotten a taste of Nathan's fists, the remaining mob members quickly lost any interest in continuing. Limping and lurching, a few of them tossing weakhearted curses, they withdrew in ragged formation and went straggling back toward town.

Watching them go, Nathan, Red Buffalo, and Montclief stood in their own somewhat ragged formation. Red Buffalo and Montclief still gripped their makeshift clubs, Nathan held his scraped, bloody fists balled tight. All were breathing heavily and were a bit scuffed—most notably Montclief's velvet collar torn loose—but otherwise none too worse for wear.

"Given the hardware we'd just got done threatening them with, Nathan," Red Buffalo remarked, "you think there *might* have been an easier way to deal with that situation?"

"Could be," Nathan allowed, still puffing a little. "But no other way would have been near as satisfying as it was to drive my fist into Ramsey's fat face."

A low rumble, starting deep in Montclief's broad chest, built slowly to a chuckle and then a booming laugh. When he could get some words out past the laughter, the Jamaican said, "I lamented earlier about missing the show you and Big Beauregard put on at the Telford House last night, Stark. I must say, speaking strictly for myself, how grateful I am for the chance to have participated in tonight's encore."

Grinning wryly, Nathan said, "Glad to be so accommodating . . . I guess."

Red Buffalo's gaze traveled back and forth between the two men. Then, slowly shaking his head in a dismayed manner, he muttered, "Speaking strictly for *my*self . . . I think you're both crazy."

Chapter 30

"I must say, Captain Earl, that I am both surprised and disappointed to discover you not only have such limited control, but, by your own admission, an alarming lack of awareness when it comes to the comings and goings of the men under your command."

These admonishments were being issued by Bennett McGreevey from where he sat, leaning back very comfortably and confidently, in a chair behind a cluttered desk. The fact that the chair and desk were located in the front-office area of the jail building, making them spaces more properly occupied by either the town marshal or his deputy, sent a clear message.

It was McGreevey who was truly in charge here, as he was throughout most of the town of Telford. Marshal Feeney stood meekly off to one side, quietly leaning against a wall while McGreevey conducted the proceedings.

For his part, Captain Joshua Earl stood straight and tall before the desk and let McGreevey have his say. Except for a slight reddening of his ears, he gave no outward sign of his objection to the claims being stated. He'd learned long ago that a junior officer must often endure unfavorable comments from a higher-up, no matter how unwarranted.

Not that McGreevey was a higher-up, militarily speaking, but it had been made clear that he was a man of stature with a certain amount of pull in Washington and should therefore be treated accordingly.

When McGreevey paused now, signaling he expected some kind of response to what he'd said, Earl replied in measured tones, "I naturally regret the involvement of my men in any of the trouble that occurred last night and will reprimand those concerned as soon as I am able."

"I should think," McGreevey said haughtily, "that would be immediately upon your return to the encampment."

"Under normal circumstances, that would be true," Earl agreed. "But you see, the men in question—scouts Stark and Red Buffalo—left at daybreak to pursue a mission that likely will keep them away all day, maybe longer."

"How convenient for them," McGreevey said, sniffing.

"Actually, I hope it proves convenient for all of us," said the captain. "Despite the poor impression these men have made on you and the town, they have a well established reputation for being top-notch scouts. In the wake of the events yesterday that left the Raymer couple and one of my troopers dead, there is hope that the renegades responsible left enough of a trail for Stark and Red Buffalo, in the light of a new day, to be able to pick up and follow. It could be the break we've been needing in order to take some meaningful action against Thunder Elk."

"Well, I certainly can't deny *that* would be most welcome," McGreevey stated. "But that still would not absolve the two scouts of their misbehavior here in town."

"I never said it should or would."

"In addition to the brawl last night, the same pair was also involved in a somewhat lesser incident the night before."

"Yes, you mentioned that at the outset," Earl said, a hint of testiness edging into his tone. He cut his gaze over to the marshal. "Remind me again, Marshal Feeney, has anyone filed charges against either of my men?"

Feeney straightened from his slouch against the wall, clearly not expecting to be pulled into the conversation. "Well, uh . . . I . . . Well, no. No formal charges have been brought."

"How about any of the townsmen who were involved in last night's brawl, the one that included my men?" Earl wanted to know. "Were any of them identified or charged in any way? From what I heard when I first arrived in town this morning, I understand there was an earlier spot of trouble in one of your local restaurants. Was that connected in some way to the later incident my men were part of?"

"The entirety of the matter is still under investigation by the marshal and his deputy," declared McGreevey, injecting himself back in. "There are still details to be ironed out. But there's no doubt about your men being part of the two incidents we've brought to your attention. That's all you need concern yourself with, Captain."

"I appreciate that, Mr. McGreevey. And trust me, I am concerned," Earl assured him. "But it's a certainty my men didn't engage in a brawl all by themselves. In order to thoroughly and properly reprimand them, it seems only fitting I know as much as I can about other things that figured into it."

A scowling McGreevey pressed his palms down flat on the desktop. "Now see here, Captain. As a delegate working hard to see Montana granted statehood, I fully understand there are many back East who still see us as part of the Wild West. Gunfights and range wars and Indian raids and all the rest. Yes, there are still a few left-over rough edges, but by and large most of that is patently untrue. Yet here I sit in Telford, practically my own back-yard, experiencing Indian raids and brawls and near riots. Can you understand how frustrating that is for me?

"When you first arrived here, I explained how instru-mental I was in getting your company assigned and how crucial it is that you quickly address the Blackfoot prob-lem. I've been patient with your progress, knowing full well what a crafty devil Thunder Elk has proven to be. And believe me, if these newly arrived scouts of yours are the key, then they will have no bigger champion than me. But in the meantime, is it too unreasonable to ask that they, or any of your other men, *not* add to unrest or un-ruliness on other fronts while they're in the area? Isn't fighting the damn Blackfeet enough to keep them busy!?"

Earl set his jaw firmly and there was a faint narrowing of his eyes. "I assure you, Mr. McGreevey, that the Black-feet remain very much the focus of me and my men. If there was any doubt before, the loss of the young trooper I came to town this morning to make burial arrangements for, helped reinforce our mission. Now, if you're quite finished with this meeting you requested, I need to finish those arrangements and get back to my men. Good day to you."

* * *

As soon as the captain had departed, McGreevey balled one hand into a fist and rapped it down on the desktop. "That insolent pup! He'd damn well better concentrate on getting rid of those Blackfeet—and quick—or I'll cost him his stripes!"

"You think having those scouts on hand will help him get those Injuns took care of?" asked Marshal Feeney.

"How the hell do I know?" McGreevey snapped. "If they track Indians as good as they apparently brawl then, yes, they ought to make a difference."

The heavy door to the cell block opened and Rafe Ridgway stepped through. He said, "I came in the back, heard part of what you was saying to the soldier boy. Rather than walk into the middle of it, figured it best to hold off."

McGreevey frowned. "I don't know that it would have mattered that much. What did matter, though, was that half-baked notion you cooked up with Ramsey and his friends to take another stab at running that blasted Bannister woman out of town. All it accomplished was creating another attention-getting row that sucked the army away from what they should be paying attention to and caused them to take a closer look at things we don't want them concerned with."

"How was I supposed to know those stupid scouts were gonna show up back in town and stick their noses in?" the deputy protested. "You keep saying you want to keep things calm around town and it was obvious all the hard feelings that had gotten stirred up over that gal— she calls herself Fontinelle, by the way, not Bannister— weren't going to die down overnight. So, instead of letting it start up all over again this morning, we figured we could scare the hell out of her, haul her out of town a ways and dump her, put enough fear in her so's she'd never come back. And we'd use fellas who'd keep quiet about ever being involved."

"Keep quiet!" McGreevey echoed scornfully. "Half of the whiskey-soaked sots you used would sell out their own mother for their next shot of rotgut."

"Say what you want," Ridgway said somewhat smugly. "Maybe it didn't go as smooth as aimed for, but the Fontinelle brat is gone, all the same."

"What do you mean?"

"I mean *gone*. Lit a shuck, flew the coop, made dust out of here . . . However you want to say it, she ain't in town no more."

"How do you know she isn't still just hiding out at Miss Marvelle's?"

"Because a little bird told me," Ridgway answered, the smugness in his tone transferring to a smile. "I laid for Marvelle's little Cajun number, the soiled dove they call Corrie, who goes out first thing every morning to get fresh milk from Jink Crowley's dairy for all of Marvelle's girls. I've leaned on Corrie before for information on what goes on behind those walls. She knows better than to not be straight with me."

"You sure you can trust her?"

"Like I said, she knows better. The way Corrie told it, that Fontinelle gal went off with Haliway, that big trapper who comes to town every month or so and who Miss Marvelle is sweet on. He's gonna take her up in the mountains to find her 'squaw man' uncle."

"Good," McGreevey said, snorting. "I hope the whole bunch run afoul of the Blackfeet while they're having their little family reunion. That's one bit of Indian blood-spilling I wouldn't mind having happen at all."

"So, all in all, that's good, then. Right, Mr. McGreevey?" Feeney said eagerly. "Rafe's plan worked out. Now we don't have to worry about no new mob trouble again today over that squaw lover's niece or whatever she is."

"I hope to hell not," McGreevey said grudgingly. "Be nice for something to start going better. Now if the damn army can do its job and Fallow and Messingill can get the last of those stubborn nesters out of my hair, maybe I could go back to Washington for a while to do some arm-twisting without worrying about everything here going to hell while I'm away."

Ridgway cocked an eyebrow. "Look, I don't pretend to be no Indian fighter. But like I've offered before, any time you want me to pitch in and give Lester and Curly a hand at putting some pressure on those sodbuster holdouts, all you got to do is say the word."

"I've contemplated that before when you've brought it up," McGreevey admitted. "I appreciate the offer, and it's tempting. But I don't want to compromise your badge too much more than we already have at times. At least for now, it's important to keep that angle appearing mostly on the up-and-up."

Ridgway chuckled nastily. "That's me. Mr. Law and Order."

"Besides," McGreevey said with a scowl, "I pay Fallow and Messingill top wages. There's no reason they can't handle their own chores. The biggest clog in the drain remains that hammerheaded Swede, Knudsen. If we could get him to budge, then I think the rest of the holdouts would give up without too much more trouble. But, as it happens, I have plans for Mr. Knudsen."

He pushed back from the desk and stood.

"Speaking of which, I need to get on out to the M-Slash-G and see how that whole thing is coming together. It ought to be about ready to set in motion. While I'm gone, I want you two to keep an eye on that young army captain for however much longer he remains in town. Make sure he doesn't show signs of getting too nosy about things."

"You got it, Mr. McGreevey," promised the marshal with an eager bob of his head.

Ridgway nodded and said, "I'll make sure he don't stick his nose anywhere it don't belong."

Chapter 31

"Yeow!" Nathan howled, jerking his head back sharply. Then, glaring up at a close-leaning Red Buffalo, he said, "I thought all redskins were natural-born to using a skinning knife as delicately as a fine seamstress uses a sewing needle! The way you're hacking around in there, you're gonna end up sawing off the whole bottom half of my jaw . . . unless that's what you're aiming for."

Glaring back as good as he got, the Crow replied, "Hadn't thought of it, but at least that might keep you from bellyaching so much. And if you hadn't jerked away right when you did, I would've had that stubborn piece of broken tooth out of there."

Nathan turned his head to one side and spat a bloody gob down toward the base of the flat rock surface he was braced against. After working his mouth around, he said, "Yeah, I can feel that blasted chunk with my tongue but I can't quite pry it loose the rest of the way."

Leaning back on his heels and backhanding some sweat from his brow, Red Buffalo remarked, "Well, if you'd let Montclief do some more talking with his Greener last night, instead of insisting on knocking heads with that

Ramsey character, we'd all have woken up less scraped and bruised this morning."

"Maybe," Nathan grunted. "But I still say, for me anyway, it was worth it for the sake of smacking that fat Ramsey square in the mouth."

"Yeah." Red Buffalo sighed. "That was a mighty fine punch, I got to give you that. I only wish I'd have gotten in my own lick at that blowhard."

It was the middle of the day. The sun overhead was centered high and hot amidst a few wispy clouds, and the air, after all of last night's bluster, was still. The scouts had spent the morning working their way from the rocky western foothills up into the beginnings of the Wolfhead Mountains proper. The Wolfheads rose high to the east and north from their present position, dappled with the greenery of shrubs and trees until the higher peaks gave way again to barren rock.

Having had some success following yesterday's renegade trail this far, Nathan and Red Buffalo had called a halt for some jerky and corn bread and to give the horses a chance to graze a bit in the fresh grass.

It was while biting into a piece of jerky that Nathan's damaged tooth from last night's brawl had given him enough grief to make him ask Red Buffalo to try and dig it the rest of the way out.

Now lifting a flat, leather-bound flask that he held in one hand, Nathan poured some of the whiskey it contained into his mouth and sloshed it around thoroughly, wincing at its sting to the gum area that had been sliced, out of necessity, by Red Buffalo's knife. Turning his head to one side again, he spit out the bloodied mouthful then once more brought his gaze back to the Crow.

"That ought to have numbed it a little bit for another go-round. You ready to finish playing dentist?"

Red Buffalo made a face. "I wasn't exactly ready to ever start."

"Yeah, I noticed. Just go in and get the damn thing out of there, will you, so we can go on about our business."

Bracing himself once more against the boulder, Nathan tipped his head back and opened his mouth wide. Red Buffalo leaned in, hooking the thumb of his free hand in the corner of his partner's mouth to stretch it wider still, then slowly, carefully, eased the point of his knife into the gaping cavity until its tip slipped in under the broken tooth in its bloody socket. There was the faint scraping sound of steel against bone and then, abruptly, the stubborn chunk lifted and finally popped free.

"There! It's out," Red Buffalo proclaimed, heaving a sigh of relief as he withdrew both the knife and his thumb and was able to lean back again. "Now hurry up and spit it out before you swallow it and I have to go digging next in your windpipe."

Nathan did as suggested and this time the piece of tooth was included in the mouthful of bloody mucus that splattered against the base of the boulder.

"Good riddance!" the scout declared. Then, after spitting out another mouthful of whiskey and blood, he again raised the flask to his mouth, saying, "Now, after wasting too much of this fine nectar, I'm going to pour some down and keep it down, the way it was meant for."

With that, he tipped the flask high.

"So," said Red Buffalo, grinning as he screwed the cap back on the canteen he'd done his own drinking from while Nathan was making use of his flask, "do I send my bill for dental services directly to you, or to the army?"

Nathan cocked an eyebrow. "Not the army, that's for sure. You was to do that, I'd have to come up with some kind of explanation to the captain for how that tooth got busted in the first place. I doubt he'd approve of our little excursion into town last night."

"Trouble with that," Red Buffalo pointed out, "is since the captain's gone into town this morning to make arrangements for Private Selkirk, ain't much doubt he'll hear about it anyway. I figure that hatchet-faced deputy will make sure he does."

Nathan made a sour face. "Yeah, that skunk. You know he was behind sending Ramsey and that bunch to Miss Marvelle's last night, whether he figured on us being there or not. And then he was conveniently nowhere around when the trouble broke out. He's another one I'd like a chance to belt in the mouth."

Lifting his brows, Red Buffalo said, "Before you get too big a list made up of all the men in Telford you want to punch, hadn't we better get back to concentrating on the task at hand? Mainly trying to run down some renegades. If we can at least narrow it down to a closer idea where Thunder Elk's camp is, that would also go a ways toward smoothing the captain's ruffled feathers over our trip to town last night. Plus, as bad as you want another crack at the deputy and whoever else rubs you wrong in town, I'm wanting a crack at some Blackfeet."

"Don't worry, I ain't far behind you in that department, either," Nathan told him. "I can have two targets in mind at the same time. But you're right, what we need to stay focused on for the moment is Thunder Elk and his cussed followers."

"We caught a break," Red Buffalo mused aloud as he gazed ahead at the Wolfhead peaks rising before them, "by them having the team of shod horses when they traveled through that rocky stretch. Those horseshoes left rock scrapings that the unshod ponies never would have, and gave us enough sign to track them even after all that wind. The underbrush and high grass coming up ain't going to be so accommodating. We'll be hard pressed to tell which broken twig or patch of flattened grass was made by the wind and which was caused by the passage of men and horses."

"You ain't saying you're ready to give up, are you?"

"Not hardly," Red Buffalo grunted. "The only thing you need to worry about me giving up is my dentist career. Now let's get a move on."

As the Crow started to turn toward their horses, Nathan stopped him, saying, "Moses?"

Red Buffalo looked back. "Yeah?"

"About that tooth . . . All kidding aside, I'm obliged to you for digging it out for me like you done," said Nathan. "Ain't just anybody I'd trust to go carving inside my mouth with a knife. Especially not . . . well . . ."

A corner of Red Buffalo's mouth lifted. "Especially not a treacherous redskin, you trying to say?"

Nathan looked almost as uncomfortable as when the broken tooth was being dug out.

"I said what I meant to say, doggone it. I'm obliged. Now let's get a move on."

Chapter 32

As the day edged into late afternoon, Red Buffalo's concerns about the difficulty of continuing to follow the trail they were on through the changing terrain and over-growth proved increasingly warranted. There were a few times when they actually lost all sign, but by proceeding for a ways on guesswork and logic, managed to pick it up again.

It was slow, painstaking going. And the higher and deeper they went, the prospect of getting closer to the Blackfoot camp meant needing to stay more and more on guard against being spotted in their approach.

And then, abruptly, a whole new wrinkle was intro-duced. They were skirting the edge of a small, meadowlike clearing, headed toward a ridge of higher ground that rose above a distant line of trees, when they came upon a set of fresh tracks running across the meadow perpendicular to the way they were headed. These tracks, as opposed to the sparse sign they'd been straining their eyes to pick out for the past hours, were relatively recent and quite distinct.

Nathan and Red Buffalo both dismounted and knelt to examine the new markings.

"Not more than three hours old, maybe closer to two. Moving north to south," Red Buffalo said.

The Wolfhead Mountains, shaped like a lumpy, elongated oval, ran at a slight southwest-to-northeast angle. The rocky spur where Nathan and Red Buffalo had started out jutted away from the southernmost tip; at the northernmost end, the high ground tapered quickly and then ended in a cluster of blunt cliffs.

The trail the scouts had been following all day had held for the most part to a northeasterly angle, gradually climbing to the highest, widest part of the overall sprawl. It made sense to expect that Thunder Elk's camp would be somewhere in the heart of this high ground. For lookout and defensive purposes, it faced populated areas to the south. Escape routes from it most likely branched into the wilderness and Canada to the north.

But if the main camp still lay somewhere up ahead, to the northeast, then what was to be made of these tracks coming down from due north?

"I count a dozen unshod ponies," said Nathan. "But what does it mean? Where are they headed? And unless this trail we've been following makes a sudden turn to the left somewhere up ahead, meaning the camp lays more that way, to the north, than we've been figuring . . . where are these riders coming from?"

Red Buffalo frowned thoughtfully. "It could be a hunting party that branched off west from the main camp and then later swung down this way. But there's quite a spread to these hoofprints. They were moving awful fast for a hunting party."

"Too fast," Nathan said conclusively.

The two men regarded each other.

"Figuring the raiders from yesterday, the trail we've been following, and knowing they'd had a close call with our patrol, we didn't expect Thunder Elk would send anybody out again right away," said Red Buffalo. "But whoever this new bunch is—a lean pack of riders headed for the flats at a pretty good clip—that sure has the feel of meaning trouble for somebody."

Nathan nodded. "Yeah, it does. Could be Thunder Elk is trying to outthink us, counting on our expecting he'd keep his horns pulled in for a while, and aiming for a surprise by making another quick strike."

Red Buffalo straightened up. "One way or the other, we can't afford to tarry here playing guessing games. Do we stick with the trail we've been following—or do we switch to this new one and see what it leads to?"

Nathan pushed to a standing position also. "If we keep picking our way along like we have been, there's the chance this bunch could turn back around and come up behind us at some point. I don't like the thought of that much at all. On the other hand, if we was to take out after 'em, might be we could interfere with whatever they're fixing to do . . . and possibly even nab ourselves a captive we could get some valuable information out of."

"I favor the notion of finding out what might be in that 'other hand,'" said Red Buffalo. "Let's play it that way."

Nathan and Red Buffalo were able to follow this new trail with ease, never having to leave their saddles in order to check closer for sign and able to hold their horses to a steady, distance-eating gait. They had descended well down into the foothills, the slope of the ground leveling off more and more and the trees and underbrush thinning, when they heard the sound of gunfire from up ahead.

The scouts slowed their horses but continued forward. The sun was hanging close to the western horizon by now, leaving open areas still awash in plenty of light, yet within the trees, even though spaced out more sparsely than higher up, a nice thickening of shadows enveloped them. Cloaked in this murkiness, they were able to move to the edge of the trees and pause there, unseen, while they scanned what was taking place across the open expanse that spread before them.

This flat, grassy apron was dotted with a scattering of sun-bleached, broken, oddly shaped boulders ranging in size from that of a pumpkin to a buckboard. A little more than a hundred yards out, a notable grouping of mostly larger, somewhat oblong rocks were heaped together in a natural mound that rose about eight feet high and then split apart at the top. Out of this unique feature bubbled an underground spring, likely connected to a lake somewhere higher up in the mountains, feeding into a good-sized stream that twisted away to the south, toward where could be seen a distant cluster of buildings and fences and a few head of nervously milling livestock.

The source of the shooting that had drawn the attention of Nathan and Red Buffalo—punctuated by much cussing and yipping that they could also hear now that they were closer—was a sort of running battle being played out across pretty much this whole panorama.

The nearest combatants to their current vantage point were the survivors of the Blackfoot war party whose trail had brought the scouts here. Five of these were bunched in around the spring-ruptured mound, furiously pouring rifle rounds and arrows after three wrangler types who were frantically retreating toward the distant buildings. Five more Blackfeet were spread out to either side of the mound, also shooting at the retreating men from behind the cover of some of the odd-sized boulders strewn around.

Two blood-spattered Indians lay motionless in the grass. And a few yards beyond the mound, the still bodies of two cowboys were sprawled. The larger lumps of four slain horses—three with saddles, one with only an Indian blanket across its back—were also in evidence.

As for the three trying to get away, they were doing so by making quick, desperate runs from one scattered boulder to the next, one man dropping back while the other two covered him. The Blackfeet fanned out to the sides of the mound were advancing on them in much the same manner.

"Looks like the first side to start running low on ammunition might be what swings the tide in this fun little game," remarked Nathan.

"Uh-huh. Meaning if any more Blackfeet have their bows with 'em," Red Buffalo said, "the whole thing might come down to a few lowly flint arrows."

"If I didn't know better, I'd say that almost sounded like you were rooting for the Blackfeet."

"Not hardly," Red Buffalo snorted. "Besides, it ain't going to swing that way no how. In addition to us, those white boys down there are about to get some reinforcements even if they don't know it yet. Look yonder toward those ranch buildings across the way."

Nathan did as suggested, his gaze sweeping out toward the distant buildings. He saw what Red Buffalo was referring to. Three men on horses were breaking away from the buildings and headed in their direction, pushing their mounts hard and gaining speed as they came. The two outside riders were brandishing long rifles.

"Well, hell," said Nathan. He reached to wrap his fist around the Winchester '73 at his knee and swept it out of its scabbard with a flourish. "We ain't going to sit here twiddling our thumbs while everybody else has all the fun, are we?"

Chapter 33

The first thing Nathan and Red Buffalo did was to seek out the Blackfoot ponies. The way they figured, the Indians had emerged from the trees and surprised the small group of wranglers involved in some activity around the mound where the spring-fed stream originated. When the attack met with more resistance than expected and turned into a prolonged shoot-out with the wranglers using the widely scattered boulders for cover, the Blackfeet resorted to the same tactic but only after moving their ponies to safety in order to keep any more from being shot down.

Expecting that their presence now, along with the added reinforcements coming from the other direction, would likely break the back of the Indian attack, the two scouts sought to eliminate those hidden ponies as a means for the hostiles to get away.

Shifting a short distance down the tree line, they found the animals as anticipated. They were hobbled just within a fringe of trees. A few swipes of bowie blades cut the restraining thongs and the ponies wasted no time wheeling about and fleeing deeper into the trees and up into the foothills. All the gunfire had spooked them.

Not wanting to risk their own mounts catching a bullet out in the open, Nathan and Red Buffalo took time to secure them at a separate spot and then, rifles swinging loosely at their sides, trotted out onto the flat. Instinctively fanning several yards apart, each moved toward a sizable boulder from behind which they would commence joining the fight.

By now, many of the Blackfeet seemed to have spotted the riders coming from the distant ranch. Two or three of the warriors grouped at the mound altered their aim and foolishly shot at those approaching horsemen. The distance was too great for any accuracy and almost beyond reach of the weapons being used.

What these wasted shots did accomplish, though, was to alert the three retreating wranglers to the fact they had some potential help on the way. This caused them to cease their flight and instead stay where they were to concentrate a heavier barrage of return fire on their attackers.

It was at this point that Nathan and Red Buffalo also opened fire. Two Blackfeet immediately jerked from bullets slamming into them and toppled to the ground. Seconds later, two more smooth trigger strokes from the scouts brought down two more Indians.

The realization they were now under fire from the rear, in addition to a growing number of shooters coming at them from the front, sent a ripple of panic through the Blackfoot braves. A couple of them simply dropped flat, seeking cover from all sides while they regrouped. Others kept pouring it on the three wranglers they'd been focused on before. Still others spun around and tried to pinpoint the source of the deadly new threat that had already cut down four of their number.

One of the latter came close to succeeding where Nathan was concerned. His shot blew away a chunk of the boulder Nathan was crouched behind, mere inches from the scout's head. This near miss not only caused Nathan to jerk away reflexively, but it also made him pull his own shot and send a slug sizzling harmlessly wide and high.

Cursing, Nathan dropped low and rolled to the end of the rectangular slab of rock he was using for cover. Squirming around the end of the boulder at ground level, he leaned out with his Winchester and swung the muzzle in a frantic sweep, looking to draw a fresh bead on the varmint who'd spoiled his last shot.

The warrior was in the midst of making a dash to a different boulder when Nathan's front sight centered on him. As the Blackfoot was making a diving leap that would have gained him new protection, Nathan's rifle roared and the bullet it hurled hit the man in midair. His body folded like a half-closed jackknife and dropped heavily into a lifeless heap on the ground.

The volume of gunfire had rapidly increased well beyond the relatively sporadic shooting that was being exchanged between the hostiles and the three retreating wranglers only minutes ago. The crash of rounds being triggered now came so close together, often overlapping, that it was like an extended growl emanating from deep in the throat of a great beast. The accompanying powder smoke rolled thick and blue in the still air.

The three riders drew close enough to join in the shooting. The two outside ones brought their rifles into play, while the middle one extended an arm and cut loose with a large-bore pistol.

This deadly surge, combined with the realization their ranks had been depleted by more than half, was too much for the Blackfeet to even try and hold their ground any longer. With the five at the mound being the only ones left, they all sprang away from the pile of rocks as if it had suddenly turned scalding hot. All five wheeled and broke into desperate flight back toward the trees and the horses they believed were waiting there.

This presented an opportunity that was almost an embarrassment of riches for Nathan and Red Buffalo. It should have been easy for marksmen of their skill to pick off all five before they even came close to covering the necessary distance. Only the swirling clouds of powder smoke and the erratic running style of some of the braves made it any challenge at all—that, and one provision Nathan felt it was important to make.

"Try to take a couple of them alive!" Nathan hollered over to Red Buffalo, even as he lowered his own aim at one of the runners and triggered a round meant to take out the brave's legs but not kill him.

Somehow, the nimble Indian managed an awkward-looking but effective skipping maneuver that avoided the bullet and left it plowing into the ground in his wake. What was more, as he continued running, his arm blurred in a windmilling motion that launched a stone-headed war club straight for Nathan's head. Nathan ducked to one side, but just barely in time. He felt the wind-rip of the menacing weapon stir the hair around his ear as it flew past.

Righting himself, pivoting, levering a fresh round into the Winchester, Nathan snap-fired from his hip, once more aiming low, and this time saw a flash of red appear on the brave's thigh as he was knocked to the ground.

But putting down that one stubborn warrior had taken more precious seconds than it should have. Nathan knew the other four Blackfeet who were making a break had to be gaining ground while he was occupied.

Except they still had Red Buffalo to deal with. And while he'd been busy, a part of Nathan's senses had been registering the familiar bark of the Crow's Henry repeater cranking out lead in a steady rhythm.

Turning now to assist Red Buffalo in bringing the retreat to an end, he wasn't surprised to see that his partner had things under control. What he didn't expect to see was that only one of the Blackfeet was left alive. The others lay in bloody sprawls and the lone survivor, a lad not yet out of his teens, had dropped to his knees with empty hands held high and a pleading look on his face.

But even more unexpected was the look on Red Buffalo's face—an expression of cold, pure, bottomless hatred that was in no way curbed by the youth's tender years nor the silent pleading in his eyes.

"Good, now we've got two captives to try and get some answers out of."

Nathan never knew for sure if his words registered at all with Red Buffalo. If they did, if the Crow scout ever even heard them in his depth of seething hatred, they made no difference.

Because a fraction of a second after Nathan spoke, Red Buffalo's finger tightened on the Henry's trigger and the young warrior's face disappeared in a scarlet mist.

Chapter 34

Everything went quiet.

Red Cloud's Henry spoke the final word of harsh gun-fire and the abrupt silence that came next seemed loud in its own peculiar way. Nothing moved except for the slowly swirling clouds of powder smoke that hung in the still air.

Then one of the wranglers initially attacked by the Blackfeet shouted, "He's getting away!" and it all suddenly, jarringly kicked back into noise and motion again.

Nathan knew instantly what the warning shout must mean, and sure enough, when he spun around to look he saw that the brave he'd knocked down with a leg shot was up and running once more. There was a jerkiness to his stride, but despite that, he was covering ground faster than Nathan would have believed possible and was already nearly to the trees. Damn!

Shouting "Don't shoot—we need him alive!" Nathan hurled himself in pursuit. He was fairly confident the other men out on the flat would hold their fire, and they were too far away to be very effective anyway, but he couldn't be sure what Red Buffalo might do. Hesitating to make certain wasn't something he could afford, though, because the fleeing brave had too much of a start and was moving too fast.

Nathan broke into a full-out run, half expecting to hear the crack of Red Buffalo's rifle again and to see the Blackfoot up ahead go into a death tumble. But it didn't happen. The running warrior reached the tree line, plunged on in, and Nathan rushed after him.

The shadowy murkiness within the trees that had offered welcome concealment to Nathan and Red Buffalo just a short time earlier now presented a very *un*welcome impairment as Nathan's eyes tried to make the adjustment from the bright sunlight out in the clearing. He could hear the wounded Blackfoot crashing through the underbrush somewhere up ahead but couldn't make out a distinct shape or accurately judge the distance separating them. Still, he pounded on, slapping aside twigs and low branches, dodging around tree trunks.

The ground began to incline upward and the vegetation grew thicker. The deadfall that cluttered Nathan's way grew thicker also, some of the more recent debris lying atop the thick bed of dead leaves that covered everything, older pieces half-buried but with twisted, bare, and rotting branches that poked up to snag at him like menacing claws.

His vision had adjusted to the dimness by now but that proved of little help in identifying the course taken by his quarry. The bramble was too dense and Nathan didn't have the luxury of being able to stop and more closely examine for sign. He spotted a splash of bright red blood on a thorny leaf at one point, but that and a freshly bent twig here and there were pretty much the extent of anything worthy of being called a *trail*.

But Nathan kept on. He wasn't sure how much time

had passed. He kept thinking that the wounded man up ahead of him should be weakening and slowing down from blood loss. Though he remained unable to catch sight of him, from time to time he heard sounds of his quarry not that far off.

Whether the Blackfoot brave knew the terrain well enough to have purposely chosen this rugged stretch once he was denied access to the horses, or whether he was just lucky in his desperate flight, Nathan had no way of knowing. But it didn't matter, really—what did was that he'd picked a damn good route for throwing off anybody on his tail.

Upon reaching the spot where a narrow, deep gully finally slashed a break in the trees, Nathan halted and dropped to partial concealment behind a fat birch trunk. He was breathing hard and sweating harder.

Carefully scanning the depth and the opposite rim of the gully, the scout willed his puffing slower and quieter so he could focus his hearing intently on trying to pick up any other sound. But there was nothing. Only the faint creak and whisper of the natural noises that belonged to the forest on all sides. Nor, hard as his eyes scoured, could he spot the slightest sign to indicate which way the young warrior had gone or where he might lay hiding.

Nathan mouthed a silent curse.

He'd lost him. Galling as it was to admit, he'd allowed a scrawny, weaponless youngster with a bullet in his leg to give him the slip.

He remained there, motionless, for another minute or so. Then, slowly, he straightened up, turned, and headed back to Red Buffalo and the other men.

* * *

When Nathan came out of the trees, he saw that every-one was congregated by the odd mound from which the underground spring gushed. Red Buffalo sat on a flat-topped chunk of rock slightly apart from the others, his Henry rifle resting across his lap. He'd fetched his and Nathan's horse and the animals were ground-reined a few yards way.

Nathan could feel all their eyes on him as he crossed the open area strewn with boulders and dead Blackfeet to reach them. The sun was partially below the horizon now, casting a long shadow beside him that rippled atop the grass.

When he got close enough, a broad-shouldered, fair-haired man of about fifty, one of the riders who'd come from the distant buildings, said, "Ended up having to kill him after all, eh?"

Nathan replied tersely, "Nope. He got away."

He looked over to see what Red Buffalo's reaction would be and got nothing for his trouble. Gone was the mask of unbridled hate Nathan had last seen on his face and in its place was the flat, mostly unreadable expression that was usually there. He said nothing, merely lifted a canteen from the rock beside him and held it out to Nathan.

After tipping the canteen high and gulping thirstily, Nathan handed it back with a nod of thanks. Then, shifting his gaze to more closely examine the others and mean-ing to inquire about any injuries, he noticed for the first time that three of the men—the ones he had earlier taken for wranglers who'd been set upon by the Blackfeet—

were bunched together in a rather awkward way, jammed shoulder to shoulder, and their wrists were tied in front of their belt buckles with lengths of rope.

"What's that about?" Nathan wanted to know as he nodded toward the bound men. "I thought we were all on the same side?"

"We were . . . against the Blackfeet," answered the big-shouldered man who'd spoken to Nathan earlier. "But the only side these low-down snakes are on is the slimy underside of Bennett McGreevey's dirty dealings. And if I'd've recognized who they were at the outset I would have left 'em to the Injuns!"

"Take a closer look, Nathan," Red Buffalo suggested calmly. "I think you'll do some recognizing of your own."

Taking his advice, Nathan quickly saw—past the dusty, disheveled condition the trio's running fight with the Blackfeet had left them in—that he indeed knew two of them.

"Well, I'll be," he said. "If it ain't our old pals from back on the trail . . . Lester and Curly." He noted that all of them had been stripped of their gun belts. "And if that don't beat all, fellas, I see you've gone and lost your shooting irons again. I swear, me and Moses dropped 'em off at the marshal's office, just like we promised. So you can't blame us this time around."

"You go to hell!" snarled Fallow through bared teeth. "All of you! You're acting high and mighty now, 'cause you think you're holding a winning hand. You got nothing! McGreevey owns the whole deck and what he's gonna deal to the lot of you before he's through is gonna make you sorry you ever stuck your pathetic noses in his business!"

The big-shouldered man suddenly stepped closer and

swung his fist in a backhand motion that cracked like a pistol shot across Fallow's jaw.

"I told you once before to keep that filthy gob of yours shut! You pop off again, I'll have one of my boys snatch a breechclout off one of those Blackfeet and stuff it in your face to keep you quiet."

Fallow's head sagged and a worm of blood crawled out one of his nostrils. Both Messingill and the unidentified third man stood very still, looked straight ahead, and said nothing.

The big-shouldered man locked eyes with Nathan. "Your partner, Mr. Red Buffalo, told us about your past encounter with two of these mutts. You're Nathan Stark, also an army scout. Me"—as he thrust out a big, calloused paw—"I'm Carl Knudsen and pleased to meet you."

Nathan took the hand and pumped it in a hearty shake.

"These lads are my sons, Ben and Ivan." The young men Knudson swept a thick arm to indicate were spitting images of him, tall and stout and blond, about a year on either side of twenty. "And the land we're standing on for as far as the buildings you can see and a bit beyond, belongs to us and we intend to keep it. That means from Indians and it sure as hell means from the greedy clutches of McGreevey."

"I don't blame you," said Nathan. "Looks like a right fine place."

"But to McGreevey we are only lowly 'sodbusters' who don't deserve even a few acres of the land he sees as being fit for only his precious cattle to eat and defecate on!"

Nathan jabbed a thumb to indicate the tied-up trio. "I take it these hombres were sent to preach that message to you?"

Knudsen grunted. "They've already preached it plenty of times in the past. Today, before the Blackfeet showed up to interrupt them, they were here to do a lot more than just talk. Show the man, Ivan."

The younger of the Knudsen sons leaned over to pick something up from amidst the rubble at the base of the mound. Straightening, he walked over and held out the item for Nathan to have a closer look at it.

It was a tightly wrapped bundle of four dynamite sticks.

Chapter 35

Nathan emitted a low whistle. "Lordy. That would do a whole lot of talking . . . and in a mighty loud voice."

Red Buffalo had left his perch and walked over to stand beside Nathan.

"That's not all," he said. "There's three more bundles just like that placed all around this mound."

Nathan frowned. "Not sure I understand. They were . . . what? Hiding 'em here, meaning to bring them down later and blast you out of your house and buildings?"

"They were fixing to blast, all right," said Knudsen, "but not somewhere else." He turned and pointed with his thick arm before adding, "See how that stream feeds out of this underground spring and meanders right down through the heart of my property? That water is crucial to my crops, my livestock. Everything. If it was to dry up, that would almost certainly do to our operation what neither the bad weather or the Indians or McGreevey's thugs or anything else has been able to do before now."

Nathan saw it then. "They were going to choke off this spring with explosives and starve your stream."

"That's exactly what the low-down curs were up to,"

Knudsen said bitterly. "A week ago, Fallow and Messingill came around with what they said was McGreevey's final offer to buy me out. When I told 'em what they could do with it, they sort of hinted at what a shame it would be if our water dried up. I figured they were bluffing but, even still, we kept a pretty close eye on this mound for several days. After some time passed, I'm afraid we let our guard down some."

"If those Blackfeet hadn't showed up when they did," said Ben, the older Knudsen son, "the sneaky rascals might have got away with it. We saw and heard the ruckus with the Injuns when it started, and that brought us running. If we'd known who it was getting attacked, we likely would have stayed out of it."

The elder Knudsen heaved a sigh and his weathered brow puckered above a scowl. "Well, what's done is done. What we're left with now is how best to deal with the leftovers."

In a flat, emotionless tone, Red Buffalo said, "Could always fix it to look like the Blackfeet got to these three before anybody was able to save 'em. Be a way to make sure they never bothered you again."

Neither Knudsen nor his sons looked particularly shocked by the suggestion.

"That's a mighty tempting thought," the father allowed. "The main trouble with it is that it would still leave McGreevey, the boss mongrel who sent 'em in the first place."

"If these three would testify to that," pointed out Nathan, "you'd have some mighty serious legal charges to bring against the whole bunch, including McGreevey."

Messingill's lip curled and he wasn't smart enough to hold back, not even after the earlier rebuke to his partner. "Fat chance of that! Nobody's ever gonna to talk out against McGreevey. He's got you beat seven ways from Sunday and you're just too stubborn and stupid to know it."

Knudsen glared at the man but made no move to strike him like he had Fallow. He seemed frozen in his frustrated anger.

"Maybe," Red Buffalo said quietly, his dark eyes fixed on Messingill, "you're the one being stubborn and stupid. You'd be surprised how willing you'd be to testify, given the right kind of persuasion."

Messingill's sneer faded and so did most of the color in his face. "What kind of talk is that? You other men, you hear that? You're hanging around with a savage who's no better than those Blackfeet we just killed."

"He might even be worse," said Nathan. "That's the kind of thing you need to take into consideration."

Knudsen grimaced and heaved another sigh. "That's the bigger problem, though. We could stack up testimony as high as the tallest man here and where would we go with it? To the marshal in Telford? That's a joke. For starters, we're out of his jurisdiction, as he's reminded us many times in the past. And even more than that, both him and his deputy are in McGreevey's pocket as bad or worse than anybody around."

"Especially with the push for statehood, ain't there some territorial marshals that could be called in?" asked Nathan.

"There's been a U.S. Marshals office down in Helena for a few years now," replied Ivan. "But our territory is a whale of an area to cover and they never seem able to keep badges on very many men. Sometimes as few as only two or three. That's expected to change with statehood, but for now it's mostly the law in different towns or so-called range detectives hired by one of the big stockmen's associations who deal with rustlers and sometimes other law-breakers."

"Vigilante justice, in other words," muttered Nathan.

"That's the way it's been in Montana since the loggers and cattlemen came," Knudsen said bleakly. "Wouldn't begin to know how to get a for-real U.S. marshal called up to these parts. As far as one ever having come around . . . I ain't ever heard of it, let alone seen one."

"Sounds more and more," Ben said, "like Red Buffalo's idea about claiming these three fell victim to the Blackfeet might be the best way to make sure the skunks get what they deserve."

"Be a sure way . . . for these three anyway," allowed Nathan. Then he added, "But it still wouldn't address the matter of McGreevey."

Knudsen scowled. "Nobody's forgetting that, least of all me. But sometimes you have to settle for half a loaf. Bide your time for a chance to get the rest later on."

Nathan eyed him. "No doubt you've got plenty of grounds to cook these rancid slabs of meat over a slow fire, if that's the call you want to make. Hell, I'll hand you a match. But there might be a better way, a more thorough one, that will bring in the right kind of law and, along with it, the kind of attention focused on McGreevey that will put him in his place, too."

"You really think so?"

"I said 'might,'" Nathan reminded everybody. "It all hinges on the captain of the army company me and Moses are scouting for. He's young, but he's got sand and has his head on straight. Most of all, he's got a healthy dose of that rare thing called integrity. Unless my impression of him is way off, I got a strong hunch he sees his assignment to protect the folks of this area as not stopping with just the Indian threat. If this situation of yours, and others like it, which I figure wouldn't be hard to come up with, was put before him, I'm betting he'd see it his duty to set things in motion for fetching a U.S. marshal up here."

"I got to go along with Nathan as far as Captain Earl," Red Buffalo said. "I still think my way would be quicker and easier, but if you want to throw a bigger net and stand a chance to catch McGreevey in it, too, then involving the captain would be the way to go."

Knudsen looked at his two sons for a minute, then brought his gaze back to Nathan and Red Buffalo.

"You fellas are laying out some notions that need to be chewed on a bit. Along those lines, swallowing it down with some supper don't seem like a bad idea. My wife, Nora, sets a fine table. Since it's getting late"—he jabbed a finger at the pinkish-orange glow along the irregular western horizon where the sun had by now disappeared— "why don't you come take a meal with us and spend the night? Afraid we don't have any spare beds, but we can spread you a couple comfortable pallets on the floor. By morning, we should have it gnawed to a decision on how we proceed."

Nathan tipped his head toward the tied-up men. "What about these three?"

"I've got a half-empty corncrib and some nice sturdy lengths of hauling chain that will hold them real secure until we make up our minds on what to do with 'em next."

Nathan looked over at Red Buffalo. "You got any other plans for supper?"

"The beef jerky and corn dodgers in my saddlebags can wait another day . . . or three or four," Red Buffalo answered.

Chapter 36

After the Knudsen men had seen to their evening chores and the three captives were secured in the corncrib, Nora Knudsen served a fine supper of ham, potatoes, greens, cherry cobbler, and pitchers of chilled fresh milk or buttermilk to wash it down. The men in the corncrib got some bread, a few slices of ham, a pitcher of water.

With the meal finished, the table cleared, and the descent of quiet darkness giving a temporary sense of calm, the few idle hours left before bedtime were pursued in different ways. Nora Knudsen took her sewing basket and sat in the parlor, mending work clothes; Ben and Ivan broke out a board and chess pieces and commenced a series of very intense battles at the kitchen table; Carl Knudsen invited Nathan to the front porch to share with him a pipe of tobacco blend that he bragged was one of the best he'd ever come across; Red Buffalo had excused himself for some unspoken pursuit and was nowhere to be seen.

"Tell me if you figure it's none of my business," said Knudsen as he puffed an aromatic cloud that rolled up past the edge of the porch overhang and lifted toward the starry sky, "but could it be that your Indian friend is out there on the flat doing what I think he's doing?"

After a slight pause, Nathan replied, "If what you think he's doing is taking Blackfeet scalps, then I figure you're right."

Knudsen puffed some more smoke, then said, "Was a time that struck me as a much more ghastly practice. After enough years on the frontier, I guess a body grows hardened to more than a few things they never thought they would."

"The frontier has a way of making some harder and harsher than they ought to be, that's a fact," Nathan allowed. "Others, if they *don't* harden up some, it breaks them. The best kind—and that's most folks, I try to believe—sort of hover in the middle. But even for them, the lines get kinda blurred at times."

"From what I gather, you've done a lot of scouting for the army. That must mean you've seen your share and more of Indian conflict, long before today. You ever take up a scalping knife?"

"Back in the day, yeah, I did it pretty regular," Nathan admitted. "I needed the money it paid, for one thing. It was also part of my rage for personal revenge . . . Can't say my thirst for vengeance is satisfied all the way, but the taste for scalping as part of it don't appeal to me much anymore."

"All of us—me, my boys, McGreevey's hired thugs—were trying as hard as we could to kill Blackfeet out there today. You and Red Buffalo accounted for most," said Knudsen. "I can't say I saw it in you, but for him—the fury with how he went at it, the look on his face—it sure seemed like something awful personal for him."

Nathan nodded. "It was. I don't know the whole of it, but a deep hatred between the Crow and Blackfoot people goes way back. So far and so deep that it's like Moses was *born* to it. No matter what you think you saw or didn't see in me, don't doubt that I'm driven by my own demons. But what took over Red Buffalo today—hell, I saw it, too—was a side I never witnessed before . . . And unless I'm mistaken, I don't think it's a side he's entirely comfortable with himself."

"Yet he's still out there taking scalps."

Nathan had no response for that. After a while their talk drifted to other things. In the end, it settled on Nathan agreeing that Knudsen's tobacco blend was a particularly fine one.

Later, after the family had gone to bed and he and Nathan lay on sleeping pallets spread for them in the parlor, Red Buffalo spoke quietly into the darkness.

"You awake, Nathan?"

"Mostly," came the answer.

"We ain't had a chance to talk alone much since things busted wide open this afternoon."

"No, we haven't."

It was clear that Red Buffalo wanted to talk now, yet there were several seconds of quiet before he continued, "You think Knudsen is going to go along with the idea of involving Captain Earl?"

"I think he's leaning that way, yeah. It's about the only option he's got without either letting things go on like they have been, or him and his sons going flat out to war with McGreevey all on their own."

"Much as I'd be pulling for the Knudsens, I fear it would be a short, lopsided war."

"Uh-huh."

A few more seconds of quiet. Then: "You figure we're on the mark with our opinion of Captain Earl? That he's the right one to not be cowed by McGreevey and will push for a proper investigation into his high-handed tactics?"

"Ain't like we put our heads together and cooked up that impression of him like a stew. We arrived at it each on our own . . . and I don't think either of us is in the habit of being dazzled by anybody simply due to their stripes or shiny buttons."

Another pause before Red Buffalo finally got around to what, Nathan judged, he really wanted to talk about. "That Blackfoot attack today . . . what did you make of it?"

"Which part? The attack *by* them? Or the attack by you *on* them?"

"That's a fair question. I guess I got a little carried away, didn't I?"

"It happens. If anybody knows, I do. I've been there."

His voice seeming to come from more of a distance, Red Buffalo said, "I haven't. Not ever before . . . And now that I have, remembering how it felt, thinking about how I told myself it was what I wanted and then how the bodies kept falling with their hot blood splashing on me and the way I kept leaning in for more . . . I'm not sure I want to go back."

"Go back to how you were before . . . or back to that 'carried away' feeling?"

"Do I really have a choice? Once that kind of rage takes

hold . . . When you felt it and you became the Indian Killer . . . has the rage ever left you?"

"Don't know that I ever wanted it to," admitted Nathan. "But I will say this. In the early years after my folks and wife were massacred, the rage burned in me constantly, with a fury. I wanted every painted-up savage walking the earth to be dead, and I wished I could be the one who made it happen. My hatred for the kind who caused me that terrible grief hasn't died. And my ache for the lost sister who may still be living a captive life somewhere never eases. But at the same time I recognize how, over the years, the intensity, the urgency, inside me has cooled some."

"Like trying to let that young Creek warrior live, you mean?"

Nathan made a sour face in the darkness. "Don't remind me."

"So what you're saying," Red Buffalo said, choosing his words carefully, "is that I may not necessarily be destined to become the next Indian Killer."

Nathan grunted. "If that's what you want, probably be best to steer clear of Blackfeet after this."

Things were quiet again for a stretch. Then Red Buffalo said, "Something more about the ones from this afternoon . . . You know I went back out there to scalp them, right?"

"Figured."

"Only the ones I'd killed. But I didn't even finish all of them."

Nathan gave no response.

Red Buffalo went on. "I noticed something, something I don't think any of us paid attention to before but bears thinking about. That was no hunting party, nor was it meant to be a raiding party. For one thing, they were all very young, not yet out of their teens. And remember, there were only twelve of them."

Nathan pushed up on one elbow. "So what's that supposed to mean? What are you trying to say? Plenty of young braves are put to the test before they're—"

"But not strictly on their own, not a group of *just* younger braves," Red Buffalo argued. "I don't know what it means. I just know there's something odd about it. We were expecting that Thunder Elk wouldn't send out a raiding party again so soon. I guess what I'm saying is that I ain't so sure he had anything to do with this bunch."

"But they *were* Blackfeet, right?"

"No doubt about it."

"So what are you suggesting, that there are *two* packs of renegades running loose through these parts now?" Nathan's voice was strained. "Are you sure you didn't chew on some locoweed while you were out there doing your scalping?"

"All I'm saying is that, come morning, you might want to take a closer look for yourself, if it ain't too much to ask," Red Buffalo said testily.

Nathan sighed. "All right, if you want me to, of course I will. I know better than to think you'd try to make something out of nothing. But we ain't exactly lacking for other stuff already lined up to deal with tomorrow."

"Like they taught me in that Christian school—'Idle hands are the devil's workshop,'" said Red Buffalo, his voice now taking on a sardonic tone. "How's that, coming from a star pupil who recently finished keeping himself busy with a round of killing and scalping?"

* * *

Miles away, in the town of Telford, Bennett McGreevey was pacing furiously back and forth across the thick carpeting in Elke Klein's plush apartment. He was in his shirtsleeves, tie undone, some unruly strands of the hair he always kept combed carefully in place poking out at his grayed temples.

Elke sat watching him from a high-backed, overstuffed chair, appearing distraught, as if unsure what to say and not daring for it to be the wrong thing. Also present in the room, seated backward on a wooden chair with his forearms folded across the top of the backrest, was Rafe Ridgway.

"Something is wrong. Something must have gone to hell," McGreevey muttered as he paced. "Some way or other, those lamebrained idiots Fallow and Messingill found a way to ruin everything! Otherwise I should have heard from them long before this."

"Would they have gone to the ranch or come here to town?" asked Ridgway.

"The ranch is where we had it set up for them to return," said McGreevey. "They had three other wranglers with them—including Peevey, the old Confederate dynamiter who learned his craft blowing up Union bridges during the war and now clears stumps and such for the M-Slash-G."

"You got somebody there who'll send word in case they do show up?"

"Yes, yes, of course," McGreevey snapped. "I was out there myself until not too long ago. I finally rode into town thinking they might have misunderstood somehow and came here instead. But there's no sign of any of them."

Ridgway's mouth twisted wryly. "Excuse me for asking, but in case something did go wrong and the question comes up . . . do you have a solid alibi for the necessary period of time?"

McGreevey went to the mantel, where a chunky glass and a tumbler of amber liquid rested. Pouring a healthy splash of the brandy into the glass, pointedly making no offer to anyone else, he said over his shoulder, "Tell him, Elke. Have I been out of your sight since early this afternoon?"

"Not at all, my dear," Elke replied dutifully.

Turning back to the deputy, McGreevey took a pull of his drink before saying, "That answer your question?"

"Loud and clear," Ridgway stated.

"Okay. Here's what I want you to do," McGreevey instructed. "First thing in the morning—assuming the worst, that there's still no sign of those other idiots—I want you to ride out to the Knudsen place. It's no secret that I've been making regular offers to buy him out. My story will be that I sent Fallow and Messingill out again yesterday with my latest bid. Nobody's seen hide nor hair of them since. That's plenty of cause for suspicion . . . and reason enough for you to show up asking questions."

"Then what?" Ridgway wanted to know. "If there *was* some kind of trouble, which is how it's looking, the Knudsens are bound to have a story ready."

McGreevey grimaced. "Then find out what it is. See what you can see. After that, come back here and report. We'll have to take it from there, figure out what our next move should be."

Ridgway nodded. "All right. I can do that. Unless, by some quirk of luck, Fallow or Messingill manages to show up before the night's out."

"I have a bad feeling," McGreevey said, pausing with his glass raised partway to his mouth, "that any quirk of luck concerning those two won't be one that will turn in our favor."

Chapter 37

"I've talked it over with my family, and we're in agreement that involving this captain of yours sounds like it gives us our best chance to stand up to McGreevey and see proper justice done."

That was the proclamation that greeted Nathan and Red Buffalo when they sat down at the Knudsen breakfast table the next morning. It came from Carl Knudsen, seated at the head of the table with his determined-looking sons at either elbow. As she placed a platter of steaming pancakes and a jar of molasses in the center of the table, his wife, Nora, appeared equally resolved.

"So how do we proceed with seeing if he's interested?" asked Knudsen, spearing one of the pancakes with a fork and dragging it to his plate, gesturing with his free hand for the others to follow suit.

Amidst the eager scrape of forks on plates that followed, as the men cut dripping bites of the molasses-drenched fare that they pushed into their mouths and then washed down with strong coffee, Nathan said, "First thing is to send for the captain and get him here. He'll want to view the site of the engagement and assign a burial detail anyway, so that won't be hard. Then we'll find out if Moses and I are right about him."

Knudsen frowned. "All of a sudden you don't sound so sure."

"I never gave a guarantee," Nathan was quick to point out. "The only thing I'm sure about is the captain's integrity and sense of right and wrong."

"But that still leaves a little thing called chain of command," Red Buffalo said. "Every officer is given that weight to carry . . . but the good ones sometimes are slower to pick it up."

"Meaning we can't be sure this captain of yours won't feel obligated to try and clear things with his higher-ups before he commits," said Ivan.

Nathan stopped eating and leaned back in his chair.

"George Custer was a lot of things. Some good, some bad," he said. "But either way, he darn sure made an impression. One of the things I remember him saying—and maybe this kind of outlook worked against him at the end—was that, in the army as in life, it is sometimes better to ask forgiveness rather than permission . . . My hunch, what I'm betting on, is that Captain Earl views the chain of command pretty much that same way."

Knudsen considered this and then, slowly, a corner of his mouth lifted in a half smile.

"I like the sound of that better. As a matter of fact, I kinda like that *ask forgiveness, not permission* thing, too." He looked intently at his sons. "Although it's not something I'd want to take root in too many places."

Nathan said, "So the quickest way to find out how the captain is going to react is to get him here. Could one of your boys ride to the army encampment and carry word to him? Moses and I would like a chance to go over the scene of yesterday's fight a little more thoroughly before it gets too trampled by more people showing up."

"Sure," Knudsen said. Immediately his two sons pinned him with pleading looks, wanting to be the one chosen for the task. Their father quickly settled it, saying, "Ben, you had the chance last week to accompany your mother into town. Ivan, that makes it fair for you to skip morning chores and be the one to fetch the captain. So eat up, boy, and set to it. And no tarrying along the way, you hear?"

Both sons accepted the decision with no sign of either disappointment or overt satisfaction. It was clear that the father's say-so was accepted with little or no dispute.

"Speaking of the missus going into town," Red Buffalo said, "I wonder if that might be something you'd want to consider more of. Going in and staying for a few days, I mean. No matter how much Captain Earl is willing to get involved and no matter the general presence of the army in this area, the fact that a dozen Blackfoot braves were killed on your property ain't something Thunder Elk is apt to take lightly. Never mind who else might have shared in the responsibility for what happened, he's going to look at this place and everybody in it as deserving of payback."

Nora Knudsen, who'd finally gotten around to sitting down and fixing a plate for herself, promptly lifted her face and thrust out her chin defiantly at Red Buffalo's words.

"Your concern for my well-being is much appreciated, sir," she said. "But I'm a Knudsen, too, just like my husband and sons. Together we made this place what it is, and together we'll stand and fight to hold on to it, be it against the shenanigans of McGreevey or the Indians or any other threat that comes along. So I'll be staying nowhere else but right here, thank you."

Nathan glanced at Knudsen, half expecting he might speak up in support of Red Buffalo's suggestion. But all he did was put his head down and keep eating. Nathan smiled inwardly. Apparently the patriarch wasn't quite the *only* one who had some say-so around here.

Twenty minutes later, with breakfast finished and Ivan on his way to the army encampment while the rest of the family got busy with their morning chores, Nathan and Red Buffalo walked out to the flat area around the mound where yesterday's battle had taken place. Overhead a trio of buzzards circled in the morning sky, impatient to get at the feast scattered below.

Red Buffalo squinted up at them. "Is it me, or do we spend too damn much time with buzzards eyeing us hungrily?"

"Ain't us they're eyeing," countered Nathan. "If it was, that'd be the time to start worrying about it."

They moved slowly from one Indian body to the next, examining each, toeing some of them over onto their backs for a better look. It wasn't pretty and it wasn't pleasant, and the pattern that emerged didn't make it any more so.

"You see what I mean?" Red Buffalo said as they reached the last few to have fallen up near the tree line. "Each one seeming almost younger than the next. A couple who looked like they couldn't have been much more than fifteen and not a one, I'd say, who'd yet seen twenty."

"But their intent to kill was plenty mature, no getting around that," Nathan said. Then, as if reassuring something to himself, he added, "All the Indian killing I've done, I never raided a village and slaughtered innocent women and children like others were known to do. By the same token, any who were old enough and of a mind to come looking for my blood, I had no compunction about spilling theirs first."

Red Buffalo shook his head. "Nobody's saying otherwise. I got no problem with what we did here yesterday. Well, except maybe for my part, what came over me, like we already talked about last night. My main point is that every single one of 'em is so young. If there'd been a third or even half like this, mixed in with some more seasoned warriors, I wouldn't question it so much . . . but not this. Something about this is plain off-kilter."

"Yeah, I see your point. I've got to agree, it's damned odd," said Nathan. "Another thing, look at the weapons they had. Most of 'em with rifles. Not top-of-the-line repeaters maybe, but all of 'em plenty serviceable. Where did a pack of youngsters get their hands on that much firepower?"

"Didn't matter in the end, though, did it? Not against you two."

The voice coming unexpectedly out of the trees caused Nathan and Red Buffalo to suddenly spring apart and drop into crouches, their own rifles swinging to the ready.

"Rest easy, I'm friendly," said the voice, its words wrapped in a deep, booming tone that had some familiarity to it. "If I wasn't, you'd both already be goners."

The two scouts relaxed only slightly, their eyes continuing to try and penetrate the trees in order to spot the source of the voice. Then, out of the green-tinted shadows, the hulking form of Beauregard Haliway appeared.

"Beauregard!" Red Buffalo said, breaking into a smile.

"Haliway," growled Nathan. "How the devil did we miss

spotting you? It should have taken the whole mountain for you to hide behind."

The big man threw back his head and laughed. "Ha! I am one with the mountain and its forest. I can hide behind a leaf and move as quietly as the flutter of a dove's wing."

Nathan finally showed a grin of his own. "Sounds a sight different than the way you operate in town," he said, rubbing his jaw. "That wasn't no fluttering dove's wing I ran into the other night at the hotel."

"That's the key to survivin'," declared Haliway. "I know how to be one thing in one place, another thing in another. It's what you call *adaptable*."

Red Buffalo's smile faded. "That may be. But what you're not, old friend, is subtle. Not even a little bit. You got a particular reason for showing up here this morning?"

"Is Miss Fontinelle all right?" Nathan asked.

"Miss Andrea is fine," Haliway assured him. Then, addressing Red Buffalo's question, he said, "A particular reason for showing up here?" He made a sweeping gesture with one hand, indicating the open expanse strewn with dead bodies. "Don't you think this rates as reason enough to take some interest?"

"It rated a lot more interest yesterday. We could have used you then," Red Buffalo replied.

Haliway grunted. "Looks like you made out okay . . . 'cept for the one who got away."

Nathan cocked a brow sharply. "And you know about that how?"

"I know about it," Haliway answered, "on account of we found him wounded and near bled out."

"We?"

"That's right. He made it as far as Ned Bannister's

place," Haliway said. "He came crawlin' out of the bushes last night and it's lucky for him something kept me from pluggin' him before I saw how bad off he was."

"Why didn't you plug him anyway?" Nathan wanted to know.

"Might have," Haliway admitted. "But Shining Water stopped me."

"Shining Water? You mean Bannister's woman?"

"Uh-huh. Turns out the pup is a cousin of hers. That's how he knew to come there, looking for help when he got hurt."

"Did he tell you and the Bannisters *how* he got hurt?" Nathan demanded.

"Yeah. He spilled it all. Was too weak and too afraid of dyin' to go with a lie on his lips," Haliway said.

"So he's dead anyway," Red Buffalo muttered.

Haliway shook his head. "No. He hung on, leastways so far. Shining Water doctored him all night, poured some kind of medicine into him that she brewed up. Gal's got the touch of a healer."

"He's still there, then, at the Bannisters'? Will you take us to him?" Nathan asked.

Haliway cocked a brow skeptically. "So you can finish killin' him?"

"That bullet in his leg, I put there on purpose," Nathan snapped. "I was aiming to take him alive or he wouldn't have got away in the first place."

Haliway's gaze made a slow sweep out across the body-strewn flat, then swung back. "Don't hardly look like the notion of takin' any of those boys alive caught on in a very big way."

"There was also a little matter of keeping ourselves alive," Nathan grated.

"Nathan's telling it true, Beauregard," Red Buffalo spoke up. "He was definitely trying to take that Blackfoot alive and he was even shouting for the rest of us to do the same. He wanted captives for the sake of leading us to Thunder Elk."

Haliway's eyes came to rest on Red Buffalo, and there was a strange look—a sadness or maybe a touch of pity—in them.

"But you made no such attempt, did you, friend Moses? The wounded boy—he is called Kicking Cub, anxious to earn a renaming to Kicking Bear, for what it's worth—spoke of you in particular, Moses. 'The Crow with the killing fire in his eyes' he called you. You might find satisfaction in knowin' he said it with a kind of fear, maybe even a touch of reverence."

Red Buffalo averted his eyes, looked down at the ground.

"I saw you kill plenty of times back in the day, Moses," Haliway went on. "But I never knew you to get caught up in it the way that boy described. And I damn sure never saw you finish it off with scalpin'. Or . . ." He turned his gaze to Nathan. "Was that part your doin'?"

"If it was, it'd be none of your damn business, now, would it?" Nathan was quick to respond.

Red Buffalo lifted his face. "Stop it," he said. His voice was quiet, but it held force. "Yeah, Beauregard, I guess you could say I went a little crazy yesterday. 'Bout like the boy described. And it was me who took those scalps, not anybody else. All I can say is that I don't feel very good, and for damn sure not satisfied, about any of it today. My only excuse is that it was the Crow blood . . . all the ancient hatreds . . . boiling up in me. I know how pathetic that probably sounds, but there it is. What's more, I can't guarantee that if I face more Blackfeet in battle, it won't boil up again. All I can say, for now, is what's done is done. Next time will have to play out for itself." He tossed a fatalistic shrug. "Maybe it will be decided by some Crow-hating Blackfoot looking to settle things for his side of the ledger."

Haliway thumbed back his hat and deep seams creased his broad, pale brow.

"Could be," he said, "there's a chance—only a chance, now, is all I'm sayin'—that this whole thing could get worked out a mite smoother."

Nathan took a turn at puckering his own brow. "What are you talking about? If you got something to say, spit it out plain."

Chapter 38

"I'll make it as plain as I can, but it gets a mite complicated," grumbled Haliway.

"Between the two of us, we'll try to keep up," Red Buffalo told him.

"All right, listen then. We'll start with Shining Water. Remember when I told you how she rates kinda high among the Blackfeet, even Thunder Elk, on account of her pa bein' one of the old chiefs leadin' the tribes up in Canada?" It was a question not really seeking a response, so Haliway went on, "Well, that wasn't the whole of it. In addition to ol' Blue Otter bein' her pa, she's also a cousin to Thunder Elk."

Red Buffalo frowned. "You said she's also a cousin to the wounded boy."

"That's right." Haliway gave him a look. "A body can have more than one cousin, can't they? And I told you it gets complicated, so listen and try not to interrupt too much until I get it all laid out. Thunder Elk and Kicking Cub are brothers, you see. And Blue Otter was brother to their pa, who is no longer alive. In other words, he's their uncle."

Haliway paused to give that much time to sink in before he continued. "Thunder Elk was always a hothead and a problem, even when his pa was still alive. After that, he just got worse, more rebellious, until he finally broke away with some followers and turned renegade, came down here to hide out in the mountains and commence raiding to keep his people provided for. His mother and Blue Otter hoped that the hardships of the life he'd chosen would bring him back soon. But it didn't. And the longer he was away and the more stories about his raids and such got back to the reservation, the more the younger bucks there found them exciting and started talking about wanting to become warriors just like Thunder Elk."

"Including his little brother," Nathan guessed out loud.

Haliway nodded. "Him most of all. He'd always been the quiet, obedient one, always living in his brother's shadow. But because of who he was, the other restless young bucks looked to him as kind of a leader. He saw that as the nudge he needed to strike out and earn the name Kicking *Bear* . . . to step out of his brother's shadow and instead stand beside Thunder Elk as an equally fierce warrior and raider."

"So, just like I thought, this pack of youngsters *wasn't* part of Thunder Elk's bunch, at least not yet," said Red Buffalo.

"That's right," confirmed Haliway. "They left the reservation just a few days ago and came lookin' to join. Just this side of the border, up above the Bear Paw Mountains, they attacked a loggin' camp. They saw that as their chance to lay claim to bein' blooded by the time they reached Thunder Elk, and it's also where they picked up the extra rifles."

"The wounded kid told you all of this?" asked Nathan.

"Like I said, he thought he might be dyin'. I can't say he was feelin' remorse, tryin' to clear his conscience or any such. That I got no way of knowin'." Haliway shrugged. "What I can say is that he seemed to want to get it all off his chest, tell everything to Shining Water."

"But he never made it to Thunder Elk, did he?" prompted Red Buffalo. "Instead, he ended up here."

Haliway snorted. "Ain't that a hell of a thing? All their plannin' and high-mindedness, all the hard miles they covered . . . but when they got here, the young fools couldn't find Thunder Elk's camp. So yeah, they ended up here instead. And when they got to this clearing and saw some men workin' out there by that mound, they went ahead and attacked, partly out of hate and frustration over bein' lost, partly lookin' to be able to impress Thunder Elk by havin' done more killin'."

All three men went quiet for a moment, reflecting on the waste and pointlessness of it all.

Until Nathan finally said, "So how does what you just told us come around to what you said at the outset about a chance for everything to work out in some smoother way?"

"It's on account of Shining Water. She's on her way to meet with Thunder Elk."

"Meet with him about what?"

"She has a notion," Haliway explained, "that she can use this bad turn of events—Kicking Cub being seriously wounded, the other young men all dead—and claim it's a sign for Thunder Elk to end his wild ways and return to the reservation. Force him to face how much harm he's done and how hopeless it is to continue this war he's wagin' with no chance to win anyway, but only the promise of more pain and sufferin' if he keeps it up. Them's her words, or as close as I can remember."

"She speaks with a sharp tongue. And wise one," said Red Buffalo.

"But how much influence can she really expect to have over Thunder Elk?" Nathan wondered out loud.

Haliway shook his head. "That I can't say. Shining Water believes that much of the respect Thunder Elk has for her pa, his uncle, carries over to her. And she says he has always been very fond of his little brother. All of that, plus heapin' on the heavy news about the eleven hero-worshippin' boys bein' lost along with the hard conditions Thunder Elk has already put his followers through these past months . . . It might be enough to break his spirit, make him ready to turn back."

"Or," Nathan said somewhat ominously, "it might whet a thirst for vengeance in him like he's never shown before. Up until now, from what I gather, the raids by Thunder Elk and his men have been mainly to gather provisions. Yeah, they included some killing, but that was seldom the primary purpose. If what we did here yesterday triggers the *wrong* response and Thunder Elk decides to deliver some bloody payback and go out in a blaze of glory . . . Well, it wouldn't be pretty. And it's something we ought to keep in mind, that's all I'm saying."

"Boy, you're a real ray of sunshine, you know that?" Haliway growled.

"That's our Nathan," agreed Red Buffalo. "But he

knows something about being fueled by vengeance, you can't deny that. So I think his point is well worth keeping in mind."

"Well, in case you want something more to put a blot on our sunny morning, take a look yonder down by the Knudsen house," Nathan said, pointing.

"Rider comin' in," muttered Haliway, cocking his head for a better look. "Something seems familiar about him."

"It should," said Red Buffalo. "We've all had our recent run-ins with him and that shiny badge on his chest—it's Deputy Ridgway out of Telford."

"That no-good skunk!" spat Haliway. "What's he doin' way out here?"

Nathan looked equally displeased at the identity of the new arrival. "I can make a pretty good guess. We'd best get down there to give the Knudsens some backup."

"You might want to come along," Red Buffalo suggested to Haliway. "Apart from the news you've told us, there are some other things going on around here that we haven't had the chance to fill you in on."

"Gonna have to wait for another time," Haliway said. "I have to get back to the Bannister place. Ned went with Shining Water, so until they return, Miss Andrea is there by herself lookin' after Kicking Cub."

"What!?" exclaimed Nathan.

Haliway held up a palm the size of a frying pan, saying, "Calm down. He's too weak to pose any threat to her. But all the same, I don't want to stay away too long until we hear what kind of reaction Shining Water gets from her cousin."

"No matter what, we need to get Andrea out of there as soon as possible!" Nathan insisted.

"I'd say that oughta be up to her," Haliway responded. "And if I had to bet on it, I'd put my money on her not bein' too willin' to pull out. She's hittin' it off real good with her pa *and* Shining Water. What's more, until we find out for sure how Thunder Elk is gonna take what he hears from Shining Water, then the Bannister cabin might be the safest place in the whole territory for Miss Andrea to be."

"I can think of some serious arguments against that," Nathan bit out through gritted teeth. "But we don't have time to argue about it now. You just look out for her, you hear?"

"And get word to us as soon as you can," Red Buffalo added, "about how things turn out between Shining Water and Thunder Elk."

"You'll be hearin' from me on both counts," Haliway promised. Then he turned back to the trees and, in a matter of seconds, disappeared into the green-tinted shadows.

Nathan and Red Buffalo watched him fade, then they started for the Knudsen ranch buildings.

Chapter 39

"I'm telling you to release those men, and be damned quick about it!" demanded Rafe Ridgway, his face purple with anger and his teeth bared in a menacing snarl.

He still sat his horse in front of the Knudsen house. His words were directed at Carl Knudsen, who stood in the shade of the front porch, but all the while the deputy's blazing eyes were whipping back and forth between Knudsen and the corncrib about fifteen yards away where the three M-Slash-G men had their sorrowful faces pressed into the open slots. Voices wailed from behind their sorrowful expressions.

"You tell him, Rafe!"

"That coldhearted varmint kept us penned up here all night, like rabid dogs!"

Nathan and Red Buffalo came striding up in time to hear Knudsen's calm response, issued in a level voice under a flat, defiant glare.

"Who do you think you are to gallop up here and start shouting orders at me in the middle of my own property?"

This answer only angered Ridgway more.

"Who do I think I am?" he sputtered. "You know blasted

well who I am. I'm *the law*, you oatmeal-brained Swede! And what I surely am *not*, if you know what's good for you, is a man to be trifled with!"

"Say now," drawled Nathan. "That sounded an awful lot to me like a threat. Was it supposed to have some sort of legal weight behind it . . . or was it just the blowing of some loudmouth who has no legal standing at all out here where he's making so much noise?"

As Ridgway's eyes raked the approaching Nathan and Red Buffalo, the men in the corncrib did some more loud wailing.

"Watch out for those two, Rafe!"

"Don't let 'em work around and set you up for a cross fire. You can see what they did to those Blackfeet out there on the flat!"

"They can slink around all they want," Ridgway sneered in response. "I know their kind for what they really are. Big, bad army scouts, they're supposed to be. What a joke! Yeah, they maybe killed a handful of red devils unlucky enough to get caught out in the open, with plenty of help from you boys and the Knudsens. But the truth is, their kind usually sniff out some mangy Indian village full of old men and papooses, then stand back and let the blue-bellies ride in and trample what they later claim were fierce savages."

Nathan surprised everybody by replying calmly, "You're right about some who've done exactly that kind of thing. Just like I'd be right if I spoke of certain so-called lawmen who line their pockets taking bribes from town fat cats while skimming cheese from the mice . . . and at the same time building a reputation for toughness by gunning down saloon drunks."

He paused long enough to raise and lower his shoulders in a nonchalant shrug.

"But none of that would really matter unless one of us happened to fall into one of those categories, would it? Tell me, how was Bennett McGreevey this morning when he patted you on the head and sent you out to do his bidding?"

Ridgway held very still except for a muscle twitching under one eye. Then he said, "You really believe in pushing your luck, don't you, mister?"

"Didn't know I was pushing anything. Just asking a question, that's all."

"And a fair one it is. What *does* bring you out this way, Deputy?" Knudsen wanted to know.

It took a long time for Ridgway to drag his eyes off Nathan. When he did, he said to Knudsen, "It's no secret than Bennett McGreevey has been trying for some time now to buy your spread and he's sent Fallow and Messingill with several different offers."

"And I've told 'em where they could stuff each and every one," Knudsen huffed.

"Yeah, you have. That's exactly the point," Ridgway told him. "You've shown yourself to be hotheaded and threatening."

"Only when they wouldn't take no for an answer and wouldn't get off my property quick enough to suit me!"

"See, you're owning up to it and showing exactly why Marshal Feeney sent me out here," claimed the deputy. "Mr. McGreevey went to the marshal and told him how he'd sent his men out yesterday with his latest offer to buy you out. But when they didn't return all night and nobody anywhere has seen hide nor hair of 'em since they headed this way, he was worried things might have got out of control, what with your temper and past threats you've made. He was concerned there could have been serious trouble."

His tone dripping with disdain, Knudsen said, "But McGreevey was still too gutless to come and ask for himself . . . so he sent you."

"In the first place, it was the marshal who sent me," Ridgway insisted. "In the second place, by the look of things, McGreevey was right to expect trouble and it only made good sense for him not to stick his own neck out and risk getting caught directly in it."

"You finally got around to saying a couple things that had some truth in 'em," Nathan said. "You bet there was trouble here yesterday. And, yeah, plenty more is headed McGreevey's way."

"What makes you think any of it is your stinking business?" Ridgway snapped.

"I'll ask the same of you."

"You damn well know the answer. But just in case you're even more thickheaded than I thought, what makes it my business is right *here*!"

Ridgway jerked the front of his shirt out away from his chest and thrust forward the deputy's badge pinned to it.

Knudsen reacted to that, stepping down off the porch and for the first time showing some outward anger on his face and in his tone.

"Thickheaded?" he echoed. "Am I being thickheaded when I recall the times I came to you and Marshal Feeney with complaints about McGreevey's threats and high-handed tactics against me and some of the other small homesteaders in the area? Many who ended up getting driven off! You told us in no uncertain terms then that it *wasn't* any of your business because it was out of your jurisdiction! You telling me now that I remember wrong, or has something drastically changed?"

Ridgway threw his shoulders back and went more rigid in his saddle. "An illegal act is more than just a matter of jurisdiction. You can't chain men up like animals and expect to get away with it!"

"But harassing and threatening and beating and *blasting with dynamite* . . . none of that matters as much? Or is it that the only thing that matters, in your book, is which end McGreevey is on?"

"Your mouth and your accusations are pushing your luck awful close to the edge, mister," snarled Ridgway.

"And now," said Nathan, his glare drilling into the deputy, "we're right back around to you making threats that neither your badge or none of the rest of you is capable of backing up. So unless you're ready to try and prove me wrong . . . and providing Mr. Knudsen don't object . . . I'd say it's time for you to turn around and leave."

"Don't do it, Rafe! Don't leave us here like this," pleaded Fallow from the corncrib. "They're all crazy! We won't see another sunrise if you ride off on us. You can see all those Injuns out there they cut down and then just left laying, along with a couple of our boys the redskins had done for."

"No! Go ahead and *do* ride off," argued Messingill. "Tell McGreevey, he'll know how to get us out of this! Tell him we did our best to do everything like he—"

"Shut up, you damn fool!" Ridgway cut him off.

Messingill clamped his mouth closed and pulled back

away from the gaps in the corncrib wall so suddenly it was like he'd been slapped.

"You may be able to shut him up for right now, Ridgway," said Nathan. "But that don't mean it can last. And think about this: if we intended for those varmints to be dead, that's what they already would be. So here's a couple of questions you can ask yourself and then take back to McGreevey. What reason do we have for keeping them alive? And just because you and your fat marshal don't have jurisdiction out here, does that mean *nobody* does?"

"Of course nobody does. Who else is there?" Ridgway sneered.

"Oh, maybe a little outfit called the United States Marshals Service," said Red Buffalo. "Ever hear of them?"

Ridgway's sneer widened. "Yeah, I heard of 'em. I heard of Santy Claus, too. But I ain't never seen either one, sure as hell not around these parts."

"Don't surprise me none that a lowlife like you never crossed paths with Santa," Nathan grunted. "I wouldn't hold out much hope for that to change. But a U.S. marshal? Now, there's an overdue visit I think has a good chance of taking place."

"The only person with enough pull to get a U.S. marshal sent all the way up here is McGreevey," Ridgway mocked. "If you say *pretty please*, you expect he'll do that as a favor to you?"

"Maybe not as a favor," Nathan replied coolly. "But the way we got it figured . . . yeah, McGreevey is gonna play a real big part in getting a marshal sent up here."

"And until then," Knudsen reminded the deputy, "you've been invited to make dust leaving here."

Ridgway hung a long glare on the now-empty gaps where Messingill's face had been. Then he brought it back to rake over Knudsen, Nathan, and Red Buffalo.

"Okay," he growled. "You cluster of fools might think you've won this round. Enjoy it while you can. Because before this is over—and I guarantee that's coming soon— the lot of you is gonna be finding enjoyment in damn short supply!"

Chapter 40

"So you just rode away and left them there!?"

Ridgway bridled at the accusatory tone in Bennett McGreevey's question. "What was I supposed to do? What else could I have done?"

"You have a badge and a gun, don't you?" McGreevey demanded. "Did you suddenly forget how to use them?"

"You know damn well this badge means nothing clear out there," the deputy countered. "We've made sure to tell them that often enough in recent months. And as for my gun, those two scouts were primed for me to try something, the Indian especially, with that damn Henry repeater he carries with him everywhere. For all I knew, Knudsen had a gun handy, too, plus his two sons were likely lurking somewhere close by. I've proven I ain't afraid to go up against almost anybody you put in front of me, but that don't mean I'm willing to buck odds that are suicidal."

"No, of course not," muttered McGreevey, relenting somewhat. He ground his right fist into his left palm and went back to the pacing that had become an unwelcome habit of late.

Once again, he and Ridgway were holding their discussion in Elke Klein's apartment. She was also present, sitting quietly for the most part, watching and listening as she sipped tea from a delicate, flower-patterned cup.

"Having Fallow and Messingill in their custody for any length of time is very concerning," McGreevey said as he paced. "Who else did you say is with them?"

"I couldn't see for sure through those corncrib slats, but I think it was that Winslow kid," said Ridgway.

"I barely know who he is. He hasn't been around long enough to be able to spill anything too harmful." McGreevey scowled thoughtfully. "That means the two dead men, the ones who got killed by the interruption from the Blackfeet, must have been Barnes and Peevey. That's who Fallow and Messingill planned on taking along when I talked to them. They're mostly just ranch hands, except for Peevey having a way with dynamite. Otherwise, they didn't know a hell of a lot about any of the other matters. It's a shame the stupid Blackfeet left alive the two men who can cause me the most grief if they end up breaking under the pressure and running their mouths."

Elke looked aghast. "That's a dreadful thing to say. Fallow and Messingill have been two of your key men for some time now."

"Key men only matter when they are successful at performing key duties." McGreevey stopped pacing and glared at his mistress. "When they start failing at what's expected of them, and worse yet, make themselves vulnerable, they are not key at all. They are a liability. And comments from you on my assessment of such matters are hardly welcome."

"Unwelcome to the point of perhaps making me a liability, too?"

"That can be achieved . . . if you don't learn when to keep your mouth shut," McGreevey said harshly.

Elke looked stricken. Slowly, she put aside her cup of tea and rose gracefully to her feet.

"Very well. It seems the wisest course for me at this time is to retreat. Let me know when you are in better humor and when I might be allowed to speak."

"I'll tell you what you *can* be allowed to do," McGreevey told her. "Bring me some of my headache medicine. You're half the reason I get the damn things, it's only right you're part of the treatment."

Elke strode purposefully from the room. McGreevey glared after her for several seconds after she was gone.

When he turned back and caught Ridgway looking at him somewhat bleakly, he warned, "Just as her opinion on my assessment of Fallow and Messingill was not welcome, neither is yours on my treatment of her."

Without changing his expression, the deputy said, "Had no intention of giving one. You don't pay me for opinions."

"That's right, unless I specifically ask." McGreevey went back to grinding fist into palm. "I guess it shows that having those two incompetent boobs penned up and the talk of a U.S. marshal being called in has me a little on edge," he admitted. "It's not a feeling I like, not one I'm used to."

"Do you really think there's any chance of them getting a marshal to come up here? And how would they even get in touch with one?"

"Getting in touch with the main office in Helena is simple enough. Just send a wire. The trick," McGreevey said, "would be finding an available marshal. There are so few of them allotted to the territory to begin with and the roster, from what I understand, is seldom full. Even with my connections, I suspect it wouldn't be easy to get one to show up."

"So what I'm hearing, then, is that whole thing is a pretty empty threat."

"My first inclination is to believe so, yes. But the fact they were so bold about bringing it up can't help but make me wonder if they don't have something up their sleeves." McGreevey started pacing again. "That damn stubborn Swede! He's been a thorn in my side from the beginning. If not for him, the rest would have all been routed easily and there wouldn't be a sodbuster left anywhere on the rim of the basin by now!"

"Maybe it's time to pull out all the stops. Get rougher even than trying to dynamite his water supply."

"What have you got in mind?" McGreevey wanted to know.

The deputy shrugged. "A few different possibilities come to mind. You've got a couple dozen men riding for your brand. Couldn't you whip 'em up and send in the whole horde to free their pards who are being held prisoner? Me and the marshal could ride out on the pretext of trying to stop it and from there it wouldn't be hard to sort of guarantee that some gunplay broke out and one of the bullets accidentally caught Knudsen.

"Or you could wait until the next time Knudsen comes to town, give me a chance to start harassing him on some trumped-up technicality, see if I can't goad him into a fight. If he's the nail holding everything together, let me yank out the nail and then watch the rest, starting with his family, collapse.

"Another possibility—if you're willing to up the ante because I don't like doing ambush work—is I could slip out to the Knudsen spread some dark night when we've rigged me an airtight alibi for being elsewhere and simply put the stubborn squarehead out of our misery with a slug from the shadows."

McGreevey continued to pace, saying, "Those are all very tempting ideas and I've considered variations on each of them at one time or other. Trouble is, they're all bound to draw more attention than I can afford. The blasted homesteaders, even the ragged handful that are left, have got too many sympathizers in town by this point. I'm afraid they'd raise too loud of a ruckus, exactly the kind of thing I've been trying to avoid for the sake of my state-hood push. Pressuring and squeezing out the nesters and homesteaders one at a time, like we've been doing, is one thing. But too bold a move, especially on someone as pop-ular as Knudsen, I'm afraid could seriously backfire."

Ridgway frowned. "What does that leave, then? If they get Fallow or Messingill to spill their guts about some of the stuff they know, you think that won't roust up the townsfolk and draw a lot more attention?"

"I know, I know. What the hell you think has me so on edge?" McGreevey stopped pacing abruptly. Slowly, his face took on a new, shrewder expression. "But it occurs to me . . . your question just now might have also con-tained the answer."

Having no idea what he meant, Ridgway simply stayed quiet and waited to hear more.

"While Knudsen taking a slug out of the darkness would surely raise too much of a ruckus," McGreevey explained, "such would hardly be the case if the same thing happened to Fallow and Messingill, wouldn't you agree? Hell, they're even more disliked around the territory than I am. If them getting gunned down raised a ruckus at all, it would probably be the ruckus of a celebration."

Ridgway frowned in thought, warming to the idea. "Yeah, a good number would look at it that way."

"Any reason to think that Knudsen and those scouts won't be holding our men in that corncrib for at least a while longer?"

"Don't know that they have a better place to move them to."

McGreevey's eyes narrowed. "You have any particular loyalty to Fallow, Messingill, or that Winslow kid?"

"None that you meeting my ante for ambush work can't overcome," Ridgway answered flatly.

"They were . . . useful . . . to me for a long time. I genuinely regret that it came to this." McGreevey's tone was without emotion. "But when something . . . anything . . . becomes a liability, only a fool continues to hang on."

"An explanation is something you don't owe me," Ridgway told him.

McGreevey nodded. "Very well. I'll meet your 'ambush price' as long as it's not unreasonable. I want a little more time to think on this, chew it extra fine. But right now I think you should start planning for tonight, before the liabilities *do* get moved. I'll give you final confirmation by midafternoon and also have a suitable alibi arranged."

"I'll check with you then."

"In the meantime, get word to our lard-butted marshal.

Don't tell him any more than you have to, but what I want him to do is lean on Crippins down at the telegraph office. I want a guarantee that if Knudsen or any of his crew tries to put a wire through to the U.S. Marshals office it gets squelched. It doesn't go through, but I want to know what it was meant to say. Every word."

"Consider it done."

"I shall." McGreevey walked to the mantel and poured himself a strong measure of brandy. Keeping his back to Ridgway, he said, "Go make your preparations. We'll talk again this afternoon."

Chapter 41

Captain Joshua Earl stood with his hands clasped behind his waist, shoulders squared and back straight, feet planted at shoulder width. Perfect military bearing that he'd conditioned himself to adopt as a standard pose. His gaze was focused out across the flat area of the Knudsen property that stretched around the mound. Soldiers from the patrol he had brought with him, faces shiny with sweat from the hot midday sun, were gathering the bodies of fallen Blackfeet braves and carrying them up closer to the tree line, where other soldiers were digging a mass grave.

Earl's eyes followed this activity with moderate interest even as the words he was speaking were directed to Nathan and Red Buffalo, who stood slightly in back of and off to one side of him.

"Ocean sailors and offshore fishermen especially along the southeastern coastline of our country," he was saying, "have long held a belief—one increasingly subscribed to also by the most recent science—that even the fiercest hurricanes or cyclones have, at their very center, an amazingly calm space. With the storm raging on all sides, this *eye*, as it is called, remains quite still, almost soothing. Have either of you heard of this phenomenon?"

Nathan and Red Buffalo exchanged glances and then said no, neither of them had.

"You two gentlemen," Earl went on, "seem to have traits similar to a hurricane's eye. I had considerable hope for your arrival to my command and the meetings and discussions we've subsequently had always seemed to bolster that hope with the promise of steady progress.

"It now seems, however, that *around* those calm, promising meetings, you two have been involved in a whirlwind of activity that's been anything *but* calm. An altercation on the trail, before you ever arrived, with some admitted miscreants from the area; a second altercation your first night in town that left much of the hotel lobby in shambles; a near riot the following night outside a, er, house of ill repute; a close call and a subsequent chase of hostiles your first day out in the field that resulted in three tragic deaths; a more significant skirmish with hostiles here yesterday that left eleven Blackfeet and two civilians dead . . . and now you've inserted yourselves into a local legal matter pitted against one of the most powerful men in the territory, for which you are seeking my support and assistance."

Slowly, the captain turned and faced his two scouts. "Would you say that adequately sums it up?" he asked.

Nathan and Red Buffalo once again exchanged glances before Nathan replied, "Yessir, that sounded like it covered everything pretty good."

"Except the part about the appeal Shining Water is making to Thunder Elk that could have an important impact on this whole Blackfoot matter," Red Buffalo added.

"*Could* have," Earl echoed. "An impact that might miraculously soothe everything. Or, by Nathan's own estimate, turn what have already been destructive, life-taking raids into even bloodier revenge strikes."

"All I was pointing out," Nathan said, "is that nobody can guess how a renegade like Thunder Elk will react. But it don't necessarily mean I don't think—or hope—that Shining Water may have some luck."

The captain's mouth pressed into a tight, straight line.

"I, too, want to hold out that hope. Nevertheless, planning for the one event—that Thunder Elk will relent— takes no planning or preparation at all.

"On the other hand, should he be moved to lash out more savagely than ever, we must make certain we are as ready as we can be for such an eventuality. That means, as a first step, I'm going to insist that all homesteaders and smaller spreads left on the rim of the basin—starting immediately, with the Knudsens—gather up their families and limited personal belongings and move to the safety of the town, closer to which we will also relocate our main encampment."

Frowning, Nathan said, "Can't you wait until we hear back from Haliway on what kind of response Shining Water got?"

"If it's the wrong response," Earl stated firmly, "then we will have lost precious time that might mean lives lost."

"He's right, Nathan," said Red Buffalo. "Lot easier to move folks *back* if there's no trouble, than to try and get 'em out if everything starts busting loose."

Further discussion on the matter was interrupted by the

approach of Lieutenant Benton and Sergeant Purdy, coming from the direction of the Knudsen house. Purdy was clutching some sheets of paper in one hand.

"We got all the statements you wanted, sir," the young sergeant announced, waving the papers.

The captain nodded. "Good. And you got them each individually, right?"

"Of course," Benton answered rather curtly. "I'm quite familiar with the procedures on how to properly interrogate multiple subjects concerning a significant event."

Ignoring his tone, Earl said, "I'll want a full report from your notes, Sergeant. Signed by both you and, after his review, the lieutenant. In the meantime, give me the bare bones of it. In particular, any inconsistencies or serious conflicts."

Purdy started to respond, but then stopped and deferred to the lieutenant. The latter, scowling, said, "There certainly were conflicting versions. Not so much as far as what happened after the hostiles showed up, but big differences on events prior to that. Specifically, about the purpose for the M-Slash-G men being on the property."

"From what the Knudsens were quick to let me know when I first arrived," said Earl, "I'm aware they believe the men were here to destroy the spring that supplies crucial water to their land. Did they stick to that claim?"

"Right down the line."

"And the other side, McGreevey's men?"

"They say they came with McGreevey's latest bid to buy the Knudsens out. But before they could present the offer, the Blackfeet came boiling down out of the foothills and it turned into a fight for life."

"It took five men to bring a purchasing bid?" Earl said skeptically.

Benton shrugged. "All I can tell you is what they said."

"What was the amount of the bid?" asked Earl.

For some reason Benton hesitated to answer, so Purdy said, "Nobody seems to know, sir. They said it was in a sealed envelope that they weren't supposed to open."

"So where's the envelope now?"

"Nobody seems to know that, either," Purdy said. "They never got a chance to give it to Knudsen before the Indians hit. Then, during the fight, it somehow disappeared . . . or so they said."

Earl arched a brow. "You sound rather suspicious, Sergeant."

Purdy shot a quick glance over at Benton, then said, "I guess I am, sir. I know an interrogator isn't supposed to make judgments, but . . . well, those three wranglers seemed awfully ill at ease and not terribly believable. It was like they were trying to remember things they'd made up only a short time earlier. The Knudsens, on the other hand, were straightforward and steady and told everything the same, but not in a copycat kind of way."

The captain looked at Benton. "How about you, Lieutenant? Was your impression anything like that?"

Benton shrugged. "Like the sergeant said, as interrogators we're not supposed to judge. I was there to inquire and document. As for the M-Slash-G men acting ill at ease, what the hell else could anybody expect? They've been caged up like rabid dogs, poorly fed, and treated in an uncivilized manner. What's more, they remain in those conditions even now and I'm afraid I must formally protest our part in allowing it."

"Duly noted," Earl said somewhat wearily. "Put it in the report, Sergeant, make sure the lieutenant initials that portion."

"Will the statements of these two men"—Benton gestured disdainfully toward Nathan and Red Buffalo—"be taken and included in the report?"

Earl answered, "I'll take into consideration my review with them and, from it, add anything I deem pertinent."

"May I ask, sir, if you deem the scalping of some of the slain hostiles to be pertinent?" said Benton. "Because I certainly do, and accordingly, I wish to add another formal protest against allowing such conduct from any member of our company."

"Again . . . duly noted, Lieutenant," Earl responded, this time terse and chill. "In the interest of time, let's establish that you may initial and enter into the report any further protests you think warranted. I will review and initial in kind. Now, before we move on to what I consider has become the bigger matter of the day, I want to know what was said about the dynamite found at the spring. I already know the Knudsens' claim regarding the how and why of it. What about the M-Slash-G men?"

Benton said, "They swear they know nothing about it. Not how it got there, no idea what it might be for."

The captain issued a quick, bitter laugh. "What a surprise."

"A couple more things to add, sir, if I may," said Purdy. "For starters, if the purpose of those dynamite charges was to try and choke off the spring as the Knudsens claim—and I'm basing this on some work I did with explosives while employed years back at a rock quarry—then the placement and strength of the charges was well suited to ensure that. Also, we found a partly used coil of dynamite fuse in the saddlebags of one of the horses carrying an M-Slash-G brand. It matches the shorter pieces of fuse in the dynamite bundles nested around the base of the mound."

"And what did the three wranglers have to say about that?"

"They had no answer for how it got there. Claimed it must have been planted to try and make them look bad."

"Another big surprise," muttered Earl. Then, in a stronger voice, he said, "But enough of that for now. As I already indicated, my opinion is that developments possibly stemming from the skirmish that occurred here demand we focus with increased intensity on the Blackfoot problem we were sent to quell. Part of that, of course, means protecting the civilian population in the immediate area until such time as the hostiles are subdued. With that in mind and suspecting that this recent incident might spur Thunder Elk into a wave of bloodier activity, I'm making the call that all of the remaining outlying homestead families— there are four, counting the Knudsens here—must be gathered up and brought into the safety of Telford. In conjunction with that, we will also be relocating our main encampment closer to the town."

"You think what happened here is grounds for increasing the threat from Thunder Elk that much?" questioned Benton.

"I think it has the *potential* for that, yes," said the captain. "I'd rather err on the side of caution than lose lives unnecessarily because we waited to be certain."

"Very well. How shall we proceed?"

Earl looked in the direction of the mass grave where all of the Indian bodies had been placed and were now being covered over. The blanket-wrapped forms of the two slain M-Slash-G wranglers, Barnes and Peevey, lay on the grass closer to the mound.

Bringing his gaze back to those grouped about him, Earl said, "As soon as that burial is complete, Lieutenant, you take four men and return to the encampment. Begin striking the tents and loading equipment, making preparations for the move closer to town.

"I'll join you there directly, but first I intend to make a trip into Telford. It's only reasonable I give the city fathers some notice of these measures I'm taking, plus I want to send out some wires. Accompanying me will be Private Marley, who has the telegrapher skills to ensure the privacy of the messages I wish to send, and one other man. We'll also deliver those bodies"—he indicated the blanketed forms—"for proper disposition."

"What about the three men being held as prisoners?" Benton wanted to know.

"For the time being, I'm putting them in your charge. I want them kept secured and I mean for them to continue being treated as prisoners," Earl told him.

"But with all due respect, sir, I remind you that I—"

The captain cut him short. "Your formal protest has been duly noted, Lieutenant. I needn't hear it repeated. As a reminder, part of the army's role on the frontier includes policing the population where no local law exists or has jurisdiction. That obviously applies here. Also obvious, to me, is that there's sufficient evidence of criminal activity regarding an attempt on the Knudsens' crucial water supply to make it worth bringing to the attention of territorial authorities, which is part of what I intend to do with the wires I'll be sending out. Now, you've been given your orders. I expect you to focus on carrying them out minus any more time wasted with unnecessary questions and explanations I'm no longer in any mood to provide. Is that understood?"

Benton's face reddened and his mouth pulled tight, except for a downward turn at the corners. "Understood, sir," he managed in a hoarse voice.

"You're dismissed, then. Go pick the men you'll want to accompany you. They can release the prisoners from the corncrib and otherwise secure them in preparation for the ride back to the encampment and necessary containment once there."

When Benton had left, the captain turned his attention to Purdy, Nathan, and Red Buffalo. "That leaves you, Sergeant. You take the rest of the men, including Stark and Red Buffalo, and swing out to gather up the rest of the homesteaders. I'll tarry here long enough to take the Knudsens in with me. Hopefully we're well ahead of any trouble that might develop, but just in case, I encourage all of you to keep a sharp lookout."

"The biggest trouble we're apt to face," said Nathan, "might come from stubborn folks who won't want to be uprooted, even temporarily. Expect you'll get a dose of that yourself, Captain, from the Knudsens."

Earl winced. "Be as persistent as you can, that's all I can say. I guess we can't hog-tie them and haul them away in a wagon, but try every method short of that. By the same token, don't drag out any argument to the point of jeopardizing yourselves. The idea is to try and get every-body gathered safely together and to accomplish it with all haste."

Pointing off toward a bank of dark gray clouds climbing higher in the sky over the northwest end of the Wolfheads, Red Buffalo said, "There's another reason for us to get a move on, lessen we want to end up rowing our way back to camp. Short of 'em emptying out over the mountains before they make it this far, I judge those big uglies to be packing quite a storm."

Following the line of Red Buffalo's finger, Captain Earl's smooth brow creased and he said somberly, "If that's the only kind of storm that rolls down on us in the next couple of days . . . I'd settle for that just fine."

Chapter 42

Marshal Fergus Feeney pushed ponderously through the moderate-sized crowd that had gathered in front of Telford's Lutheran church. In the generously wide wake left by his passing walked Bennett McGreevey, followed by Deputy Ridgway.

"What's going on here? What seems to be the trouble?" Feeney demanded gruffly as he reached the foot of the stairs leading up into the church.

Looming in the open doorway at the top of the steps, his own girth one of the few in town close to equaling Feeney's, was Pastor Gerald Claypoole. He had a round, pink face made even rounder and broader by cottony white muttonchop sideburns that curved around his fleshy cheeks. His eyebrows, also like tufts of cotton, pinched slightly together now as he gazed down at the lawman and his entourage.

"Good afternoon, Marshal," he greeted in the famously booming voice that shook the rafters of the church regularly when he was laying down his sermons of fire and brimstone. "Let me first assure you that any trouble visited upon us, especially here on these blessed grounds, my flock and I trust in the loving hand of Jesus to see us through. However, that's not to say that your interest and aid is not also welcome, just as the same is equally true for the good captain here."

With his closing words, Claypoole gestured to indicate Captain Earl, who sat his horse nearby, reined up alongside a heavy, stout-wheeled work wagon with a team of thick-chested plow horses in the harness. The wagon was pulled up near one of the church's side doors, and in addition to a heap of their hastily gathered personal possessions, it contained the dour-faced Knudsen family.

Tied to the rear of the wagon were two horses each carrying a blanket-shrouded dead body draped across its back. Behind them, two soldiers sat straight and motionless on their mounts; the only departure from their statue-like stillness was the slow, steady sweep of their eyes, registering everything about their surroundings and those who made up the crowd.

Scowling, Marshal Feeney said, "Well, it's real nice to hear that the good Lord is looking out for all of us. But you still didn't say what this is all about. What's the trouble needing His loving hand?"

"How about letting me address that?" said Earl. "I was just in the process of filling in Pastor Claypoole and these other interested folks, so the timing is perfect for you to hear it, too."

"If you have something to say that's of wide interest to the citizenry of Telford," spoke up a frowning Bennett McGreevey, "then why didn't you come directly to the marshal instead of staging this public rally? And, out of simple reverence if nothing else, couldn't you at least have avoided parading the slain bodies of two of my men as part of it?"

The captain's eyes turned brittle. "How do you know those shrouded bodies are two of your men?" he asked bluntly.

McGreevey was clearly caught off guard by the challenge. His mouth opened and closed, gaping like a fish out of water, as he struggled to find a suitable response.

Before he could come up with one, Earl spoke again.

"You know who they are," he said, "because you sent them out to the Knudsen property yesterday to carry out an errand for you. Somewhat curiously, even though they and the other three men you sent with them never returned last night, you showed no concern for what might have happened to them. Until, that is, you sent Deputy Ridgway around to check this morning. He found out then that these men were dead, killed in an Indian attack, and certainly must have reported that back to you. Yet again you showed no apparent concern, at least not enough to send anyone out to retrieve the bodies. So isn't it a little late for you to be worried about showing some respect or reverence to them?"

By the time the captain was finished, everyone gathered around had their eyes locked on McGreevey, watching for a reaction, waiting to hear a response.

For a moment, some of the color seemed to drain from McGreevey's face. But then the color returned in a rapid flush, and as it did, his eyes blazed with a glare that he first aimed at Earl and then swept to cover the others crowded around.

"Everybody knows what a busy man I am," he snapped,

finally finding his voice. "I've been in town all morning, tending to my various business interests here. I haven't had a chance to get back out to my ranch in order to send some riders to fetch the bodies of the fallen men, that's all. I was just now preparing to leave for the sake of seeing to that very matter when we spotted this gathering and came to find out what was going on."

"If you ask me," spoke up Ridgway, judging by the expressions on the faces of many of the onlookers that McGreevey's explanation sounded weak, "there are some bigger questions to be answered. Like why were the Knudsens so eager to run me off when I went out there and not give *me* the chance to bring those poor fellas in? Or why didn't they bring 'em in themselves before now?

"But the biggest question of all is what good did it do us to have the army brought up here? What have they done to help with our Blackfoot problem? You heard the captain say these men were killed in an Indian attack. There were two others—that innocent young couple, just arrived to our area—the day before. The way it's going, we're losing more folks since the army got here than we did when we were on our own! Why ain't you out there chasing down those red devils right now, Captain?"

This did exactly what it was meant to do: divert attention away from McGreevey and stir up simmering Indian fears that quickly got turned on Captain Earl in the form of a ripple of concerned murmurings that ran through the crowd.

But the young officer refused to be flustered.

"The Blackfoot situation is exactly why I'm here," he responded in a clear, steady voice. "What the deputy failed to mention is that eleven of the twelve Indians who staged that attack were killed. Carl Knudsen and his sons joined the fight bravely, and the M-Slash-G wranglers who were initially set upon fought back as well. But it was two men from my company—our two scouts, who were nearby because they were already on the trail of the hostiles—who showed up to turn the tide. So no one can say the army isn't out there on the job!"

"The captain speaks true," proclaimed Knudsen from the seat of his wagon. "If his men hadn't been there, I fear the savages would have taken a far bloodier toll."

"What's more," continued Earl, "my entire company is on the move even as we speak. That's what I'm here to inform the town about. I have a patrol sweeping the area all across the base of the Wolfheads, temporarily bringing the remaining outlying homesteaders to safety here in town."

"We are even now preparing accommodations for them here inside the church," interjected Pastor Claypoole. "It may be a bit crowded, but everyone will be dry and warm and safe. And my flock and I will see to matters of food or any unexpected needs that might arise."

The collective murmur that had passed through the crowd just minutes earlier, one of concern and questioning, now became a supportive, reassuring ripple of compassion.

"You should also know," Earl said, again addressing everyone, "that our main encampment is moving in closer to town. That's under way even as we speak. I have minimal reason to think Thunder Elk would be bold enough—or have a large enough force—to pose any threat to the town. But it is a precaution I chose to take, nevertheless. I'll leave it to you, Marshal, to see that word is spread adequately.

"The reason for all of this, everyone needs to understand,

is the belief by me and my men that the killing of those eleven braves yesterday will prod Thunder Elk one of two ways. Because his raiding force, by our best previous estimates, has only been between thirty and forty men, losing a third or more in one fell swoop may be enough to break his spirit; or, just as important, the spirit of his followers. In that case, we're hoping, he will finally give up and withdraw across the border to the reservation in Canada. In that case, we'll be following close behind all the way, making sure."

Earl paused, his expression turning grimmer. Then: "The other possibility—and I repeat, it's only a possibility, one I think is a lot less likely than Thunder Elk withdrawing— is that the killing of those braves may spur a backlash of revenge from him. That's why I want the outlying homesteaders safe. Once that's done and our main camp is also in closer, then I'll begin putting a series of patrols out, constantly sweeping the flats to the north. Thunder Elk can't seek revenge unless he comes down out of the foothills. If he does that, we'll be waiting to engage him. All the while, my scouts will be scouring the higher ground, monitoring his movement so they can alert us."

"Sounds like you've taken into consideration everything except for the bigger cattle spreads out in the basin," pointed out a scowling McGreevey. "What about us? What if Thunder Elk and his raiders make it past your patrols and go for our ranches?"

"Other than snatching a few head of cattle from the outer fringes of your herds," Earl replied, "my understanding is that the larger outfits haven't been bothered by the Blackfeet very much. I suspect that was partly due to Thunder Elk being able to more easily get what he needed from the smaller spreads, but also because you bigger operations have enough men and guns to make it too costly for him to go against you. I don't see where that's changed, especially now that his force has been so badly diminished. Naturally the men of my command will ride to your protection if the need arises. But until such time, I think you and the other big ranchers will be generally safe if you stay alert and armed and remain as close as you can to your central buildings. One way or the other, this should be over in a matter of a few days. Riders should be sent out carrying that message. If any of the ranchers feel too uneasy, they can always bring their people to the safety of town as well."

A fresh round of murmuring that ran through the crowd seemed to convey that most felt this was a reasonable response.

Earl made a final sweep of the scene before announcing, "Very well. I need to take care of a couple more things here in town and then get back to my command. If all you folks stay alert and sensible, we'll get through this just fine." He turned to glance up at Carl Knudsen on his wagon seat. "Same goes for you and your family, Mr. Knudsen. My men will do everything we can to protect your place— and the others—while you're gone from it."

"We have trust in you, Captain," Knudsen said.

"You'll be back to look after it yourselves in no time," Earl told him. "Meanwhile, you're in good hands here with Pastor Claypoole."

The holy man smiled reassuringly. "And remember, we are each of us in the most wonderful hands of all . . . those of the Lord."

Now Earl turned to McGreevey and his two pet

lawmen. "I expect you're ready to take charge of your deceased now. But before you do that and before I pay my visit to the telegraph office, there's a particular matter we need to discuss. I've a strong hunch it's not something you want aired out here in front of everybody, so if you'll suggest some better place we can adjourn to . . . Maybe the marshal's office, where you can put your feet up on the desk and feel at home . . ."

Chapter 43

The dark clouds that had been out over the northwest end of the mountains a few hours earlier had rolled on in now, thicker and blacker and beginning to pulse with flashes of lightning followed by loud belches of thunder. Ahead came a surge of rapidly cooling air carried by strong wind gusts.

Those were the conditions Nathan and Red Buffalo and the diminished patrol of men led by Sergeant Purdy now found themselves in as they urged along the three wagonloads of homesteaders they had rounded up and were trying to get to the safety of town ahead of the storm's full fury.

Each wagon represented one of the families—the Malones, the O'Briens, and the Ketchels—Captain Earl had sent them after. Somewhat to Nathan's surprise, none of them had protested overly much once the situation was explained, and all had cooperated in hurriedly getting some essentials loaded up and falling in line with the column of mounted soldiers.

"One good thing about this storm hitting now," Red Buffalo, his voice raised to be heard above the wind, called over to Nathan as the two of them rode a few yards ahead of the column, "is that it ought to discourage Thunder Elk from starting out immediately if he decides to ride for revenge, no matter how hot his blood boils. Having until the weather breaks should give us plenty of time for the captain's plans to all be set in place."

"Can't argue that," Nathan replied. "Don't mean, though, that I ain't wishing we didn't have to get ourselves caught out here in this howler. We sorta lucked out last time, when all that wind the other day failed to bring down any rain. Pretty much a guarantee that, starting any minute now, we ain't gonna avoid that again this time."

Red Buffalo waited to answer until a reverberating crack of thunder finished rolling across the sky. "Even still, apart from the drenching we're about to get, you've got to admit that things are flowing along mostly favorable. Best of all, we got almost exactly the reaction we were hoping for out of Captain Earl. I know, a lot of details remain to be worked out, but at least there's a better chance than before for some proper justice in the end."

"Yeah, that's a good feeling," Nathan allowed. "But it will be an even better feeling to find out for sure which way Thunder Elk is going to jump. Hell, it was better before when everybody knew he was a renegade and there was no question about going straight at him at any chance. This in-between stuff—this hangin' fire, wondering if he's going to slink away with his tail between his legs or come roaring out with a renewed thirst for blood—that just puts me on edge. I don't like it worth beans."

"Yeah, I know what you mean."

Neither man spoke again for a minute. Until, right after

a stutter-flash of brilliant lightning revealed his sharply etched features to appear locked in stern contemplation, Red Buffalo said, "What if the option Thunder Elk chooses is to be broken spirited and head back to Canada, slink away with his tail between his legs, like you said a minute ago? Are you going to be satisfied with that?"

Nathan frowned. "Not sure I follow you. What do you mean 'satisfied'?"

"Just what the word says. Satisfied," Red Buffalo answered somewhat impatiently. "Will you, Nathan Stark, the Indian Killer, be willing to let a renegade who's raided and robbed and murdered say he's had enough and then . . . simply turn his back and walk away?"

Nathan eyed him in the murkiness of early evening hurried by the overcast sky. "You make it sound like you've already made up your mind, like you think the only right answer is for me to say, *No, I wouldn't be satisfied with that.*"

"No, I haven't made up my own mind at all, that's why I'm asking," said Red Buffalo. "But I admit to being surprised at the notion of the Indian Killer *not* being dissatisfied over such an outcome."

"I see what you mean. And yeah, I reckon you're right. Not too many years back, that kind of thing—letting a hostile who'd shed white folks' blood surrender and then live off the government on a reservation somewhere— would have gone against my grain. Any redskin who found himself out in front of me, the only way it was going to end was with one of us dead." Nathan paused, as if reflecting on a scene such as he'd just described.

Then, sighing, he went on, "But like I told you the

other night, the rage inside me don't burn quite as hot or urgent as it used to. We got sent here being told the goal of Captain Earl's command was to rid the area of renegades, either by killing 'em or driving 'em back to Canada. So I accepted those conditions from the get-go. The thing to remember is"—here he bared his teeth in a wry, wolfish smile—"as long as there's white men who keep pushing the edge of the frontier and red men who keep trying to hold on to a slice of it for themselves, there'll always be conflict that will continue giving me the chance to kill more Indians."

"I guess that's one way of looking at it," Red Buffalo said.

With the first fat, cold, widely scattered drops of rain starting to fall, Nathan eyed him again and said, "Now, how about the question you were really trying to work your way up to? Are *you* going to be satisfied letting Thunder Elk and his Blackfeet simply withdraw back over the border, if that's what it comes to?"

Red Buffalo shook his head. "I don't know. You're right, that's the question aching inside of me . . . but I don't have the answer."

Moments later the sky opened up all the way and slashing sheets of rain came slamming down. The two scouts bent their heads against the wind and the wet and plodded on ahead of the column, their conversation finished for now.

Miles away, in a shallow, wind-buffeted draw not yet reached by the rain, Lester Fallow stood buckling his gun belt around his waist, enjoying a sense of smug relief at having it once more on his person. Damn, it felt good!

A few feet away, Curly Messingill was likewise occupied, his mouth also curved in a satisfied smirk.

On the grassy ground around them lay sprawled the bodies of six men, all but one clad in U.S. Army blue and each further adorned with still-seeping bullet holes. Immediately at Fallow's feet lay the lifeless, twisted form of Lieutenant Kirby Benton.

In addition to the red-rimmed black hole in the middle of his forehead, a flat-headed length of rusty metal—what had once been a five-inch flooring spike—protruded from high in his throat, leaving a funnel-shaped pattern of wet crimson all down his front that seemed curiously excessive compared to the minimal leakage from his head wound. The spike that had done such messy damage, painstakingly plucked at and tugged at until it finally pulled free from the floor of the Knudsen corncrib, had become the element of surprise and desperation initiating the rest of the gory scene now laid out under an appropriately ominous sky.

Working alternately, until their fingers were gouged raw and bleeding, Fallow and Messingill had tugged at the slightly exposed sliver of steel throughout much of their first night locked in the corncrib. Once they had it free, they knew they had a serviceable if primitive weapon that might make an escape possible . . . but only if they were patient and waited for the right opening.

None presented itself while they were still locked in the corncrib. But once they were taken from there and put on horseback for relocation to the army encampment, it was a different story.

The lieutenant, much to his severe regret, would realize in his final moment of life that he proved to be an obliging ally. Having made no secret of his displeasure for keeping the men prisoners at all, he'd demonstrated his halfheartedness for the task he'd been given to transport them by allowing them to have their wrists tied in front during the time they were mounted. This allowed Fallow easy access to the spike, which he had by then hidden in the waistband of his trousers.

Once they were on the trail and several miles apart from all the others, Fallow set in motion the plan he and Messingill had put together. Fallow started pretending to be violently ill, blaming it on some spoiled food he must have been given by the Knudsens. He acted so weak and doubled-up by cramps that he fell from his saddle.

Benton and one of the other soldiers, the two riding closest to the fallen man, dismounted and attempted to try and help him. As soon as the lieutenant leaned in close, Fallow—who by then had slipped the spike from his waistband—slammed it up into the soft pad of flesh directly under Benton's chin. As he jerked back, spasming in agony, Fallow yanked his sidearm from its holster and began firing. He immediately killed the other man who'd dismounted and then swung to cover the remaining troopers.

The instant he saw Fallow thrust up with the spike, Messingill launched from his saddle and threw himself on the soldier mounted closest to him, dragging them both to the ground. Stunned by the fall, the trooper had no chance to resist Messingill seizing his pistol and also opening fire. All five soldiers were dead in a matter of seconds, most of them without ever fully realizing what was happening.

Eddie Winslow, the third prisoner but a young man lacking experience at gun work or the ways of violence, was himself dumbfounded by the explosive burst of shooting and sudden death. When Fallow put the muzzle of the lieutenant's own gun to the officer's head and fired a round through his already dying brain, Winslow was too repulsed to hold back. He leaned to one side in his saddle and vomited uncontrollably.

Fallow and Messingill exchanged looks. "The kid flat ain't got what it takes," said Messingill. "No way he'll hold up for what we've got to do next."

"You're right." Fallow's words were spoken to Messingill, but his eyes were locked on Winslow. "And I've had a gutful of crawfishin' varmints we can't trust to have our backs."

With that, he once more raised Benton's Army Colt, extended his arm, and this time it was Winslow's brain the slug he triggered went through, entering at the temple and knocking the young man out of the saddle, soaking the ground where he landed with what sprayed from his wound as well as what was still dribbling out of his mouth.

Once the shooting with confiscated guns was finished, Fallow and Messingill wasted no time digging out their own hardware from the soldiers' saddlebags. Now, with their captors dispatched and their gun belts snugged back in place, it came time to decide what their next move should be. It didn't take long to find out they were of similar minds as far as who deserved their focus.

"That low-down McGreevey hung us out to dry," snarled Fallow. "Ain't no other way to look at it. First, he held off all night long without sending anybody around to check on what happened, leaving us penned up like dogs in that rat-infested corncrib. Then, even after Ridgway finally *did* come around and saw what was what, he left us there. Seems plain enough to me McGreevey was willin' to sacrifice us while most likely puttin' all his attention to makin' sure he was alibied seven ways from Sunday and never mind what we had to face."

"It's always been about him and his high standing, keepin' himself pure and lily-white while we did his dirty work," agreed a scowling Messingill. "There was never a clearer message than when he stopped us from settlin' with those two scouts who took our guns and even sent Ridgway around to warn us off goin' after 'em. Never mind us havin' to eat crow, he had his precious little schemes he wanted to protect, that's all he cared about."

Slapping the six-shooter holstered on his hip, Fallow said, "Well, now we've got our guns again and this time I say we put 'em to use the way *we* want. Paying a visit to McGreevey is our first order of business. That snake owes us for what he put us through . . . owes us big enough so we can shove this whole stinkin' area behind us and move on to set ourselves up good in some new place. But before lightin' out all the way, I also say we take time to pay another visit to those army scouts. That'll give us a chance to square our old score and to cure them once and for good from stickin' their noses in anybody else's business!"

Messingill grinned slyly. "I like the sound of that." But then the grin faded and he added, "Only what about Ridgway? If he's still dancin' to McGreevey's tune, can't we expect him to try and stand in our way if we show up to do some crowding of the big man?"

Fallow snorted. "You said the right word—*try*. Ridgway might try. He's got his reputation, but who's he ever proved himself against outside a few saloon drunks? Me and you ain't without our own credentials, Curly. If Ridgway figures to get in our way . . . well, I say we might have to square things with him, too."

Messingill's grin returned and slowly became a throaty chuckle. "I like the sound of that even better. Let's get to it!"

Chapter 44

Bennett McGreevey was fuming. "That pompous, uniformed young pup! I don't know who he thinks he is, but before this is done I will damn sure show him who *I* am! I'm the one responsible for him being here . . . an assignment he could have parlayed into a big career boost simply by swatting away a handful of ragtag savages. But no, that's not enough for him. He believes he has the right to police the whole territory while he's at it! Yes, I'm the one responsible for him being here, and by the time I'm through with him, I'll be the one responsible for him spending the rest of his military career swamping out mule stalls!"

For a change, McGreevey wasn't pacing while he spewed this rant. Nor was he in Elke Klein's apartment. Rather, he was seated behind Feeney's desk in the marshal's office, his fists balled white-knuckled on the desktop in front of him. A burning cigar rested in an ashtray close by, piles of loose ash scattered around it from when McGreevey had banged his fist down so hard he'd dislodged the stogie a time or two.

Rafe Ridgway sat in a wooden chair in front of the

desk, legs extended out straight, fingers laced across his flat stomach. Over by the shuttered front window, Feeney stood fidgeting, shifting the weight of his considerable bulk from one foot to the other as he gazed out through a peephole in the shutter. Gusts of banshee wind howled down the street outside, sending bits of sand and gravel rattling against the outer panes of glass.

"Boy, that wind's a corker," the marshal muttered. "By the look of the lightning moving in from the north, it's gonna be a real frog-strangler out there before much longer."

"Yes, Feeney, you said that three times already," growled McGreevey. "So we're going to get a storm, so what? Who gives a damn?"

Feeney turned from the window, looking dismayed. "Just sayin', that's all, Mr. McGreevey."

"Well, you said it enough. No need to say it any more." McGreevey took a long pull on his cigar, puffed a thick cloud of smoke. "What I wish you could tell me is what was in those telegrams our boy captain sent out. Blast it, I told you to lean hard on Crippins and keep a lid on any outgoing wires."

"I made sure he understood that. And he would have done just like you wanted," said the marshal, "except that captain told him he was commandeering use of the key and he had his own man send out his messages."

"And Crippins couldn't make anything out, couldn't catch at least part of what was being said by listening to the dots and dashes or whatever the hell they call that racket they do their talking with?"

Feeney shook his head. "They chased him clear out of the office. He couldn't hear nothing."

"You think he's telling it straight?" asked Ridgway. "Any chance those soldier boys put a little more fear in him than you did, Fergus?"

"No, I'm convinced he wasn't trying to put anything over on me."

"We're all clear on what might have been contained in those wires, right?" said McGreevey. "You both heard the captain's spiel when he marched us here after leaving the church. He all but accused me flat out of hiring Fallow and those other fools to blow up Knudsen's water source, and implied almost as strongly that you two were complicit. If he convinces the wrong people with those kind of claims, it could bring some very unwelcome attention our way."

"But you got influential contacts back East and practically everywhere in between," pointed out Ridgway. "Why don't you get in touch with some of them, get ahead of the captain, put him in a bad light, and muddy the waters about his claims? Dispute them before they get a chance to take root?"

"But how can I dispute what I don't know?" protested McGreevey. "I don't know what he sent—or to who! If I cast about blindly and end up mentioning the wrong thing to the wrong person, I could do more harm than that tin soldier's wailing is able to."

Feeney looked perplexed. "So what are you going to do?"

"For starters, it's what *you're* going to do." McGreevey stabbed out his cigar stub in the ashtray. "First thing in the morning, I want you to lean on Crippins some more. He may not be able to tell us what the captain sent out, but he'll be the one who receives any responses. Benton can't afford to station a man at the telegraph office full-time.

So as soon as something comes in, I want Crippins to make sure I get a copy right away. Maybe that way I can decipher at least some of what that snot-nosed bluebelly sent and then I can start making some defensive moves."

Feeney bobbed his head eagerly. "Good thinking, Mr. McGreevey. You can bet I'll see to it that Crippins gets a copy of any incoming wires straight to your hands right away!"

A loud clap of thunder pounded down out of the sky and made even the sturdy jail building shudder.

McGreevey stood up. "Sounds like I'd better make tracks to Elke's place before that frog-strangler starts coming down. Walk with me, Rafe. We need to discuss a change in plans for our friends Fallow and Messingill. It complicates things if they've been moved to the army encampment, but at the same time it also increases the chance for them to be inclined toward blabbing. We have to think of a way to counter that."

Ridgway rose to his feet and followed McGreevey out. The two men began hurrying up the street with lightning ripping through the sky overhead, followed by booming peals of thunder. Feeney stood in the open doorway for a moment, rocked by wind gusts and feeling the first droplets of rain.

"Hope you don't get too wet, fellas!" he called after them.

Chapter 45

A grim-faced Captain Earl glared down at the sodden, blood-spattered cavalry hat he held in one hand. He stood behind the folding table in his command tent, the pulsing glow of a lantern perched near one edge of the table painting his features with contrasting patches of soft gold and dark, sharp-edged shadow.

Lined up before him on the other side of the table were a dour-looking Sergeant O'Driscoll and the bedraggled trio of Nathan, Red Buffalo, and Sergeant Purdy. Outside the trembling walls of the tent, the wind howled and sheet after sheet of rain came slapping down.

"I guess this gives a pretty stark explanation for why the camp hadn't begun being struck when I arrived from town and why Lieutenant Benton hadn't shown up with the orders to do so." There was an uncharacteristic huskiness in the young captain's voice when he spoke. "I fear my annoyance at the time was as ill-founded as my concern was lacking. I never dreamed the lieutenant's delay would be due to something so severe."

"There was no way you could have suspected such an outcome, sir," stated Purdy. "Lieutenant Benton and the men he chose to accompany him were all seasoned and competent. I don't think any of us—except maybe for Stark and Red Buffalo—would have been any better prepared for the degree of desperation shown by the prisoners."

"Knudsen also recognized them for what they were," Earl said. "He managed to raise some suspicion in me, though not nearly strong enough. It's not hard to believe strongly now, however, that the rest of what he claimed is true. Namely that the man those murderers work for, McGreevey, must have a side to him every bit as ruthless."

"You can put money on it," Nathan declared firmly. "He's the crafty old wolf hanging back in the lair, eyeing the landscape for prey. Lester and Curly are the prowlers who go out for the kill. That wedge-faced town deputy is part of the pack, too, unless I miss my guess, and to a lesser degree, that fat, waddling marshal as well."

"I got a certain amount of respect for wolves," muttered Red Buffalo. "What you're describing sounds more like a tangle of diseased coyotes."

"Categorize them however you choose," Earl said bitterly. "The bottom line is that five good men wearing the uniform of our country are dead, and I want every mother's son who had anything to do with it—either directly or indirectly—to pay a heavy price. Where are the bodies now?"

"They'll be along shortly, sir. I left some men behind to gather them up and get them loaded on horses," reported Purdy. "I thought it best to continue on with the homesteaders we were escorting in. There are women and children in those wagons who didn't need to see any more than what they already were exposed to. It was only by accident we happened on the dead men at all, nearly rolling right over the poor devils if Red Buffalo hadn't been sharp enough to spot 'em in a lightning flash."

"And the homesteaders? Where are they?"

"They're outside, waiting out the storm in their wagons. I know we need to get them on into town, but when I saw that the encampment was still in place here I thought it best to make a quick report."

"Yes, of course," Earl agreed. "When I got here and saw nothing had been done to start relocating the camp, the lateness and the approaching storm caused me to decide to hold off starting our move until tomorrow, when hopefully the weather will break. But by all means, those wagons need to be taken on to town. Proceed with that immediately, Sergeant. There are good people waiting to take them in at the Lutheran church. Stark, Red Buffalo, O'Driscoll, you men remain here."

The sergeant snapped off a salute, spun on his heel, and plunged back out into the storm.

As soon as Purdy was gone, the captain allowed his shoulders to sag somewhat, as if no longer feeling the need to maintain his rigid military bearing quite so strictly. He waved one hand wearily toward some folding camp chairs within the tent, saying, "Seat yourselves if you wish, gentlemen."

The men before him elected to remain standing. So did Earl, though he placed his palms flat down on the table and leaned slightly forward, shifting some weight off the small of his back.

Hanging his head a bit, not looking directly at any of the others, he said, "Stark, Red Buffalo, based on your past encounters with the scum in question—though it's been quite limited, I realize—what's your best guess where they might head after doing what they did?"

"I don't see it as much of a guess," Nathan replied without hesitation. "They'll make a beeline straight for McGreevey. They'll expect him either to protect them, hide them out somewhere, or pay them off big enough so's they can light a shuck for parts long gone from here."

Neither Red Buffalo nor O'Driscoll had anything to add to that assessment.

The captain lifted his face. "The question then becomes: Where are they most likely to find McGreevey?"

"Wouldn't his ranch be the logical place?" said O'Driscoll. "It's away from prying eyes except for other men already riding for the M-Slash-G brand."

"Under normal circumstances, yes, that would seem logical," Earl agreed. "I wish we could count on finding the fugitives there. That would again be outside the boundaries of any established legal authority, just as at Knudsen's. As I've already demonstrated, I have no compunction about broadening the scope of my command to include taking police action over apparent criminal activity in a setting such as that. My concern, however, is that the ranch isn't where the men we want will catch up with McGreevey. At least not tonight, or in the immediate future."

"What makes you say that?" Red Buffalo wanted to know.

"For one thing, when I left Telford not too long ago to return here, McGreevey was still in town," Earl told him. "In the time we've been stationed here, I've heard that he frequently spends some nights in town rather than always going home to his ranch house. Considering how fast this storm was moving in when last I saw him, it seems unlikely he'd risk trying to reach the ranch ahead of it."

"But that don't mean the killers we want didn't still go there, expecting that's where they'd find him," argued O'Driscoll.

Earl nodded thoughtfully. "True. But *not* finding him, would they stay and wait . . . or would they head to town to brace him there? This storm provides good cover for them to move around in."

"Yeah, it does," agreed Nathan. "And all things considered, I can't picture those polecats Lester and Curly having the patience to sit around waiting in one place for very long."

"Same here," added Red Buffalo. Then he pointed out, "But to be safe, you've got plenty of men to cover both places."

"I'm aware of that," the captain responded crisply. "Which is why, as soon as we conclude this discussion, Sergeant O'Driscoll will be leading a patrol of men to the M-Slash-G ranch headquarters for the express purpose of apprehending the fugitive murderers if they're found there."

At this announcement, the veteran sergeant couldn't suppress a wide, satisfied grin.

"That," Earl continued, "leaves the town. And it also leaves me in a bit of a quandary. Since Telford *does* have an established and recognized legal authority, even though we suspect it of being highly corrupt, there are strict limits governing any action allowed to be taken by me or anyone in my command while operating within said jurisdiction. Without digging out my manual and checking to make certain, I don't recall the verbatim wording. But I'm fairly sure it prohibits blasting away at suspected human vermin or squashing reptiles masquerading as local big shots.

"Again, all of that applies quite clearly to officers and soldiers in uniform. It's always baffled me, though, how distinct the manual can be about so many things and yet in other areas like . . . oh, for instance, civilian scouts . . . it can be strangely vague. Have you ever noticed that, Sergeant O'Driscoll?"

"Aye, the very thing!" exclaimed O'Driscoll, scowling shrewdly. "Why, those shiftless rascals—other than when they're hoppin' about amidst a pack of hair-hungry Injuns—they get to come and go practically at will. And the other thing about 'em is the fact that, besides knowin' how to dodge Injun traps and such, most of 'em ain't overly bright. Take a night like this, when me and some boys are gonna be sloggin' out because it's our assigned duty—I bet there's certain scout types who might take a notion to head out in such sorry conditions for no better reason than to go to town merely for the sake of some pointless revelry."

A long, rolling grumble of thunder held everyone's tongue for a minute.

After it had passed, Nathan drawled, "Fortunately for this outfit, you've got a couple of scouts who wouldn't think of acting so foolishly." The sarcasm in his tone made it clear he fully recognized the performance that had just taken place for what it was. Then he added, "Although, Moses and I *have* been talking about getting into town for a visit with our friends Amos and Esther Handley, the folks we spent some time with on the trail." He cut a glance over at Red Buffalo. "What do you think? This might be the last chance we get for a while."

Red Buffalo shrugged. "We're already soaked, going back out in the storm ain't gonna get us any wetter. And Miss Esther is bound to serve up a fresh pot of coffee and maybe have some leftover pie on hand to go with it."

"Reckon that settles it, then," said Nathan. His gaze went first to the captain, then came to rest on O'Driscoll. He cocked one brow sharply. "Sure hope you and your patrol have luck catching up with those killers out at the ranch, Sarge, and don't accidentally flush 'em into town where they might show up and interrupt our pie eating."

O'Driscoll's shrewd scowl turned into a shrewd grin. "I hope so, too. But as long as one or the other of us ends up running into those curs . . . I'll settle for that."

Chapter 46

Rafe Ridgway stood in the recessed doorway of Flannery's Boot Shop, the narrow, cramped space providing adequate shelter from the storm that continued to hammer Telford, its wind-lashed sheets of rain turning the town's main street into a shallow river of foaming, churning water. From his vantage point, the deputy had a full view up and down the darkened street.

On most nights, the series of lanterns that hung from posts positioned along the edge of the boardwalk at regular intervals on alternating sides supplied at least a few patches of meager illumination. But tonight the lanterns had long since been drowned out so everything was black except for the brilliant, bluish-white flashes thrown by the lightning bolts streaking overhead.

Since most downtown businesses were closed at this hour, they loomed in rows of silent, undefined shapes other than during the lightning bursts. A couple of exceptions were, of course, the saloons—Kerrigan's Keg, located diagonally across from where Ridgway stood, and the High Plains Palace, next block down but on his same side. A good-sized drinking crowd was present in each, hardly deterred by the storm. Probably in more than one case, some thirsty husband was using the downpour as an excuse for having to wait for a letup before venturing out to return home.

At any rate, the smears of yellow-gold light pouring out through the rain-beaded windows of these establishments gave a touch of more constant illumination than just the intermittent lightning.

In addition to that provided by the saloons, there was one other source of steady light on the street that night. It was, in fact, the reason for Ridgway holding so steadfastly to his post. The light he was so focused on came from the curtained windows of Elke Klein's apartment on the second floor over her dress shop, directly across from where the deputy now stood.

A short time earlier, Ridgway had left that apartment after escorting Bennett McGreevey there and then departing at the completion of the discussion they'd been having. Before leaving, he had caught Elke's eye long enough to give her one of the discreet signals they'd worked out, letting her know he needed to see her in private as soon as possible. Since McGreevey remained behind, however, he knew it would take some time before she'd be able to respond. Until then, all he could do was watch and wait with an impatience that was churning as restlessly inside him as the storm rolling over the land.

The deputy took a long drag on the cigarette he was smoking, then flipped the remains out into the rain, a moment later releasing the plume of smoke he'd pulled out of it.

Damn! Was this storm ever going to let up?

How long had he been wedged in this dripping doorway? Wasn't Elke ever going to find a way to excuse herself for a few minutes?

Those wind gusts were getting cold! *Damn this stinking weather . . .*

Ridgway had just hooked a finger in his shirt pocket, hoping his makings weren't too damp to get another cigarette going, when he saw a flicker of movement in the high window across the street. The curtains were drawn wide for a moment, then pulled back closer until they hung about four inches apart. That was the signal he'd been waiting for. Ridgway shoved the makings back in his pocket and flipped his collar up, getting ready to shove out of the doorway.

With an oil lamp raised in one hand while his other gripped the hickory cane he used to steady his frailness, Miles Rafferty stepped back from the door he had opened to his visitors.

"Come in, come in," he urged them. "Good heavens, get yourselves in out of that wretched night!"

Chased by wind and rain, Nathan and Red Buffalo gladly ducked inside. But even with the door closed quickly behind them, there were still rivulets of rainwater pouring off the brims of their hats as well as dripping from the shiny slickers they were wrapped in.

"I'm afraid we're making a mess all over your floor," Nathan apologized, his voice raised in order to be heard over a reverberating boom of thunder.

"Don't worry, that's what mops are for," Rafferty told him. Then, chuckling, he added, "Besides, having it to clean up tomorrow will delight my sister. Ever since arriving, she insists on fussing around to improve what she calls my 'bachelor digs' and acts disappointed to find that I am quite tidy on my own."

"Then this muddy puddle we're making ought to tickle her pink," remarked Red Buffalo.

"Can I fix you some hot tea to warm you up some?" Rafferty said. "Or if you want to take a more direct route, perhaps a touch of brandy?"

Red Buffalo arched a brow. "Offering firewater to an Indian? That could land you in heap big trouble in a lot of places."

"Not to mention risking our scalps," Nathan deadpanned, "in case a jolt of the stuff was enough to trigger the demons in Moses and set him straightaway on the warpath."

"You'll have to forgive me for not giving proper consideration to the worry of getting scalped," said a mildly grinning Rafferty, reaching up to pat his thoroughly bald dome. "But if spirits are to be left aside, then the offer of some hot tea still stands."

"No thanks, Mr. Rafferty," replied Nathan. "We appreciate your hospitality, truly, but we didn't barge in to take up too much of your time, and the fact is we don't have a lot of our own to spare, either."

Rafferty's eyebrows lifted. "Of course. I should have known. I heard about the recent Blackfoot activity and how your captain has been bringing in families from the outlying homesteads. Naturally, you must be involved in that."

Nathan nodded. "We are, yes. But our reasons for stopping by tonight are only indirectly related to that matter. You see—"

"The prisoners!" Rafferty exclaimed, interrupting him. "Yes, that is even more fitting. I heard how the captain is holding three M-Slash-G men as prisoners on some kind of criminal charge he feels is a rightful concern for the army while it's in the area. And two of the men he's holding are your old pals Fallow and Messingill. Certainly you'd want to take a particular interest in anything concerning those two."

"More so now than ever," Red Buffalo said solemnly.

"Because," Nathan added, "it happens that those two pet coyotes of McGreevey have escaped." He then went on to quickly furnish the rest of the bloody details.

Rafferty was left shaking his head in dismay. "What a tragic waste. Five men cut down in such a ruthless manner. I always knew that Fallow and Messingill were capable of violence, yet . . ." Here the frail old man's voice trailed off and he frowned as he swept his gaze over Nathan and Red Buffalo. "But I'm not sure why you've come to me. Is there some way you think I can be of help in recapturing those murderous dogs?"

"As a matter of fact, there is," said Nathan. The corners of his mouth lifted in a thin smile. "I was saying to your sister just the other day how you seem to have your finger on the pulse of things around town better than anybody. Especially for a fella who claims not to get out and about very much."

Rafferty sniffed. "It's not like I go out of my way to stick my nose in things. Folks tend to talk freely around me, that's all. I guess I'm just a good listener. Actually, it's kind of a compliment that—"

"Yes, it is. And I didn't mean to sound at all negative," Nathan assured him. "In fact, your knowledge of the town and the things that go on in it is why we came here, what we're counting on to help us out."

"How so? What do you need to know that I can perhaps tell you?"

"We suspect, though we don't have any proof, that Bennett McGreevey was behind the attempt to dynamite the Knudsens' water source," said Red Buffalo. "But whether he was or not, we suspect even stronger that Fallow and Messingill will go running to him for some kind of help."

"Sounds reasonable," Rafferty agreed. "And I figure you're on the money, too, thinking that McGreevey was behind that dynamiting business."

Nathan scowled. "We've got time to get to the bottom of that. But first things first, and that means stopping Fallow and Messingill from making good on the rest of their getaway. We figure the best way to do that is to get between them and McGreevey."

"Is McGreevey in town?"

"We're not sure. Given the weather, we think so. The captain has also got men headed out to his ranch, just to make sure. But our question for you is: When McGreevey spends the night in town, like we've heard he often does, where does he stay? Where would Fallow and Messingill go looking for him?"

Rafferty burst out in what was almost a giggle. "That's the information you need from me? The answer is so simple and so well known you could get it by asking practically anybody."

"Well, we ain't asking just anybody—we're asking you," growled Nathan. "So how about spitting out the answer so we'll have a chance at maybe getting there in time to stop Fallow and Messingill?"

Chapter 47

At the rear of Elke Klein's dress shop was a service door leading in to a small storage area. An enclosed stairway led up from there to the second-floor apartment.

When Rafe Ridgway lunged out of the storm and into the storage area, Elke was there waiting for him. She stood off to one side, near the stairway, holding a lantern. The pulsing illumination it gave off cast her in a soft, golden glow that only enhanced her blond beauty.

Ridgway removed his sodden hat and hung it on a nearby woman-shaped wire framework before shrugging out of his wet slicker and letting it fall to the floor. Then he stepped forward as Elke moved to meet him and he wrapped her in an embrace. She held one arm extended rather awkwardly, still holding the lantern, the other snaked up and her hand cupped the back of his head, pulling his lips to hers.

When the kiss ended, Elke said breathily, "It's been so long since we've had even a moment alone together!"

"You think I don't know that?" Ridgway muttered. "It's been driving me crazy."

They kissed again and this time when their lips parted

Ridgway shot a glance over toward the stairway, saying, "Where's McGreevey now?"

"After you left earlier, he came down with one of his headaches," Elke answered. "I gave him some laudanum that I keep on hand for such times. He'll sleep now for hours, maybe the rest of the night."

Ridgway grimaced. "Yeah, I think you can figure those headaches are gonna start coming more and more regular."

"What do you mean?"

"It's why I wanted to see you so bad, what I've got to talk to you about," the deputy said. "I got a bad feeling about how things are headed. I think all of McGreevey's big plans are on the brink of falling apart. That means our plan—our dream of getting away, of going off together while he's back East making his final push for statehood—is at risk, too."

Elke set the lantern aside, placing it on a wall shelf, and took both of Ridgway's rough hands in hers. "How? What makes you think so much has suddenly gone so wrong?"

"It's that blasted army captain and the way he's sticking his nose into things," Ridgway said through clenched teeth. "It looks to me like he may succeed in pulling in some outside attention that could be real damaging. A U.S. marshal, maybe even a federal judge. If they start asking around and get people talking about the way we've been doing things around here, it won't be good. Too many people around town and all through the area got no love for McGreevey, and that goes likewise for me and Feeney. And if that ain't bad enough, then the way McGreevey is reacting—panicking, getting even crazier ideas—is only gonna make it worse."

"Crazier how?" Elke wanted to know.

"You heard how Fallow and Messingill got caught trying to dynamite Knudsen's spring, right? So now the army is holding them as prisoners waiting to see what kind of responses the captain gets back from the wires he sent out. If Fallow and Messingill end up facing a federal marshal and judge, how long do you think they'll be willing to keep their mouths shut about McGreevey being the one who sent them to do that stupid dynamiting job in the first place?" Ridgway's expression turned anguished. "And do you know what his idea is to stop them? He wants me to sneak into that army encampment and kill them before they can squawk!"

Elke's fingers dug into his arm. "That sounds like a suicide mission."

"You think I don't know that? Before, when they were being held out at the Knudsen ranch, I was willing to give it a try. But now, to slip in and out of the army encampment when I don't even know where they're being held and the soldiers are already on full alert due to the Indian trouble . . ."

Ridgway let his words trail off and he just shook his head as if in hopelessness.

"So what did you tell him?" Elke wanted to know.

"I told him yeah, I'd do it. Just to get him off my back, give me time to think." The deputy's mouth twisted with frustration. "But don't you see? That's what I mean about him panicking, being willing to act even crazier. If it's not this business with those two fools Fallow and Messingill, then what will he come up with next? That's why I say it's all getting ready to fall apart around him. The only question is: Are you ready to face that fact with me, and to go ahead and make our move to get away while we still have a chance?"

Elke looked startled. "What do you mean? Go away where? How? What will we do for money?"

Ridgway pulled her hard against him. "We can always get money. For starters, I've got a decent amount saved up. You must have, too, the way McGreevey's been lavishing things on you. Right? And hell, I bet he probably keeps some of his own stashed up in your apartment."

A flood of emotions—surprise, indecision, concern—poured over Elke's face. "But this is so . . . so sudden. So impulsive! Are you sure we wouldn't also be panicking? You said you needed time to think. Don't I deserve at least a moment of the same?"

"What's to think about?" Ridgway demanded, suddenly impatient and angry. "It's what we've been wanting, ain't it? The chance to get away. Together. No, it's not the ideal way we were planning. But I'm telling you, it's the best chance we're likely to get, and if we don't take it we may end up caught in the rubble McGreevey is gonna bring down on himself and everybody around him!"

Elke's expression had now become one of pure fright.

But then, before she could say anything, the door burst open and two men came charging through!

Elke screamed, but it was lost to the storm's howling wind and another clap of almost-constant thunder before the door slammed shut again. With his arms full of Elke, Ridgway had no chance to go for the Colt holstered on his hip. Especially not with the gaping muzzles of two already drawn revolvers aimed squarely at his face.

On the trigger ends of those revolvers were the sneering, rain-drenched faces of Lester Fallow and Curly Messingill.

"Except for pokin' your hands up slow and high, you hold real still, Rafe," ordered Fallow. "And if you think that German floozy in front of you will keep us from pullin' these triggers, you'd be makin' an awful bad mistake."

"Don't hurt the girl, I'm doing exactly like you say," Ridgway responded as he proceeded to do so. But he couldn't keep from asking, "How did you get away from the army?"

"By showin' them what I just got done tellin' you—that we ain't at all shy about pullin' triggers when we need to," Fallow answered.

"And sometimes when we just plain *want* to," Messingill added.

"Now you, Miss Elke. Be smart and listen close, just like the deputy. Take half a step away from him," Fallow instructed, "then turn back, real slow, and unbuckle his gun belt. After it falls to the floor, move all the way away from him and step over here closer to us."

Elke did as she was told, her fingers trembling as she fumbled with the gun belt buckle.

"C'mon, you can do better than that," jeered Messingill. "We was watching through the window a minute before we invited ourselves in, and the way you two was plastered against one another made it plain this ain't hardly the first time you've reached to undo his belt buckle."

"I always said that mouth of yours was going to get you killed one day, Curly," Ridgway snarled. "Now it just brought you one step closer."

"I'll worry about that when I hear it from somebody who ain't got his hands full of empty and his gun layin' at his feet," snorted Messingill.

"Never mind that crap," said Fallow. Then, his eyes

whipping back and forth between Ridgway and Elke, he added, "The fact you two are down here rubbin' together all sneaky-like tells me McGreevey must be upstairs asleep. That the way it is?"

When he didn't get an answer quick enough to suit him, Fallow barked, "All I need is one of you to speak up—and if it takes puttin' a bullet in the other one to loosen a tongue, then we can do it that way if we have to."

"You trigger a round in here it will draw attention you can't afford," Ridgway challenged him.

Fallow didn't buy it for a second. "Bull! With all that thunder bangin' around outside, I could empty my whole wheel and nobody would pay any notice, except maybe McGreevey. But if he took a dose of his headache medicine, like it now occurs to me is probably the case, then even he won't be roused."

"What do you want with him? Or any of us?" Elke wailed.

"Money. And lots of it, for what that greedy skunk put us through!" Fallow told her. "Enough to leave this lousy town and McGreevey and all his big plans in our dust for good."

"But since you mention it, Miss Always-with-Her-Nose-Stuck-in-the-Air," said Messingill, narrowing his eyes, "now that we see clearer what you really are, maybe from you we'll want a little something extra."

Ridgway spoke hurriedly. "You're right, McGreevey is upstairs. And like you guessed, he's deep under a dose of his headache medicine."

Fallow nodded. "That's more like it. See, was that so hard?" He jerked his chin toward the stairs. "So it's time for all of us to go up. You lead, Rafe. Keep your fingers laced behind your head and take one step at a time, real slow. Miss Elke will be behind you and we'll be right behind her. I shouldn't have to tell you again that we won't hesitate to cut her down and then blast you if you try anything funny. So start movin', slow and easy."

Chapter 48

Outside the storeroom's only window, the small, curtainless square that Fallow and Messingill claimed to have peeked through a short time earlier, two new faces hung back cautiously so as not to be revealed by a lightning burst. They gazed through the rain-beaded glass as the procession of people inside started up the stairs.

Dropping away from the window altogether and crouching against the outer wall slightly to one side, Red Buffalo said to Nathan, "If timing was money, we wouldn't have a Confederate copper between us."

Sleeving rainwater off his face, Nathan could only agree. "Yeah, it would've been better if we could have got here a few minutes sooner. But the good news is that we got three quarters of what we're after—Fallow, Messingill, and Ridgway—right here in a box. And it seems a safe bet that somewhere at the top of those stairs they're climbing is the rest of it, the he-bull himself, McGreevey."

"Too bad that gal is in the mix," Red Buffalo said with a scowl. "And just incidentally, did you happen to notice they appear to have a fair amount of firepower inside the box with them? I bring that up just as a reminder that it might make coaxing them *out* of the box a little more difficult."

Nathan grunted. "I also noticed they're pointing some of that firepower at each other. What do you reckon that's all about?"

"No idea," Red Buffalo replied. "But I got a pretty strong hunch that if we were to poke our heads in and ask why, they'd quick-like decide to all aim in the same direction— at us."

"Ain't like we don't have some firepower of our own to aim back," Nathan said stubbornly.

"In that case, since you seem to think we got 'em right where we want 'em, how do you propose we go about convincing them of that?" Red Buffalo wanted to know.

Nathan frowned. "I'm thinking on it. We could see if Sergeant Purdy is still in town after bringing in those homesteaders. With him and his men, we could surround the joint, sort of lay siege and give everybody inside a chance to give up. Or you and me could wait right here until they come out on their own and hope they give us an opening to get the drop on 'em. How about you? You got any thoughts on how to play it?"

The Crow's sharply cut facial features, etched deep by the brilliance of a stuttering lightning flash, were also pulled into a frown.

"Well, laying siege to force 'em out or waiting for 'em to come out on their own . . . either way seems like a notion cut from the same blanket. Both involve more waiting, and I've had about a bellyful of that. Especially in this cold rain." He paused, then added, "The only good thing, considering the spotty bathing habit of us redskins, is the fact I'm soaked thoroughly enough to have the next ten years or so already covered."

Nathan groaned. "Are you really bringing that up all over again? And especially at a time like this?"

"Just sayin', that's all."

"Well, you've said it enough. If you want to keep jabbering, how about coming up with an idea for how we can flush the rats out of this box before we both end up drowning out here waiting for 'em?"

After a minute, Red Buffalo said, "Okay. The only way I can see is to not wait. To rip the box open in a couple different places and go in after the rats."

"Sounds terrific. But how we gonna manage that?"

Red Buffalo made a sour face. "You're going to love this part. You get to work inside where it's dry. That means slipping in and cat-footing up those stairs. The sounds of the storm will help cover any noise you make. Meanwhile, I'll be making like a squirrel out front. When we came down the street a minute ago, I spotted a big tree growing right beside the front of this building. I figure I can shinny up that, then hop over onto the strip of porch roof that juts out above the entrance to the dress shop. That will put me level with the second-floor windows. You ought to have made it to the top of the stairs by the time I'm in position outside. I'll start the ball by busting out one of the windows, then we'll both boil in and have 'em pinned between us."

Nathan had been listening intently, head bent close. When Red Buffalo was done reeling off his plan, Nathan lifted his face and said, "Moses, that sounds crazy enough to maybe work."

"I figure it's better than squatting here and drowning like a couple turkeys staring up at raindrops."

"You know, you could make it easier on yourself by

being the one to take the stairway," Nathan pointed out. "It's your plan, you got the right to adjust it some."

"I got it adjusted the way I want," Red Buffalo told him. "So if we're gonna go with it, best we start." He paused, arching one brow before quipping, "And if it comes to having to throw some lead, be sure to remember I'll be somewhere across the room from you. I know that Colt of yours is used to shooting at Indians. Try to remind it that things are a little different this time around."

Nathan grinned wryly. "I'll do my best to make it behave."

"That's preposterous! I can't put my hands on that kind of money. Not cash, not at this time of night! It's simply impossible, even if I was willing."

"Even *if* you was willing? You think this is a game, you damn fool skinflint? We're wanted murderers, thanks to you. Killers of federal soldiers! You think we've got any more to lose by killing you?"

"If you kill me, you'll never get your money. *That's* what you've got to lose. And I never told you idiots to kill those soldiers."

"No, but you left us rotting in their custody, didn't you? What did you figure we was supposed to do?"

From where he crouched at the top of the stairs, Nathan could hear this exchange plainly. The door now in front of him, opening to the apartment beyond, had been left slightly ajar by whoever passed through last. That was helpful as far as *hearing* what was taking place on the other side, but the narrow opening provided no useful visibility, no sign of any of the people within the living quarters.

Of those talking now, Nathan recognized the one doing all the threatening as Lester Fallow. The other, he judged, had to be McGreevey.

McGreevey spoke again, saying, "If you had stayed calm and given me a chance, I could have come up with something to help you. Bribed somebody, pulled some strings to get that overambitious captain jerked into line . . . something. But not now. You're right, by killing those soldiers you've left yourselves nothing to lose. Your only option is to run as fast and far as you can."

"Ain't we already made it plain we know that?" snarled Fallow. "That's what we're here for. Money from you to make that run in style. And if we don't get it, we take you down with us!"

Now another voice—Messingill's—joined in. "To hell with not gettin' it! You want to talk options? Well, that *ain't* one. You're the big wheel around town, around this whole territory, McGreevey. You've told that often enough to everybody who'd listen, remember? So I don't want to hear about how much cash you can't get your hands on. What you're gonna do is go with us to the bank president or whoever it takes, trot us all down *to* the bank, and once we're there you'll be able to get your hands on all the cash you want. See how easy that will be? And the cash you'll want, of course, is the amount me and Lester are askin' you to fork over to us so we can go ahead and take our little ride."

"You're insane!" McGreevey said.

"No, you're the one who's loco"—now it was Fallow's voice again—"if you think one word of that was a bluff. So are you ready to take us to Mr. Bank President . . . or would you rather limp there with a bullet where your kneecap used to be?"

"Or maybe," suggested Messingill, "a couple bullet holes in your German floozy, even if she ain't quite the private property you think she is, would make you even more cooperative."

"For God's sake, Bennett! Do what they want!" wailed Elke.

Nathan's gut tensed a little extra at that. Even if the gal in question appeared to be a conniver in her own right, resorting to rough tactics on a female went against his grain. Damn, how much time had passed? Shouldn't Red Buffalo be in place by now and about ready to—

As if bidden by Nathan's thoughts, the sound of shattering glass, sudden and startling even against the outside backdrop of moaning wind and growling thunder, sounded from within the apartment.

Nathan thrust up from his crouch and slammed his left shoulder against the door, ramming it open wide as he charged through with his Colt extended in his right fist. His gaze made a fast sweep, taking in the expanse of the elegantly appointed living quarters.

On the opposite wall, the shattered window gaped wide, its curtains streaming inward, billowing straight out, driven by the wind and lashing sheets of rain. In between, the room's occupants were bunched to Nathan's left. Ridgway, Elke, and McGreevey crowded toward a dining area; Fallow and Messingill stood more toward the middle.

In that moment, all faces were turned toward the gaping window and the inward-blowing curtains. Nathan's entrance was barely noticed until he shouted, "Everybody freeze! I'll shoot down the first one who twitches wrong!"

As eyes whipped around to focus on him, a second

window about six feet down from the first burst open and Red Buffalo plunged through with his Henry rifle sweeping at waist level until its aim came to rest on the two gunmen.

Addressing the same pair, Nathan said, "You know we mean business, boys. We've been here before. Drop the hardware and nobody has to get hurt!"

The eyes of Fallow and Messingill were wild, desperate. But not suicidal. Their bodies were half twisted around, torn between whether to face Nathan or Red Buffalo. The guns they'd previously been holding leveled on the other three now sagged uncertainly downward.

A long, ragged moment passed. Then another.

The only sound was that of the rain splashing on the windowsill and a distant grumble of thunder.

Every indication was that it was going to end like that, with Fallow and Messingill lowering their guns the rest of the way and surrendering to the two scouts . . .

But then, totally unexpected, McGreevey pulled a short-barreled hideaway gun from the pocket of his silk dressing gown and shouted, "What are you waiting for? Shoot them!"

And acting on his own words, he triggered a round in the direction of Red Buffalo.

The range of the peashooter, even in a skilled hand, wasn't effective for the span of the room. McGreevey's frantic shot went high, drilling a slug into the ceiling a full three feet short of Red Buffalo.

Nathan's response, however, was lacking in neither range nor accuracy. His .44 slug entered a quarter inch above McGreevey's right eye and sent the boss of the territory staggering back a step and a half, spraying gore from the back of his head where the bullet had exploded out, before he toppled and fell heavily to the floor.

Elke screamed, this time high-pitched and piercing enough to cut through even the sounds of the storm.

McGreevey's desperate attempt and Elke's scream were enough to propel Fallow and Messingill into trying their luck after all. Trying and failing. They got their bodies turned—Messingill toward Red Buffalo, Fallow toward Nathan—and were in the act of bringing their pistols level again. But that was as far as they made it.

Nathan's Colt spoke twice more, as fast as he could cock and squeeze. His bullets pounded into Fallow's chest an inch apart, sending the man into a death spin and then a collapse.

The first round from Red Buffalo's Henry hit Messingill on the tip of his sternum, lifting him up on his toes and sending him staggering back against Ridgway, who was turned to wrap Elke in a protective embrace. Messingill's insistence on still trying to raise his gun, though feeble, gave Red Buffalo no choice but to fire again. This second slug passed through Messingill's rib cage and struck Ridgway in the back. Both men fell into a heap, with Elke pinned partially underneath Ridgway.

As the echoes of the shots died away, everything went quiet again.

Except for the splash of the rain on the windowsills and the thunder that seemed to finally be fading some . . . and Elke's soft sobbing.

Chapter 49

Two mornings after the shoot-out in Elke Klein's apartment, a gathering took place on the property of Carl Knudsen and his family.

In that short interim of time, much had changed in and around the town of Telford, much was still in the process of change, and more was yet to come.

Captain Earl had declared the whole area under martial law until the scheduled arrival, as arranged via telegram, of a U.S. marshal and federal judge out of Helena. Meanwhile, Sergeant Purdy and a small contingent of soldiers would maintain day-to-day law and order in the town. Elke and former marshal Fergus Feeney would remain under house arrest until such time as the judge could determine their knowledge and/or involvement in any underhanded dealings by McGreevey.

The same determination would be made for Rafe Ridgway, except he would be awaiting it while healing from his back wound in the jail lockup. As for McGreevey, Fallow, and Messingill, as well as the five soldiers slain by the latter two, along with the young wrangler Wilson, funeral arrangements were pending.

But the gathering this morning on the flat plain north of the Knudsen house and buildings had nothing to do with any of that. Yet it was certainly of no less significance.

Thunder Elk had agreed to end his renegade breakout and return to the Canadian reservation. This decision was reached thanks to the intervention of Shining Water and given further impetus by an unexpected visit from the old chief Blue Otter—father to Shining Water, uncle to Thunder Elk—who had journeyed down from the north hoping to coax back the dozen youths who had most recently fled to join Thunder Elk's group.

The tragedy of how that had turned out had weighed heavily on Thunder Elk's decision and continued to weigh heavy on the hearts of all Blackfeet now present.

The purpose of this morning's ceremony, as brokered by Beauregard Haliway, was for Thunder Elk to officially announce to Captain Earl his intended withdrawal and to establish, as necessary, any related terms. Captain Earl's only requirement in the way of terms was that the Blackfeet withdrawal take place immediately and with the understanding that a force of his soldiers would follow along as far as the border, to ensure the departure was complete. There was no objection to this.

A request by the Blackfeet, as first voiced by both a somber Thunder Elk and a very sad-faced Blue Otter and then translated by Haliway, was that they be allowed to retrieve the bodies of the eleven slain young braves and take them for reburial in accordance with their tribal customs. To this, Captain Earl agreed without hesitation.

With Haliway continuing to speak for the Blackfeet, it came down to one final piece of business. Their group, which included Shining Water, Ned Bannister, and Andrea

Fontinelle in their midst, stood about ten yards from
Nathan, Red Buffalo, O'Driscoll, and a half-dozen soldiers
who stood with Captain Earl.

Working his way up to it, the hulking old trapper first
eyed the captain for a long moment and then slid his gaze
over to Nathan and Red Buffalo.

"The onliest thing left," he said, "is, well, a sort of favor,
I guess you could call it, being asked by Thunder Elk."

"A favor?" echoed Captain Earl, scowling. "We owe
him no kind of favor. What he's already been granted
should be considered quite sufficient."

"I know that, Captain," agreed Haliway. "And so does
Thunder Elk, rightfully. He ain't askin' this as any part of
the settlement between the Blackfeet and the army. It's
strictly a, uh, personal thing."

"Get to it, man," growled Nathan. "What are you driving at?"

Now Haliway's gaze locked squarely on Red Buffalo
and he said, "It's you, Moses. Thunder Elk is lookin' for
what he calls atonement, and he sees you as the only way
he has a chance for gettin' it."

Red Buffalo's expression immediately hardened. "Not
that I'm inclined to do that wretch any kind of favor but
what, exactly, is he talking about?"

"He's claimin' a kind of blood rite, see," Haliway explained. "He knows he messed up with this whole renegade thing, draggin' his people down here, puttin' 'em
through the hardship and sufferin' they had to endure . . .
but most of all he blames himself for causin' the deaths
of all those young braves, him bein' the one they came
to join and try to be like. For that, he fully expects to be
banished from the tribe when they get back across the

border and then be left to wander in a cloak of shame that will keep him out of the afterlife.

"But if you'll meet him in a fight to the death—you, Moses, *'The Crow with the killing fire in his eyes'*—that's how Thunder Elk is hoping to atone. If he kills you, he has avenged those young lives you took so many of; if you kill him, he has given his life *trying* to right the tragedy of his mistakes. Either way, it maybe gives his soul a chance to be accepted in the afterlife."

"Too damn bad," muttered Nathan. "Let his stinkin' soul *rot* while it drifts between the winds forever. Why should Moses put his neck on the line to ease that heathen's mind?"

"I agree," stated Captain Earl. "Honoring such a request is out of the question."

But then, his voice sounding wooden and distant, Red Buffalo said, "Not so fast."

All eyes turned to him. The hardened expression he had adopted only a moment ago was still in place but his own gaze had taken on a strange, faraway look aimed generally off toward the mountains, yet, at the same time, nowhere in particular. Slowly, that faraway look pulled back into closer focus and came to rest on Nathan.

Quietly, Red Buffalo said, "Only you are aware of the demons I have been struggling with. The ancient feelings and voices that drove me into a killing frenzy that day. Here, on this very ground, only a short time ago. The frenzy that put the killing fire in my eyes and brought about many of those same deaths now tormenting Thunder Elk . . . Maybe I, too, am in need of atonement. Maybe by focusing all of my ancient, blind Crow hate on a single

Blackfoot—Thunder Elk—I can purge myself from continuing to carry it around inside me."

Nathan met his gaze and looked deep into his eyes, not saying anything for a minute. Then, in a low voice: "No, that kind of hate don't suit you, Moses. It will always be cause for torment . . . I guess maybe you would be better off trying to purge it out."

"What are you talking about?" Captain Earl demanded. "Surely you're not advocating for such a thing to take place. I can't allow it."

Nathan turned to him, saying, "Captain, a couple nights ago, you spoke at some length about all the loose ends when it comes to army regulations covering civilian scouts. I suggest you let this thing Moses reckons he has to go through with fall into that same category."

A handful of minutes later it was set and ready to start. Each man was armed with only a knife, their left wrists bound together by an eight-foot length of leather thong. Intentional severing of the thong was forbidden, anything else was allowed. They would fight until one was dead.

As the combatants separated to the full length of the thong and got ready for the start signal from Haliway, Nathan stepped close to Red Buffalo at the last second and said, "For what it's worth, you've proven to be as good a partner as any man could ask for. And my hatred for Indians in general . . . the way I've acted toward you at times and some of the things I've said . . ."

When he couldn't find the words to finish, Red Buffalo showed him a brief smile. "I know, Nathan. I know."

Turning away, Nathan said over his shoulder, "And something else for you to know, atonement or not . . . if you fall to Thunder Elk, I'm gonna kill him."

What took place next played out like something surreal in the eyes and minds of many looking on. The two groups, watching silently and with a limited display of outward expression on their faces, moved farther apart to give the fighters plenty of room. The sun shone down high and bright from a cloudless cobalt sky and the green of the grass and in the trees along the base of the foothills seemed to have been polished a brilliant emerald by the recent rain.

Both Red Buffalo and Thunder Elk were stripped to the waist and their bronze backs quickly took on a sheen of sweat under the hot sun. Thunder Elk was taller and leaner, Red Buffalo more thickly muscled. They moved with equal grace and speed as they circled, taking turns feinting, judging each other's balance and reflexes.

Thunder Elk suddenly made a more serious thrust. Red Buffalo parried it, knocking the Blackfoot's blade aside and then immediately sweeping his own blade in a slashing backhand, its tip passing less than an inch from Thunder Elk's throat.

They backed away as far as the thong would allow and resumed moving in a slow circle. The chest of each man was rising and falling more rapidly now and their sheens of sweat had begun dripping more freely.

Red Buffalo abruptly stopped circling, planted his feet, and swung his left arm hard across his chest, using the thong to yank Thunder Elk toward him. Caught off guard, Thunder Elk came staggering forward.

He managed to check his momentum, however, in time to pull back from another sweep of Red Buffalo's bowie. This brought the combatants' torsos thudding together. They stayed like that for several seconds, both leaning in hard, grunting loudly with effort as their free hands groped frantically to grab the wrist of the other's knife hand.

It didn't take long for Red Buffalo's greater strength to begin winning this struggle. Thunder Elk backed up a step, then another. The hand trying to hold the Crow's bowie blade at arm's length began losing ground, too. To counter this, Thunder Elk suddenly lowered his center of gravity, dropping into a crouch and throwing himself backward, pulling Red Buffalo along with him. As his back slapped hard onto the ground, Thunder Elk sank his feet in Red Buffalo's stomach and kept pulling, bringing his opponent forward and over in an unintended somersault and then straightening his legs to shove him off in the opposite direction.

Red Buffalo landed hard enough on his back to drive a good deal of air out of him. But he knew he couldn't afford to lie still, not even for a second. He twisted around and scrambled momentarily to his hands and knees, finding himself face-to-face with Thunder Elk gaining the same position. Both men still gripped their weapon but each had lost his restraining hold on the wrist of the other's knife hand.

Immediately, Thunder Elk swung his blade in an uppercut motion that succeeded in laying open a long gash through the middle trapezius muscle running from the side of Red Buffalo's neck to his right shoulder. Screaming pain shot down the length of the Crow's arm, all the way down to his knife hand. It was a telling stroke and Thunder Elk knew it. His eyes blazed as he sensed victory.

But Red Buffalo still had one good hand. And in their present close proximity, with the connecting thong hanging slack, he didn't hesitate to use it. He brought his fist up and across in a smashing left hook to Thunder Elk's jaw that nearly snapped the Blackfoot's head off his neck.

Then, continuing to reach across Thunder Elk's face, Red Buffalo looped the thong under his chin and around the back of his neck until he could grasp the dangling portion of the strap again in order to twist the loop tighter.

Though still stunned by the left hook, Thunder Elk suddenly realized he was being strangled. In panicked desperation, he foolishly let go of his knife and brought both hands to his throat, fingers clawing frantically to try to loosen the choking strap. As his opponent flailed at this, Red Buffalo had all the time he needed to raise his throbbing, weakened arm with the bowie still gripped in its fist . . . and to plunge the blade deep into Thunder Elk's tormented heart.

A ripple of elation naturally ran through the knot of soldiers looking on. But in view of the somber faces on Blue Otter and Shining Water, already so closely surrounded by so much tragedy and death, it was kept respectfully subdued.

But there was no holding back the wide grin on Nathan's face as he rushed to kneel beside where Red Buffalo still lay. Haliway and Andrea Fontinelle were also approaching, the latter brandishing a cloth for bandaging.

Before anyone else arrived, Red Buffalo reached up and clutched Nathan's shirtfront with his good hand. "I did it, Nathan . . . I got rid of my demons."

"I'm glad for you," Nathan told him. "Someday I hope I'll be able to say the same."

Managing a weak smile through his pain, Red Buffalo said, "That's something we can work on together . . . partner."

Keep reading for a special excerpt

National Bestselling Authors
WILLIAM W. JOHNSTONE
and J. A. JOHNSTONE

RED RIVER VENGEANCE
A PERLEY GATES WESTERN

JOHNSTONE COUNTRY. VENGEANCE IS HERE.
*A good man like Perley Gates knows that when you race
with the devil, you'd better cross the finish line first—
or you won't finish at all . . .*

They rode into town like the Four Horsemen
of the Apocalypse. Four armed outlaws
bringing their own brand of hell to Paris, Texas. First
they rob the First National Bank. Then they take a
woman hostage as insurance. When Perley Gates learns
that local waitress Becky Morris is in the hands of these
tough customers, he joins a posse with the Triple-G
ranch hands to get her back. Problem is, the outlaws are
heading toward Red River—straight into Indian
territory. That's where the ranch hands draw the line.
But Perley won't give up. He manages to rescue the girl,
but not before killing the gang's leader.
Now he's incurred the wrath of the other three . . .

The race is on. Come hell or high water, Perley has to
get Becky across the Red River—before three vengeful
devils make it flow with their blood . . .

Look for *Red River Vengeance*,
On sale now, wherever Pinnacle Books are sold.

Chapter 1

"Reckon we'll find out if Beulah's cookin' tastes as good as it did when she called her place the Paris Diner," Sonny Rice announced as he drove the wagon carrying supplies behind Perley, who was riding the bay gelding named Buck.

"How do you know that?" young Link Drew asked. "He just said he wanted to see the new hotel."

"I know 'cause he always eats at Beulah's place when he comes to town for supplies," Sonny replied. "Why do ya think I volunteered to drive the wagon in?"

"I bet the food won't be a whole lot better'n what Ollie cooks," Link said. It was his honest opinion. The gangly orphan had never eaten as well as he did now, ever since Perley brought him to live at the Triple G after his parents were killed. Although most of the crew at the Triple G complained good-naturedly about Ollie Dinkler's lack of compassion, they had to admit that he had taken a special interest in the welfare of the young lad.

"It'll be a whole lot fancier," Sonny said, "and it'll look better comin' from a pretty woman, instead of an old man with tobacco juice in his whiskers."

Ahead of the wagon, Perley reined Buck back to a halt and waited for Sonny and Link to come up beside him. "They built it right next to the railroad tracks," Perley stated the obvious. "That'll be handy, won't it? Get off the train and you can walk to the hotel." He nudged his horse and rode up to the rail in front of the hotel and stepped down to wait for the wagon. "Park it on the side, Sonny," he directed. "You and Link go on in and get us a table. I'm just gonna walk through the hotel and take a look." The hotel had been completed while Perley and Possum Smith were down in Bison Gap, and he was curious to see what kind of place it was going to be. According to what his brother Rubin told him, the fellow who built it made his money in cotton. Amos Johnson was his name and he thought the little town of Paris was ready for a first-class hotel. Rubin said he had talked Beulah Walsh into moving her business into the hotel. Perley figured what Rubin had told him must have been right because the little Paris Diner building was vacant when they had ridden past.

When Sonny drove the wagon around to the side where the outside entrance was located, Perley walked in the front door. He was greeted by a desk clerk, smartly dressed in a coat and vest. "Can I help you, sir?"

"Howdy," Perley replied. "I'm on my way to your dinin' room and I just wanted to get a look at the hotel. My name's Perley Gates. I work at the Triple G and your hotel opened while I was outta town."

"Pleased to meet you," the young man said. "I'm David Smith. If you're looking to see the owner, that's Mr. Johnson. He's in the dining room eating his dinner."

"Oh no," Perley quickly responded. "I don't need to

bother him. I just wanted to see what the hotel looked like on the inside. It looks like a first-class hotel."

"Would you like to see what the rooms look like?" David asked. "I'd be glad to show you one."

"No, no thanks," Perley replied. "I won't have much occasion to rent one, anyway. I'll just go on to the dinin' room, but I thank you for offerin'." He pointed to the entrance to a hallway. "That way?" David nodded. "Much obliged," Perley said, and headed down the hall.

The first door he came to wore a sign that said it was the entrance to the dining room. Perley stepped inside and stood there a moment to look the room over. Still looking and smelling new, it was about half again bigger than Beulah's original establishment. Unlike Beulah's original location, there was no long table in the center of the room, only little tables with four chairs at each one. He saw Sonny and Link sitting at one of them over against the outside wall. He started toward them but stopped when Sonny waved his arm and pointed to a table beside the outside entrance, holding several weapons. Perley nodded and unbuckled his gun belt, looking toward the kitchen door as he walked over to leave his weapon with the others.

He was curious to see if Becky and Lucy had come to the hotel with Beulah, but if they had, they must all be in the kitchen right now. He rolled his holster up in his gun belt, and when he put it on the table, he noticed there were three others there. One he recognized as Sonny's six-gun. It was easy to guess who the other two belonged to. He glanced at a table near the center of the room where two men were attacking the food in front of them as if they were afraid someone might try to take it away from them. One of the holsters caught his eye. It was a well-oiled fast-draw holster. He glanced again at the two strangers and tried to guess which one belonged to that holster before going over to join his friends. "I thought you would already be eatin'," he said when he sat down at the table.

"It's on the way," Sonny replied, and nodded toward the kitchen just as Lucy Tate, carrying two plates, came out the door. "We're havin' the pork chops, since we don't get much pork at the ranch. It's either that or stew beef today. You don't usually have a choice at the midday meal, but Lucy said today you do because it's Beulah's birthday."

"Well, how 'bout that?" Perley replied. "Don't reckon she said how old she is today."

"Nope, and I sure ain't gonna ask her," Sonny responded. Perley had to laugh at his response. Beulah had reached the age where she was no longer young, but she didn't consider herself old. And only she knew how many notches she had actually acquired.

"Well, there you are," Lucy Tate greeted him. "You haven't been to see us in so long, I figured you'd found someplace else to eat."

Before Perley had time to answer, one of the men at the table in the center of the room blurted, "Hey, Red, where the hell's that coffeepot?"

"Keep your shirt on, cowboy," Lucy yelled back at him. "Got a fresh pot workin' and it'll be ready in a minute." Back to Perley, she said, "I heard you had been gone for a while. You back to stay?"

"Far as I know," he answered. "At least I ain't plannin' to go anywhere right now." He looked at Link and winked. "I expect my brothers are thinkin' it's about time I did my share of the chores at the ranch." Back to Lucy, he said, "Those pork chops look pretty good, I expect I'll try 'em, too."

"Right," Lucy replied, "I'll tell Becky to bring you a cup of coffee." He hadn't asked, but she figured he was wondering where Becky was.

As she walked past the table with the two strangers, one of them stated loudly, "The coffee, Red."

"I told you," she replied, "it's making. And don't call me Red. I don't have red hair and my name's not Red."

"I reckon she told you what's what," Leonard Watts japed, and reached over to give his partner a playful jab on his shoulder.

Not to be put down by the cocky waitress, Jesse Sage called after Lucy as she continued on to the kitchen. "What is your name, Sassy Britches?"

There were only a few other patrons in the dining room, but Lucy didn't respond to Jesse's last attempt to rile her, sensing an air of discomfort among those diners already. When she went into the kitchen, she met Becky Morris on her way out with a cup of coffee for Perley. She knew the young waitress must have recognized Perley's voice when he joined Sonny and Link. "He wants the chops," Lucy said.

"I heard," Becky said, "but I thought I'd take him some coffee while Beulah's fixing up his plate."

Lucy chuckled, unable to resist teasing her. "You do have good ears," she japed. "I could have waited on him."

Accustomed to her friend's joking, Becky didn't respond while she went out the door, hurried over to Perley's table, and placed the cup of coffee down before him. "I know how you like your coffee," she said, "so I brought it right out. It's the first cup out of a new pot. Beulah's fixing your plate right now."

The warm smile she always caused to form on Perley's face blossomed into a beaming grin of embarrassment as he tried to think of something intelligent to say. Failing to come up with anything, he settled for, "Howdy, Becky."

His response was not loud, but it was enough to be heard at the table several feet away. "Yeah, howdy, Becky," Jesse demanded, "where the hell's my coffee? If anybody got the first cup, it oughta been me. Hell, he just walked in."

Leonard chuckled. "I swear, Jesse, you sure are feelin' ornery today, ain'tcha?"

"Damn right I am," Jesse said. Then to Becky, he ordered, "Tell that other gal, Miss Sassy Britches, I want some fresh coffee right now."

It had already gone too far. Perley was not happy with the obvious disrespect shown the two women and now he could see that same resentment building in Sonny's eyes. Afraid Sonny might get into an altercation with the two drifters, he thought he'd better try to see if he could defuse the situation before it blew up. "Hey, there ain't no problem, friend," he called out to Jesse. "Becky, here, didn't know you were supposed to get the first cup. You can take this one and I'll wait for the next one. We don't talk to the ladies here in the dinin' room like you might talk to the ladies in the saloon, so it doesn't set too well with 'em. Whaddaya say? You want this cup of coffee?"

Both drifters looked at Perley in disbelief for a long moment before Jesse responded. "Mister, in the first place, I ain't your friend and it ain't none of your business how I talk to a woman anywhere. So you'd best keep your mouth shut and mind your own business. I don't want your damn cup of coffee. If I did, I woulda already come over there and took it. Whaddaya say about that?"

Remaining unruffled, Perley paused and shrugged. "Well, I'd say that wouldn'ta been necessary, since I offered to give it to you, anyway."

Jesse looked at Leonard and asked, "Do you believe this mealymouthed jasper?" Looking back at Perley then, he warned, "Like I told you, keep your nose in your own business and stay the hell outta mine."

"Don't fret yourself, Perley," Becky said. "I'll run get the man some more coffee. There's no reason to have any trouble."

Jesse didn't miss hearing the name. "*Pearly*, is that what your name is?" When Perley nodded, Jesse declared, "Well, it sure as hell suits you. *Pearly*," he repeated, laughing. "What's your last name? Gates?" He looked over at Leonard and gave him a playful punch on the shoulder.

"Matter of fact, it is," Perley said.

That caused Jesse to pause for a moment. He was so surprised to find he had guessed right when he thought he had made a joke of the fellow's name. He looked at Leonard again, then they both howled with laughter. "*Pearly* Gates," he repeated a couple more times. "If that ain't a perfect name for a jasper like you, I don't know what is." He paused then when it occurred to him that the innocent-looking cowhand might be japing him. "Or maybe that ain't really your name and you're thinkin' you're pretty funny." He was about to threaten Perley but was interrupted by Lucy, who came from the kitchen at that point, carrying two fresh cups of coffee.

"Sorry to make you boys wait," she said. "I had to clear my throat first." She glanced at Becky and winked. "Now,

I hope you two will settle down and act like you've been around decent folks before."

Having caught Lucy's quick wink at Becky, Jesse was at once suspicious. "I don't reckon there's anything in that cup but coffee, right?"

"Of course, that's right," Lucy answered. "Did you want something else in it?"

He looked at his friend and gave him a wink. "Then I don't reckon you'd mind takin' a little drink of it first," Jesse said.

Lucy shrugged and without hesitating, picked up the cup and took a couple of sips of coffee. Then she graced him with a broad smile as she placed the cup back on the table. "Fresh out of the pot," she said. "Satisfied?" She turned to Becky then and said, "Come on, Becky, let's let 'em eat so they can get outta here. Perley's plate is ready now, anyway."

Becky started to follow her to the kitchen, but Jesse grabbed her wrist and pulled her back. "To hell with Perley's plate. You can stay here and keep company with me and Leonard."

That was as much as Perley could abide. "I reckon you've gone far enough to make it my business now," he said as he got up from his chair. "We don't stand for that kinda treatment to the ladies in this town. Let her go and we won't send for the sheriff. You can just finish your dinner and get on outta here and let decent people eat in peace."

Jesse gave him a big smile as he released Becky's wrist. She shot one worried look in Perley's direction before running out the door to find the sheriff. "Well, well," Jesse asked Leonard, "did you hear what he called me?"

"He called you a dirty name I can't repeat in front of these citizens settin' in here eatin'. And he said you was a yellow-bellied, scum-eatin' dog," the simple man answered, knowing what Jesse was fixing to do. Judging by the foolish grin on his face, it was easy to guess he possessed mere childlike intelligence.

"I'm thinkin' a man ain't no man a tall, if he don't stand up to a yellow snivelin' dog callin' him names like that. Whaddaya think I oughta do about it?"

"I reckon you ain't got no choice," Leonard said. "A man's got a right to stand up for his honor. If he don't, he ain't got no honor. Ain't that what Micah always says?" They both got to their feet and stood grinning at Perley. "Maybe if he said he was sorry and admitted he was a yellow dog and crawled outta here on his hands and knees, you could let him get by with what he said," Leonard added, excitedly.

Perley patiently watched their little parody for a few minutes before responding. "You two fellows are puttin' on a good little show over one cup of coffee. If you think I'm gonna participate in a gunfight with you, you're mistaken. I came in here to eat my dinner, just like the rest of these folks. So why don't you sit back down and finish your dinner. Then you can go to Patton's Saloon and tell everybody there how you backed me down. That way, nobody gets shot and we can eat in peace."

Since it was fairly obvious that Perley was not inclined to answer his challenge, Jesse was determined to force him to face him in the street or acknowledge his cowardice. He was about to issue his ultimatum when Sheriff Paul McQueen walked in with Becky right behind him.

"What's the trouble here?" McQueen asked as he walked up to face the two strangers still standing.

"Ain't no trouble, Sheriff," Jesse answered. "I ain't got no idea why that young lady thought there was and went and got you for nothin'. Me and my friend, here, was just tryin' to enjoy us a nice dinner. Then this feller"—he nodded toward Perley—"came in and started bellyachin' about a cup of coffee."

"That ain't exactly the way I heard it," McQueen replied. "I heard you two were disturbin' the peace. We don't stand for any rough treatment of the women who work in this dinin' room, or any rough language, either." He looked at Perley then, knowing he hadn't started any trouble. "Perley, you got anything to say?"

"Not much, Sheriff," Perley replied. "I think these fellows just forgot their manners. They're new in town and don't know how to act in a peaceful place of business. But there ain't any need to lock 'em up, if they'll just finish their dinner and get on outta here. That oughta be all right, wouldn't it, Beulah?"

Beulah Walsh, who was witnessing the confrontation from the kitchen door, shrugged and answered. "I reckon, if they agree not to cause no more trouble."

"Seems to me you ain't hearin' but one side of this argument," Leonard Watts declared. "That feller, there, is the one oughta go to jail. He as much as called Jesse out, but we'll finish up and get on outta here, anyway. Ain't no need to put us in jail."

"Leonard's right," Jesse added. "We ain't gonna start nothin', but I ain't gonna back down if he calls me out."

McQueen couldn't suppress a little smile. "Well, that would be a different matter. If Perley called you out, you'd have a right to defend yourself." He looked at Beulah to see if she was satisfied to let them remain.

She nodded and asked, "You wanna sit down and have a cup of coffee or something, Sheriff?" He had already eaten there earlier, but she figured it would ensure the peace if he stayed awhile.

"As long as I'm here, I might as well," McQueen said. "I'll just sit down over here." He walked over and sat down at a table near the one that held the weapons. "I'll make sure Perley don't call one of your customers out," he couldn't resist saying.

"I'll get you some coffee," Lucy sang out, and went into the kitchen with Beulah and Becky.

Beulah fixed up a fresh plate for Perley, since the first one had begun to cool off. While she dished it out, Becky stopped Lucy on her way out with the sheriff's coffee to ask a question. "I thought I knew why you winked when you said you had to clear your throat. Why did you take a gulp of that coffee when that man dared you to?"

Lucy laughed. "'Cause it was just my spit in it. I was just glad he didn't want me to taste the other fellow's coffee. Beulah spit in his."

"That fellow was really puttin' the challenge out on you," Sonny said to Perley, his voice low so as not to be overheard at the table where the two strangers were rapidly finishing up their meal.

"It's just mostly big talk," Perley said. "He probably owns that gun on the table in the fast-draw holster, so he's always lookin' for some excuse to shoot somebody. I didn't want it to be one of us."

"I reckon it was a good thing Becky went to fetch the sheriff," Sonny said. "You mighta had to meet him out in the middle of the street."

"I wasn't gonna meet anybody out in the middle of the street," Perley insisted. "That's one of the dumbest things a man can do."

"I reckon you're right," Sonny allowed. He had heard rumors of how fast Perley was with a six-gun, although he had never witnessed it, himself. And he once overheard Perley's brother John telling Fred Farmer about an incident he had witnessed. Fred was older than the rest of the hands at the Triple G and had been with the Gateses the longest of any of the men. John told him that Perley was like chain lightning when backed into a corner. He said Perley didn't know why he was so fast, something just fired in his brain when he had to act. John figured because he didn't understand that "gift," he was reluctant to use it. Thinking about that now, Sonny thought he would surely like to have been there with John to see for himself.

"Ain't you afraid they might go braggin' around town that you were too scared to face that bigmouth?" Link asked. Perley was his hero and he didn't like to think there was a flaw in his hero. The man called Jesse had openly laid down a challenge to Perley and Perley just tried to talk his way out of it.

"Doesn't make any difference to me what they say," Perley told him. "It's just words, and words get blown away by the first little breeze that comes along. Sometimes you might get caught where you ain't got no choice. There ain't much you can do then but try to do the best you can. Anyway, it ain't nothin' but tomfools that pull a gun on another fellow just to see if he can get his out quicker.

The folks that count are the folks you see and work with every day. And they know who you are, so it doesn't matter what some stranger passin' through town thinks about you. You understand that, don'tcha?"

"Yeah, I reckon so," Link answered, but he was still thinking he would have liked to have seen how fast Perley really was.

Chapter 2

When the two drifters finished eating, they left money on the table and walked toward the door. As they passed by the table where the three Triple G hands were eating, Jesse reached down and knocked Perley's coffee cup over, causing him to jump backward to keep from getting his lap filled. He just managed to catch himself from going over backward with his chair. "Damn, Perley," Jesse mumbled. "Sorry 'bout that. That was kinda clumsy of me, weren't it? I'll be down at the saloon if you wanna do somethin' about it."

Perley reached over and grabbed Sonny's elbow when he started to jump to his feet. "No need to get excited," he said. "I didn't get any on me and it needed warmin' up, anyway." He looked at McQueen and shook his head when the sheriff got to his feet.

As a precaution, the sheriff walked over to stand beside the weapons table while Jesse and Leonard picked up their guns. "You two are gettin' close to spendin' the night in my jail. You're damn lucky the man you been pickin' away at is a peaceful man or you mighta been sleepin' in the boneyard up on the hill."

"We ain't gonna cause no more trouble, Sheriff," Leonard was quick to assure him. "Come on, Jesse, we don't wanna spend the night in jail." They went out the door and McQueen followed them to watch them as they walked away.

When the two troublemakers reached Patton's Saloon and went inside, McQueen returned to the dining room. He was met at the door by Becky Morris. "You should have put them in jail," she said, "especially when that dirty-looking one knocked Perley's cup over."

"Perley's after the same thing I am," the sheriff told her. "And that's to keep from havin' gunfights in our street and endangerin' the good folks in this town. I'm beholden to him for not answerin' that saddle tramp's challenge." He glanced at Perley and nodded his thanks. He was well aware of Perley's skill with a six-shooter, but he also knew that the young man's lightninglike reflexes were not something Perley liked to display. He slowly shook his head when he thought about Perley's dilemma. McQueen had never met a more peaceful man than Perley Gates. His father had placed a tremendous burden on his youngest son's shoulders when he named him for the boy's grandfather. McQueen could only assume that God, in His mercy, compensated for the name by endowing the boy with reflexes akin to those of a striking rattlesnake.

When he realized Becky was still standing there, as if waiting for him to say more, he thanked her for the coffee. "I'd best get back to shoein' that horse," he said, referring to the job he was in the middle of when Becky came to find him. It brought to mind a subject that had been in his thoughts a lot lately. The town was growing so fast that he felt it already called for a full-time sheriff, instead of one who was also a part-time blacksmith.

"Thanks for coming, Sheriff," Becky said, turned, and went back to the table where Lucy and Beulah were already warning Perley to be careful when he left the dining room. "They're right, Perley," Becky said. "Those two are just looking for trouble."

And like John and Rubin like to say, if there ain't but one cow pie in the whole state of Texas, Perley will most likely step in it, was the thought in Perley's mind. To Becky, however, he said, "Nothin' to worry about. We've already got the wagon loaded with the supplies we came after, so we'll be headin' straight to the ranch when we leave here. Besides, I've got Sonny and Link to take care of me. Ain't that right, Link?" Link looked undecided. Perley continued, "So, I'm gonna take my time to enjoy this fine meal Beulah cooked. By the time I'm finished, those fellows probably won't even remember me."

"I hope you're right," Becky said, and turned her attention to some of the other customers, who were waiting for coffee refills. The room returned to its usual atmosphere of peaceful dining.

Just as he said he would, Perley took his time to enjoy his dinner and some idle conversation with Becky and Lucy, plus a pause to stick his head inside the kitchen door to wish Beulah a happy birthday. Unfortunately, it provided enough time for his two antagonists to think of another way to entertain themselves at his expense. "We saw them two fellers ol' Perley met with when they drove that wagon around to the side of the buildin'," Jesse recalled as he and Leonard walked out on the porch of the saloon. "But he came from that inside door from the hotel."

"Yeah, he did," Leonard replied, wondering what that had to do with anything.

"Look yonder at that bay horse tied out front of the hotel," Jesse said, a grin slowly spreading across his unshaven face. "I'm thinkin' that's ol' Perley's horse. I bet you he ain't got a room in the hotel. He just tied his horse out there."

Still not quite sure what his friend was driving at, Leonard asked, "Maybe, so what about it?"

"I'm thinkin' about borrowin' his horse for a little ride," Jesse answered, his grin spreading from ear to ear now. "See if that don't get his dander up enough to make him do somethin' about it."

"Damned if you ain't got the itch awful bad to shoot somebody, ain't you? How do you know how fast he is?"

"I know he ain't faster'n me," Jesse crowed. "I just don't like his attitude—like he's too good to have to stand up like a man." He continued to grin at Leonard, waiting for him to show some enthusiasm for the caper. When Leonard remained indifferent, Jesse announced, "Well, I'm gonna take that bay for a little ride up and down this street a few times, till ol' Perley shows his yellow self."

"What if it ain't his horse?" Leonard asked.

"Then I'll just say, Beg your pardon, sir, and if whoever owns him don't like it, we can settle it with six-guns." Jesse didn't wait for more discussion but headed straight for the hotel. Thinking it was bound to provide some entertainment, no matter who owned the horse, Leonard followed along behind him. He didn't think it was a good idea and Jesse's brothers wouldn't like for him to draw any more attention to them. But he knew better than to tell Jesse not to do something.

When he walked up to the hitching rail, Jesse took a quick look toward the front door of the hotel. Seeing no one, he untied Buck's reins from the rail and turned the bay gelding toward the street. "You're a good-lookin' horse for a jasper like that to be ridin'. It's time to let you feel a man on your back." He put a foot in the stirrup and climbed up. While he was throwing his right leg over, Buck lowered his head toward the ground and reared up on his front legs, causing the unsuspecting Jesse to do a somersault in midair and land hard on the ground in front of the horse. "Damn you!" Jesse spat as he tried to gather himself. "You like to broke my back!"

It only made matters worse when Leonard whooped and hollered, "Hot damn, Jesse! You never said nothin' about flyin'. Looks to me like that horse don't wanna be rode."

"Well, he's gonna be," Jesse announced emphatically, and got back up on his feet. "C'mere, you hardheaded plug." Buck didn't move but stood watching the strange man as he advanced cautiously toward him. "You fooled me with that trick, but I ain't gonna be fooled this time." The horse remained stone still as Jesse walked slowly up to him and took the reins again.

Leonard bit his lip to keep from laughing, urging Jesse on. "Watch him, Jesse, he's waitin' to give you another flip."

"He does and I'll shoot the fool crowbait," Jesse said. "He ain't as ornery as he thinks he is." Buck continued to watch Jesse with a wary eye, but he remained as still as a statue. Trying again to approach the stone-still horse, Jesse kept talking calmly. "You just hold still, ol' boy, till I get settled in the saddle. Then I'll run some of the steam outta you." With his foot in the stirrup again, he took a good grip on the saddle horn, then stood there on one leg before attempting to climb into the saddle. Still he paused, waiting to catch the horse by surprise. When he was ready, he suddenly pulled himself up to land squarely in the saddle. Buck did not flinch. He remained still as a statue. "Now, you're showin' some sense, horse." He looked over at Leonard and grinned. "All he needed was for . . ." That was as far as he got before the big bay gelding exploded. With all four legs stiff as poles, the horse bounced around and around in a circle while Jesse held on for dear life. When that didn't rid him of his rider, the incensed gelding started a series of bucks that ended when Jesse was finally thrown, landing on the hotel porch to slide up against a corner post.

With the fuse on his temper burning brightly now, Jesse rolled over on the rough boards of the porch, his hands and knees skinned under his clothes. He scrambled on all fours to recover his .44, which had been knocked out of his holster when he landed on the porch. When he had the pistol in hand, he turned to level it at the offending horse. "Damn you, you four-legged devil, I'm sendin' you back to hell where you came from!" He cocked the pistol at almost the same time his hand was smashed by the .44 slug that knocked the weapon free.

Jesse screamed with the pain in his hand as he turned to see Perley standing in the doorway, his six-gun trained on him. "I'm willin' to ignore your childish behavior when it ain't doin' any harm," Perley said. "But you're goin' too far when you mess with my horse." He glanced over at

Leonard, standing in the street, to make sure he wasn't showing any signs of retaliation. He wasn't, after having witnessed the swiftness of the shot just fired. Perley looked back at Jesse. "I'm sure Sheriff McQueen heard that shot and he'll be up here pretty quick to find out who did the shootin'. My advice to both of you is to get on your horses and get outta town before he gets here. If you do, I'll tell him it was just an accidental discharge of a weapon. If you don't, you're goin' to jail. So, what's it gonna be?"

"We're gettin' outta town," Leonard said at once. "We don't want no more trouble." He hurried over to the edge of the porch. "Come on, Jesse, he's right, it's best we get outta town. You can't go to jail right now."

Jesse was in too much pain to argue. He picked up his pistol with his left hand and let Leonard help him off the porch. "I might be seein' you again, Perley," he had to threaten as he went down the one step to the street.

"Come on," Leonard urged him. "Let's get outta here and find a place to take a look at that hand."

Perley stepped out into the street to watch them hurry to the saloon, where their horses were tied. They galloped past the blacksmith's forge just as Paul McQueen came walking out to the street. He paused to take a look at the two departing riders. Then, when he saw Perley standing out in front of the hotel, he headed that way. By the time he walked up there, Sonny and Link were there as well. "Wasn't that those two in the dinin' room before?" the sheriff asked.

"Yep," Perley answered. "They decided it best to leave town before they wound up in your jailhouse." When McQueen asked about the shot he heard, Perley told him he fired it and why. "I did the best I could to avoid trouble with those two, but that one that kept pickin' at me was fixin' to shoot my horse. So I had to keep him from doin' that."

"You shot him?" McQueen asked.

"Just in the hand," Perley replied. "I told 'em you'd be on your way to most likely put 'em in jail, so they decided to leave town."

"Good," the sheriff said, "'cause it don't look like I'm ever gonna get done shoein' Luther Rains's horse."

"Sorry you were bothered," Perley said. "If you do get called out again, it won't be on account of me. We're fixin' to head back to the Triple G right now."

"I know it ain't your fault, Perley. You don't ever cause any trouble," the sheriff said. To himself, he thought, but damned if trouble doesn't have a way of finding you. He turned away and went back to finish his work at his forge. He had put his wife and son on the train the day before for a trip to visit her family in Kansas City. So he was trying to take advantage of the opportunity to catch up with some of his work as a blacksmith. Maybe if Perley stayed out of town for a while, he could get more done. As soon as he thought it, he scolded himself for thinking anything negative about Perley.

"He was gonna shoot Buck, so you had to shoot that feller, right, Perley?" Link was eager to confirm. His admiration for Perley had wavered a bit after having witnessed Perley's reluctance to fight before. But now his faith was restored.

"That's right, Link. There wasn't any time to talk him out of it. It's too bad it takes a gun to talk somebody outta doin' something stupid." He glanced down the street to see a few people coming out into the street, curious to see what the gunshot was about, so he climbed up into the saddle. "Let's go home before Rubin sends somebody after us."

When they reached a small stream approximately five miles south of Paris, Leonard Watts said, "Let's pull up here and take a look at your hand." He dismounted and waited for Jesse to pull up beside him. "Is it still bleedin' pretty bad?"

"Hell, yeah, it's still bleedin'," Jesse complained painfully. "I think it broke all the bones in my hand." He had bound his bandanna around the wounded hand as tightly as he could, but the bandanna was thoroughly soaked.

"Come on," Leonard said, "let's wash some of the blood off and see how bad it is." He helped Jesse down from his horse and they knelt beside the stream to clean the hand. After he had cleared some of the blood away, he said, "The bullet went all the way through."

"Hell, I know that," Jesse retorted, "you can see the mark on the grip of my Colt. And I can't move my fingers."

"Well, quit tryin' to move 'em. That just makes it bleed more. Lemme get a rag outta my saddlebag and I'll try to bind it tight enough to hold it till we get back to camp. Micah can take a look at it and see what we gotta do. You might have to ride down to Sulphur Springs. They got a doctor there."

"That sneakin' egg-suckin' dog," Jesse muttered. "I oughta go back and call him out with my left hand."

Leonard shook his head. "I don't know, Jesse, that was a helluva shot that feller made, comin' outta the doorway when he done it. You weren't lookin' at him when he shot you, but I was lookin' right at him when he opened the door. And his gun was in the holster when he started to step out. I don't know," he repeated.

"I reckon that was the reason you never thought about pullin' your gun," Jesse grunted sarcastically. "He was just lucky as hell," he insisted. "He was tryin' to shoot me anywhere and just happened to hit my hand."

"I don't know," Leonard said once again, thinking he had seen what he had seen, and knowing he had never seen anyone faster. Finished with his bandaging then, he said, "Maybe that'll hold you till we get back to the others." Jesse's two brothers were waiting at a camp on the Sulphur River and that was fully ten or eleven miles from where they now stood. Leonard didn't raise the subject with Jesse, but he was thinking Micah and Lucas were not going to be very happy to learn of the attention he and Jesse had called upon themselves in Paris. Their purpose for visiting the town was to take a look at the recently opened bank while Micah and Lucas rode down to Sulphur Springs to look at that bank. Their camp was halfway between the two towns and the plan had been to go to the towns in the morning, look them over, and meet back at the river that afternoon. It was easy for Leonard to forget his part in encouraging Jesse's behavior and then blame him for causing them to be one man short in the planned robbery. I reckon he can at least hold the horses while we do the real business, he thought. "We'd best get goin'," he said to Jesse.

* * *

  Leonard was right on the mark when he figured that Jesse's older brothers were not going to be happy to hear the cause for his wounded hand. "What the hell were you two thinkin'?" Lucas demanded. "We told you to lay low while you were up there and not attract any attention. So you decided to challenge somebody to have a gunfight out in the middle of the street? I swear, no wonder Ma and Pa decided not to have no more young 'uns after you popped out." He looked at the eldest brother, who was busy examining Jesse's hand. "Whaddaya think, Micah? Think we just oughta hit that bank in Sulphur Springs? It's been there a lot longer than the one they looked at, but there is a damn guard."

  "Yeah, and they got a pretty tough sheriff, too," Micah replied. He turned to Leonard and asked, "Tell me what you did find out when you weren't tryin' to get everybody to notice you."

  "I swear, Micah," Leonard responded, "we did look the town over. It didn't take long. It ain't a big town, not as big as Sulphur Springs. The bank's new and they ain't got no guards workin' there. It'd be easy to knock it over. They got a sheriff, but he's just part-time. Most of the time he works in a blacksmith shop. I don't think they'd be able to get up a posse to amount to much. And there weren't but a few people that got a look at me and Jesse. Besides, we'd be wearin' bandannas over our faces, anyway."

  "Right," Lucas scoffed, "and one of the bandannas would be blood soaked on the feller with a bandaged-up hand. How 'bout it, Micah? Is he gonna have to go see a doctor about that hand?"

"Well, it ain't good, but it coulda been busted up a lot worse. Just feelin' around on it, I think it mighta broke one of them little bones in there but not all of 'em. It just went straight through. If he can stand it, I think a doctor can wait till we get the hell outta Texas." He turned to Jesse then. "What do you say, Jesse? Can you make it?"

Jesse took a look at his bandaged right hand and cursed. "Yeah," he decided. "I can wait till we get our business done here and get gone."

Micah studied him for a long moment before deciding Jesse was not just blowing smoke. Considering what he now knew about the two possible targets for bank robbery, he made his thoughts known to the others. "Right now, I'm thinkin' that Paris bank is the smartest move, especially since we're short a man. It's smaller, not well guarded, and they've got a part-time sheriff. There's one other thing I like about it, it's a lot closer to the Red River, only about sixteen miles and we'd be in Indian Territory. I'm thinkin' that right there would discourage any posse they might get up to come after us. Sulphur Springs is more like fifty miles before we could slip into Oklahoma Indian Territory. It's been a while since we were up that way, but ol' Doc O'Shea is most likely still over at Durant Station. If your hand don't show signs of healin', we can let him take a look at it."

"If the old fool ain't drank hisself to death by now," Lucas said. Dr. Oliver O'Shea was a competent physician when he was sober, so it was said. They knew that he was adequate even when drunk, since that was the only state in which they had ever seen him.

There was no disagreement on the plan from any of the four after they discussed it a little further. They decided

Micah was right in his opinion that there was less of a gamble on their part if they struck the smaller town. "All right, then," Lucas declared, "I reckon we'll ride on up to Paris tomorrow, camp outside of town tomorrow night, so the horses will be rested up good. Then we can go to the bank the next mornin' to make a withdrawal. That'll be a Friday. That's a good day to go to the bank."